Kris Webb and Kathy Wilson are sisters who grew up in Brisbane.

Inheriting Jack is their second novel and is the result of even more coffee and wine than their first one.

INHERITING JACK

KRIS WEBB & KATHY WILSON

PAN
Pan Macmillan Australia

First published 2004 in Macmillan by Pan Macmillan Australia Pty Limited
This edition published 2005 in Pan by Pan Macmillan Australia Pty Limited
1 Market Street, Sydney

Reprinted 2005 (twice), 2006

National Library of Australia
cataloguing-in-publication data:

Webb, Kris.
Inheriting Jack.

ISBN 0 330 42153 0.

1. Motherhood – Fiction. 2. Toddlers – Fiction.
I. Wilson, Kathy. II. Title.

A823.4

Typeset in Bembo by Post Pre-press Group
Printed in Australia by McPherson's Printing Group

Papers used by Pan Macmillan Australia Pty Ltd are natural, recyclable products
made from wood grown in sustainable forests. The manufacturing processes conform
to the environmental regulations of the country of origin.

The characters and events in this book are fictitious and any resemblance
to real persons, living or dead, is purely coincidental.

To Neil and Stephen

ACKNOWLEDGMENTS

Our thanks go to our agent Margaret Connolly, who saw something in *Sacking the Stork*, our first book, long before it was ready to show the world and has guided us ever since. Thanks also to Cate Paterson, who believed in us enough to ask for two books and without whom *Inheriting Jack* wouldn't exist. And to Brianne Tunnicliffe and Julia Stiles, who helped turn our manuscript into a book – thank you for caring about our characters and worrying so much about Jack.

ONE

This had to be the worst blind date imaginable.

Clutching a large brown teddy bear, I watched apprehensively as the passengers off the flight from Rome began filtering into the arrivals hall.

I tried to ignore the sick feeling in my stomach and focused instead on a pair of bedraggled backpackers who had obviously taken advantage of the free airline alcohol. They squinted painfully in the fluorescent glare as they felt the full force of their first Australian hangover. Behind them was a woman who looked more like she'd been in a beauty salon than an aeroplane. She had to be Italian, I thought to myself, not without some bitterness.

Suddenly I craved a cigarette, despite the fact that I had never had more than an occasional drunken puff. A new wave of terror shot through me as I realised that now I would never be able to take up smoking – even if I wanted to.

'Maybe the bear is a mistake.' I turned to Patrick. Despite my own panic, I noticed that his eyes, which usually sparkled with fun, were decidedly worried. 'I think it looks too much like a bribe.'

Patrick ran his hand through his sandy hair; his silence spoke volumes. While I reacted to pressure by talking, my brother's response to stress was silence. Consequently I'd been babbling nonstop to a wordless Patrick since the phone call and there wasn't much left for me to say on any subject.

The teddy bear had been an afterthought, bought at the airport gift shop five minutes ago.

'But then again, it might help to break the ice,' I muttered. Patrick managed a nod in response and, encouraged, I continued. 'I mean, what do you say to an eighteen month old you've never met who has travelled halfway across the world to live with you? "Did you see any good movies on the flight?"'

The words died in my throat as I saw a child toddling towards us.

'Oh God. Here we go,' I croaked.

Finally, Patrick had something to say. 'Julia, I don't know much about kids, but I think it's unlikely that a boy called Jack would be wearing a pink dress with strawberries on it.'

He had a point. I unclenched my hands and tried to look casual.

When the telephone had rung at six o'clock on Saturday morning, I hadn't realised my life was about to change forever.

Several of my good friends had moved to London and developed the unfortunate habit of phoning to tell me they were having a drink for me. The time difference meant that these calls came at spectacularly antisocial times and almost always woke me up. So when the harsh bleating of the telephone broke through the layers of my alcohol-induced sleep, I assumed it was my friends, clustered around a table in another smoky London pub.

Cursing, I stumbled out of bed and into the living room, trying to locate the mobile handset. I finally tracked down the shattering noise and pressed the talk button.

'Joanne, do you really have to call me every time you get drunk?' I said by way of greeting as I walked unsteadily back to my bedroom.

There was silence on the line and then the caller cleared his throat.

'Hello, is that Julia Butler?'

The voice was definitely not Joanne's. I stopped walking.

'Ah, yes,' I answered hesitantly, not entirely sure of that fact this morning. My hangover had just caught up with me and I pushed my fingers against my temple, trying not to move my head.

'Julia, this is Robert Neilsen.'

I tried to force some rational thought into my murky brain. Why would my best friend's brother be calling me? Robert lived in London and I hadn't spoken to him for several years.

'I'm afraid I have some bad news,' Robert said.

Something in his tone made it past the pounding in my head.

'Anita died this afternoon.'

I heard the words but felt nothing. Anita couldn't be dead.

When I didn't respond, Robert continued miserably. 'There was an accident outside her school . . .' He stopped and it was several seconds before he spoke again. 'I'm not sure of the details, but apparently a school bus lost control.'

My neck suddenly felt unable to hold up the terrible weight of my head and I leaned against the wall. I closed my eyes and then opened them, trying to get a bearing on a world that had been turned upside down in the time it took to answer the phone.

I groped for an explanation. Obviously the whole thing was a mistake – they'd just confused Anita with someone else. 'Are you sure?' I heard my voice echo back on the tinny line. 'Maybe it's a mix-up? You hear about that kind of thing happening. A guy I went to school with disappeared in India a couple of years ago during some floods. His family went mad trying to find him and then it turned out he was on a beach in Thailand the whole t–'

I could almost believe what I was saying as long as I didn't stop talking. But Robert interrupted me mid sentence.

'There's no mix-up,' he said leadenly. 'One of the other teachers she worked with saw it happen.'

I thought suddenly of Anita's son.

'Oh God. What about Jack?'

'He's fine. She'd already dropped him off at the daycare centre. I'm catching the first plane to Rome in the morning.'

My sense of relief that Jack was all right lasted for only a second before Robert's terrible news finally registered. My hands began to shake and I missed what he said next as I slid down the wall and pulled my legs into my chest.

Closing my eyes, I saw Anita as she was when she was last in Brisbane, several years ago. We had arranged to meet at a cafe in the city and I'd almost walked past her. The long dark waves she'd had since she was a girl had been cropped and bleached almost white and she was wearing a flowing skirt that could only have come from Europe.

Robert's voice brought me back to the present. 'Did you know that Anita appointed you Jack's legal guardian in the event of her death?' The words seemed oddly formal, as if he were reading them from a document.

'Sorry?' I asked, convinced I'd misheard.

'Anita wrote a will just after Jack was born – she left a copy with me. She stipulated that if anything happened to her, you were to take care of Jack. She didn't talk to you about it?'

More blurred flashes of that last visit came back to me. Anita had been in Brisbane for her mother's funeral and had flown back to Rome via Sydney, where I was living at the time. A quiet drink turned into many more and we'd ended up in Baron's in Kings Cross, sitting on velvet-covered sofas that bore testament to the number of drinkers who'd preceded us. I vaguely remembered us professing undying friendship and promising that we'd be godmother to each other's unborn children.

When Jack was born, Anita had asked whether our agreement still applied. I'd been delighted, thinking that being his godmother meant an excuse to buy him fabulous presents. I'd given very little thought to the religious side of things and none whatsoever to what might happen if she died. Given that Jack's father had never even seen him, maybe I should have.

Now I had no idea what to say.

Fortunately Robert didn't seem surprised by my lack of response. 'Look, this is a lot for you to take in. Why don't I call back in a few hours?'

After muttering some kind of affirmative response, I pressed the off button. I looked around. Everything was the same as it had been before I'd answered the phone. My bedroom door was still only half painted. My new white shirt, which lay in a crumpled heap on the floor, still had a red wine stain on it. Last night that had seemed like such a tragedy.

My best friend was dead. Anita. Gone. I knew there was more I needed to deal with, but I couldn't make my mind focus.

Slowly I pulled on some jeans and a crumpled T-shirt, not caring that I looked more than a little bit slept in. I thought briefly about brushing my hair but dragged my fingers through it instead. My usual morning concerns about whether my shockingly expensive styling product was winning the battle to subdue the kinks in my short hair seemed ridiculously unimportant.

I glanced in the mirror. Like the house, I looked much the same as I had yesterday. Dark hair, brown eyes – although the red tinge to the whites of my eyes hadn't been there before the excesses of last night.

As I pulled the front door shut behind me, I looked up at the light breaking across the pale blue sky. I couldn't believe that Anita would never see another morning sky. It just didn't seem possible.

Mindlessly, I turned out of the gate and started walking. There was something soothing about just putting one foot in front of the other and I concentrated on counting my steps until I lost track around a thousand.

When I looked up, I realised that I was near New Farm Deli. Although the doors were unlocked, the chairs were still upside down on the tables. I hesitated and then pushed open the glass doors, breathing in the warm smell of coffee.

I knew I should be thinking about what Robert had told me. Anita was dead and Jack was my responsibility. There were things I had to do and decisions I had to make. I tried to force myself to concentrate, but it was no good. Something in my brain still refused to believe this was happening.

What had Anita been thinking when she'd decided I should be Jack's guardian? I was thirty-one, single and a solicitor in a law firm that monopolised ninety per cent of my waking hours.

The man behind the counter smiled and I tried, but failed, to smile back.

'Is it too early for a flat white?'

He shook his head. 'Never too early for a coffee here.'

I handed over my money. This was all wrong. Anita was dead. How could I be standing here paying for a coffee as I had a thousand times before?

Automatically I turned around and headed for my usual table on the footpath. I hauled a chair off the top and slumped into it.

I'd dropped my wallet on the table in front of me. Slowly I opened it and pulled out a photo I always carried. It was the first one of Jack that Anita had sent me; it had been taken when he was only hours old. Anita was sitting on a hospital bed, a swaddled Jack cradled in her arms.

Anita had been part of my life for as long as I could remember. We'd gone to primary school together in Manly, a laid-back suburb on the shores of Moreton Bay, had swapped sandwiches at lunchtime and ridden home together on matching Malvern Star bikes. Our friendship had outlasted adolescent romances, teenage angst and survived the stresses of university while Anita studied to become a teacher and I'd done a law degree.

We'd always planned to travel through Europe together, but it wasn't until Anita had been teaching for several years and I'd emerged from university that our dream had finally become a reality.

From our first night in a terrible hostel in Rome, Anita had loved Italy. We'd been travelling for several months by that stage and I'd decided to head to London to find some work to boost my flagging finances. I'd left her in Rome, where she revelled in wandering the ancient streets, stopping only to drink espressos in the shade of thousand-year-old buildings.

'A little longer,' she told me, and stayed another ten years, having learned Italian and found work in an English language school. She immersed herself in the Italian way of life and I'd been sure she'd marry an Italian and never come home. That was until Jack came along.

It was this photo of Anita and Jack that had made me realise that for the first time there was a real difference between us. She was a mother. I could only guess at the nature of the love that filled her face as she touched a tiny hand that had escaped the midwife's efficient wrapping.

And now, after only eighteen months of her son's life, she was dead.

The ache in my chest moved up to my throat and I rested my forehead on my hand, suddenly wishing I had stayed at home. Tears leaked out of my tightly screwed eyes and I pressed my hand over my mouth. A sob burst through and was followed by another. Dimly I registered someone putting a coffee on the table and hovering uncertainly for a few moments, but I could focus on nothing but the fact that my friend was gone forever. Blindly I pushed the chair back and stumbled away, wanting to be by myself. I made it as far as a side street, where I sank onto the edge of the gutter, head buried in my hands, crying uncontrollably.

I snapped out of my reverie as I saw a little boy holding tightly onto the hand of a red-headed man emerge from behind the screen and enter the arrivals hall.

Jack had spent the night Anita died with the woman who ran the daycare centre. A lawyer friend had told Robert that although Jack had an Australian passport, the best plan was to get him out of the country quickly in case the Italian welfare system decided it should get involved. So without giving anyone a chance to argue, he'd picked Jack up on Saturday morning, spent a day I didn't even want to think about in Anita's apartment, and got them both on the flight to Australia that night. Twenty-four hours later, here they were.

Robert had changed little in the last few years. While Anita had inherited their mother's tawny hair and brown eyes, Robert had picked up the red hair and pale skin that appeared every couple of generations. He was tall and lanky and his loud laugh and dramatic gestures had always seemed at odds with his bookish appearance. But now all he looked was very tired.

My gaze travelled down further to Jack. Without meaning to, I found myself searching his face for a likeness to Anita. He had olive skin, dark eyes and light brown hair that curled slightly at the ends. If I hadn't known better I'd have bet his father was Italian. A little belly pushed out his grubby yellow T-shirt and he trudged along in jeans and tiny sneakers, showing no interest in his surroundings. Alongside Anita he probably would have looked like her son, but there was no feature that seemed to be exactly hers. Strangely I felt relieved.

Jack rubbed the knuckles of one hand into his eye and I saw a tiny dimple on his chubby hand. He looked lost and utterly confused and his vulnerability took my breath away.

He was barely more than a baby, certainly not old enough to understand what had happened. All he knew was that, suddenly, his mummy wasn't there anymore.

Could there be anything more terrible than to suddenly be taken away from the person who had always provided you with love and protection – always been there ready with a cuddle to make things seem all right again?

Up until that moment, I'd never understood what it meant to feel your heart breaking but as I gazed at my best friend's baby, I felt my chest contract, weighed down by sadness. My lungs felt incapable of taking in air and I had a terrible sensation that if I didn't move quickly, I'd never breathe again.

Grabbing Patrick's arm like a lifeline, I dodged several clusters of people and stepped into Robert and Jack's path.

When Robert saw me he managed a weary smile. 'Hello Julia.'

The trip had obviously not been an easy one.

Robert had his own business in London, selling wine from a number of premium Australian vineyards. As a single and childless thirty-six year old, he had a large disposable income and I'd never seen him anything but immaculately dressed. But now his shirt and trousers, which had no doubt looked the cutting edge of fashion twenty-four hours ago, were crushed and covered in a variety of stains. Behind his rimless glasses, his eyes were bloodshot.

I couldn't think of anything to say and hugged him instead. Pulling back, I looked at the little boy by his side.

Jack was standing staring up at Patrick and me. I couldn't begin to imagine how he must be feeling.

His mother had disappeared from his life three days ago. He'd been shunted to the other side of the world with an uncle he knew only vaguely and he was about to be left with a woman he'd never seen before.

I dropped into a crouch in front of him. 'Hi Jack. I'm Julia. How are you?' I asked quietly.

Jack tightened his grip on the toy he was holding and turned away from me, burying his face in Robert's legs.

I tried again.

'Now what's that you've got there?' I asked, pointing at the toy clutched in his arms.

Jack held a large brown plastic frog out towards me with a pride that almost broke my heart.

'That's Harold, apparently,' Robert supplied.

Feeling like the Horse Whisperer, I shuffled forward on the pretext of taking a closer look at Harold.

'He's . . .' I struggled for a word to describe the very large and very ugly toy. 'Excellent,' I finished lamely.

Suddenly the creature emitted a loud croak and I lurched backwards in fright, landing on the floor.

Why couldn't Anita have given her son a nice cuddly stuffed dog like a normal mother, I wondered as I stood and dusted off my trousers. It was clear that now was not the time to present the bear I'd hastily thrust at Patrick when Jack had appeared.

Patrick and Robert nodded at each other awkwardly.

'Sorry, Robert. This is my brother Patrick,' I said, and they shook hands briefly.

'You must both be tired,' I continued, desperate to get this excruciating scene over with.

Patrick took the trolley that contained a suitcase and folded-up stroller. Robert was obviously travelling light and his luggage seemed to consist only of a leather backpack he had slung across one shoulder.

Torn between feelings of sadness and abject terror of what lay ahead, I followed them to the car.

TWO

As we approached my silver European car I cursed, once again, the impulse that had made me buy it new, for a ridiculous sum, two years ago. At the time I had managed to convince myself that it would be reliable and last me for years and that I wasn't just buying it because it looked cool. Instead, it had spent more time in the mechanic's than on the road, as one thing after another went wrong. To add insult to injury, the parts all had to be shipped at great cost and low speed from the other side of the world.

Thankfully the first year's worth of repairs had been covered by the warranty. But now I was on my own and I was in constant fear of what disaster my temperamental set of wheels was going to throw at me next.

I'd once read about a man in China who'd had similar problems with his car. He had drawn attention to his plight by towing it behind an ox through the centre of Beijing and having several men set to it with sledgehammers. It was only with regret that I'd given up on the idea of a similar performance in the Queen Street Mall, oxen being pretty hard to come by.

My sole consolation, that the car looked cool and classy, was wearing very thin. As Robert tried to cram Jack into the back seat, I realised that the disadvantages of a two-door car were about to take on a whole new dimension.

Finally Robert managed to deposit Jack into the car seat I'd bought the day before. He wrestled with the harness for a few minutes before withdrawing his head and looking over his shoulder at Patrick and me, hovering uselessly behind him.

'Do either of you have any idea how this works?' he asked wearily.

Patrick shook his head vehemently.

'The woman in the shop did explain it to me,' I admitted. 'Although I wasn't paying much attention – I figured it would be pretty obvious.'

'Right, your turn then.' Robert straightened and gestured towards the back seat.

As I leaned over Jack, he started screaming at the top of his lungs. The noise felt as though it could burst my eardrums and it was almost impossible to concentrate. I fumbled uselessly with the two straps, unable to click them together in the way that had seemed so easy when the shop assistant had demonstrated it.

Admitting defeat, I stood up. 'What do we do now?' I asked hopelessly, wondering whether it would be criminal to drive home without strapping him in.

A woman pushing a child in a stroller walked past and unlocked a car several metres away.

After a moment's hesitation, I followed her. 'Excuse me,' I began.

She looked up and smiled.

'This is going to sound really strange. But none of us has any idea how to do up the baby seat.' I gestured towards the car. 'Would you mind giving us a hand?'

The woman looked over at a stained and exhausted-looking Robert, a terrified-looking Patrick, who had positioned himself on the far side of the car, and then back to me.

'Sure,' she replied, obviously having decided that we all looked too incompetent to be dangerous.

Pushing her stroller over, she leaned into the car and spoke soothingly to Jack who stopped crying instantly. She clicked the belt into place with one easy movement.

'Thank you so much,' I gushed.

'No problem at all,' she answered. Turning to go, she stopped and looked back around. 'Is there anything else I can do?'

'No. We'll be fine, thanks,' I lied.

With a doubtful look she headed back to her car.

By some miracle we finally managed to fit the three of us, plus the luggage and the stroller, into my car. This was despite the fact that it was designed to carry about one and a half people. As the smallest, I'd squeezed into the back seat with Jack, who had resumed crying as soon as the helpful woman had left. Patrick slid into the driver's seat and turned the key in the ignition.

I could deal with this, I told myself, pulling a plastic shopping bag off the floor. I'd spent a hellish hour in Baby World the day before. For some reason I couldn't bring myself to tell the truth about Jack to the shop assistant. Instead, I'd made up some crazy story about my nephew arriving and my sister-in-law having forgotten to pack anything but his clothes. The woman obviously thought I was mad but was more than willing to help me fill my trolley.

Nearly a thousand dollars later, I walked out with what I was assured were 'the basics'.

Before I'd left home this morning, I'd filled a bag with a random selection of my purchases. Opening it now, the first things I saw were an empty drink cup, a carton of cupboard safety locks and a set of swimming floaties (I hadn't been paying much attention by the end). Digging further I found a small cardboard book with pictures of babies and a rattle on it.

I offered this hopefully to Jack. My spirits rose when he took it, but fell when he flung it to the floor. The next three toys met the same fate. I abandoned my useless bag of purchases and tried talking to him. Unable even to hear my voice I gave up and spent the remainder of the trip looking miserably at him, feeling utterly useless.

After what felt like an eternity but was only about fifteen minutes, Patrick pulled up outside the house. Fortunately unbuckling the car seat was relatively easy. I hesitated, unsure whether to pick Jack up. A glance ascertained that Robert and

Patrick were fully occupied unwedging the luggage from my tiny boot. 'Right,' I muttered under my breath.

I tentatively pulled Jack's arms out of the straps and held him, still crying, to my chest as I scrambled out of the car and hurried towards my house.

The Queenslander, which I'd bought a year earlier, was set up high on a hill in New Farm about two kilometres from the CBD. While it looked quite impressive from the road, it had definitely seen better days and I lived in fear that it was going to take notes from my car and start costing me a lot of money.

The main selling point for me had been the enormous deck, which looked over a small overgrown backyard. The combined kitchen and dining room ran off the deck with the living room, two bedrooms, a study and bathroom looking as though they had been afterthoughts.

Although he was six years younger than me, Patrick and I had always got along well and, to help me pay the crippling mortgage, he'd moved into the bedroom downstairs.

Despite the fact that I now subscribed to three different home-renovating magazines and had magnificent plans, I hadn't managed to do more than paint one side of my bedroom door fire-engine red.

Patrick struggled briefly with the front gate and then our small convoy headed up the long flight of stairs. I carried a still-crying and struggling Jack, while Robert and Patrick brought Jack's gear.

I twisted the key in the lock and pushed the front door open with my shoulder. Jack finally stopped crying. With relief I set him down and he headed off at great speed towards the steps that led down to Patrick's bedroom.

In panic I ran after him and deposited him back in the middle of the room, only to see him tear off towards a pot plant, somehow managing to shove a handful of dirt into his mouth before I caught up with him. After frantically scraping out the largest clumps, I looked around at Patrick and Robert, who stood in the doorway watching wordlessly.

'What do I do now?' I asked, trying to be calm. 'Is dirt dangerous?'

Robert looked embarrassed. 'Well, he ate about half a pot plant in Rome airport and seems to have survived,' he admitted.

Slightly reassured, I released Jack. Anticipating his sprint-star acceleration this time, I caught him just before he pulled over the large terracotta pot next to the front door.

'What on earth do I do with him?' I asked Robert and Patrick as I held a wriggling Jack in my arms.

I was met with blank looks. It was fast becoming clear that Robert and Patrick knew even less about children than I did, a situation I hadn't thought possible.

Patrick's face lit up.

'What about feeding him?' he exclaimed, obviously impressed by his flash of brilliance.

At this stage any ideas were welcome and I nodded vehemently. 'Great idea – food. When did he last eat, Robert?'

Again Robert looked embarrassed. 'Well . . . It depends what you call eating . . .' His voice trailed off. 'Once we got to Singapore I remembered the lollipops I'd thrown in my bag before we left and . . . Well, he ate a few of them on the Brisbane leg and didn't seem to want anything else.'

'How many lollipops?' I asked suspiciously.

'Ah, a few,' he replied, not meeting my eyes.

I raised my eyebrows and waited.

'All right, probably around ten,' he admitted.

'Right . . .' I said slowly. Any vague hope I'd had that Robert would be able to help me look after Jack vaporised as I realised he'd had his nephew chain-sucking lollipops for the last eight hours.

Looking around for somewhere to put Jack, I discovered that somehow my excited shop assistant had omitted a high-chair from my 'essential' purchases.

I spotted the stroller, which was stacked next to the suitcases.

'Patrick, could you open that?' I asked as I headed for the kitchen, still holding Jack.

Yesterday, credit card still shuddering from the Baby World

experience, I'd gone to the supermarket. With no clue about what an eighteen month old would eat, I'd been hit by a burst of inspiration and bought anything I could see with cartoon characters on the packaging. Consequently, two shelves in my fridge were crammed with miniature yoghurts, cheese sticks and other things I couldn't even identify.

Grabbing a yoghurt and a spoon, I stepped back into the living room to see Patrick struggling with the as yet unopened stroller.

'The damn thing won't undo,' he muttered through gritted teeth as he tried to pull it apart with brute force.

'Robert, you must have opened this, surely,' I pleaded.

'No, I couldn't get it open either. I just stuck Jack on the top of the luggage trolley.'

Thrusting Jack at Robert I grabbed the stroller. As I did, I was reminded of a strategy a married friend of mine had once let slip after too many drinks. Swearing me to secrecy, he had confided that the approach many a groom takes to his wedding arrangements is to seize with great enthusiasm a difficult job and then proceed to make a total and absolute hash of it. The result, my friend grinned, was that the bride-to-be immediately removed any form of responsibility from the groom.

If Patrick and Robert were using a similar strategy, it was clearly very successful.

After struggling for a couple more minutes, I managed to accidentally depress and twist a latch at the same time as undoing a clip, and the stroller sprung open. I made a mental note never to fold it up again.

Banging it down purposefully on the floor, I took Jack back from Robert and deposited him in the seat. After pulling the top off the yoghurt, I handed it to Jack and placed a spoon in his free hand. He looked at the carton with great interest and then inverted it, pouring the entire contents into his lap.

'Right,' I pronounced heavily.

Ten minutes later I had opened and discarded just about every packet and tin I had bought and Jack still hadn't eaten a thing.

In desperation, I looked at Patrick and Robert. 'What do I do now?'

They both shrugged.

'Maybe he's not hungry,' Patrick volunteered.

'Surely if he hasn't eaten in nearly twenty-four hours he needs something in his stomach?'

Robert cleared his throat. 'Um, one of the airline hostesses took a shine to Jack and made him some fairy bread. You know, bread with hundreds and thousands? He was pretty happy with that.'

'Yeah, well it's handy to know, but my pantry doesn't quite stretch to hundreds and thousands. I haven't even seen any since I was a kid. I wouldn't have thought there'd be a huge demand for them on international flights either.'

'She told me it was her secret remedy for stroppy kids. She gave me the bottle. I think she figured I needed all the help I could get.'

I looked at Jack and decided today was not the day to worry about his dietary intake. 'Sounds good to me.'

I picked up the loaf of bread sitting on the bench.

'Julia!'

'What?' I looked over at Patrick.

'You cannot make multigrain fairy bread. It has to be white.'

Robert nodded his agreement as he rifled in his shoulder bag and pulled out a small bottle. 'It was definitely white on the plane.'

'Okay.' I held up my hands in defeat.

I reached for the loaf of white bread, which, together with frozen pies and sugar-laden breakfast cereal, seemed to constitute Patrick's sole grocery needs.

Jack accepted the brightly coloured piece of bread, smiled enthusiastically and wolfed down two slices. I handed him a third for good measure. Hunger pangs obviously stilled, he began to lick the tiny balls off the bread.

'All right, I think I might put him to bed.' I figured that everyone was tired when they came off a long-haul flight but that didn't make me any less nervous at the prospect of trying to get him to sleep.

'Why don't you head off?' I suggested to Patrick. 'Won't you be late for work?' Somehow it seemed better to have as few witnesses to my incompetence as possible.

After Patrick had headed downstairs, Robert cleared his throat.

'Julia. There are a couple of things we need to talk about.'

'Yeah, I know.' I looked at him, not knowing where to start.

'Did Anita ever mention Jack's father to you?'

I bit my lip hard, trying not to burst into tears again. In the last two days I had cried more than I had in the rest of my life. Now that Jack was here I had to try to get it together.

'Um.' I tried to force the shakiness from my voice. 'His name was Thomas Driscoll. He broke her heart.'

'Do you know how they met? Or if he knows about Jack?'

I nodded. 'He was a teacher at her school, out from England for a twelve-month stint. He had separated from his wife and he and Anita were together for a few months. But then his wife came over and asked for another chance. They had two kids – girls, I think. Didn't Anita ever tell you any of this?'

Robert looked sad. 'She told me bits, but not the whole story. I don't know, we never seemed to talk about that kind of stuff.'

'Well, Thomas flew back to the UK with his wife and Anita found out she was pregnant a few days later.'

'Did she ever tell him about Jack?'

I nodded again. 'She sent him a letter. He sent one back with a cheque for five thousand pounds saying he didn't want to be involved.'

'God, what a wanker!'

'Yeah – Anita was really hurt. Although I think once she got over the rejection, she realised that she was probably better off without him.'

'But there was never anyone else?'

I shook my head. 'Not that she ever told me about. I think her job and Jack kept her pretty busy. And I guess not a lot of guys want to jump into a relationship with someone with a small child.'

I tried not to think about the consequences for my own love life.

'So does that mean this Thomas Driscoll doesn't have any claim over Jack now?'

'I really don't know,' I answered, slightly embarrassed. People frequently assumed, not unreasonably, that I had some knowledge of practical legal matters. Unfortunately, as a lawyer who had spent her whole career focused on the dealings of huge companies, my knowledge of anything useful was rather sketchy.

Had one of my friends asked me how to list a company on the stock exchange, I'd have been just the girl. But somehow none of them ever seemed to be in need of that kind of information.

'Um, I think as he's had nothing to do with Jack, it would be pretty unlikely that he would just step in now – assuming he wanted to,' I answered. 'But he is Jack's father so I guess he needs to be notified.'

How someone could not even want to see his child defied understanding. I felt a fresh wave of anger for the man who had hurt Anita so badly and abandoned Jack.

'My lawyer in London did Anita's will, so I can see if he knows what we need to do,' Robert suggested.

'Okay – and I'll find someone at work who can tell me what we have to do this end. So it was you who arranged for Anita to have her will done?' I asked.

To Robert's frustration, organisation had never been Anita's strong point. I remembered her telling me that he'd given her an electronic diary one Christmas. She'd tried it briefly and then returned to her old system of an envelope full of phone numbers written on scraps of paper. So the fact that she'd managed to do a will had seemed out of character.

Robert nodded. 'When I went to Italy just after Jack was born, I talked to her about it. I'm sure she only did it to shut me up.' He paused. 'The other thing I did was make her take out life insurance. I think there will be about $300,000. Some of it is to be kept in trust for Jack and the rest is to be used for looking after him and his education.'

'That's good news,' I said without a lot of enthusiasm.

I hadn't even thought about how I was going to afford to look after Jack. This whole thing had happened so suddenly, I still hadn't got my head around it.

It sounded like a lot of money, but I was sure Jack would rather have his mum around. I knew I certainly would.

Jack had obviously grown bored of eating and started lunging forward against the chest straps of the stroller.

I tore off a piece of paper towel and gave his hands a half-hearted wipe. Reluctantly I lifted him out of the stroller. He immediately walked over to the only pot plant I'd managed to keep alive for longer than a week and started tearing off the leaves, systematically working his way upward. I was pretty sure it wasn't poisonous and figured if it made him happy for a little while, it was worth the sacrifice. Happiness was in short supply in his life at the moment.

Robert obviously agreed with me as he just raised his eyebrows and continued. 'She wrote you a letter as well, although I don't think she ever believed you'd see it.'

Robert handed me an envelope. My name was scrawled across the front in Anita's familiar writing. I stared at it for a couple of seconds then slipped it into the back pocket of my jeans.

I took a deep breath. 'I still don't really understand why Anita made me Jack's guardian. I mean, what about your family? Or one of her friends in Italy?' As soon as the words were out of my mouth, I knew they sounded terrible but I also knew we were way past being polite. This was my life, and Jack's, we were talking about here.

To my relief, Robert didn't look offended, just sad. 'There's not much family to talk of really.'

I winced inwardly. Anita and Robert's parents had been a lot older than mine and had both died – their father when they were children and their mother only a few years ago. A reminder of how little family Robert had left was the last thing he needed. But if his thoughts had followed mine, he gave no sign.

'The only relative we . . .' He paused for a moment and corrected himself. '. . . I keep in contact with – is Carla, Mum's younger sister. She runs a shop over in Paddington, but she never had any kids and must be at least sixty-five.'

I remembered Anita mentioning an exciting aunt who used to bring them back presents from exotic places. She didn't sound like the kind of person who would want to take on a toddler.

'And that's it?' I felt as though the walls were closing in on me. I glanced at Jack, relieved to see he was still engrossed in destroying my plant.

'Pretty much. Anita probably told you that Dad had a big falling-out with his family years ago, so we never really knew them. Other than that, there's just me.'

'And what about you?' It was the question that had been going over and over in my mind for the last two days.

The look on Robert's face confirmed my fears, but I kept talking. 'Look, I don't think I can do this by myself.' My words tumbled over each other. 'Maybe Jack should be with you, not me. You're his uncle, for God's sake – I'm just a friend. I could understand it if I had kids of my own or something, but I know absolutely nothing about bringing up a child. I work eighteen-hour days and have no idea how I'm going to manage Jack as well. It's pretty obvious Anita didn't think all this through properly because she just didn't think it would ever happen. Or maybe she assumed that by the time anything happened to her I'd have my own family. She can't possibly have contemplated this situation.'

I looked again at Jack, who was now pulling the dirt out of the pot. A stab of guilt hit me but I ignored it, trying to tell myself that Anita wouldn't have wanted Jack to be part of the life I currently lived.

Robert's eyes didn't quite meet mine. 'Julia, you don't understand. My life is in London. I have a flat that doesn't even have a spare room. Jack just wouldn't fit.'

My eyes widened. 'Does this place look like a childcare centre to you? C'mon, Robert, that's not an excuse.'

'Julia . . . I just can't take Jack. I can help you – take him on holidays to give you a break but . . .'

There it was. Confirmation that I really was on my own. Robert had been my last hope but he couldn't be much clearer than that. I swallowed my reply. The things I wanted to say to him weren't going to help the situation and the last thing we both needed was an argument.

'There's something else,' he said. From his tone, this wasn't going to be good news. 'Anita's funeral is on Thursday. She's being buried in Rome.'

The funeral. Strangely, thinking about that made her death seem more real than her son's arrival on my doorstep.

'She's being buried in Italy?'

'It was her home,' Robert said simply. 'I really want to be there. And there are lots of things that need to be sorted out. But it means leaving tomorrow morning.'

I tried to be charitable and think about the situation from his point of view, but it wasn't easy.

Although I was certain he was as devastated as I was, Robert had kept it together enough to deal with everything to get Jack out here. He'd just endured a long flight with a terrified nephew he hardly knew and now here I was harassing him. But I knew if we didn't have this conversation now, we never would.

'Will you come back?'

'After I sort out Anita's affairs, I'll go to London and deal with some business that I just can't ignore. I'll come back again in a few weeks. I can help you out for a while. How does that sound?' He looked as though he was trying to convince us both he was doing the right thing.

It sounds ratshit! I wanted to scream. Don't leave me here all alone. I have no idea what I'm doing and I'm terrified I'm going to get it all wrong.

But something, possibly pride, forced me to nod. 'That sounds fine.' I tried unsuccessfully to speak with conviction. 'It's not like you're an expert anyway.' I tried to smile, remembering the lollipops.

I turned my head to the side, rubbing my hand across my eyes. When I opened them I saw Jack looking at us, a very dirty thumb in mouth.

Anita was dead. She wanted me to bring up her son. So I would. It was that simple.

'Right, there we are then.'

I looked back at Robert, whose face was tight with fatigue.

'You must be exhausted. Patrick should be gone by now – why don't you go and have a sleep on his bed?'

Robert shook his head briefly. 'I said I'd go and see Carla when I got in. She loved Anita – saw something of herself in her, I think. Anyway, seeing her for the first time since – well, since the accident, isn't going to be great so I want to get it out of the way.'

Looking like a man on his way to the gallows, he picked his bag up and headed for the door. He turned around at the top of the steps.

'Julia – thanks.'

I smiled faintly.

'That's okay. It will all work out.'

I just hoped I was right.

THREE

The reality of the situation hit me like a shower of icy water. This was it. I could no longer walk out the door and do whatever I wanted whenever I wanted. This noisy whirlwind of a child and his hideous toad were mine forever. I felt as though I was going to throw up.

I didn't even have my parents to help me as they'd just left for a three-month tour of New Zealand. It was a trip they'd been saving for as long as I could remember, putting money aside each week. I hadn't wanted my mum this badly since Amanda Jacobs stole my tuckshop money in year four, but I couldn't ruin their holiday of a lifetime.

Patrick had told me I was mad, that they'd be livid when they returned. But I was determined not to tell them and made him promise not to as well. I knew if I did, there'd be no talking them out of coming home early to help me. They'd probably never have an opportunity to do this trip again, and besides, this was my problem, not theirs.

Mum was from Melbourne; her brother and his family still lived there but I hadn't seen them in years. Dad was an only child and none of my grandparents were alive, so I was on my own. Except for Patrick, who was possibly more clueless than I was.

Squashing the panic rising in my chest, I looked at my

watch and saw with disbelief that it was only eight-thirty. The whole day stretched ahead endlessly.

I pulled Anita's letter out of my pocket. Slitting the envelope with my finger, I took out the single sheet of paper. Judging by the date at the top, Jack must have only been a couple of months old when Anita wrote it.

Dear Julia,

If you're reading this then I'm no longer around. Given my organisational skills, it's highly likely that Jack is forty-five and I never managed to update my will. In which case, please consider your guardian duties fulfilled . . .

But if he's not, then you must be wondering what on earth I've done.

As I write this, Jack is still tiny and not exactly doing a lot, but already he's the most precious thing in my life. If I can't be around to show him the world, then you're the person I want to do it. What I hope is that I'm not being too selfish and that you'll love Jack and get as much joy out of him as I do.

Thank you.

Love always,

Anita.

Tears dropped off my chin and onto the letter.

Jack was looking at me quietly.

'Well, my little friend, it's just you and me from now on. How do you feel about that?' I asked softly.

If this had been a telemovie, Jack would have smiled at me and held out his arms for a hug. Instead, he grabbed hold of the stroller, causing the whole thing to tip over on top of him with a resounding crash. There was a brief silence while he inhaled, followed by an ear-splitting wail.

Convinced he'd broken something, or at the very least needed stitches, I picked him up, trying to remember where the nearest hospital was. To my relief, I couldn't see any blood or any limbs poking out at unnatural angles. My first-aid certificate had long since lapsed, but I didn't think internal bleeding was likely.

I gently pushed his head towards my shoulder, but his crying increased and he struggled to be put down. He stood there sobbing, his little shoulders shaking. I swallowed, trying to move the lump in my throat. If a complete stranger tried to hug me when I was upset, I'd set her straight too. I was just going to have to take this slowly.

Still hiccupping, Jack rubbed the knuckles of his hand into his eyes.

'All right, I think it's time for bed. What do you think?'

His little T-shirt and jeans were covered in yoghurt. Gingerly I eased his elbows out of the T-shirt and pulled it over his head. So far so good. I realised I'd been holding my breath and forced myself to exhale.

Shoes next. The laces were tied into double bows and I wondered for a moment if that was the way Anita had always done it. Was he still wearing the clothes she had dressed him in, thinking she was getting him ready for another ordinary day? The thought snagged at my mind and I felt close to tears again.

I'd just managed to slip his shoes off when Jack decided he'd stood still for long enough. Pushing past me, he headed for the deck. Again I was surprised at his speed and I only just caught hold of him before he reached the kitchen.

I carried him into the bedroom, awkwardly pulling his jeans over his bottom as I went. The sight of his nappy reinforced just how far out of my depth I was. I wondered how often they had to be changed and articles I'd read about neglected children being discovered with cockroaches in their pants sprang to mind. However, I simply couldn't deal with a nappy change just yet.

I'd do it just as soon as he'd had his nap, I promised myself. The cot was already made up, the sheets still bearing the creases from the packets I'd pulled them from at four o'clock this morning. Gingerly I laid him down, unhooked the jeans from his feet and held my breath. Immediately he sprang to his feet, grabbed the bars and started wailing at the top of his voice.

Rushing out of the bedroom, I closed the door behind me. I sank onto the sofa and put my head in my hands, trying to figure out what to do now. His crying grew even louder.

I recalled hearing somewhere that picking a crying child up out of bed ruined their sleep patterns forever. But it didn't seem right to leave a little boy who'd just lost his mother, and had been sent to the other side of the world, to cry.

I walked back into his room and lifted him into my arms. He stopped crying instantly. I spoke soothingly to him and then, without any real hope, started lowering him back into the cot. His legs and arms tightened around me like a vice and I was left half bent over the cot with him clinging to me like a limpet.

What the hell did I do now?

Relenting once again, I carried him back into the living room and sat down on the sofa. As I pondered my tactics, the telephone rang and I answered it absently.

'Hello Julia. It's Jonathon Earl,' announced the senior partner of Jennings Walker, the firm of solicitors I worked for. Jonathon and I weren't exactly buddies. I was pretty sure that he'd been unaware of my existence until recently, despite the fact that I'd worked in the firm for years.

'Jonathon!' I jolted upright.

'How are you, Julia?' he asked.

'Oh fine, just fine,' I answered with forced joviality.

'Very good,' he replied, obviously having exhausted his notoriously limited small talk. 'Mark has just informed me that you have taken two weeks off work.'

His tone left no doubt as to what he thought of that. I wondered whether Mark, the partner I worked for, had explained what had happened, but decided that it wouldn't make any difference. There were a lot of stories told about Jonathon Earl and if they were even half true, he had no concept of any form of life outside the office.

I looked apprehensively down at Jack, who was sitting quietly in my lap.

'Um, yes. A family emergency came up over the weekend.'

'Gordon has just called wanting an update on the trial. I said I'd speak to you.' Gordon Farley was one of my clients and also, to my great dismay, one of Jonathon's personal friends.

I tried to sound businesslike. 'I was planning on calling him this afternoon to tell him about my . . .' I hesitated, 'situation. I still have control over everything even though I'm not in the office.'

Jonathon's reply was drowned out by a sudden wail from Jack.

Jumping up, I jiggled Jack desperately on one hip, phone glued to the opposite ear.

'Julia. Can you hear me?' Jonathon's words had an edge of irritation.

'Yes, yes,' I lied.

He continued talking, but I couldn't hear a thing.

'Ah, actually Jonathon, do you think I could call you back?' I yelled into the telephone.

The only parts of his reply that I caught were 'no' and 'meeting'.

Sprinting into the kitchen, I looked around wildly. With relief I spotted a half-eaten piece of fairy bread and shoved it into Jack's mouth. His noise stopped instantly and I realised with relief that he couldn't eat and cry simultaneously.

'I'm glad to hear that you are confident you have everything in hand.' Jonathon's tone clearly implied that he had serious doubts about this. 'I don't need to remind you how important this matter is to the firm. I think you should meet with Gordon on Wednesday. We need to reassure him that his case is your priority. Do you have any problem with that?'

Did I have any problem with that?

On Saturday I'd called Mark, who was technically my boss but who still had to report to Jonathon, to tell him what had happened. He'd instantly given me two weeks off work and agreed that I could work from home a couple of days a week while I settled Jack in. But my assumption that I'd be able to easily arrange daycare for the other days crumbled when Mark called back to say that his wife doubted I'd be able to find anywhere to take Jack on less than six months' notice. As it had been the weekend, I hadn't been able to call and check and consequently had no idea what I was going to do with Jack when my leave was over.

I cursed whatever whim of fortune had made one of Jennings Walker's most important clients decide that I was his favourite lawyer.

But Jonathon's question was clearly rhetorical, so I answered as he expected. 'No, of course not, Jonathon. Wednesday is fine.'

'Excellent. My secretary will call you with the time.' He rang off without saying goodbye.

I pushed the disconnect button as Jack choked down the last crumb of fairy bread and immediately resumed crying. Drained, I slumped back down onto the sofa. As my adrenaline levels subsided, I registered that I was sitting on a large object. I leaned over and pulled Harold, the world's ugliest frog, out from under me.

Jack grabbed it with both arms and buried his face in its plastic neck, his crying miraculously silenced.

A vague hope stirred. Carrying Jack back into the bedroom, I laid him down on his back in the cot. To my great amazement he immediately closed his eyes, arms clasped tightly around the frog.

'Thank you, God,' I muttered, trudging to my bedroom and sinking onto the bed, unable to think about Jonathon, Gordon or their accursed trial right now.

FOUR

I woke up two hours later to find Jack still fast asleep. I had no idea what I was going to do when he woke up and was terrified by the prospect. Unable to focus on any activity for more than a few seconds, I flinched each time the dog next door barked, or the noise of trucks grinding past to a nearby construction site echoed through the house. Suddenly the sound of the front doorbell pierced the air.

Trying not to make any noise, I hurried down the hall, praying whoever it was wouldn't ring again.

'Maggie!' At this point even the postman would have made my day, but Maggie was like a lifeline – a reminder that normal life was continuing outside this house.

Shoulder-length brown hair corkscrewing madly around her face, my visitor looked as though she'd only just climbed out of bed – a highly likely scenario, despite the fact that it was now almost eleven. She was wearing black trousers, a tight white T-shirt with sequins all over the front, and her familiar silver choker from which a turquoise pendant dangled today. Maggie was always hard to miss.

I'd known her since she'd hired me soon after I'd started university. In the first two weeks of my first term I'd managed to spend all the money in my bank account, money I'd been hoping would last until the next holidays. On scouring the job section of the newspaper, I'd spotted an advertisement for bar staff at the King's Head, a popular pub on Edward Street in the city. Despite the fact that I'd only passed the legal drinking age three weeks earlier and had never pulled a beer in my life, I decided to give it a go.

The ad had said to come any time after nine. Thinking I'd make a good impression, I arrived at eight-thirty the next morning to find the pub closed and empty except for a cleaner who was about my age. She laughed and told me the interviews started at nine that evening. Feeling decidedly stupid, I turned to go.

'But if you leave your details and the hours you want to work, I'll see if I can get you some shifts,' Maggie added.

It turned out that, far from being the cleaner, Maggie was the boss's daughter and in charge of the staff.

After a few terrible mistakes, I got the hang of bar work and the job suited me perfectly. I worked there for almost five years and Maggie and I became close friends.

Maggie's father had retired three years ago, leaving her in charge of the whole place. As one of the very few women in the hotel industry, she was always getting propositioned and worked hard to live down the jokes about the pub making her the best catch in Brisbane.

Now, face full of concern, she stood on the top step holding two jumbo cups of takeaway coffee and a tub which I knew from past experience had come from the King's Head.

'I didn't know what to bring but I figured you can never have too much caffeine in a crisis . . .'

I smiled, only just resisting the urge to throw myself into her arms. 'Come out to the deck. But be quiet – Jack's asleep and I'd like to leave it that way until I figure out what to do when he wakes.'

She slipped off her shoes and tiptoed up the hall behind me, depositing the tub in the fridge before following me onto the deck.

I closed the folding doors behind us, leaving a small gap so I could hear Jack if he woke.

'So how's it going?' she asked as we sat down around the huge pine table that was the focal point of the house.

I took a large mouthful of the delicious coffee.

'Oh great, just great. So far Jack's almost pulled three heavy objects onto his head and has pulled his stroller down on top of himself. I have also just had a conversation with one of the most important partners at work, which I have no doubt confirms his general opinion that women should never have been given the vote.'

'Well Jack's asleep now – that's good, right?' Maggie was clearly searching for something to be positive about, but I was not in the mood for optimism.

'I have no idea. What if he's too old for a daytime sleep and now he'll stay awake all night?'

'But what's the alternative – waking him? Aren't kids really grumpy if they're woken up before they're ready?'

I looked at her desperately. How was I to know? 'Maggie, I have never been so out of depth in my whole life. What am I going to do?'

'Have you thought any more about asking your folks to come home early? Your mum is going to have kittens when she realises what you've been keeping from her.'

I shook my head again, this time with more conviction. 'Nope – this is my problem. I can't expect to always go running to my folks when something goes wrong. I'm thirty-one, for God's sake.'

'Yeah, well this isn't exactly an everyday situation. It's not like you forgot to pay the rent.'

'I know. It's just they've been saving for this trip forever. I don't want to ruin it for them.' Despite my brave words, I had been having serious thoughts about asking them to come home.

'What about when they call? How are you going to explain the sound of a child in the background?'

'That one's easy. Mum has discovered the joy of text messaging. She keeps sending me updates on my mobile telling me where they are. I figure all I have to do is keep texting them back complaining about how much work I have on and they won't notice anything.'

Suddenly I didn't want to talk or think about my problems anymore.

'Brighten up my day a bit. Did you go out last night?'

Maggie rolled her eyes. 'Yeah, although I wish I'd stayed home. I went out with this guy who's head of marketing for some company producing a new boutique beer.'

As if on cue her mobile phone beeped. She pulled it out of her bag casually and then dropped it with a clatter on the table.

'Aaah,' she yelled.

I expected to hear an answering scream from Jack, but it was beginning to appear that he slept like Patrick did after twenty beers.

'What?' I asked, knowing Maggie's extreme reactions well enough not to panic.

'It's him!' She jabbed her finger towards the table. 'Barry – the guy from last night. He's text-messaged me!'

I picked up the phone.

Had a gr8 time last nite. Fancy doing it ag -n?

I looked at her. 'I thought people only sent that kind of message in *Sex in the City*.'

'Not quite the same as a dozen red roses, is it?'

'So did you have a gr8 time too?'

'Hardly – he spends more on his clothes than I do. He called me babe and talked about his favourite designers all night – and he wore his sunglasses inside.'

'So why don't you just send back a message saying, *Not while I'm breathing*?'

'Well it's a bit complicated. He's arrived in town with an enormous budget and he has to pick which pubs are going to get the big promotions. I can't really afford to piss him off.'

'So what are you going to do – keep going out with him until he's made his decision and then tell him you hate him?'

She looked embarrassed. 'Well, I had a plan. It just doesn't seem to have worked.'

'Yes?'

'Well, I decided it would be better if he dumped me.' She shifted uncomfortably in the chair.

'And?'

'And I spent the whole night being a pain in the arse. I whinged about the food, I talked about my allergies. Hell, I even told him my favourite band was Bon Jovi! He agreed with me that nothing has ever come close to *Bed of Roses*!'

I doubled over laughing. 'Nice plan. So based on this experience, he's decided you're his soul mate. He must be quite a catch.'

Reluctantly she started laughing. 'Fine. I'm pleased to see I have at least lifted your spirits. Now what am I going to do?'

'Don't look at me. Do I look like I am in a position to hand out advice?'

She sighed and glanced at the keypad on her phone. 'Ideas on how to respond?'

A call of 'Mama!' floated out to us on the deck.

We looked at one another. My hollow feeling of unease, which had subsided while we were talking about Maggie's dramas, returned.

'Oh God. He thinks Anita is here,' I whispered.

Slowly I walked into the house. Jack was standing up in his cot, Harold tucked under one arm.

'Hi.' I forced a smile, sure that like dogs, children could smell terror. 'Remember me? I'm Julia. You're staying with me now.'

He looked at me without expression and then his lip quivered and his face crumpled.

'Mama!' he sobbed. 'Mama!'

'Oh Jack. Your mum's not here. She would do anything to be, but she can't. But it will be all right, it really will.'

I wasn't sure I believed it myself.

One side of Jack's face was creased with the line of the sheet and his eyes were bleary. Half awake and groggy, all he wanted was Anita.

Tentatively I reached my arms out towards him.

'No!' he yelled, pushing at my hands and crying even

louder. Throwing himself on top of Harold, he put a thumb in his mouth and, still crying, began sucking desperately.

I tried to tell myself that his rejection was completely understandable, that it wasn't personal, but I couldn't help feeling terribly hurt by it.

He looked so helpless lying curled around Harold. I would have given anything to take away his misery, but I knew the only way to do that was to bring back Anita.

Out of the corner of my eye I saw Maggie in the doorway and turned towards her, mutely appealing for any ideas.

She shook her head.

Jack's cries gradually subsided, but he didn't move.

Not knowing what else to do, I knelt on the floor next to the cot and talked not to Jack but to Harold. 'So Harold, what do you think of your new room? I'm sorry about the walls, we'll paint them something much nicer soon.'

The room had been painted a lurid blue when I bought the house and keeping the door closed had always seemed like an easier option that doing anything about it.

'It needs a bit of decoration too, doesn't it? What does a frog your age like? Winnie the Pooh, or maybe Astro Boy?' I had a feeling Astro Boy had gone out with hula hoops, but I was working with whatever I could. 'I was thinking maybe you'd like to come and have a look around the rest of the house. No ponds, I'm afraid, but the bath's nice and big.'

Jack struggled to his feet on the soft mattress and held Harold in front of him; his thumb was still firmly in his mouth and tears stained his face.

Holding my breath, I lifted the pair of them up. Not wanting to push my luck, I set Jack on his feet straightaway.

Maggie had disappeared – I hoped towards the start of the toad speech.

'Come and say hello to Maggie.'

I put a hand on his back and gently guided him out the doorway and onto the deck.

'Hey Jack.' Maggie greeted him in a much softer voice than normal.

Ignoring her, he headed towards a bucket in the corner, dropped onto his bottom beside it and placed Harold next to him. Intently he picked up some pegs, dropped them in, tipped them out and started again.

I looked at Maggie with raised eyebrows and she gave a small smile, neither of us game to say a word. Gradually I lowered myself into a chair and soon, totally ignored by Jack, Maggie and I began a quiet conversation.

'Well it's a big improvement on five minutes ago,' Maggie offered.

'Yeah. I guess so. I've got to do something about that nappy though. How long can you leave those things on?'

Robert had said that the airline hostess who'd provided fairy bread had also taken pity on him and changed Jack's nappy during the flight, but it was a long time since he'd got off the plane.

Maggie shook her head. 'No idea – maybe he'll tell you when it starts to get uncomfortable.'

Somehow I didn't think it worked like that but I figured it was probably so disgusting by now that a couple more minutes wouldn't make much difference.

'I brought some seafood chowder from the pub. Do you fancy some?' Maggie asked.

'That'd be great.' I hadn't eaten anything all morning and was suddenly ravenous.

'All right. You stay here and I'll get it.' Maggie eased herself out of the chair and crept across the deck, slipping between the doors. A few minutes later she appeared with a large tray bearing three steaming bowls of soup, a plate of bread and a pile of paper serviettes with the King's Head logo on them.

'That smells fantastic.'

'Do you want to give Jack some?'

I looked over at Jack who was inspecting the various objects my poor housekeeping had left lying around on the deck. 'I don't know. He seems happy, so I think I should just leave him, don't you?'

'Yeah, probably. It needs to cool down anyway.'

The smell had obviously reached Jack though, as he looked

over and headed towards the table. I blew on a spoonful of soup and held it out to him.

'Hang on!' Maggie yelled and I jumped, spilling the soup over my legs.

'What?' I demanded.

'What if he's allergic to seafood?'

'He probably isn't,' she continued. 'But it's not worth trying until you know.'

I stared at her. 'God, Maggie, I could kill him with what I don't know. What about other things like . . . I don't know, peanuts and things? How on earth can I look after a child when I don't even know what he can eat?'

'Robert must know,' Maggie said with confidence.

I snorted. 'I doubt it. And even if he did, he's made it very clear he's just the courier. He's leaving tomorrow.'

'You're joking!'

I felt a bit guilty about how bitter my comment sounded and was gratified by Maggie's look of shock.

'Is he coming back?' she asked.

'Well, he says he's going back for Anita's funeral and to get his business in order and then he's coming out for a while. It's pretty clear, though, that he's happy leaving Jack to me, so I'm not going to hold my breath.'

'How could he just leave?'

I shook my head. 'No idea. It's not just that, though. It's . . .' I struggled for words. 'Everything. I feel like I'm stuck in the middle of a jungle without a map.' Tears spilled out of my eyes again and I wiped them away furiously with the side of my hand. 'I've never felt so alone in my whole life.'

Jack had clearly decided he wanted some soup and let out a cry.

'I'm sorry,' I sniffed. 'Here, try some bread.'

Jack took the bread only to throw it on the floor and start bellowing.

'And to make the whole thing worse,' I raised my voice so Maggie could hear me over the noise, 'I've even stopped feeling sad about Anita. I just wish she was here so I could yell at her and tell her to go find someone else's life to ruin. Pretty nice, huh?'

Maggie looked unsure how to respond. Clearly deciding the first priority was reducing the noise level in the room, she picked Jack up. He cried harder and she put him down again.

'Do you have anything else he could eat?' she asked anxiously.

I blew my nose on a serviette. 'All I've managed to get him to eat so far is fairy bread. Surely I can't give him any more?'

She raised her eyebrows.

'You're right. I definitely can. At least I know it won't kill him.'

Again Jack stuffed the fairy bread into his mouth, but he started crying the moment he'd finished and pushed away anything else I offered him.

'Look, Maggie, why don't you head off,' I finally said over his crying. 'I've got to figure this out for myself, no point in ruining your afternoon too.'

'Absolutely not,' she answered vehemently. 'I want to help.'

'No really, I have to do this myself. Jack needs to get to know me and to figure out that I'm going to be around all the time.'

'I just don't think you have to do it alone.'

I shook my head, biting my lip to stop myself from crying. 'You know, the worst thing is not knowing what I'm up against. If I can get to feel like I have it at least partly under control, then maybe I won't feel so scared.'

Maggie nodded. 'Okay. But give me a call if you change your mind. Tanya's really worried about you too, but she didn't want to call in case Jack was sleeping.'

'Okay. I'll call her later,' I promised.

Jack wouldn't even look at the toys I offered him and seemed less agitated when I wasn't too near. Trying not to take it personally, I kept as much distance as I could while removing potentially lethal objects from his path as he and Harold explored the house.

Everything was going fine until he tripped over the wire from a speaker and fell onto his knees.

I'd only known Jack for a few hours but I was pretty sure he was crying not because he'd hurt himself but because he was lonely and confused and didn't know what else to do. Hell, I was thirty years older than him and I hadn't come up with a better way of dealing with what was going on.

One of my earliest childhood memories was of lying in my grandmother's lap, sobbing because I'd been stung by a bee. It felt so good being safe and warm, pressed against her soft body, that I'd stayed there long after the pain had faded.

Wanting to give the same comfort to Jack, I sat on the floor and tried to pull him into my lap. Instead of relaxing against me, his whole body tensed and he pushed himself away.

Feeling an utter failure, I could do nothing but watch the pitiful little figure sit on the floor and cry.

Eventually he stopped and stood up again, wiping a mixture of tears and mucus across one cheek.

Despite my grand statement to Maggie about wanting to be by myself, I suddenly wished I'd asked her to stay.

I picked up the phone, figuring I had at least a couple of minutes before the next bout of crying.

'Hi Tanya, it's Julia.'

Tanya had been working at the King's Head when Maggie hired me. One of the downsides of the job was that by the time we finished work, most of our other friends were ready for bed. As a result, the three of us had started going out together. After graduation, Tanya had found a job as a journalist and had been well and truly on the career track until she'd met Greg while she was researching a story on women in the bush. She'd accused him of being a chauvinist; he'd insisted he was a roman-tic, and somehow, six months later, they were married. To everyone's great surprise, she'd happily moved to his sheep property in Central Queensland and set about writing a novel.

Greg was tall and sandy-haired. He had worked on the fam-ily property since he'd left school and only ventured into town a few times a year. But bizarrely, although they seemed totally unsuited, their differences seemed to make them complement each other. They both loved a good party and Tanya told great stories of the rodeos and musters they travelled for miles to attend. Their wedding was the stuff of legend and had lasted for three days.

For a born and bred city girl, Tanya had adapted well to the isolation and the dramatic change in lifestyle. One part of outback life Tanya refused to accept, however, was moleskins, maintaining that they accentuated every bulge she owned. She was always trying to drop a dress size, despite Greg's constant assertions that he loved her exactly as she was. I'd tried to tell her that in my opinion the most important thing was that with her long blonde hair she looked good in an Akubra. The opposite was true for me. I figured that even if a devastatingly handsome farmer proposed to me I would simply have to turn him down or live with a lifetime of hat hair.

'Julia! I'm so glad you called. How is it?'

I pondered how to answer that question. 'Not great.' I pushed my fingers against the bridge of my nose, determined not to cry. 'Jack's tired and sad and he just wants Anita. I feel like some terrible apparition he thinks has taken her away.'

'The poor darling. How are you doing?'

'Not too well.' My voice broke and I swallowed before continuing. 'I swing between feeling terrified and feeling incredibly sad for Jack.'

As I spoke, Jack spotted the stairs which led to Patrick's room and headed straight for them.

'I've got to go,' I cried. 'I'll give you a call when things get a bit better.'

'Okay. Julia? We're thinking of you – I just wish I could help some more.'

Greg was having most of the outhouses on the property rebuilt and there were tradesmen all over the place. Tanya was needed to cook for the masses and wasn't able to get to town for a couple of weeks.

'Thanks. I know. Talk to you soon.'

Just as I reached Jack, he put his hand on the wall and launched his little right leg into the air.

'Down,' he chanted as his foot miraculously hit the step below.

I paused. Maybe he was okay on steps.

As I hesitated, he kicked his leg out again. 'Down.'

This was a game or a kind of routine he must have gone through with Anita. Suddenly I felt a rush of pleasure, as if I'd been given an extra moment with her.

Slipping beside Jack, I stood on the landing where the staircase doglegged to the left.

'Come on, Jack,' I encouraged him with a smile. 'Down!'

He looked at me for a moment, foot poised above the next step.

'Nooo!' he cried, and swayed against the wall as he lost his balance.

My light-hearted feeling vaporised. Reaching out, I picked him up and carried him to the top of the steps.

'Here, Jack, give Harold a cuddle.'

Knowing I couldn't help, I handed him the frog and went to find some nappy-changing paraphernalia, figuring I may as well make the awful day even worse.

FIVE

I now had a meeting at nine-thirty on Wednesday and no one to look after Jack. Leaving him with someone even less familiar than me seemed an incredibly unfair thing to do to him. But I just couldn't see a way around it. Patrick's job seemed to consist mainly of arranging a venue for Friday night drinks, so with great trepidation I asked if he'd mind taking a morning off work to look after Jack.

'Yeah, okay,' he answered slowly. He opened the fridge door, but not before I'd seen the look of terror on his face.

'I'm really sorry. I just can't think of anything else to do. Maybe it won't be as bad as you think,' I added hopefully.

Patrick raised his eyebrows and I looked away. It was Tuesday morning and I'd only now mustered the courage to raise the topic. Patrick had witnessed enough of the last twenty-four hours to know how little grounds there were for my forced optimism.

Things hadn't improved when Robert had reappeared late on Monday afternoon. He'd had a sleep at Carla's and had come back intending to take Jack around to see her. But Jack seemed to have decided that Robert was responsible for the terrible direction his life had taken. Forgetting he'd travelled halfway around the world on Robert's lap, his face crumpled whenever his uncle came near. I couldn't console him either, and he cried almost continually until Robert decided to leave and spend the night with Carla.

Even though I knew that food wasn't the answer, cooking at least made me feel like I was doing something that might help. By evening the kitchen was littered with a variety of different meals, all of which had been noisily rejected. I was close to tears myself a lot of the time, appalled that I couldn't do anything to help this sad little boy whose world had just collapsed around him.

Finally, at ten o'clock, he'd fallen into an exhausted sleep. I'd briefly considered cleaning up, before deciding I was too tired to do anything but go to bed myself, relieved that, at least for a little while, Jack wasn't unhappy.

But his distress even penetrated his sleep and if anything the night had been worse than the day, with him waking up crying half-a-dozen times. The first time he woke, I'd tried to gently explain who I was. But that approach had resulted in half an hour of hysterical crying before he fell back asleep, tears coating his face and the sheet. After that I left the room dark and pushed Harold into his arms silently, hoping he'd assume I was Anita. That seemed to work until 4 a.m. when he was so wide awake that it was clear that sleep was no longer an option.

By the time Patrick had surfaced, I'd been up for three hours and had held my breath through two toxic nappy changes. Jack's eyes had dark circles under them and he looked as if he just couldn't figure out how things had suddenly gone so terribly wrong.

Yesterday's pattern had started again. He would be fine for a little while, but then some tiny problem would cause him to collapse in floods of tears and my attempts to comfort him were worse than useless. Finally he'd put his head down on the floor and closed his eyes. I'd scooped him up and put him into his cot where he'd mercifully gone straight to sleep.

'All right,' I conceded to Patrick. 'It probably will be as bad as you think, but it will only be for a couple of hours. My meeting is at nine-thirty, so if I leave here at nine, I should be back by eleven-thirty.'

I figured I might as well prepare Patrick for the worst, but I was fervently hoping things would have improved by tomorrow.

Jack was still asleep later that morning when Robert called around on his way to the airport. He looked as tired as he had the day before and just shook his head when I asked how his night had been.

I knew that being on another long flight and then having to deal with Anita's funeral would be awful. But even that seemed better than what I was facing and it took all my self-control not to break into tears and beg him not to leave.

Jack woke soon after Robert left, crying miserably, and he didn't stop when I took him out of bed. He wouldn't let me hold him and nothing else I could think of seemed to comfort him. Finally he climbed onto the couch, his thumb in his mouth and Harold held tightly under one arm, and the sobs eventually stopped.

The rest of the morning passed slowly and Jack slept again after lunch. With eyelids that felt like sandpaper I lay down too, but found myself unable to sleep until what seemed like moments before he woke again.

Tanya called midway through the afternoon.

'He's just so sad,' I told her. 'A little boy should just be running around chasing – I don't know – butterflies or something. Not sitting crying in my lounge room.'

'You've got to take it slowly, Julia – you can't expect miracles,' she insisted. 'He's lost his mum and he's jet-lagged to hell. Just hang in there, it's got to get better.'

The slight uplift in spirits her words gave me disappeared as soon as I hung up the phone. But our conversation had given me an idea.

Ignoring Jack's protests, I picked him and Harold up and carried them down the steps that led off the deck into the backyard.

'Sorry about the grass,' I apologised. Patrick and I usually avoided mowing the small lawn until it was impossible to get to the clothes line. While the grass wasn't the longest I'd seen it, it still came up over Jack's knees.

Undeterred, Jack explored the garden, Harold tucked firmly

under his arm. I left him to it and leaned against the back gate which opened onto some parkland, enjoying the sun on my face.

A highpitched giggle brought my attention back to Jack. I jogged to where he was standing and followed his gaze towards a snail, which was stretching its slimy head towards him. Crouching down beside him, I tried to summon some enthusiasm about the revolting creature, which was no doubt engaged in destroying what little remained of our garden.

Jack touched my arm with one hand and pointed at the snail with the other. He giggled again and suddenly I laughed too. Of course the owner of the horrible Harold wasn't going to be interested in ephemeral butterflies.

We admired the snail for what seemed like forever, but eventually Jack tired of it and headed off in another direction. It was only a matter of minutes before he tripped over a branch and dissolved into tears, but the brief glimpse of something beyond this horrible time helped me to get through the afternoon.

By the evening I'd given up any pretence of trying to feed Jack real food and put a stack of fairy bread slices on a plate on the coffee table, figuring he'd eat when he was hungry. A rummage through his suitcase had revealed a bottle and Jack had guzzled the first bottle of milk I handed him. At least he was now getting calcium, I told myself.

Finally he went to sleep just after Patrick arrived home. Even though I'd been counting the hours until my brother walked in the door, I found myself unable to muster the energy to hold a conversation and he marched me to my room and told me to go to bed.

Wednesday started at 4 a.m. Even though I'd been in bed for a long time, Jack's crying had wrenched me from my sleep so often that I found it hard to concentrate my thoughts long enough to butter his breakfast bread and cover it with the coloured sprinkles.

Eight o'clock felt like midday and I took Jack into the bathroom with me. He made a beeline for the cupboard under the sink and with one lunge gathered a tube of hair remover, a container of jewellery-cleaning liquid and a packet of aspirin. I shoved them all back onto the shelf and tied the two handles together with a scarf, making a mental note to check all of the low cupboards in the house for lethal products.

Thwarted, Jack looked around for his next disaster, his eyes brightening as he spotted the toilet roll. About to remove it, I reconsidered. A ruined toilet roll seemed a small price to pay for a peaceful shower.

I wet and lathered my hair quickly, peering through the shower screen to make sure he was still safely occupied. About half of the paper was curled on the floor and Jack was still delightedly spinning the roll. I relaxed slightly and massaged the conditioner into my scalp, then put my head under the jet of warm water and closed my eyes.

A minute or so later, my foggy mind registered the fact that the whirring noise of the spinning toilet roll had ceased and in its place was an ominous silence. Wiping steam off the shower screen, I saw Jack teetering on his stomach on the edge of the bathtub. I jumped out of the shower and lunged across the room, grabbing his legs with one hand just before his head hit the bottom of the bath.

With my other hand I pulled him backwards and picked him up. I winced as he began the now familiar wind-up, taking a deep breath and screwing up his face.

'Jack!' I exclaimed, desperately trying to distract him.

'What about the . . .' I looked around in search of a distraction. 'Toothpaste!'

I stuck the tube in front of his face, drawing a deep sigh of relief as he exhaled and reached for it. It immediately went in his mouth. After watching him for a moment I concluded that squeezing the tube was beyond him and that the amount he could lick out of the top wouldn't kill him. Kids needed fluoride anyway, didn't they?

I deposited him on the floor with the tube, towelling myself dry and combing my hair. Blow-drying was definitely an optional extra today. Reaching for my make-up bag, I applied a quick layer of foundation and was brushing on mascara when Jack lunged at my legs.

I wiped the mascara, which had jolted across my eyebrow, but only ended up with a black smudge. By the time I had repaired the damage, finished my make-up and herded Jack back into the bedroom, it was half-past eight.

Throwing open my cupboard doors, I tried to focus on what I should wear.

A glance ascertained that Jack's interest in the contents of my bottom drawer was fading and I grabbed a black suit without further prevarication. I pulled on some underwear and then stepped into the last pair of black pantyhose in the drawer. A wide-collared white shirt went on next and then the suit.

Although I occasionally managed to look groovy on weekends, my work wardrobe could only be described as safe. Despite my protestations that I worked for a conservative law firm, Maggie and Tanya had recently taken me shopping, insisting I buy a pair of strappy shoes to loosen up the suits. But today I pulled out my old court shoes, figuring I could save the time it took me to do up the buckles on the new pair.

'Right,' I breathed as I slipped on the jacket and looked at my watch. 'Eight-forty. Mission Get Dressed successfully completed.'

Before I had even carried Jack into the living room, I realised my mistake. He grabbed at my shirt, leaving a smear of toothpaste down the front. That was okay, I decided, trying to be positive – white on white I could live with. Wriggling to be set down, Jack tipped his head into my shoulder and wiped his face on my jacket. I pulled him away and looked down. White on black – not so good.

A few dabs with a wet paper towel resulted in a white smudge embedded with flecks of paper. Suppressing the urge to scream, I looked at my watch and decided there wasn't time for an outfit change. I'd just have to carry a file over my left breast and then whip the jacket off as soon as we reached the conference room.

Where was Patrick? It occurred to me that maybe he had left the country to avoid this morning's babysitting duty. But he appeared, a pad of paper and a pen in his hands, as I was pouring milk into a bottle.

Taking the day off hadn't been a problem as Patrick had spent the last few months conducting a highly charged affair with his married boss. While I'd never met her, our house being dismissed as an insufficiently clandestine rendezvous point, I had regularly been regaled with torrid sex-on-the-boardroom-table type stories. Patrick had declared only last week that it was the best relationship he'd ever had.

'Great sex, no issues. What more could you ask for?' he'd gloated. Apparently Jennifer's husband was a highly intelligent psychology professor and, according to Patrick who had seen a photo, looked like Woody Allen's long-lost brother.

My theory was that it was the dramatic contrast between her husband's weedy frame and Patrick's footballer build that appealed to Jennifer. Although his handyman skills were stretched by a tricky light bulb, Patrick looked like someone who could knock you up a decent shack if the need arose. The fact that Jennifer had recently bought him a designer flannelette shirt only confirmed my suspicions.

'Hi,' he managed feebly, looking like he'd rather be anywhere but here. 'How was your night?'

'Fine, just fine,' I lied, not wanting to scare him any more than he was already.

'Okay.' He visibly braced himself, pen poised over the paper. 'Give me the drill.'

'All right,' I replied. 'Here's the deal. I'm going to put him into bed with a bottle now. He should go to sleep and, with a bit of luck, sleep for an hour or so.' I decided not to tell him that I wouldn't be putting large sums of money on this chain of events actually occurring.

'Uh huh.' Patrick nodded while making notes. He looked up from the pad. 'What then?'

'Pick him up and put him out on the deck. Don't leave him in any other room, he'll tear it apart and find every life-threatening object within thirty seconds. He should just play out there. You can give him some fairy bread if you think he's hungry.' I paused to let Patrick finish scribbling.

'What do I do if he cries?' he asked.

'Well, you can pick him up,' I suggested half-heartedly, given my limited success.

Reading upside down, I saw him scrawl the words 'Crying – pick up'.

'And what then?'

'Jiggle him or something. Say nice things . . . maybe sing him a nursery rhyme?'

'Nursery rhymes . . .' Patrick mused, trying to bring one to mind.

'You know, Baa Baa Black Sheep, Humpty Dumpty, something like that,' I supplied helpfully, naming the only two I could recall.

Patrick read back what he'd written and nodded. 'All right. I'm with you so far. What about,' he swallowed, 'nappies?'

I'd thought about this earlier that morning. 'Just leave them,' I said decisively. 'You can ignore his nappy until I get home.'

A look of relief swept across Patrick's face. 'Right then,' he said with forced bravado. 'We'll be fine then, Jack, won't we?' he asked, bending down and talking to him.

Jack burst into tears.

Patrick took two steps back and I picked up Jack quickly.

'He's just tired, Patrick,' I assured him. I had no idea whether this was true or not but sensed that I was in serious danger of losing my babysitter down the front steps. 'I'll put him into bed and then get moving.'

I grabbed Jack's bottle and bent down to pick Harold up off the floor, but he slipped out of my hand and slid down the front of my jacket. His claws caught in my pantyhose and he hung there, one wart-studded leg on each of my knees.

Jack shrieked and lunged out of my arms. I only just managed to prevent him falling headfirst to the floor.

'Ah, Patrick, could I have a bit of help here?' I asked, trying to remain calm.

Patrick looked at me, obviously unsure as to what to do.

'Can you pick the toad off my legs?' I asked, as if it was a normal request.

Patrick squatted in front of me and pulled at Harold.

'Gently!' I yelled. 'These are my last pair of pantyhose.'

Patrick gingerly gripped Harold and lifted him up. My pantyhose rose in little peaks with the claws and Patrick looked up at me enquiringly. Jack peered down, enthralled by the devastation that Harold was causing.

'Can you just push the material off?' I asked, holding my breath.

Transferring Harold to his right hand, Patrick pushed at the fabric caught on the left claw, which slid off and sprang back onto my leg.

'Excellent,' I breathed.

Patrick didn't look up. He moved Harold slowly to his left hand and then tried to repeat the manoeuvre on the other side.

'It's stuck,' he said.

'Push a bit harder,' I instructed.

As he did, I felt the material give way and the ladder race from my knee to my calf.

'Bugger, bugger, bugger,' I exclaimed.

Another look at my watch showed it was 9.05. Definitely no time for a change, but I didn't have an option. Snatching Harold from Patrick, I raced to my bedroom. I flung the cupboard door open and deposited Jack at the bottom. Too stunned to move, he sat there surrounded by shoes as I ripped off my clothes and replaced them with a pair of navy trousers and a matching jacket.

I grabbed Jack and whirled into his room. Dropping him into his cot, I shoved the bottle into his mouth and wedged Harold in beside him. Pulling the door shut behind me, I flung my handbag over my shoulder.

'I've really got to go, Patrick. I'll see you in about two hours.'

'Yes, okay then,' he replied. His face bore a twisted expression which I assumed had been intended as a smile.

Miraculously the car started first go. One benefit of being late was that I had missed the morning rush and had a clear run into town. I stepped out of the lift at 9.29 and took a deep breath, trying to find some semblance of calm.

'Hi Ellen,' I greeted the receptionist.

'Hi Julia. Mr Farley is in conference room two.'

'Right.'

After a quick detour to pick up his file from my desk, I walked into the large conference room. Gordon was standing at the window, looking at the view over the river.

'Hello Julia,' he smiled, extending his hand.

'Nice to see you, Gordon.'

Gordon Farley was the chief executive officer of a huge manufacturing corporation. I'd met him the previous year when I'd advised him on the company's takeover of one of its competitors. For some reason, obvious to no one but himself, he had decided I was a genius. When he'd decided he needed some legal help on a personal matter, he had decreed that I was the only one to handle it.

There were two major disadvantages to this. The first was that the personal matter involved a neighbour, a tree branch and Gordon's Tuscan statue. While the $10,000 claim was a pittance to someone as wealthy as Gordon, he had lost all sense of perspective and was nothing short of obsessive about it.

The second disadvantage was that Jonathon Earl was watching the process every step of the way and had made it very clear that an adverse result would be very bad for my career. The partners I worked with had agreed earlier in the year to put me forward for partnership in July. The indications so far were that I had a strong chance of being accepted, but a bad word from Jonathon could change that in a flash.

The situation was a source of great amusement to my colleagues who did their utmost to have absolutely nothing to do with the whole thing. Many theories as to why I was Gordon's golden-haired child abounded, the obvious being quickly discarded as he was widely rumoured to be gay.

To make matters worse, I knew almost nothing about litigation, a fact Gordon had dismissed with a wave of his hand and an assertion of my legal genius.

'So what's new?' Gordon asked as he sat down.

I sat opposite him and opened the file, despite the fact that I knew the contents backwards.

'The original statement from Enrico Guilo has arrived. Other than that, no, there's nothing new.'

We had a trial date in the Magistrates' Court, which was the lowest court in the state system, in just over a month. Most people appearing in the Magistrates' Court represented themselves on small debt or drink-driving claims. We were going to march in there with a senior barrister and a trolley full of documents. If this matter weren't quite so career-threatening, it would have been embarrassing.

The case was between Gordon and his neighbour, Leonie Baker. We were claiming that Leonie had been negligent in not removing a tree on her property. Our argument was that this negligence had resulted in a branch dropping over the fence onto a very expensive statue, which Gordon had bought on a recent trip to Italy.

To add insult to injury, the hand of the statue, which was a replica of Michelangelo's *David*, had fallen into the pool. By the time Gordon saw it there two weeks later, it had stained the bottom of the pool.

Leonie had pulled in her own legal entourage and arguments about the validity of the claim had been flying back and forth for the last six months. The amount spent by both sides had already far exceeded the amount of the claim. Its scope had even gone beyond Australia and the latest statement I'd obtained was from an art buyer in Venice.

I took a deep breath. If I didn't explain to Gordon why I was out of the office, I'd have Jonathon Earl on my back every two days.

'Ah, Gordon, I have had to take leave for the next two weeks. It's a, uh, personal matter.' My choice of words had been deliberate. As I'd expected, Gordon looked away, clearly worried that a request for any further details would result in a lurid description of a terrible female medical complaint.

'Right. Well as long as I can rely on you to stay on top of everything.'

'Yes, of course,' I replied, with more conviction than I felt.

'Is there anything more we should be doing?' he asked, a question I'd heard more than once.

We'd still been unable to obtain clear evidence that the tree had been dying, or that Leonie was aware of the statue's presence, two problems that had given me some sleepless nights.

'No, Adrian is very comfortable about how things are progressing.' I mentioned the barrister's name in what I knew was a fruitless attempt to spread responsibility.

'That's fine then,' Gordon replied, springing up and heading for the door. 'Please just let me know if there are any developments.'

'Certainly, no problem, Gordon,' I said to the door after it closed behind him. Why, I wondered, thinking of the chaos this meeting had caused in my life, couldn't that little update have been conducted in a five-minute phone call?

SIX

I drained the last drop of coffee from my cup and looked down at Jack playing happily at my feet on the deck. He was completely absorbed by the set of drink coasters I had given him half an hour earlier and the quiet coffee had done wonders for my state of mind.

It was Saturday – day six. Jack seemed to have accepted that I was the provider of his needs. I put him into and took him out of bed, fed him fairy bread, gave him bottles of milk and made sure Harold was always within arm's reach. Beyond that he wasn't interested. He continued to reject any form of comfort from me and when he became upset, the best I could do was to stand nearby and talk to him.

He hadn't cried much since he'd woken that morning and the previous night had been good, relatively speaking. And it was Saturday, so I wasn't looking at an endless string of hours to get through by myself. Things were definitely looking up.

Patrick dropped the weekend papers on the table. For the first time since I left uni, I reached for the employment section of the *Courier Mail* before anything else.

'Well let's just hope that fabulous part-time nannies all over Brisbane are flipping through the job advertisements right now.' I was only half joking. This was a serious business.

About the only thing I'd managed to achieve since Jack's

arrival was to be knocked back by every daycare centre this side of Cairns. Each centre was very helpful, telling me at great length about the philosophy of the centre and the staff-to-child ratio, but they all had trouble hiding their amusement when I asked if there were any places available straightaway.

In desperation I had even begun to call the same places I had started with, hoping some kind of miracle had occurred. I was now finding it very difficult to be put through to anyone more senior than the cleaner and was convinced that more than one of the people I'd been calling were screening their calls to avoid me.

It seemed pretty clear that without his mother putting in a seriously good word upstairs, Jack wasn't going to get a place in a daycare centre before I had to go back to work. So I had high hopes for the advertisement for a nanny I'd put in today's paper.

'Can I see the ad?' Patrick asked.

I flicked to the place where it should have been. Should have been, but wasn't. I felt as though I'd been kicked in the stomach.

'No! How can they have done this to me? Patrick, it's not there!'

My peaceful state of mind disappeared. Saturday was the day for job ads and I was already woefully late to find someone available to start in a week's time. Next Saturday would be hopeless.

'Hang on. Maybe it's somewhere else.' Patrick took the paper from me and paged through it slowly. 'Okay, you're right. It's not there. But don't panic,' he added fruitlessly.

'How can this have happened?' I thundered. 'I sent the email well before the deadline . . .'

My voice trailed off and I ran into the study. I logged onto the computer, pacing the room in agitation as it loaded up. Finally my email program came up and I clicked on the sent box. There was no email to the newspaper. Even before I looked in the draft emails I knew what had happened.

On Thursday morning I'd been reading the ad one last time when I spotted Jack climbing on top of the coffee table. Saving the email as a draft, I'd pulled him off and taken him for yet another walk in the stroller. And completely forgotten to do anything more about it.

'Didn't send it?' Patrick was looking over my shoulder.

'No.' Anything else I could think to say wasn't fit for Jack's, and probably not even Patrick's, ears.

This was a disaster. A complete and unmitigated disaster. My work was being spread among a number of other lawyers for the two weeks I was away. But everyone was already flat out and there was no way I could ask them to manage the load for any longer. Without anyone to look after Jack, though, I didn't have a lot of options.

What was wrong with me? I worked with deadlines for a living and had never forgotten one before.

'Julia, it will be all right. We'll figure something out.'

My eyes filled with tears and I nodded wordlessly.

'What about bribery – maybe if you slip the owner of one of the centres a couple of hundred dollars in small bills?' Patrick was obviously concerned that he would find himself pulled in for some heavy-duty babysitting if we didn't find a solution. 'Or we could start a rumour that one of the centres is on the site of an old asbestos factory. Bet that'd cut down the demand.'

I made a mental note to make sure Patrick didn't have anything to do with Jack's ongoing education. If these were his solutions to get Jack into daycare, I was terrified to think what lengths he would go to to secure him a university place.

Patrick was suddenly serious. 'Look, Julia, you need some help. If you won't tell Mum and Dad, I will.'

I had received two messages from our parents since Jack's arrival. Both times I'd replied quickly with no mention of Jack.

Mum was great with babies and kids and the thought of her arriving and sorting this mess out was like a blissful dream. But I had to be realistic. Mum worked full time, so even if I asked her to come home, she would only be able to help until she'd used up all the holidays she'd saved for this trip. She and Dad lived on the Sunshine Coast, which was over an hour's drive away, so it wasn't like she could just pop in when I was having a bad day.

No matter which way I looked at it, this was my problem.

'Leave it a bit longer. I had a text message from them this morning. Apparently they're about to start the Milford Track walk and will be out of mobile range for a few days. Let's wait until they get back. If things are still bad then, I'll ask them to come home, I promise.'

He looked doubtful. 'Okay – for now. But we've got to sort something out.' He paused. 'Jack's going to have a sleep now, isn't he?'

'Yeah, I guess so,' I replied, looking at my watch.

'You need a break. Why don't you put him to bed and then head out for an hour or so – I'll stay here while he sleeps.'

Patrick's confidence was obviously still high after Wednesday's babysitting success. I'd arrived home after my meeting to find a still-sleeping Jack and a very happy Patrick.

'You're not telling me he's slept the whole time I've been away?' I asked disbelievingly.

'Yep,' Patrick replied proudly, as if he'd managed the event himself.

'You didn't slip some rum into his mouth just to make sure, did you?' I asked suspiciously.

'Julia, as if I'd do something like that!' His tone of righteous indignation made me feel as if I'd questioned Mary Poppins' spoonful of sugar remedy.

Jack hadn't slept again the entire day, but I'd figured it was a small price to pay for the huge boost it had given Patrick's child-minding confidence.

'Are you sure?'

'Absolutely,' he replied.

'That would be fantastic. Thanks.'

Maybe some exercise would help clear my head. After settling Jack, Harold and a bottle in the cot, I opened my cupboard and pulled out a pair of black lycra leggings and a matching purple and black gym top.

The Healthworks gym was on the river about a kilometre away, theoretically the perfect distance for a warm-up jog. After a momentary hesitation I picked up the car keys, telling myself I needed to drive in case I had to get home quickly.

The gym was two-thirds empty, which seemed strange until I realised it was only nine and normal people would still be fast asleep in bed.

I stepped onto the closest running machine and threw my towel and backpack on the floor. The machine flashed at me, asking me to enter my weight. My hand hovered over the control panel uncertainly. I always felt the urge to lie to running machines. The desire to lie about my weight was not unfamiliar. But what was odd here was that I was torn between subtracting a few kilos – my natural reaction – and adding a few extra – which would mean that the automatic calorie counter would tell me I had burned more than I really had. After checking that no one was watching, I added an extra five kilograms to my true weight.

Time was a strange thing, I reflected philosophically as I increased the speed and moved into the shuffle I liked to call a jog. Twenty minutes spent over a cup of coffee with Maggie and Tanya went by in the blink of an eye, while twenty minutes on a running machine felt like an eternity.

Eventually the machine proclaimed that I'd reached the end of the workout. I slowed to a walk, glad of the pounding music that masked my gasping breath. Resisting the urge to call it a day and head home, I pointed my shambling wreck of a body in the direction of the weights corner.

Picking up some very small dumbbells, I surveyed the weights corner, which was reflected in the mirror in front of me. About to turn back to my own reflection, I caught a glimpse of a man doing bench presses in the corner and stopped mid bicep curl. I'd noticed him on a visit to the gym a couple of months earlier, but hadn't seen him again. This was probably not surprising, considering that by no stretch of the imagination could I be described as a regular gym user.

He was tall and had brown curly hair that was just a bit too long. Mentally adding a breastplate, I decided that he looked like a Roman gladiator in shorts and a T-shirt.

Realising I was staring, I looked away and rehefted my weights, wishing that they were slightly more significant looking.

Glancing back again, I noticed that the object of my attention had the sleeves ripped out of his T-shirt. I'd have to knock a couple of style points off for that one, but would be prepared to let it pass, I decided magnanimously.

Resolutely keeping my eyes to myself, I finished my weights. Sit-ups next.

After wiping my red face with my towel and pushing my sweaty hair behind my ears, I headed for the mats, which just happened to be in the corner next to the bench press. Spotting a large ball against the wall, I decided to do my sit-ups across it, something I'd never done but had always thought looked very cool.

Not looking at the gladiator, who was midway through another set of bench presses, I picked the ball up and moved it to the centre of a mat.

'Now what?' I muttered. Tentatively I sat on top of the ball and lowered myself backwards. As my head tipped upside down, I felt the ball roll sideways. My body started to follow and I scrabbled with my feet in a desperate attempt to keep my balance. As I did, the ball and I rotated like an inverted crab trying to flip itself over. My body tipped further sideways and I increased the speed of my feet until I was moving quickly in a large arc across the mats. Suddenly my feet lost their grip and I fell off the ball onto my side. There was a resounding thump, followed by a groan as the air was forced out of my lungs.

I kept my eyes closed for several seconds and tried to breathe. When I opened my eyes, I was looking straight at a pair of legs. Forcing my head up, I saw the gladiator's head and torso. Despite the ache in my chest, I noted that he had green eyes and slightly crooked front teeth.

'Um . . . are you okay?' he asked tentatively.

'I'm . . . fine,' I forced out, dragging myself to a sitting position. 'Just a little bit winded.'

Glancing around, I saw that I'd managed to attract the attention of the whole gym. I'd always known that the bad karma I'd generated years ago by laughing at a man who'd fallen off a running machine would come back to haunt me.

'Do you think you can stand?' the gladiator asked, holding out a hand.

I seriously doubted it but wasn't going to miss a chance to hold that hand. I stretched out my arm.

He hauled me up, depressingly with decidedly more strain than he'd shown while bench pressing.

'Thanks, I'm fine now,' I muttered, too embarrassed to look at him. 'Guess I should get back to it,' I added, while vowing never to go anywhere near one of those balls again.

'Yeah, okay then.' He smiled and returned to stacking the weights he'd been using.

Deciding that I'd finish my sit-ups in private, I headed for a mat behind one of the mirrored poles. The sight of a toned woman doing rapid crunches was too much for me though. Abruptly I reversed my steps and headed for the exit.

Looking down, I rummaged in my backpack for my car keys, wondering what chaos was waiting at home. I stopped as I stood on the back of someone's heel.

I saw with horror that it was the gladiator.

'Sorry,' I apologised, wondering why I was unable to walk and operate like a normal human being at the same time. 'Miles away . . .' I volunteered vaguely.

'No problem,' he said, smiling.

He walked out the door and turned left. I followed him, my steps slowing as he turned down the small side street where my car was parked. This guy was going to think I was stalking him.

He stopped next to an old MG and looked up as I passed. I smiled and jingled my car keys loudly in an attempt to show that I had a legitimate reason for being there.

I opened the door of my car and slid into the driver's seat. Twisting the key in the ignition, I heard the motor turn over several times without catching. My heart sank. After several seconds I tried again, knowing it wouldn't do any good.

'Come on, come on, you dog of a car,' I fumed.

A car slowed down beside me. I looked out of the window to see the gladiator looking over at me.

'Is everything all right?' he asked.

'Fine thanks.' Pasting a confident smile on my face, I prayed that he would drive away. I hadn't humiliated myself this much in front of anyone since the time I threw up on a date after a particularly turbulent roller-coaster ride. 'Sometimes it just takes a few goes to start.'

Either he believed this highly unconvincing lie or, more likely, he had just decided I was beyond help.

'Okay then, good luck.' With a wave he took off. As I watched his car disappear, I reflected that it was at least twenty years older than mine and yet it had started first go.

Past experience had taught me that once my car decided not to start, there was no point in trying any further. I needed a mechanic.

I looked at my watch. Despite Patrick's confidence, I was worried about leaving him alone with Jack for too long, and arranging a mechanic now could take hours. Walking home and dealing with the car later seemed like the best option.

I opened the door and stepped onto the road, just as the gladiator's ancient car came hurtling back around the corner. I cursed under my breath as he pulled up on the other side of the road.

'My mother told me that I was never to leave a damsel in distress,' he said. 'Still not having any luck?'

'No, but it's all right, thanks. I'm going to walk home.'

'Well if you're going to walk, it can't be far out of my way. Jump in and I'll give you a lift.'

I hesitated for a very short moment. If this guy was a homicidal psycho, he'd done a magnificent job of orchestrating this situation.

'That would be great,' I answered.

'I'm Tony.' The gladiator held out his hand as I squeezed into the passenger seat.

'Julia,' I responded.

'Okay. Where to, Julia?' he asked as he put the car into gear and moved off.

I gave him directions and he nodded.

I tried surreptitiously to sniff my armpit, unsure as to

whether I'd remembered to put deodorant on that morning. While I couldn't detect any BO, I decided I shouldn't get too close and pressed myself against the car door.

'So, have you been going to the gym for long?' he asked.

'Well . . . I've been a member for about a year but I really wouldn't describe myself as a regular. I figured if I paid up front for a full year, guilt would force me to go.' I shrugged. 'My brother worked out that I now average about eighty-three dollars per visit.'

Tony smiled. 'I guess that explains why I haven't seen you around before.'

So he hadn't exactly been ogling me the last time we were there together. I reminded myself that some people did actually concentrate on exercising when they were at the gym and tried to think of something witty and interesting to say.

'What about you? Do you go there often?'

I could have come up with a worse conversational gambit – but not much.

'Yeah, I try to make it about four times a week. The gym helps take my mind off work.'

'Where do you work?'

'TV53,' he said, and then added with a wave of his hand, 'don't worry, you wouldn't have heard of it. It's a community television station that produces about ten hours of programming a day. Not exactly cutting-edge television, but I'm producing, which is what I really wanted to do.

'What do you do?' he asked as he turned left into my street.

I always dreaded being asked that question. In my experience, telling strangers you were a lawyer was only a step away from telling them you were an axe murderer.

'I'm a lawyer,' I mumbled, thankfully spared Tony's reaction as I gestured for him to pull over outside my house.

'Thanks for the lift,' I said, and then added impulsively, 'Would you like to come in for a cold drink?' The words were barely out of my mouth before I regretted them and I silently willed him to say no.

He looked surprised and hesitated. 'Um . . . sure,' he answered. 'I'm not due at the studio until this afternoon.'

What was I thinking? I had no idea what degree of chaos was waiting for me inside the house and Tony certainly wasn't expecting to have to deal with a confused and upset child.

As we walked up the footpath, I realised I'd forgotten my key. Not wanting to wake Jack with the doorbell, I led Tony down the side path to the steps at the back of the house. As we stepped onto the deck, I could see Patrick through the open glass concertina doors. He was standing in the kitchen with his back to us in front of a very wide-awake Jack who was strapped in the new highchair Patrick had bought yesterday.

'Okay, my man, here's what we're going to do.' Patrick paused for a couple of seconds, obviously in search of inspiration.

Jack's attention span rivalled that of a grasshopper and as we watched he drew a deep breath, preparing himself for a cry.

Patrick struck a dramatic pose with one foot in front of the other, one arm punching the air and the other held in front of his face.

Stunned, Jack breathed out again and Patrick slumped into a rapper pose, with his thumb and little fingers extended. He began waving his arms in front of his body and chanting: 'Yo, Jack. I've been hearin' that you were feelin' blue and so I figured that this is what we'd do.

'Not bad,' he said in his normal voice, straightening slightly.

I looked over at Tony, wondering what on earth he was thinking of this.

Smiling, he raised his finger to his lips and looked back at Patrick.

Seeing Jack start to squirm, Patrick turned to the pantry. Rifling through the various cans and packets stacked on the shelves, he extracted a paper box and held it above his head in triumph.

'Okay, my man!' he exclaimed.

As he turned back to Jack, I saw he was holding a packet of pancake mix. While I couldn't remember buying it, it certainly couldn't have been bought by Patrick. He'd lived without a refrigerator for six months before he moved in with me and thought tomato sauce was a raw ingredient.

Ripping the top off the box, Patrick handed the plastic packet to Jack as he searched through the cupboard next to the stove. Jack put the bag in his mouth and started chewing on it. Patrick pulled out a bowl and banged it loudly on the bench, causing Jack to jump. He took the saliva-covered plastic bag out of Jack's mouth and, holding it by one corner, slit the other with a knife and tipped the mixture violently into the bowl.

'Now this here powder is gonna make some dough; just as soon as you can,' he paused and then added, 'say yo!'

Reading the back of the packet, he muttered, 'Damn, it needs an egg. Who keeps eggs?'

Opening the fridge door he stared in surprise to see the packet of eggs I'd bought the day before. Flipping back the top of the packet, he took out an egg and tossed it over his shoulder, catching it just before it landed in front of a delighted Jack.

'But first we've got to make a crack in this egg.' He banged it on the side of the highchair and dropped the contents into the bowl, tossing the shell towards the bin in an overhead basketball shot that fell well short of the mark.

'And mix it round with this here . . . spoon.' His rhyming genius seemed to have momentarily deserted him.

He held the bowl under the tap for a slurp of water, which I was sure in no way resembled the amount required by the recipe. Picking up a spoon, he proceeded to roughly beat the mixture.

'Doosh, doosh, doosh,' he chanted, in what I presumed was supposed to be background rap music.

Patrick's performance seemed to be working for Jack, who was entranced.

'Now right here is where the good bit is gonna start. We'll heat this pan and jive on to the next old part.'

Patrick up-ended the frying pan and rubbed his left hand back and forwards across it as if he was a DJ mixing a record. He put it on the stove top and, while waiting for it to heat up, did a very passable moon walk from one side of the kitchen to the other.

Tony and I instinctively stepped back to stay out of Patrick's peripheral vision.

Touching the pan with his finger, he jumped and stuck it in

his mouth. 'Sssssss,' he imitated the sound of steam for Jack. 'Well this damn pan is hot, so let's get it movin'. We'll toss on this mix and carry on a groovin'.'

Holding the bowl up high, he poured some dollops of mixture into the pan. He pulled a spatula from the container on the corner of the bench, waiting a few seconds before sliding it into the pan.

With a flourish he flung the misshapen pancake into the air in a slow arc which looked like finishing on the floor in the far corner of the room. Snatching the pan off the stove, he dived onto the floor and miraculously caught it.

Jack let out a high-pitched squeal, never before having witnessed such a performance.

Standing up gingerly, Patrick felt his chest for bruises and hobbled back towards the stove where he flipped the remaining pancakes very carefully. Breaking one up with a fork, he blew on it for a few seconds and then handed it to Jack.

'Now, Mister Jack, there's just one rule you must know, and that is if you decide to blow,' he paused to maximise the effect of the rhyme, 'my cover with the big J, then, my son, that will surely be,' he paused again, 'the last time that you get to eat a pancake while she's, ah, not here.'

I was just storing this piece of subterfuge away for future reference when Tony's mobile phone rang.

Patrick spun around. Seeing us on the deck, the colour instantly rose to his face.

'How long have you been there?' he demanded.

'Yo, Jack, I've been hearin' that you've been feelin' blue,' I chanted with a grin as we walked into the kitchen.

'Oh no. You saw it all?' he asked with a wince.

'Yo man,' Tony answered as he switched off his phone.

'Where on earth did that routine come from?' I asked.

'Bits of it I saw on a Steve Martin movie, the rest I made up as I went along,' Patrick shrugged. 'Jack woke about twenty minutes after you left. I was going to take him for a walk, but every time I tried to put him into his stroller he screamed blue murder. I was running out of ideas.'

'Interesting pancakes,' I said, looking at the weird-shaped and half-cooked objects sitting on the bench.

'Ah, Julia . . . about what I said at the end,' Patrick squirmed.

'Yes?' I asked with raised eyebrows.

'Well, I'm just trying to create a bit of a bond here and thought that a shared secret might help,' he tried. 'You know how it is – kind of a boy thing.'

'Whatever,' I said, enjoying myself too much to get into a debate about Patrick's childcare techniques.

'Anyway, he seems to approve of the pancakes,' Patrick commented. We all looked at Jack who was trying to chew a huge mouthful of semicooked dough.

'My God! He's eating it!' About to explain why a child eating a pancake justified such a level of excitement, I suddenly realised how strange this scene must look. 'Sorry. Let me start again. Tony . . . This is Patrick and Jack,' I said.

'Hi,' he answered uncomfortably.

I realised that he must think that a married woman with a child had just invited him home for a drink.

'Patrick is my brother and Jack is . . .' I struggled for an easy way to explain the situation and decided there wasn't one. 'Jack is my best friend's son – she died in Italy a week ago and he's living with me now.'

The words came out in a rush. I felt the tears rise to my eyes and bit my lip hard.

'Oh . . . I'm really sorry.' Tony shifted from one foot to the other. I was sure he was wishing desperately that he'd tossed me out of the car and kept driving, or better still, never turned his car around in the first place.

'So . . . good gym session?' Patrick asked, clearly doing his best to change the subject.

The question reminded me of how much I had humiliated myself. I wondered fleetingly if I would have to change gyms.

'Well, that depends. Ever fallen off a sit-up ball in the middle of a crowded gym?'

Patrick paused, piece of pancake halfway to his mouth. 'You didn't?'

Beside me I heard Tony choke back a laugh but he couldn't suppress a smile as I nodded.

Patrick doubled over with laughter. 'Haven't I warned you to leave high-tech gym equipment to the experts?'

Even Jack seemed to think the whole thing was pretty funny as he continued to stuff pancakes into his mouth.

Patrick's laughter had broken the tension.

'What can I get you to drink?' I asked Tony. As I did, I reflected that unless he felt like sucking down five child-sized tetra juice packs, water was probably the best I could offer.

Tony eyed the coffee machine on the bench. 'It's probably going to dehydrate me for the next twelve months, but what I really feel like is a coffee,' he admitted.

Much to my annoyance Patrick gave me the thumbs-up behind Tony's back.

I'd long been a vocal opponent of health drinks. The only vegetable juice I could stand was tomato, and that was only when it was combined with vodka and Tabasco sauce. Energy drinks always tasted like seawater to me. Someone who craved caffeine rather than wheat juice was definitely my kind of person.

I caught myself. I'd known this man about half an hour. During that entire time I had been red of face, sweaty of hair and fully occupied in making a fool of myself. We had a long way to go before a mutual love of coffee could be of any assistance in our being each other's kind of people.

'This is a great place,' Tony said, looking around.

'Thanks,' I replied. 'I bought it about a year ago and Patrick moved in to help with the mortgage. He has his own space downstairs, so it works well.'

We chatted as I made coffee for the three of us. I spooned froth onto the last coffee and handed mugs to Tony and Patrick. Pushing Jack's highchair in front of me, I led the way to the deck. As an afterthought I threw an extra couple of pancakes on his tray. Any development on the previous week's diet was a good thing.

'Tony is the producer for a television station,' I informed Patrick, terrified that the conversation would peter out.

'Assistant producer on a very small community station,' Tony qualified.

'So you do ethnic programming and things like that?' Patrick asked.

'Well . . . no.' Tony looked embarrassed. 'Most community TV stations do that kind of stuff. The whole idea is to provide everyone in the community with access to TV. But a guy called John Abbot started TV53 about five years ago. He'd made a stack of money in the property market and always fancied being in television, but no one was interested in him. So he decided he'd buy his own station – how he got the approvals, I have no idea. So, not only do commercial stations think we're a joke, so do the real community stations. Credibility is something we are very short on.'

'What kind of shows do you make then?' I asked.

'We do all kinds of programming – mostly pretty badly. That doesn't seem to bother John, though. I'm convinced he thinks we're giving CNN a run for their money.'

'So why do you work there?' Patrick asked.

Tony shrugged. 'I finished a film and television course a year ago but couldn't find any other job in the industry. My theory was that at least it was a foot in the door, but lately I've been starting to have my doubts.'

I wondered briefly what he had been doing before that but didn't want to seem like I was prying.

'Still sounds more glamorous than being an accountant,' Patrick commented.

'You're an accountant?' Tony asked in surprise.

'Yeah, afraid so,' Patrick said glumly.

Patrick made no attempt to hide how unsuited he and the accounting profession were and was convinced he had been temporarily insane when he enrolled in a business degree. He claimed that the university social life was then so good, he gave his career little thought until three years later he found himself sitting in a suit and tie in a tiny cubicle in a big firm in the city.

'Sorry.' Tony seemed concerned that his reaction had offended Patrick. 'It's just I wouldn't expect an accountant to come up with a routine like that.'

'No, we're not exactly a wild and crazy bunch, are we?' Patrick was clearly not in the least insulted.

I looked at Tony out of the corner of my eye – he was definitely not ugly. A flash of resentment hit me. Even if there had been a vague possibility of Tony being interested in me, Jack's presence would put me in the too-hard basket. I had been lumbered with someone else's child who was going to ruin my professional and personal life.

I looked over at Jack, who was still fully occupied ripping his pancakes apart, and immediately felt a rush of guilt. It wasn't Anita's choice not to be around to bring up her child. The fact that she thought I would be the best person to look after him was the greatest compliment anyone had ever paid me.

And anyway, my love life hadn't exactly been spectacularly successful before Jack came along.

I'd broken up with Michael, my last boyfriend, two years previously. He and I had moved to Sydney together. I'd worked in Jennings Walker's office there, while Michael had found a job in a competing law firm. We'd had three great years spending every cent we made – mostly on eating and drinking. It had all been fabulous until I'd woken up with a monumental hangover one Sunday afternoon just as the sun was going down on a glorious day. I'd decided that I needed to make some changes to my life. In a rush of enthusiasm, I'd joined a gym and started a cleansing diet, much to Michael's amusement.

But when he discovered I was serious, he stopped being amused and we started fighting. Without the parties and the alcohol, we didn't seem to have all that much in common any more. I moved out shortly afterwards and requested a transfer back to Brisbane not long after that.

Two years and some spectacularly unsuccessful dates later, I had been wondering whether I'd done the right thing.

Michael had been in Brisbane for a wedding a month ago and in true ex-couple style we'd arranged to meet up for a drink one night to catch up. One drink had become two, and many hours later we had ended back in his hotel room deciding we should never have separated. That decision had lasted until morning, when we'd disagreed on where we should have breakfast and then on pretty much everything else. He'd returned to Sydney and I'd realised once and for all that we weren't meant to be together.

But my chances of finding the love of my life now seemed to have plummeted from small to infinitesimal.

Patrick's laugh brought me back to the present and I realised I hadn't heard a word of the conversation.

'You're not serious, they were really picketing?'

'Trust me, I wouldn't joke about something like that,' Tony said ruefully. 'A few weeks ago my boss gave me a bit of leeway to make some programming changes. I decided that the children's show was awful and figured that there'd only be about three mothers and a couple of insomniacs tuning in anyway. So I axed it. Every day for the last week I've had about ten women and children parading around the car park with banners demanding my head. We've got a bit of a stand-off happening at the moment. I'm going to have to come up with some kind of alternative fast – otherwise *Hooray It's Morning!* is going to be back on.'

'*Hooray It's Morning*?' I asked incredulously.

'Yup,' Tony replied with a grimace. 'What do you think, Jack?' Tony turned to him. 'Would you be seen watching a television show that has a host who dresses up as a flower?'

Jack spat some half-chewed pancake out of his overloaded mouth.

'See!' Tony exclaimed. 'My thoughts exactly. This boy has taste.'

I wasn't so sure as I watched Jack spread the masticated mess across the highchair tray.

Tony watched Jack for a few seconds before looking at me. He smiled slightly, his eyes sad.

'No wonder you're falling off gym equipment,' he said simply.

Unable to think of a suitable response, I just nodded. A silence stretched and Tony looked at his watch.

'Well, I need to get back home and try to come up with some ideas for a new show before I'm due at the station. I was hoping the gym session would clear my head, but it doesn't seem to have worked.'

He drained the last of his coffee and stood up. 'It was very nice to meet you all.'

'Thanks for driving me home,' I said to Tony at the door. 'Guess I should get onto my mechanic again – the day his company starts giving frequent flyer points, I'll be jetting all over the world.'

'Good luck with it,' Tony said as he headed down the steps. 'Maybe I'll see you at the gym again – stay off those sit-up balls!'

Well that, as they say, is that, I thought glumly, turning back inside.

SEVEN

As I realised the faint light filtering through the blinds was from the sun and not the streetlights, I drew a deep sigh of contentment.

After six almost sleepless nights, Jack seemed to have finally got the idea that dark hours were for sleeping. Last night we had both had almost seven hours uninterrupted sleep and as I stretched on the cotton sheets I felt a surge of optimism.

Maybe the worst of it was over and things were going to get better from here, I thought lazily. Turning over, I closed my eyes again and dozed happily, dreaming that I was having my arm stroked by a faceless but, I was sure, beautiful man. The dream faded but the stroking remained and became an insistent tugging. Opening my eyes I saw Jack standing beside the bed with one hand on my arm.

The first morning I'd been woken by Jack rummaging around in the study, I had just about had a heart attack. I had thought that the whole idea of a cot was that it kept a child in. It wasn't until I discovered Harold wedged against the side that I realised that Jack had used him as a step to climb over the rail. How he managed to get down from the top remained a mystery. But as he seemed to be able to do it without breaking any limbs, I wasn't going to add it to my already extensive list of things to worry about.

'Good morning,' I said softly. 'Would you like to jump into bed?'

He nodded and I pulled him up and into bed with me. He snuggled down beside me with his head on my pillow, and feeling slightly foolish I found myself blinking back tears.

This was the first time Jack had voluntarily sought me out and here he was tucked up beside me in bed.

I could feel his warm tummy against me where his pyjama top had ridden up. His soft hair tickled my face but I didn't want to move in case I spoiled the moment.

As if we did this every morning, he looked at me commandingly and said what sounded like 'boos'.

'Ah yes, I'm sure there is a bus outside, Jack,' I ventured uncertainly. A headshake and a frown made it clear this was not the desired response.

'Boos . . .' I repeated to myself. 'Ah,' I said as an idea struck me. 'Wait here a second.'

Leaping out of bed I hurried into Jack's room and gathered an armful of the storybooks that had been in his suitcase.

The smile on his face when he saw them confirmed my guesswork and I settled back into bed with him. Half an hour later I decided I couldn't read *Diggers and Dumpers* one more time. Despite the choice of all kinds of much more colourful and beautiful books, it was the only one he was even remotely interested in and he wanted to hear it over and over again.

Breakfast was a bowl of cereal for each of us. Miraculously, Patrick's pancakes seemed to have broken Jack's hunger strike. Patrick's theory was that Jack was a processed-food guy and at his suggestion I'd given him fish fingers for last night's dinner, which he'd devoured. This morning I put a bowl of Patrick's sugar-laden cereal in front of him and he scraped the bowl clean. Still not exactly a diet to brag about at a mothers' group, but I figured any development was a good one.

By 8 a.m. we'd eaten and I'd cleaned up and was wondering what on earth we would do for the rest of the day.

In my old life, which was now starting to seem as though it

belonged to someone else, my favourite way to spend a Sunday had been going to see a movie. I loved the whole experience of visiting a cinema. Loved the excitement as the lights went down. I even loved the rustle of chip packets from the row behind at the pivotal cinematic moment. But as I watched Jack work his way around the room swinging Harold above his head, I realised that I'd better find myself another hobby. Movies and Jack were just not going to mix.

Okay, so taking out long lunches and Sunday sessions at the pub, that left . . . I had no idea. What did parents with kids do on the weekend? Despite all the toys I'd bought, Jack had quickly exhausted the entertainment value of the house and I was now venturing out at least once a day, for my sanity as much as his.

He picked up a tennis ball and flung it across the room where it bounced off the television and rolled under the sofa. I pretended not to see, deciding if he didn't know I was watching there was no need to discipline him.

He scrabbled under the sofa in search of the ball, but came back out clutching a small shiny object. Toddling over, he held it up to me triumphantly. It was an Easter egg and a quick mental calculation told me that, given it was February, it couldn't be much less than a year old.

My gaze fell on the weekend paper, which, except for the employment section, I hadn't managed to even glance at.

With sudden decisiveness I unwrapped the egg, handed it to Jack and opened the lifestyle section. Not to my surprise he deemed chocolate to fall within his acceptable food range and crammed it into his mouth immediately.

At the same moment Patrick appeared at the top of the stairs and I jolted guiltily. One look at him, though, made it clear he was oblivious to anything around him.

'Late night?' I asked enviously.

Mornings weren't Patrick's best time of the day and I was used to him emerging from his room with the back of his hair sticking up and sheet marks on his face. But this morning he looked even worse than usual.

'Mmm.' He slumped morosely in the armchair.

The night before had been the first time Patrick and Jennifer had gone out for dinner together. Apparently Jennifer had only agreed to the outing on the basis that they eat somewhere no one would recognise them. After a tough negotiation over the restaurant section of the Yellow Pages, which had started with her nominating establishments halfway to the Gold Coast, they'd settled on a Greek restaurant in Greenslopes. However, judging by Patrick's appearance, all was not well in paradise.

'Don't tell me you and Jennifer had your first fight?'

Patrick shook his head and then winced at the movement. The smell of cigarettes clung to him.

'Worse,' he said, looking sightlessly at the far wall. 'Jennifer told me that she loved me and that she'd decided to leave her husband so we could be together.'

'Oh . . . what did you say?' I asked tentatively.

'Well, not much at first. I just sort of sat there.'

I stayed silent as he continued.

'And then I tried to persuade her that she should think about it before she made any rash decisions . . . that maybe if she talked to her husband they could work it out.'

'Ah . . .' I tried to keep my voice neutral. 'I'm guessing she didn't think much of that suggestion?'

'Noooo, you could say that,' Patrick replied. 'She asked me what the hell I meant. When I confessed that I just thought we were having fun, it started to get really ugly.'

'Oops.'

'Yeah – oops. She then proceeded to tell me – loudly enough for the whole restaurant to hear – how much she had sacrificed for me. Finally, she slapped my face and stormed out.'

'And that was it?' I asked, slightly disappointed.

Patrick nodded, wincing at the movement. 'I left some money on the table and slunk out of the restaurant just as our meals arrived.'

'So where did the hangover come from?'

'Well, I decided I needed a beer after all that, so I stopped at an Irish bar nearby. There was a pool competition happening so

I signed up and . . .' He trailed off. 'At least I won a hundred bucks,' he added.

I suddenly realised that Jack had been silent for way too long, something I was fast learning was never a good thing. Looking away from Patrick, I spotted him in my study.

'Jack – no!' I screamed.

Crayon in hand, he was standing over a textbook Jonathon Earl had lent me from his private collection.

In the last week Jack hadn't shown the slightest interest in pencils or crayons, despite the fact that I had bought every type of colouring book known to man. But, as I dived across the room, I saw that he had almost covered the entire front cover of the priceless book with red scrawl.

I pulled it away from him and he bellowed his protest just as the phone began to ring.

Expecting Patrick to answer it, I carried a kicking Jack towards the deck. The ringing continued and I looked back over my shoulder to see Patrick pressed back in his chair with a look of terror on his face.

'I'm not home,' he mimed dramatically to me, shaking his head violently in case I hadn't received the message.

If it was Jennifer, then she could just call back, I decided, intent upon my more immediate disaster.

The ringing stopped and then started again immediately. Unable to bear it, I left Jack on the deck and ran back into the living room, the defaced book still in my hand.

'Hello?' I was only half listening as I rubbed frantically at the cover with the bottom of my T-shirt.

'Hello. Could I speak to Patrick please?' asked a cool female voice.

'Uh, he's not, uh, here,' I stuttered.

'Fine, thank you very much,' the voice replied before hanging up.

'Was it her?' Patrick asked.

'She didn't say, but I think so.'

'Did she sound angry?'

'Well, she wasn't exactly bubbly.'

Shaking his head, Patrick turned around and headed downstairs.

I looked down at the book in my hands. It was one Jonathon had declared to be 'a timeless authority', which I was willing to bet meant that finding it for sale anywhere would be nigh impossible. Maybe he wouldn't notice if I returned it without its dust jacket, I thought without much hope. I put the book down on the kitchen bench and tried to put it out of my mind. There wasn't much I could do about it today.

Patrick reappeared, holding his mobile phone as though it was about to bite him.

'She's sent me a text message.' He held his phone up so I could see the screen.

Work car pk - 10 - pls b there.

Somehow the stark characters conveyed a strict instruction rather than a pleading request.

'Are you going to go?'

Patrick looked stricken. 'I don't really think I have any choice, do you?' He looked at me as though I could write him a note saying he was sick.

I shook my head. 'Don't think so.

'Maybe she's calmed down now that she's had time to think about it,' I added hopefully.

'Yeah, right,' he replied unenthusiastically. 'Bloody hell. The work car park . . . that place will be deserted today. Pretty damn creepy.'

I had to agree. Visions of *Fatal Attraction* filled my mind and I made a mental note never to get Jack a pet rabbit.

Only minutes after Patrick had reluctantly headed off, the doorbell rang. Picking Jack up, I walked down the hall and opened the front door.

Tony was standing there dressed in calf-length navy trousers and a white shirt. He looked even better than I remembered.

'Hi,' I said.

'Hi.' Tony smiled in return before looking at Jack. 'Hello, Jack. Still eating those pancakes?'

I did a quick mental review of my appearance. Old cargo

pants, faded black T-shirt and hair washed the day before. Not exactly glamorous, but a hell of a lot better than it could have been.

'Ah, would you like to come in?'

'Thanks.'

Tony followed me out to the deck as I tried to figure out what he was doing here. Could he be going to ask me out? I couldn't think of any other explanation.

I gestured at one of the chairs and he sat down.

'Can I get you anything to drink? Coffee, orange juice?'

'No thanks, I'm fine.'

I sat down in the chair opposite and put Jack down. Spotting a string of ants he followed them, squashing half of them with his little feet. I turned back to Tony.

'So how's the car?' he asked.

'Believe it or not, it's fine now,' I replied. 'My mechanic tells me it must have been a loose wire or something. Of course it started straightaway when he got there.'

It had cost me about a quarter of my weekly wage for the mechanic to tell me that sometimes that happened with 'these cars'.

Over a couple of bottles of wine a few weeks ago, Maggie and I had produced what we thought at the time was a breakthrough theory on cars and computers. We'd decided that there was a universal law that ensured that both cars and computers would only work when there was a technician within twenty paces. How this worked we weren't quite sure, but suspected that they were all programmed with a hidden sensor that could detect whether they were in the presence of someone who knew what they were doing. My car had obviously rubbed its spark plugs with glee when I turned up.

'That's good news.'

Tony looked around. 'Is Patrick here?'

'No, he just headed out.'

'Damn, I had an idea I wanted to run past him.'

Disappointment shot through me. He was here to see Patrick, not me.

Tony thrummed his fingers on the arms of his chair. 'Sorry,' he said. 'It must be a bit odd my arriving on your doorstep the morning after I meet you.'

Not if you fancied me, I thought. Pulling myself together, I managed what I hoped was an enigmatic smile but which I suspected made me look like I had toothache.

'It's just that it occurred to me in the middle of the night that maybe Patrick could solve my problem at work.'

I raised my eyebrows.

'You know I told you I need to find a new show – quickly?'

I nodded.

'Well, what do you think about Patrick with some kind of cooking show for kids? Doing things like the pancake scene?'

'Are you serious?' I looked at him incredulously, unable to picture my little brother as a television star.

'I'm thinking we could call it *Kids in the Kitchen*.'

I was finding it hard to hide my lack of enthusiasm as he rushed on.

'There are celebrity chefs everywhere at the moment. Why don't we come up with one for kids? The parents will love it because it will be interesting for them too; the kids will love it because they get to make a mess. We could create a whole new category of television. What do you think?'

I couldn't believe he was asking my opinion. What would I know about programming for kids? I was still having trouble getting Jack's shoes on.

'But Patrick's not a celebrity,' I said, stating the obvious.

'No. What would be ideal would be to use a soapie star, or even a well-known sports personality. Someone with a profile. But there's the little matter of money. We have none.'

I nodded. Now I was with him. Patrick was cheap.

As if reading my thoughts, Tony rushed on. 'But I really think Patrick could be great. Jack loved what he was doing yesterday, and you and I thought it was pretty funny too. It wouldn't take too much time and we could work around his schedule.'

Jack had followed the line of ants to a large pot, which had once briefly contained herbs but now was just filled with dirt. I stood up to move him, thought better of it and sat down.

He seemed to have worked out that dirt didn't taste too good and had stopped putting it in his mouth. The mess I could deal with later.

'Well, it's certainly worth talking to him. I don't know when he'll be home but you could call him on his mobile if you like.'

'Yeah, I'll do that.'

'Although,' I added, wondering how Patrick was faring, 'it might be a good plan to leave it for a couple of hours.'

I grabbed a scrap of paper and wrote down Patrick's mobile number. On impulse I added my own.

'The bottom one's mine,' I said, 'in case you can't get hold of Patrick.'

'Thanks,' Tony tucked the paper into his back pocket and glanced at Jack. Sliding off his chair, he crouched down beside him.

'Want to see something cool?'

Jack nodded.

Tony reached for the sugar bowl that was still on the table from breakfast and sprinkled a couple of grains beside the line of ants Jack had abandoned. Instantly, the nearest ones made a detour and picked them up, unable to believe their luck.

Jack giggled and reached for the bowl. Before Tony could stop him, half of it was on the floor.

'Um . . .' Tony looked up at me and I laughed at the nervous expression on his face.

'Would it make you feel better if I said that isn't the first time that sugar has been on the floor?' I asked.

He grinned back. 'No, but it would make me suggest we all eat out for breakfast.'

I tried not to look as delighted as I felt at the invitation. This guy was seriously good-looking, not to mention fun. Suddenly the day was looking pretty good.

'There's a new cafe in Spring Hill that does great fry-ups,' he continued.

'Breakfast?' I tried to pretend I was wondering if I could fit it into my busy schedule. 'That'd be great.' I decided not to mention the fact that Jack and I had eaten hours ago.

'I've got to drop in to the hardware store first. Mum and Dad are coming around this afternoon. Mum can't believe that I've been in my place for so long and still not hung the pictures on the walls. I can't face another lecture today.'

I laughed. 'Far be it for me to come between a man and his hammer. How long do you need?'

We arranged to meet at a cafe called Denby's an hour later.

'All right Jack.' I turned to him after Tony had left in search of a hardware store and I'd cleaned up the sugar. 'Your first breakfast date. We need to find some cool clothes for you. Knowing your mother, there must be some Italian designer numbers in amongst your gear.'

Anita had always dressed well and her ten years in Italy had added a European sophistication that I could only look at with envy. We had already been planning some serious clothes shopping when I visited her later in the year. My eyes stung as I pictured us cruising the boutiques on the Via del Corso, before stopping for an aperitif. Anita, of course, would have had Jack under control so he would be a perfect shopping companion.

There'd been so much I'd been looking forward to talking to Anita about when I was in Rome. Telephone calls were great, but it was all the little things that we seemed to miss. Details that weren't significant enough to mention or ask about, but that when put together, made up an important part of both of our lives. I still couldn't quite believe we were never going to have that opportunity.

Swallowing hard I picked Jack up and carried him into his bedroom. Robert had haphazardly thrown clothes, toys and books into Jack's suitcase and I hadn't yet sorted anything into drawers. Burrowing under the top layers, which I'd churned into a crumpled mess over the last week, I pulled out a pair of yellow trousers and a blue and white floral shirt.

I started to unbutton Jack's pyjamas. Although I was still a long way from competent, I was getting better at dressing him. After only a small struggle I managed to get him into his clothes and a pair of brown leather sandals. Feeling like I'd come a long way, I cheerfully added a navy cap bearing an Italian brandname.

I sat back on my heels and looked at him.

Dressed in his trendy gear he looked just like a tiny little man. I reached out my hand and pushed a brown curl back under the cap, wondering how many times Anita had dressed him in this outfit.

'You look very cool, Jack.' My voice came out husky and I cleared my throat. 'Groovy, as your mum would say.'

Tired of being still, Jack raced off. Catching him, I took him into the bathroom and handed him an open packet of cotton-wool balls. The time it took for him to spread them from one end of the bathroom to the other was just enough for a quick shower. He'd lost interest before I'd finished drying myself and I scooped them back into the bag, wondering if a jumbo pack would buy me enough time for a hair wash.

Keeping one eye on Jack as he pulled the videotapes out of a drawer in the living room, I pulled on a pair of wide-legged red trousers and a white T-shirt. I ran a brush through my hair and gave my lips a swipe of lipstick.

Even though the cafe was in the next suburb, we were ready much too early. Why not walk? I thought. It was a lovely morning and I felt like stretching my legs.

Half an hour later, neither of us was looking quite so bright or cheerful.

Having now been awake for almost four hours and eaten only some sugary cereal and a tiny chocolate egg, Jack was ravenously hungry. A hopeful scavenge through my bag had located nothing edible other than breath mints, so I had nothing to appease him with. To make matters worse, Spring Hill was further away than I'd anticipated and there were a lot of large hills on the way. My black leather mules, which were sensationally comfortable walking around the city, weren't quite so suitable for pushing a twelve-kilogram lump uphill. After they had slid off my feet for the umpteenth time some way back, I'd given up and shoved them in the basket under the stroller, electing for bare feet.

Jack's outfit wasn't faring much better. The navy cap had been hauled off his head and thrown in the dirt before we'd crossed the first road. I'd forgotten to check his hands before I dressed him and he'd managed to smear most of the front of his shirt with leftover chocolate. Worse than the fact he looked absolutely filthy was my paranoia that everyone could see I'd been feeding a small child chocolate for breakfast.

Finally we reached the street the cafe was on and I slipped my shoes back on, trying to ignore the film of black dirt covering my feet.

'We're nearly there,' I reassured Jack, who had given up wailing and was slumped in his stroller, obviously resigned to the fact that I was going to starve him to death.

Denby's had a wall along the side but was open at the front to the footpath and at the back to a courtyard. I spotted Tony sitting at a table next to the footpath, reading the newspaper.

'Hello!' His warm smile raised my flagging spirits. 'Hi Jack,' he added as he pushed the stack of newsprint to one side. 'Sit down.'

'Thanks,' I replied. 'Jack and I walked here. I think it would be fair to say Jack's hungry.'

Jack had smelt the food and decided on a last-ditch effort to make someone feed him. Wailing at the top of his voice, he threw himself backward in the stroller, struggling to get out. The coffee shop was full of people looking for a quiet breakfast to revive them from last night's indulgences. As a single unit, they turned to see who had the bad form to bring a child out into this bastion of adult relaxation.

Wrestling with Jack, I studiously ignored them and pulled him onto my lap.

Well, I thought wryly, at least it wasn't hard to attract a waiter's attention. I waved frantically to the three who were staring at us. One of them made his way to our table with obvious reluctance.

'Ah, I need some food for the baby, he's really hungry,' I yelled above his crying. There was no answering smile of sympathy and I pushed on. 'Could you just do some white toast and, ah, Vegemite to start with?'

'Sorry, madam, we only have fruit toast and seed loaf and no Vegemite,' he replied unhelpfully.

'Ah,' I said mildly, swallowing the countless curses that rose to my lips. 'I don't suppose you have any pancakes or dough-nuts?' I tried hopefully.

He shook his head in silence, a look of distaste on his face, which was intended to convey the fact that Denby's was not a pancake or doughnut type of establishment.

'All right, just make it fruit toast and jam.'

'Certainly, madam, although rosehip jam is the only jam we serve.'

'That's fine,' I hissed through gritted teeth.

The waiter disappeared in the direction of the kitchen and I turned my attention back to Jack, who was trying to throw every item from the table to the floor.

'I think maybe we'll go for a little walk while the toast is cooking,' I said to Tony, who looked slightly stunned at the abrupt turn his calm Sunday morning had taken. Standing up, I dragged Jack out of the restaurant onto the footpath.

'We'll be back,' I called over my shoulder.

Jack's attention was immediately taken by a teddy bear dis-play in a nearby shop window. Following behind, I registered the growling of my stomach and cursed the fact that I hadn't thought to order some food for myself.

After ten minutes I deemed it safe to return. As I arrived back I noticed that there were no other children at the cafe. Tony put his newspaper down again. I felt a pang of sympathy for him – this can't have been the kind of breakfast he'd had in mind.

He skyrocketed in my estimation when I saw that beside Jack's toast there was a coffee for me.

'Sensational,' I murmured, sinking into my chair and resist-ing the urge to drain it in one gulp.

'I ordered you a latte – is that okay?'

I was surprised to hear a note of hesitancy in his voice. For someone so good-looking he seemed to be surprisingly shy. 'That is definitely okay,' I enthused.

I moved one of the chairs out of the way, grabbed Jack and lifted him into his stroller. Of course I'd forgotten to bring a bib, so I tucked a serviette into the top of his shirt, smeared a piece of the fruit toast liberally with butter and jam and thrust it at him. He grabbed it like a dying man and stuck it in his mouth.

It looked as though we would have peace for as long as it took Jack to swallow the mound of toast and jam I piled on the table in front of him.

I glanced at the menu. 'I think I'll have the scrambled eggs and smoked salmon,' I decided quickly.

After calling the waiter over again, I ordered my food and Tony added an order for bacon and eggs.

I turned to Tony, determined to make the most of Jack's silence. 'Did you go out last night?'

Stupid question. Everyone went out on Saturday night. Everyone except me, that was.

'Ah, yeah. I saw a band at the Zoo,' Tony replied, naming a very hip live music place in the Valley.

How fantastic to be able to see an up-and-coming band, I thought enviously. I ignored the fact that, despite ample opportunity, I hadn't actually done so for several years.

'How's Jack dealing with everything?' Tony looked over at Jack, who was sucking on a piece of toast.

'Um . . . better I think, but some days it's hard to tell.'

'I bet.' He hesitated and then said, 'Do you mind talking about Jack's mum?'

I shook my head. Anita dominated so many of my thoughts, it wasn't as though not talking about her would reduce the pain.

'How long did you know her?'

Maggie had a theory that guys only asked you about yourself because they'd read in GQ that it was a good way to look sincere and not interested in sex, and therefore was the quickest way to get sex.

But as I told Tony about my friendship with Anita, I didn't feel it was like that. It was a relief to talk and he seemed to genuinely be listening.

I felt like I could talk to him all day, but it wasn't long before Jack decided the toast was no longer interesting and crawled under the bar at the front of the stroller. He made a beeline across the footpath towards the traffic. Springing out of my chair I grabbed him and pulled him back to the table.

'Look, why don't you walk over there?' I suggested, directing him into the midst of the tables, figuring that at least he wouldn't be in mortal danger there. Maybe his cute smile would even charm the customers.

He toddled off in the right direction. Our breakfast arrived in record time and I tried to make witty intelligent conversation while keeping one eye on Jack. He seemed to be making friends and stopped at various tables to have his cheeks pinched.

Having walked the length of the cafe he headed blissfully out the back into the small courtyard that fronted a block of shops. He rounded a corner and disappeared from sight. Dropping my cutlery with a clatter, I stood up, knocking over my water glass in the process.

I pushed my way through the maze of tables and chairs until I reached the other side of the cafe. My heart began to thump when I couldn't see Jack, only settling when I spotted him behind a large potted plant chewing on a sugar sachet someone must have handed him. Wonderful. All I needed at this stage was Jack on a sugar high.

The jolt I'd felt when I thought I'd lost him pulled me up short. It had lasted for less than a second but had given me a terrible fright. Did it really matter if my coffee got a bit cold or if the people at the next door table were unhappy?

'Come on, you,' I commanded, leading him back to the table.

I sat him down on the floor beside me and pulled out a couple of books I'd thrown in my bag. Determinedly I turned to Tony and tried to resume the threads of our stilted conversation.

'How long have you been with the station?' I asked.

'It'll be ten months next week.' He looked at his watch as though the time of day would make a difference. 'I can't believe my contract is nearly up.'

'Do they always have such short contracts?'

Tony shook his head. 'I'm a bit of a long shot for them. I didn't have any real experience and they gave me a year to prove myself.'

'And have you?'

Tony shook his head. 'Depends who you ask. I've made some pretty big changes and I think it is slowly turning around, but I'm running out of time. The trouble is that John is into instant gratification. If I don't get something big happening soon, I don't think I'll get any more time.'

'So what will you do if your contract isn't renewed?'

Tony looked down at Jack. 'To tell you the truth I have no idea. All I know is one way or another I am going to break into the industry.' His jaw was suddenly tight and I was surprised at his intensity.

'Do you think you'll be able to sell the *Kids in the Kitchen* idea?'

'Hope so. We have a production meeting scheduled for this week. John's expecting a concept proposal then. I thought if Patrick was interested, I'd see if he wanted to come along. Do you think he would be able to get time off work?'

'Um . . . maybe.'

I was starting to get the hang of doing everything with one eye on Jack. But it was hard to enjoy myself when I expected him to bolt or start screaming at any moment. I could see from the corner of my eye that he was engrossed in his books and I forced myself to sit back in the chair and relax slightly. This wasn't so bad. Maybe if I just brought enough things to entertain Jack, then I'd still be able to meet friends at places like this.

The waiter returned, bearing the bill despite the fact that we were still only halfway through our food.

Tony reached for it. 'I'll get this.'

'Okay, thanks,' I said. 'I'll get the next one.'

As I said the words, I realised how pathetically desperate they sounded.

Tony stood up and started shuffling through the newspaper. 'My wallet is in here somewhere. Can you see it?'

I lifted a few piles of paper before a terrible suspicion hit me.

Looking down at Jack, I saw that rather than reading his books, he had been quietly disembowelling Tony's wallet, which was now sitting in a puddle of jam surrounded by various credit cards and pieces of paper. As Tony and I watched in stunned silence, a gust blew a handful of banknotes through the cafe.

Galvanised into action, I dived for a fifty-dollar note under the nearest table, startling the occupants as I scuffled around under their feet.

'Sorry,' I apologised briefly. After scrambling back to my feet, I launched myself at another note drifting towards the kitchen.

Having retrieved what I hoped was all of the money, I turned to see Tony holding his sticky wallet between two fingers and trying to prise his Visa card from Jack's grasp.

One of the books I'd bought in my Baby World shopping frenzy had explained that the best way to deal with toddlers was to treat them as equals and explain to them rationally why you want them to do, or not do, something.

'Jack, that's Tony's credit card and he needs it. Please give it back to him,' I tried.

Jack clutched the card tighter.

'Jack, you're upsetting me by not giving Tony the card, please give it back,' I instructed firmly.

So much for reasoning with children. Reaching out, I yanked the card from Jack's grasp and handed it to Tony. Jack screamed in response and, grabbing handfuls of the remaining cards, threw them wildly around him.

The book, which I vowed to burn as soon as I made it home, also said that the only way to deal with a toddler's tantrums was to ignore them and let them run their course. Fine advice when you were alone in a fully soundproofed and padded room, but not quite so practical in a coffee shop full of people who were already less than thrilled with your presence.

Trying to restrain Jack with one arm, I gathered a handful of Tony's cards with the other and dumped them on the table.

It was definitely time to leave and I tried to lift Jack into his stroller. He arched his back and braced his feet on the bar,

refusing to sit down. With more force than I intended, I bent
his knees and thumped him down in the seat. He sat in sudden
silence, which I suspected was more a result of having had the
air driven out of his lungs rather than any belated obedience.

Taking advantage of what I was sure was only a momentary
silence, I turned to Tony, who was surveying the wreckage of
his wallet.

I couldn't see his face, but I was sure he was furious. 'Tony,
I am so sorry. I think the best thing for everyone is if I just get
Jack out of here.'

As I had thought, Jack had only been getting his breath back
and as soon as he did he let out another huge yell.

Tony turned to me and I saw to my amazement that he was
smiling. Taking out the few items still left inside, he handed his
wallet back to Jack. Silence descended immediately. I was sure
there was a disciplinary issue I should be concerned about here,
but as far as I was concerned Tony's act was inspired by the
wisdom of Solomon.

'Julia, it's only a wallet.' Relieved, I looked at him as he
continued, 'Of course my grandmother gave it to me shortly
before she died . . .'

I must have looked as stricken as I felt.

'I'm joking. I bought it in Bangkok for ten dollars a couple
of months ago.'

'Really?' I hoped desperately that he was telling the truth.

'Really,' he confirmed. 'Now why don't I pay so we can get
out of here? I have the distinct impression that these people
won't be too sad to see the back of us.'

As Tony went to the counter to pay, I loaded all of Jack's paraphernalia into the stroller and wheeled it outside. Even though
Tony had been very understanding about the whole experience,
I was sure he was itching to get away. When he reappeared, however, he was carrying two takeaway coffee containers.

'I thought maybe we could have our second coffee on the
move. Shall we head over there?' He gestured to a large park
across the road.

I couldn't believe how understanding he was being. I

couldn't imagine any of my friends, male or female, taking this episode so easily in their stride.

'Okay, so let me guess,' I said as we crossed the road. 'You are the eldest in a family of sixteen, all of whom you had to bring up by yourself because your parents owned a farm and had to work in the fields all day?'

Tony laughed. 'Not quite. My parents are both doctors and I have one sister. The only reason I know anything about kids is that my sister has three boys who are all under five. You should try having breakfast at their place!'

Just the idea of Jack multiplied by three made me feel exhausted. 'Your sister deserves a medal,' I said with feeling.

'I think you deserve a medal.' Tony was suddenly serious. 'What you have taken on is enormous. You must have really loved Anita.'

His words caught me off guard and I nodded, suddenly terrified I was going to cry.

I felt Tony's hand briefly touch mine and tactfully, he changed the subject. 'I don't think that wallet is going to stay in one piece long enough for us to have a peaceful coffee,' he said, looking at Jack. 'Do you have a problem with Jack eating ice-cream?'

I cleared my throat. 'Ah, actually Jack's diet is somewhat patchy. I keep telling myself that I'll feed him properly when I get the hang of everything else, but at the moment I'm concentrating on getting through each day.' I realised I hadn't managed to answer Tony's question in amongst my ramblings. 'So,' I summarised, 'ice-cream is just fine by me.'

Just then I heard the unmistakable tinkle of an approaching ice-cream van, which Tony had obviously already spotted. My smile faltered.

'Ah, let's not worry about stopping the ice-cream van. Why don't we just grab it from a shop somewhere,' I suggested in a poor attempt at nonchalance.

'Sure,' Tony answered, looking at me strangely. 'Except . . .' he looked around. 'There doesn't seem to be one nearby.' He paused, clearly wondering how to deal with someone with a soft serve phobia.

I decided I had no choice but to come clean.

'Well, it's just that . . .' I struggled for words. 'If this is the same ice-cream man who covers New Farm, then I'd rather not see him.'

Tony said nothing and I blundered on. 'A few mornings ago Jack had been up since five, after waking all through the night. I'd finally got him to sleep when what happens but the bloody ice-cream van tootles along the street playing that stupid music ridiculously loudly. Anyway, he woke up Jack, who screamed hysterically. I mean, you'd think they'd have road-tested the music to make sure it didn't terrify small children, wouldn't you?' I finished weakly.

I scuffed my shoe on the footpath, noticing idly that three of my toenails had black grime under them.

'To make matters even worse, he parked right in front of the house. After about ten minutes I'd had enough and ah . . .' I paused, embarrassed. 'Well, I went down and suggested that maybe he could move on elsewhere.'

'You abused the ice-cream man?' Tony asked with a broad smile. 'That's almost as bad as swearing at Santa!'

'No!' I exclaimed. 'I . . . well yeah, okay, I did. And as if that wasn't bad enough, I started talking while his back was to me and when he turned around I realised I had gone out with him in high school. I tried to back down but by then it was too late. I haven't seen him since, I think he's avoiding our street.'

I still couldn't believe how much I had overreacted – or what bad luck it was that the ice-cream man had turned out to be the guy I had once thought was the love of my life. The late nights and Jack's constant crying had changed me from a reasonably calm individual into a shrew who yelled at a man who made thousands of children happy. I'd slunk back into the house and tried to forget it had happened. What I hadn't expected was to have him cross my path again so soon.

Tony laughed and I managed a smile, still mortified by the way I'd acted. At least he seemed to find it funny, rather than evidence of a deep-seated personality disorder.

'All right, how about I buy the ice-cream and you find somewhere to sit?'

'That'd be really good,' I said gratefully.

Tony perched the coffees in Jack's stroller basket and I pushed it towards a bench as he headed over to the van. The day was getting hotter and I reflected idly that Jack's ice-cream would end up in a puddle in his lap pretty quickly.

Several minutes later Tony was back, walking towards us with a cone in one hand and his mobile phone pressed to his ear with the other.

'Yep, sure. No, I understand.'

I glanced around uncomfortably, trying to look as though I wasn't listening to the conversation.

'All right, I'll be there in ten minutes.' He pushed a button on the phone and slid it into the pocket of his trousers. 'I'm really sorry, Julia, but I've got to go. That was John. There's a problem at the station he needs me to sort out. I'm going to have to cancel on Mum and Dad too – Mum's going to kill me for doing this again.'

'No problem,' I answered, trying to keep the disappointment out of my voice.

'Well, I'll see you later, Jack,' Tony said. 'I hope you enjoy the wallet.'

'Are you sure you don't want it back?' I asked.

'Quite sure,' he answered, eyeing the object which was by now covered with saliva and bite marks. 'I've really got to get moving, I'll catch you later.' Tony strode back purposefully in the direction we'd come.

'Great,' I said leadenly. Realising that I was still holding the dripping cone, I thrust it at Jack. Eyeing the cooling containers of coffee, I picked one up and took a deep swallow, glumly contemplating the long walk home.

EIGHT

After eight days I was definitely getting tougher with Jack. By Tuesday I'd come to the conclusion that if I didn't get his sleeping under control, I would go mad. It seemed pretty clear that wouldn't be a good result for either of us.

He had been almost asleep on his feet this morning, but as soon as I put him into bed he'd sprung up, howling at the indignity of it all. However, after a long ten minutes he seemed to come to the conclusion that he wasn't going to be rescued. His cries became increasingly less committed until finally there was silence.

I tiptoed into the room to look at him. True to form, Harold was pressed to his face as if he were a soft teddy bear instead of a rock-hard piece of wart-covered plastic. I stood for a moment looking down at the smooth curve of his cheek, his dark eyelashes distinct against his creamy skin. Suddenly I forgave him for the 5 a.m. start to the day and the morning's tantrums. No child who looked so beautiful asleep could really be a problem – I just had to try a bit harder.

I closed the door behind me, wondering how Patrick was faring at work. I'd almost had to push him out the door the last two mornings, his reluctance to go to work reminding me of the elaborate lies he used to come up with to try to get a day off school. While Patrick had approached the rendezvous on

Sunday morning with trepidation, Jennifer had apparently been calm and collected. After making him repeat what he'd told her the previous night, she'd looked at him coolly and then asked him how important his job was to him.

'I mean, how was I supposed to reply to that?' he'd asked me. 'Oh well, it stops me living on the street, but other than that I'm not too bothered?'

'So what did you say?'

'I can't remember,' he admitted. 'It was like those job interviews where you're concentrating so hard on saying the right thing that you can't remember what you actually said. Anyway, it can't have been too good as she just turned around and walked away.'

Patrick was usually laid-back and it was strange to see him worked up. While he clearly wasn't blameless, I had the feeling that he genuinely regretted hurting Jennifer.

When I told him that Tony was interested in using him to host his cooking show, he just snorted. 'Julia, I'm an accountant. I've never done a day's acting in my life, and you know how bad my singing voice is.'

I nodded, deciding not to comment.

'I'm not exactly going to take the showbiz world by storm. My accounting career isn't in fabulous ascendancy at the moment, and I need to figure out something sensible to do about it. Getting carried away about a television show that about five people will ever see just doesn't make sense.'

'Why don't you at least talk to Tony about it – he said they could do the taping on weekends.'

'I'll call him but I'm really not interested. Anyway, why are you so keen for me to do it? Wouldn't have anything to do with the fact that it would increase your chances of seeing Tony again, would it?'

I flushed guiltily.

By the time Patrick had made it home after meeting Jennifer, I'd spent hours squirming each time I thought about the morning's debacle. I had come to the conclusion that unless I came up with a cunning plan I'd never see Tony again. No sane man would look for a repeat of that performance, nephews or no nephews. I had constructed an elaborate strategy, which included us dropping in while Patrick was taping his show. I figured that if Tony could see Jack and me having a riotously fun time together – doing what, I still wasn't sure – he might not be too terrified to ask me out again.

At Patrick's words, I had realised how sad I was being. I needed to just accept that, at least until I could get the Jack situation under control, romantic involvements were impossible.

Now Jack was asleep I picked up the weekend paper, which I still hadn't managed to read, and headed out to the deck. The January edition of *Babies and Toddlers* was lying on the table where I'd left it ever since the Baby World woman had forced it on me, telling me it was a treasure trove of wonderful parenting information.

I glanced longingly at the newspaper in my hands but I put it down and picked up the magazine. Now that it appeared I was able to keep Jack alive, I should probably try to raise the bar a little.

The first article was headed, 'How early can you socialise your child?'

As soon as your baby is strong enough to sit up, neighbourhood playgroups can be a great way to teach your child to interact.

There followed a comparison between the social skills of children who spent time with others and those who didn't. Basically babies who hadn't been socialised enough turned into boring adults who couldn't hold a conversation unless it was about them. That actually explained more than one of my past boyfriends.

Worried that I'd be responsible for Jack growing into a socially dysfunctional adult, I grabbed the latest edition of the local newspaper. Turning to the back I scanned the advertisements, secretly hoping I wouldn't be able to find anything. With disappointment I spotted one for a playgroup attached to a local kindergarten.

Unable to think of a good enough reason not to, I dialled the number.

Yes, they had a vacancy, the very efficient-sounding coordinator informed me. But only for that afternoon's session. Was I able to make it? Unenthusiastically I admitted that I could.

Apparently I'd been lucky enough to ring on the first day of term and they were having a getting-to-know-you afternoon tea. All I had to do was bring a plate of food.

My secretary rang as soon as I hung up. She gave me the unwelcome news that the opposing lawyers in Gordon's matter had delivered a twenty-page statement from some amazingly qualified engineer. Apparently he said that with the weather conditions on the day of the accident, the tree branch would have fallen two metres from the statue.

The one matter that no one had agreed to cover in my absence was Gordon's, and I finally worked up the courage to call him.

'Is Leonie suggesting that I used a rope to pull the damn thing down on top of David?' Gordon demanded.

His habit of calling the statue by the original's name was quite disturbing.

'Don't worry about it, Gordon. They're just getting desperate and pulling in useless experts.'

Gordon was still unconvinced when he rang off. I wasn't sure I believed my argument either. The evidence the other side was stacking up was definitely a worry.

Next I resumed my phone calls to bookstores in an attempt to find a replacement for Jonathon's book. Finally I spoke to the owner of a small store who sounded excited by the challenge and promised to track me down a copy.

As I put the phone down, I heard Jack stirring.

In a fit of enthusiasm I decided that it would be fun to bake a cake for the playgroup together. Why I decided this would be fun when I hadn't baked a cake since high school, I have no idea. Half an hour later, Jack had eaten a cup of flour, pulled half a dozen eggs onto the floor and was screaming because I'd taken the sugar packet away from him. I abandoned my obviously misguided efforts and tipped the odd-looking mixture into the bin.

The next couple of hours disappeared as I fed Jack lunch and fielded a couple more calls relating to Gordon's case. Looking at my watch, I realised that we were due at playgroup in an hour and I had nothing to take. Maybe I could just give it a miss. But as Jack's noise increased in volume, I realised that staying home for the rest of the day was not an option. We needed to get out.

Which meant I needed some food. So after pulling shorts and a T-shirt on Jack and wrestling him into his shoes, we headed out to the supermarket. I scanned the aisles, hoping to see a selection of home-baked goodies that I could pretend to have pulled steaming from my oven an hour ago. There was nothing and in desperation I moved on to the frozen section.

'Perfect!' I exclaimed as I spotted the quiches. Pulling out an egg and bacon version, I headed for the cash register.

'Things are under control,' I told Jack confidently. 'We're due there in half an hour – plenty of time.'

'Do you think that a "plate" is constituted by something in a box?' I asked as we walked in the door at home.

He looked up at me seriously.

'No, you're right,' I acknowledged. 'We've got to at least take off the wrapper.'

As I opened the box, I glanced at the instructions on the back. 'You've got to be kidding!' I exclaimed, freezing mid tear as the words 'Leave out of the refrigerator for two hours before cooking, microwave defrosting is not recommended' jumped out at me.

Surely that defeated the purpose of prepackaged food, I fumed. Not only did I have to cook the quiche, but I had to wait two hours to do it. Did the manufacturers not realise that if I had that kind of time I could have made the damn thing myself?

Deciding that I had no other option, I pulled the quiche out of its metal tray, slid it onto a plate and stuck it into the microwave. I hit the button marked high and, hoping for the best, headed into my room.

Standing in front of my wardrobe, I pondered the appropriate dress code for a children's playgroup. If the other women's lives bore any resemblance to mine over the last week, they probably never got to wear anything that was ironed, let alone remotely fashionable. Maybe this was their big chance to dress up?

I looked at my 'business casual' bone trousers and crisp linen shirts and back at Jack. He was smearing his jam sandwich as far up the doorframe as he could reach, and I quickly discarded that idea. Trying hard not to think about when it was last washed, I left my denim skirt on and grabbed a red T-shirt with strawberries on the front. Pulling it over my head, I carried Jack into the living room while trying to keep out of range of his sticky grasp.

When the microwave finally dinged, I opened the door gingerly, wondering what I would find.

Not too bad, I concluded optimistically. Sure, one half of the pastry had subsided rather badly and a large crack had opened across the middle, but at least it still resembled a quiche. The middle felt rather solid, while the outside was piping hot, but I was sure that would resolve itself before we actually sat down to eat.

My next dilemma was what to put it in. Where did mothers get their vast stores of Tupperware? Every mother I had ever met had cupboards bursting with all shapes and sizes of plastic containers, while my entire collection consisted of two ice-cream containers, neither of which had matching lids. Maybe women were sent home from hospital with their new baby and a crateload of plastic tubs and lids?

A plastic bag seemed to be the only option. I opened the cupboard under the sink and pulled one from the snarling mess lurking in there. Slamming the door shut in an attempt to stop the hundreds that remained from escaping, I tried to figure out why I felt as though I was being environmentally conscious by not throwing them away. At least a pelican couldn't choke on them if they were safely imprisoned under my sink, I decided virtuously.

'Right, Jack, we're off.' I grabbed him with one hand and hefted my bag and the quiche with the other.

The kindergarten that ran the playgroup was only a couple of kilometres away and I pulled up outside, glancing at my watch.

'Only fifteen minutes late,' I congratulated myself, pleased to see that my time-management skills hadn't altogether disappeared.

After inspecting a sparrow and the contents of the gutter and diving on and eating what I hoped was a sultana, Jack finally allowed me to manoeuvre him to the front of the building.

Opening the door, I hesitated as all of the adult eyes in the room turned towards me. Feeling like the new girl at school, I gripped Jack's hand tighter – for his security, I told myself. To the right of the door was a large desk, behind which sat an equally large woman with the name Marjorie written on her badge.

I stood awkwardly, uncertain how to proceed. Despite the slam of the door behind me, Marjorie scribbled intently on the paper in front of her for at least another thirty seconds before sighing and looking at me imperiously over the top of her half-glasses.

'Yes, can I help you?'

'Ah, we're here for the playgroup,' I volunteered, wondering what else she thought I and the small person standing beside me could possibly be after.

'Ah, yes . . .' She shuffled through the papers in front of her. 'You must be . . . Julia and Jack.'

'That's right.' I smiled.

'Fine,' she said without an answering smile. 'Shoes off and please put your food over on the counter out of reach of the children. Afternoon tea is at three o'clock.'

'You'd better appreciate this, Jack,' I whispered in his ear as I bent over to take off his sandshoes. I wondered whether there was any chance of escaping before the nominated finishing time of four o'clock. Right now, that seemed an eternity away.

Oblivious to our frosty reception, Jack tore off towards a tower made of plastic bars. What did I do now? I looked around hopefully in search of some form of coffee machine. None was visible and I presumed that beverages were strictly limited to snack time. Unable to think of what else to do, I followed Jack. He totally ignored me as he conquered the tower and then settled himself in a child-size car from which he gave no indication of ever moving.

For the first time since Jack had arrived, he was in a room

designed for kids and I couldn't spot one thing he could destroy. He clearly didn't need me and I felt silly hovering near him.

There were a couple of knots of mothers around the room. I sidled over to one of them and smiled at a woman standing to one side.

'Ah, hi,' I said. 'I'm Julia.'

'Hi,' she replied warmly. 'I'm Stacey. Your little boy is lovely.'

Astonished that I didn't stand out as a learner parent, I felt a quick flare of pride that this woman could think that the gorgeous little boy standing by my side was my son. I swallowed an explanation about Anita and replied simply, 'Thanks. Which one is yours?'

'The little girl in the red,' she replied, gesturing towards a rack of musical instruments where the fattest child I'd ever seen was erratically banging a musical shaker against a bookshelf. 'She goes to music class each week and I can't seem to keep her away from the musical instruments here.'

'Really?' I replied lamely, trying to hide my concern. Her daughter was barely even crawling but was already having culturally enriching lessons. I had thought I was being pretty impressive by enrolling Jack in one playgroup, but it seemed as though I was way behind.

Despite it being the first playgroup for the year, the women obviously all knew each other and while they weren't rude, they didn't fall over themselves to make me feel comfortable. The situation was not helped by the fact that my baby-related small talk was pretty shaky.

An hour later Marjorie looked up from the paperwork that had kept her so intently occupied all this time and announced, 'Right, afternoon tea time.'

Dragging my feet, I headed towards my offering, uncertain as to what I would find. I unwrapped the layers of plastic to find that it still looked vaguely quiche-like. Encouragingly, a surreptitious jab of my finger under the pastry seemed to indicate that the frozen middle section had defrosted in the last hour. Quickly I deposited the plate on the table and jumped back, hoping that no one had witnessed my association with it.

With coffees and paper plates balanced on our hands, conversation flowed easier and I was chatting amiably to a couple of interesting women when Marjorie clapped her hands imperiously.

'All right everyone, time to vote on the best dish. As some of you might already know, our parent body, Child's Play Australia, is compiling a playgroup recipe book this term to raise funds. Each group has to choose one recipe to submit. Whoever we vote for today can submit their recipe and have it published.

'You can vote first, Stacey,' she commanded.

'Hmm . . .' Stacey clearly hadn't given the issue a lot of thought. 'You know, I think my vote would have to be for the quiche.'

Unfortunately my sharply indrawn breath coincided with my swallowing a large chunk of carrot cake and I choked loudly.

'Sorry,' I apologised with watering eyes as everyone turned towards me. 'Just went down the wrong way.'

The voting continued and despite some late support for the honey and banana cake, the overwhelming majority favoured my offering.

'And who brought the lovely quiche?' Marjorie asked.

There was a moment of silence as I considered pretending it wasn't mine, but images of us all having to stand beside the table with our hands on our plates made me speak up.

'It was me,' I ventured timidly.

'Our newcomer!' Marjorie smiled at me with the first sign of approval she'd given me. 'We'll need you to bring in a copy of your recipe next week.'

Somehow I hadn't expected to face a moral dilemma at playgroup. I toyed with the idea of saying nothing and never showing my face here again. Alternatively, bringing in any quiche recipe I could find sounded like a good option. Reluctantly I decided on the truth.

'Ah, that's actually a bit of a problem.'

'Why?' Marjorie demanded. 'Don't tell me it's a secret family recipe.'

'No, it's not that,' I said, playing for time, hoping for a natural disaster to get me out of this. No flood or famine appeared to be immediately forthcoming, however. 'Actually it's a frozen quiche I bought from the supermarket,' I muttered, unable to let the silence stretch any further. 'I'm happy to tell everyone the brand, though,' I continued with sudden inspiration. 'I'm sure the box is somewhere at home.'

I braced myself for a barrage of disapproval and was surprised when, beside me, Stacey let out a loud laugh. 'Now that would be a truly useful recipe book. Bought food that can be passed off as homemade.'

'Yeah,' one of the other mothers added. 'We could call it "Don't make it – fake it." It'd be a runaway bestseller.'

Everyone laughed and after a moment I joined in. It looked as though I was going to have to take my successes where I found them.

NINE

I pulled on the handbrake and stared unenthusiastically at the corner shop across the road. This wasn't what I'd expected of Anita's globetrotting aunt.

The faded blue shop was not much more than the front room of an old worker's cottage set close to the street. Racks of magazines on either side of the open front door promised exposés of the lives of various celebrities, and a handwritten sign declared that Mrs Jones's award-winning chutney was back in stock.

Robert had said that Carla was looking forward to seeing Jack. But she'd called on Tuesday when Jack and I were in the backyard and left a message saying she was in bed with the flu and thought it would be better to wait until she was well again.

She'd called again yesterday while I was trying unsuccessfully to convince Jack to eat some mashed potato. We'd spoken briefly in between his protests and I'd suggested that Jack and I drop around today.

Unfortunately Jack didn't seem to feel like socialising. He'd cried when I strapped him into his car seat, a fact that I couldn't really blame him for, given that it still took me forever to figure out how to work the clasps. The drive hadn't improved his spirits and halfway to Carla's I realised I'd forgotten Harold. But we were late as it was, so there was no time to go back.

Unable to face chasing him around Carla's shop, I decided putting him in the stroller was the best option. But as I tried to do up the straps, he let out a squawk of indignation which turned into a full-throated yell. Abandoning the effort, I headed towards the shop. In one swift move Jack pushed himself into a crouch, teetering precariously over the front of the stroller.

'Jack!'

I stopped dead and he catapulted towards the concrete path. With more luck than skill, I hooked two fingers over the waist-band of his trousers and caught him just before his head hit the ground. I eased my way around the stroller and put my other hand under his arm, turning him up the right way and lifting him into my arms.

'Are you all right?'

The fright in Jack's eyes was clear and I pulled him into my shoulder to comfort him. Pushing away, he struggled to get down. The rejection took my breath away. I couldn't even comfort him when he was scared. What on earth did I think I was trying to do?

Jack kept struggling. Suddenly I ran out of energy. My attempts to try to look after him were hopeless. He didn't want me and I didn't want him. I was totally incapable of caring for him – I couldn't even move him five metres without almost killing him. Tears leaked out of the corners of my eyes and a sob forced its way out of my throat in a strangled hiccup.

'Why don't you come inside?'

Through my blurred vision I saw a thin woman with short grey hair put her hand on the stroller. If this was Carla, she must be horrified. I tried to think of a way to explain why her great-nephew and I were both in tears on her doorstep.

Jack screamed at the top of his voice and threw himself onto the ground. My tears turned to sobs and it was all I could do to stop myself doing the same.

The woman moved closer and touched my arm. 'Julia? I'm Carla. Please come inside,' she said gently.

I nodded, sure only of the fact that anything would be an improvement on the current situation.

Pushing the stroller ahead of her, Carla walked towards the shop door. I scooped Jack up and, holding him horizontal with arms and legs flailing, followed her inside.

I stepped through the door and stood there with Jack in my arms, trying to wipe the tears away with my forearm. His struggling slowed and I turned him up the right way, then looked around me. The entire wall space from floor to ceiling was covered in large wooden shelves that groaned under the weight of packets and bottles. Two rows of chest-high shelves in the middle of the room were equally laden. As well as the usual milk, bread and soft drinks, there were racks of olive oil, spices, pasta and interesting-looking jars. Towards the back of the shop was a long wooden counter with a cash register and a large coffee grinder. Several bar stools were lined up along the front.

Jack's screams stopped abruptly as he looked around. He wriggled to get down and I knew I wouldn't be able to hold him for long.

'You can put him down,' Carla said.

I looked at her in disbelief. Was she serious?

She saw the look on my face and smiled. 'Most of my regular customers have kids. The bottom shelves have things that are all unbreakable. Don't worry. He'll be fine.'

With trepidation I lowered Jack to the floor and watched as he headed for the nearest shelf. Unable to budge a huge tin of oil, he pulled some cans of olives onto the floor and proceeded to bang them together.

My tears had stopped and I felt a wave of humiliation that Anita's aunt had not only witnessed the ridiculous scene outside but had seen the need to come out and rescue me.

'I'm really sorry, Carla. I . . .'

Carla cut me off. 'Love, you don't have to explain anything to me. What you are going through . . .'

That was obviously all the discussion of the footpath debacle that was required and I felt myself relax.

Carla was looking at Jack, a bright smile on her face.

'He's grown up a lot since the last photo Anita sent. Somehow I was expecting a baby, not a little boy.'

She walked over to where Jack was and squatted down easily beside him. Anita's mother had been very frail before she died and I'd imagined Carla would be the same. But she was obviously a lot younger and looked strong and confident.

'Here, why don't you try this?' Carla pulled a handful of cans off another shelf and showed Jack how to stack them. He fumbled at first, but with her help managed to balance one on top of another.

'You did it! Fantastic.'

Jack looked up at her, a triumphant smile on his face, and Carla stretched out a hand and touched his brown curls gently. He turned back to the cans, knocking his tiny tower over with glee and starting again.

'It just doesn't seem fair, does it?' Carla stood up, still looking at Jack.

'No,' I answered. 'It doesn't.'

'Well,' she said briskly. 'He's having a nice time, so what about I make us a coffee?'

'That sounds lovely. Thank you.'

'Excellent,' she responded. 'Excuse me for a moment.' She disappeared through a door behind the counter, which I could see led into a living room.

'Sometimes I think I should go into business selling cups of coffee,' she said when she reappeared. 'Then at least I could justify buying a fancy machine. Mind you, my stove-top machine has brewed so many cups I'm not sure I could bring myself to retire it.'

'What are the stools for if you don't sell coffee?'

'I started offering coffee to some of my regulars a couple of years ago. It just sort of took off. Mind you,' she smiled, 'it drives the posh cafe up the road mad.'

I'd only been in the shop for five minutes and already I had a feeling as to why people stayed for coffee. Something about the place made you feel comfortable.

I looked around. 'You have some great stuff.'

'My husband Joe always just sold the standard corner-shop stuff. But when we were married, I started stocking a few different items from places I'd travelled to. Customers asked me to get certain things, and before I knew it, the place was crammed full of stuff. I don't make a fortune, but it's a lot more interesting than just selling milk and bread.'

I'd always thought that people who owned corner stores must have terrible lives, living behind the shop and working all day every day. But Carla's life sounded great. I reminded myself that I had recently thought the same thing about the woman behind the cash register in the supermarket and the guy driving the rubbish truck past our place at six in the morning. Basically, anyone's life but my own looked pretty appealing at the moment.

Carla turned her head. 'That's the coffee starting to bubble. Won't be long.'

I hadn't heard a thing, but she returned soon after with two small cups of inky coffee. We sat on the stools, both of our eyes returning to Jack, who was still happily engaged with the cans.

'I can't quite believe this has all happened,' Carla said quietly as she stirred sugar into her coffee. 'It just doesn't seem possible that someone so young could be gone. My husband died of a heart attack a few years ago. That was hard enough, but at least he'd had a life. Cutting Anita's off now just seems so wrong.'

It was strangely comforting to talk to someone else who'd loved Anita.

'I keep half expecting her to walk around the corner and for this to turn out to be a huge mistake. It just doesn't seem right that she's never going to see Jack again,' I said.

'How are things going with Jack?' Carla asked carefully.

I exhaled. Given our performance earlier, there wasn't much point in telling her anything but the truth.

'Not so good. Just when I feel like I might be getting on top of things and that Jack is becoming comfortable with me, something like that business outside happens.' I paused. 'Ah well, I'm looking for a nanny to look after him when I go back to work. It's only three days a week, but maybe she'll be able to sort us both out in that time.' I didn't really believe it, but didn't want to sound too depressed in front of Carla.

'It's a huge thing Anita has asked you to do,' Carla said. 'She obviously thought a lot of you.'

'I guess so.' My voice wobbled and I swallowed. 'I feel so useless so much of the time, like I'm failing Anita and Jack by not being able to make him happier.'

'You can only do your best,' Carla replied. 'No one can ask for any more.'

'No, I suppose not. I just wish she was here.'

Tired of the cans, Jack walked over to us.

'Would you like to sit up here?' Carla asked him.

He nodded emphatically and she lifted him onto a stool between us.

'Is it okay with you if he has a couple of lollies?' she asked.

'Sure.' If only she knew how poor his diet was, I thought guiltily.

Carla picked a few coloured jubes out of a box and set them on the counter in front of Jack. He put a red one in his mouth, delighted at the sugar coating. Wanting to give Carla a little time alone with Jack, I wandered over to the shelves, pretending to be enthralled by the range of biscuits.

After a couple of minutes Carla lifted Jack off the stool. Stepping into the living room, she brought back a box, which she handed to me.

'These are some old photos of Anita. I found them in her mother's things when I cleaned out her house. I thought you might like them for Jack.'

How strange it was going to be for Jack to grow up with only photos of his mother. I had no idea how I was going to help him deal with that.

Jack headed towards Carla's living room. Grabbing him with my free hand, I decided it was time to go.

'I think we'll head off, Carla. Thanks for the coffee.'

'You're welcome. I've really enjoyed having you both here. Well, goodbye, little Jack.' She bent down and kissed his cheek. 'Please just drop in whenever you feel like it, Julia. I'm always here.'

'Thanks. I will.'

I gathered Jack and the stroller and headed out the door.

After putting Jack to bed that night, I poured myself a large glass of wine and sat down on the sofa with a block of paper.

Questions to ask nannies, I wrote at the top of the page.

After my advertising disaster the week before, I'd discovered that the Thursday local paper had a large job section. I'd called the advertising department twice to make sure that my ad would appear the following day and was now worried they'd leave it out on the basis that I was a weirdo. At this stage I was refusing to think of the consequences if nothing came out of it.

I took a sip of wine and wrote: *Name*. Okay, that was a good start.

After that I was stumped. I thought back to my last interview and with a flash of inspiration added *Experience?*

With relief, I heard Patrick's key in the lock.

'Hi there. How was your day?' I asked brightly.

'Not so good. Jennifer spent the morning alternating between yelling at her secretary and yelling at me. This afternoon I shut myself in a conference room and didn't come out until I was sure she had gone.'

'And people still don't know about the two of you?'

He shook his head. 'Don't think so. If they do, they're doing a very good job of hiding it. The news about her and her husband splitting up seems to have leaked out, though. I think everyone assumes that explains her foul mood and they just figure I'm in the firing line.'

He sank into a chair across from me.

'But the good news is I had plenty of time to work on the nanny selection criteria for Jack.' He opened his laptop and turned it on. 'I've worked out a way to make sure we get a good nanny. This spreadsheet lets you rank each candidate against each other . . . Watch.'

Opening a program, he proceeded to show me how I could score each candidate based on a series of questions. I could then rank the questions in order of importance and compare them overall using a bar chart.

I covered my two pitiful questions with my elbow as he filled in a series of imaginary interviews and turned the information into a bar chart which demonstrated the hypothetical applicant's strengths and weaknesses.

'That's great.' I tried hard to summon the requisite enthusiasm. 'Do you feel like giving me a hand figuring out what I should actually be asking?'

He looked at his watch. 'Sorry, I've got to go. Touch football tonight.'

'Yeah of course, I'd forgotten it was Wednesday.'

In a time that would have made Superman's phone box transformation look sluggish, Patrick emerged from his bedroom in his club jersey and shorts. He obviously hadn't looked in a mirror and his hair stuck up where he'd pulled his tie over his head. About to tell him, I stopped. Patrick's hair always looked as though he'd just got out of bed and I'd lost count of the number of times I'd seen girls try to smooth it down.

I followed him as he headed out the door and stood watching him go. At the bottom of the stairs he turned around.

'I nearly forgot – I called Tony today.'

I tried to sound as though I could hardly remember who he was talking about. 'And?'

'And I told him that if he thinks I could do it, I'll give it a go.' He shrugged. 'You never know.'

With a wave he was gone and I turned back inside, trying not to feel like the little woman left at home by herself. Two Wednesdays ago I was out drinking with a bunch of friends, oblivious to the fact that my life was about to be transformed. Now here I was, a frog-obsessed eighteen month old asleep in the next room and no prospect of any social occasion on the horizon.

Well one thing was for sure, sitting in front of a virtually blank piece of paper trying to think up interview questions wasn't going to improve my spirits. Thumping the block of paper on the table, I stood up and went back to the fridge for the bottle of wine. Up-ending it, only a tiny amount dribbled into my glass. Knowing full well I wouldn't find another bottle, I nonetheless searched the fridge, throwing myself onto the sofa when I acknowledged that the place was dry.

Fabulous. No company and no wine. Maggie was working; I thought about calling Tanya but decided I wasn't a fit telephone companion. Given the lack of other options, I turned off the lights and crawled into bed, figuring I may as well catch up on some sleep.

As soon as my head hit the pillow my mind started racing. Why on earth had Anita thought that I'd be up to looking after Jack? Surely she had some friends in Italy with children who could care for him properly and whose lives wouldn't be totally turned upside down by his arrival.

As I lay there I added up in my mind the number of ways my life had changed. Going out, sleeping in, working late, long weekend lunches. They were all a thing of the past. I'd always known that having a child meant changing lifestyles, but I had assumed that by the time it happened to me, I'd have a loving man who looked like Mel Gibson to keep me company.

Instead, here I was, by myself. I hadn't been able to manage a successful relationship pre-Jack and there was no way I could see anyone willing to take on two of us. Even though I knew no sane man could be interested in a repeat of Sunday's breakfast disaster, I'd held out a small hope that Tony would call. But it was now pretty clear I wouldn't be hearing from him again.

God, even holidays would never be the same. I couldn't see Jack sitting peacefully under a tree on a tropical beach while I spent the day reading. And he'd last about two minutes in an art gallery in Rome before trying to deface ancient paintings.

At the thought of Rome, my self-pity stopped abruptly. The main reason for my trip to Europe, planned for later in the year, had been to spend some time with Anita. Anita who was now dead and had entrusted her precious son to me.

Fantastic, I thought. From self-pity to depression – this was really turning into a wild night.

With a sigh I threw back the covers and sat up. While not being able to sleep was never fun, it was doubly frustrating when Jack was fast asleep.

My usual technique when I'd found myself unable to sleep

had been to make a cup of hot milk and call Anita. The time difference meant I'd usually catch her in the early evening and we'd chat for half an hour or so, after which I'd go back to bed. We'd told each other everything since we were young and that hadn't changed even though we lived on opposite sides of the world.

I pulled the steaming cup of milk out of the microwave and leaned against the kitchen bench, looking out into the dark backyard. Because Anita hadn't been a part of my daily life, I found that, despite Jack's constant presence, I could go long periods without thinking about the fact that she was dead. But when I did register her absence, grief hit me like a physical force. I closed my eyes.

Suddenly I remembered a half-bottle of limoncello that had been in the back of the freezer for ages. Opening the door, I dug behind three ice-cream cartons which I knew from past experience would each contain no more than half a spoonful of ice-cream.

My fingers closed on the cold bottle and I banged it down on the bench. The icetray was, predictably, empty.

'Ah well, it's cold enough anyway.' I spoke aloud, ignoring the fact that the purpose of the ice was to dilute the potent alcohol. 'Just one won't hurt,' I assured myself as I sloshed a generous amount into a glass.

I tipped the milk down the sink and picked up the glass. As an afterthought, I tucked the bottle under my arm. Flicking off the kitchen light, I walked aimlessly towards the living room. A thought struck me and with more purpose I turned towards my bedroom. I pulled the box of photos Carla had given me down from the shelf where I'd put them earlier in the day. Sitting cross-legged in the middle of the bed, drink balanced on a book beside me, I up-ended the box and looked at the photos of Anita's life.

I made a pile of special photos, which grew quickly. There were some of her as a baby and a small child and her first day at school. I picked up one of the two of us at our senior formal. In the shot, Anita and I were laughing into the camera, looking young and happy. It was clearly taken early in the night, long before any alcohol was smuggled in.

Anita looked as though she'd just stepped out of *Breakfast at Tiffany's*. She had on a long emerald dress which clung to her body. With her simple pearl choker, she'd have looked great at a cocktail party on tonight – fifteen years later.

Unfortunately, my outfit hadn't withstood the test of time so well. Where Anita had gone for gentle sophistication, I had gone for effect. Elbow-length red gloves competed for attention with red sparkly earrings, making the short black dress look like an afterthought. It was only after a brief wrestle with my conscience that I deposited the photo in the pile.

There were a lot of photos of the two of us in Europe, but it was a photo of Anita taken in a small town in France that I looked at for the longest. Sitting on the grass next to a river, she was dressed in jeans and a T-shirt with her head tilted back and a smile of genuine happiness on her face. She'd had no idea that there wasn't a lifetime of happiness ahead of her.

But Anita's smile held my attention for another reason. I'd seen that smile a handful of times in the last ten days when momentarily everything was right in Jack's world. Even through my weary haze I'd been struck by the simple joy in it and the fact that it was usually caused by something I'd not even noticed, like the butterfly sitting on the rail of the deck this morning.

It occurred to me that when Jack had first arrived I'd looked for something of Anita in him. But already it was the other way around and it was Anita who reminded me of Jack. I put the photo down on the bed and stared blindly at the wall.

I'd lost my friend. Never again would I talk to her or laugh with her. But in Jack I had an unbreakable connection to her. By bringing him up I was making sure that Anita's and my friendship didn't die in that accident.

The thought gave me a rush of happiness. With determination I went through the pile a second time. The top forty shots of Anita were what I wanted and three hours later I had them chosen and stuck into one of the many empty albums I'd bought over the years. I also had an empty limoncello bottle sitting on the bedside table.

When I finally fell back onto the pillows, my eyes were bleary but I was happy. Jack was going to know as much about his mother as I did – with certain omissions I was sure she'd approve of – and this album was for both of us.

TEN

Jack's shouts wrenched me from the arms of Bill from *Playschool*. Eyes still closed, I reluctantly acknowledged that Bill's calm assurances that I should head out for dinner and leave him and Jack to make me a new car out of toilet-paper rolls were only a dream.

Before I even moved a finger, I knew that it was going to hurt. Turning my head slightly, I squinted and looked at the clock radio on the bedside table. After blinking twice, the blur of red glowing lights finally assembled themselves into numbers. 4.56.

Rolling onto my side, I slowly levered myself into a sitting position. This was clearly a mistake and my arm collapsed, depositing my head back on the pillow just as Jack let out another unmistakably cheery greeting from his cot. It'd seemed like a cruel trick that, for the first time since he'd arrived, Jack hadn't woken up screaming. At this point in my life, the sound of another person's happiness seemed like the ultimate torture. To add insult to injury, it sounded as though he was still in his cot, which meant I had to go and get him.

I slid my feet onto the floor, head still on the seductive softness of the mattress. This wasn't too bad, I told myself. Maybe if I could just keep my upper body horizontal, everything would be fine. Reluctantly I acknowledged that tending to a toddler from that angle was going to be tricky. Using every element of willpower I could muster, I pushed myself upright. I made it as far as the doorway before I realised I was going to be sick and veered towards the bathroom.

By the time I finally reached Jack, I was feeling slightly better but still in desperate need of sleep.

I lifted him up and carried him to my bed, every conceivable piece of sleep paraphernalia at the ready. Bottle, dummy, Harold.

As he happily sucked away on his bottle, I whispered into the darkness, 'If you go back to sleep now, I swear I'll let you drive my car the second you get your licence – before even. And,' I added, trying without success to imagine the warm little body beside me as a teenager, 'if a girl rings, I'll leave the room so you can have some privacy. Hell, if you let me sleep for another half an hour, you can have your own line.'

An hour and a half later I woke to the sensation of a finger being poked up my nose. Jack slid off the bed and followed me as I dashed into the bathroom again. As I leaned over the toilet he reached up beside the sink and tried to grab my bottle of Chanel No. 5. It teetered for a moment as I lunged for it and then slipped from my fingers, smashing into a thousand pieces on the floor.

Jack's 'Ooh' of delighted surprise didn't do a lot to help ease the moment and, unable to deal with the mess, I ushered him out of the bathroom and closed the door behind me.

I headed for the kitchen, where I blocked the exit with two up-ended chairs and concentrated on making coffee. What had I been thinking? Not only had I got drunk by myself, but I had managed to do so on almost pure alcohol. What would have happened if Jack had woken up through the night? Or there'd been a fire?

I was still standing, drinking strong black coffee with three sugars, when Patrick came in.

'Morning,' he said, hardly looking at me as he headed over to where Jack was playing.

'Hey man – give me five.' This was something he'd been working on with Jack since the pancake incident, so far without much success. To my surprise, Jack raised his hand, smacked it solidly against Patrick's and said something that sounded suspiciously like 'Yo'.

Delighted, Patrick ruffled Jack's hair and gave me a triumphant look. 'That's my boy!'

Jack followed him while he poured some Coco Pops into a bowl and drowned it in milk. Just watching it made me feel queasy. Obviously deciding it looked much better than the wholegrain muesli I had offered him, Jack began to climb up onto the counter stool to reach it.

Patrick helped him settle onto the seat and poured another bowl. Expecting me to object, he glanced over at me. I knew that introducing Jack to Coco Pops was setting a dangerous precedent but I couldn't find the energy to complain.

'Jack sleep all right last night?' he asked.

'Ah, yeah, I think so.'

'You think so?'

'Well I didn't hear him.'

Patrick looked confused. 'You don't look great. Are you feeling all right?'

'Ah, no. I'm a bit hungover actually,' I said in what I felt to be the greatest understatement of the century.

'Really?' Patrick looked interested. 'Who came over?'

'Ah – no one.'

'You got drunk by yourself?' Patrick looked justifiably concerned. 'I'm surprised you found enough wine in this place to get drunk.'

I was silent.

'Julia?'

'Actually I had a bit of limoncello,' I confessed.

'You got drunk on limoncello by yourself?' Patrick asked incredulously.

'Yeah, but it was kind of social,' I attempted to defend myself.

'How can getting drunk by yourself possibly be social?'

'Well, I was doing something else while I was drinking. I made a photo album of Anita so Jack could remember her and I just had a couple of drinks while I was doing it . . .' I trailed off.

'Things aren't going well, are they?' Patrick asked.

'Nope,' I replied honestly. 'I didn't realise that looking after a child could be so hard – and I haven't even gone back to work yet. How the hell I'm ever going to manage both things, I have no idea. I must be totally incompetent. Women all over the world manage with a lot more than one child.'

'Other women don't have a toddler suddenly arrive in their lives. Face it, you need someone to help – someone who actually has some clue about children.'

'Yeah, but where? At the moment it seems like I've got a better chance of winning the lottery than finding someone to look after Jack.'

Patrick looked at his watch. 'Tell you what. Go back to bed for a couple of hours. I'll go in a bit late this morning. It can't exactly make things any worse with Jennifer.'

'Really?' I felt so pathetically grateful, I had to stop myself from throwing my arms around him. About to give instructions about what Jack would eat, when he'd sleep and so on, I stopped. They'd sort it out.

I practically sprinted back to bed and fell immediately into a dreamless sleep.

I had no idea how many calls to expect in response to the advertisement, but when I switched on my mobile at nine the only message I had was from my parents saying they were back in Queenstown with sore feet but had loved the walk.

I'd promised Patrick that if things hadn't improved by the time they were back in range, I'd ask them to come home. By no stretch of the imagination could I be described as having things under control. When eleven o'clock passed without a single call about the job, I picked up my mobile.

Feeling like a failure, I sent my parents a message saying there was something I wanted to talk to them about and asking them to call me.

I was due back at work in four days' time and I still had no one to look after Jack. What on earth was I going to do?

Despite having an impressive-looking affirmative action policy, Jennings Walker had only a few female partners, none of whom had children or worked fewer than eighty hours a week. Mark had been understanding about my predicament, but I doubted the other partners would be so kind when they voted on my partnership in July. I had to come up with a workable solution very soon.

When my mobile finally rang at two, I dived for it, suddenly desperate to talk to Mum and Dad.

I took two deep breaths before pushing the button, trying to regain my composure. 'Hello, Julia Butler speaking.'

'Hello Julia. It's Carla here.'

'Hi . . . Thanks again for yesterday, we both really enjoyed it.'

'Oh, that's all right.'

The silence stretched for a few seconds.

'Look, Julia, I've had an idea. Well, weekdays aren't that busy in the shop and since Joe died it gets pretty lonely. I never had kids of my own and I know I'm not an expert, but I thought maybe I could help out by looking after Jack on the days you have to go to work.'

My tired brain was still trying to catch up and before I could think of a reply she went on.

'If you've got something else lined up then that's fine. It was only an idea. It's just that I would really love to help out if I could. You'd be doing me a favour letting me have Jack around too.'

Doing her a favour? I looked over at Jack, who was stacking books as high as he could and then knocking them over with great gusto.

This was a perfect result. Carla was lovely, Jack had loved the place and seemed perfectly happy with his great-aunt. It solved all my problems. Didn't it?

'Carla, that's such a nice offer. It's just . . .' I paused, not sure what I was trying to say.

'I don't know anything about kids because I haven't had any myself?'

I laughed. 'Trust me. That's clearly not part of the criteria or I'd be out of a job. No it's just . . .' Carla was silent as I debated whether to tell her what I was thinking. 'I was kind of hoping I could find someone who would sort everything out for me.'

I realised how pathetic that sounded and added quickly, 'It's dumb I know, but I just can't see how I'm going to be able to keep both Jack and me alive once I go back to work, even with someone to help out. I kind of had visions of Mary Poppins or, I don't know, Mrs Doubtfire moving in and taking care of both of us. Except they'd also have to be independently wealthy because I couldn't afford to actually pay someone for that.'

There was no sound from Carla's end of the phone and I was sure I'd offended her.

I shook my head in disbelief at my own stupidity. Carla had made possibly the nicest offer I'd ever heard and I'd told her that unless she could sort out all my problems I wasn't interested. If I'd had half a brain I'd have accepted gratefully and worried about everything else later.

I braced myself for the sound of her receiver being slammed down in my ear. Instead she said softly, 'I don't think it's dumb at all. What about if we just think of me helping out as a short-term thing – until Mary arrives.'

Relief washed over me. 'That would be wonderful. You may have just saved my life,' I said with feeling. 'Things have hit a bit of a low point.' That seemed like a fair comment given that I could still taste last night's limoncello. 'I'm not sure what the rate is for this sort of thing, but I may be . . .'

Carla cut me off. 'Julia, I'm not interested in doing it for money. Joe left me more than I need – I just want to get to know Anita's baby.'

I immediately felt stupid again and decided the less I said while my brain was still coping with this hangover, the better.

'Thank you so much,' I managed weakly.

We agreed that I'd drop Jack around the next day for a trial run and I hung up the phone smiling. Feeling light-headed with relief, I picked up my mobile and scrolled to Mum and Dad's number.

Problm slvd. No need 2 call love J.

Maybe something was finally starting to go my way.

ELEVEN

This was what I'd been dreaming of for the last two weeks. To be in an office full of adults whose clothes were not covered in food stains. Nine whole uninterrupted hours in which to calmly and methodically make my way through my pile of work.

So now that I was actually here, why was I calling Carla every hour and spending the rest of the time wondering when I could next call without offending her?

I knew I was being ridiculous. Jack and Carla had been great friends by the time I'd collected him after the trial run the week before and when we'd arrived that morning he'd disappeared in search of her cat without a backward glance.

'Right, well I'll be going then,' I'd said with a touch of embarrassment. Despite my plans to include fifteen minutes to make sure Jack would be comfortable without me, I was already running late.

Since the first morning he'd crawled into bed with me reading had become a ritual.

It had been surprisingly difficult to pull myself away this morning and I had succumbed to three more 'one last stories' before I'd managed it. So as I headed to Carla's front door, I told myself it was a good thing he clearly didn't need me to stay.

I'd decided the best plan was to drive across town to Carla's place in Paddington, park there and catch a bus into town. The whole trip had taken more than an hour, almost four times my normal commute time. But, I reminded myself, beggars couldn't be choosers.

Even walking to the bus stop by myself had seemed odd and I was finding it hard to relax now I was at work. Having been with Jack almost constantly for the last two weeks, it was strange not to know what he was doing.

I forced my eyes back to my foot-high in-tray. The morning had started with a procession of colleagues returning the files they'd been looking after for me while I was away. When someone else was babysitting your file, only problems that couldn't wait were dealt with. Which meant that most of them now urgently needed my attention. There was also a stack of phone messages I needed to deal with.

But instead of accomplishing anything, I'd spent the last two hours making lists and flicking from one problematic email to another. All I'd succeeded in doing was making myself feel sick at the amount I had to do and how little time I had to do it. Previously a huge workload could always be dealt with by working longer hours. Late nights and weekends came with the territory, and a whole weekend away from the office seemed like a holiday. But suddenly my available time had been slashed and all I seemed to be able to do was panic about it.

The telephone rang and I picked it up reluctantly, hoping it wasn't a client wanting to talk about something I hadn't yet glanced at.

'Julia, it's Mark. I'm in conference room two with a new client. Would you mind coming in for a while?'

'Sure. I'll be straight in.'

Excellent, I thought automatically. A new client and Mark was bringing me in at the start. That was good.

Before I'd even completed the thought, I changed my mind. That was not good – it was bad. Very bad. When in God's name would I get a chance to do anything on another matter? And if it was a new client it would have to be done straightaway. Get a grip, I thought fiercely. More work meant more hours I'd be charging which was exactly what I needed to have any chance of being made a partner.

I grabbed my jacket off the back of the chair where I'd slung it earlier. Doing up the buttons, I stopped when I reached the bottom. The jacket was dark blue, while the skirt was definitely black.

I toyed with, but discarded, the idea of not wearing a jacket. Several years ago a senior partner had seen me returning jacket-less from lunch on a baking hot day. He had berated me loudly about the importance of professional standards of dress. As a result, I couldn't even contemplate walking into the meeting 'half-naked', as he'd put it. All I could do was pray that the client was male. After all, twenty per cent of men were colourblind.

I knocked briefly on the conference room door and opened it. Mark stood up, as did our new female client.

'Ah, Julia. This is Sandra Stewart. She's the managing direc-tor of First Gen. They want to retain us to deal with the fallout from their incident.'

I paused in case more information was forthcoming. Nope. I nodded in what I hoped was an intelligent manner, despite the fact I had not the faintest idea what First Gen was, let alone what incident Mark was referring to.

Before Jack's arrival I'd spent half an hour a day reading two daily newspapers and a folder full of relevant clippings compiled by a media scanning company. These days I was lucky if I man-aged to catch the six o'clock news and wouldn't have been particularly surprised if another world war had broken out with-out my knowledge. My reading material consisted exclusively of *Diggers and Dumpers* and, at a push, *Hairy Maclary*. And given that First Gen's incident hadn't featured in the last edition of *Babies and Toddlers,* I had not a clue what was going on.

Despite the fact that to all outward appearances I was a suc-cessful female professional, I always felt outclassed in the presence of women like Sandra. Her hair fell to her shoulders in soft waves and I was sure she'd never decided that ten more minutes in bed was worth a day of greasy hair. Her fingernails were beautifully manicured and her expensive fountain pen rested on a leather-backed notepad. I hid my hands behind my foolscap block and plastic pen. Of course, underneath the confident attractive exterior, she was desperately unhappy, I decided with little conviction. Anyone who was that perfectly turned out must have issues – at least I hoped she did.

Act confident when you feel the least so. It had always been my standard tactic when I felt out of my depth and I saw no reason not to employ it now. It wasn't like I had a lot of options.

'Hello, Sandra.' I held my decidedly unmanicured fingers out to her. 'It's very nice to meet you. I'm pleased to hear we'll be acting for you.'

I flicked open the business card holder which I'd taken from my handbag. Slipping out a card, I handed it across to her.

Her forehead creased and I looked down. The top of the business card was fringed in a soft pulp. I could clearly make out the bite marks across its length and I suddenly remembered handing the holder to Jack when we were in the car last week. It seemed that having been unable to remove the tightly wedged cards, he'd decided to wreak as much havoc as was possible given the limitations he had to work with.

'Oh dear,' I laughed hollowly. 'I forgot this lot went through the wash last week. Sorry about that.'

'As you'll understand, things are pretty stressful at First Gen right now.'

Mark was speaking to me and I nodded sagely. 'Mmm,' I added as an afterthought, frantically running the possibilities through my mind. First Generator, First Generation, First Gender . . . Even if I didn't know what had happened last week, I should have at least had some glimmer of recognition of the name.

Thankfully Mark spoke again. 'I've told Sandra that I'd like to bring you in to help me with this matter.'

'Of course.' I had absolutely no doubt that Sandra had noticed the mismatched outfit the second I entered the room and was wondering just what value someone who was incapable of dressing herself could bring to the case.

Determined to show her how wrong she was, I pushed to

the back of my mind the fact that my life was in chaos and I was hardly capable of changing the sheets on my bed.

In for a penny in for a pound, I decided. 'I understand that you feel it is important that you act immediately. But in my experience it is often better to take the time to work out the best course of action.' That sounded generic yet wise, I thought.

They both looked at me strangely. 'Yes . . .' Mark said. 'Except that when you have fifteen miners stuck in a mine shaft, sooner is often better than later.'

'Ah yes, the miners.' I wondered if I should just hand in my notice now and be done with it. 'Of course – that goes without saying.' I tried to sound impatient about having to go over ground I had already taken as a given. 'But once the ground crew have done their job, we need to be ready to deal with the strategic aspects of the case.'

To my amazement Sandra nodded. 'That was exactly what I was saying before you came in. Because First Gen was only spun off a month ago, the first that most people have heard of us is that we have a mine disaster. The rescue efforts are going excellently and we're confident we'll have everyone out safely very soon. So we need to be prepared to deal with an inquiry as soon and cleanly as we can.'

Mining. Spin off. The words jogged a faint memory. My mind whirred as I tried to pull the picture together. With a blinding flash I had it. First Gen was the coal-mining company which had recently been sold off by a large Australian company. From the sound of it, I'd missed the blanket media coverage that would have surrounded a mining disaster.

I started making notes, trying not to picture my already overflowing in-tray.

By six o'clock my to-do list had reached the end of the second page. The only good news was that given the high profile of the First Gen matter, Mark had decided to handle things by himself for the moment.

But I'd told Carla I'd pick Jack up by six-thirty, so I resolutely shut down my computer, ignoring the fact that I was the first to leave. Law firms hadn't exactly switched on to the idea of paperless offices and I shoved five huge files into two supermarket bags.

The bus was late and the traffic horrific, so it was well after six-thirty by the time my plastic bags and I arrived at Carla's.

Great effort, Julia, I fumed. I couldn't even get here on time on the first day. Carla would probably throw Jack at me and withdraw all offers of help.

The shop was still open and Carla greeted me with a smile, waving away my apologies. Jack was sitting on the floor in his pyjamas, scrawling with a crayon on a large piece of butcher's paper.

'Hello Jack.'

I was faintly apprehensive about what his reaction would be upon seeing me. Screams at the thought of being taken away from the lovely Carla by nasty Julia weren't what I needed at this point in my life.

He looked up at me without expression.

The fact that he wasn't screaming was a good thing, I told myself in an attempt to be positive.

He pulled his feet under him and stood up without using his hands, a manoeuvre I admired each time I saw it. His pyjamas were half a size too big and stretched past his knees and I could see his little chest above the top button on the shirt.

He walked towards me and stopped only centimetres from my leg. Tilting his head back, he looked up at me and extended his hand. Gently I closed my fingers across his palm and allowed myself to be led to the kitchen.

'Wow, a cat! That's great,' I enthused as he pointed at it, his cherubic face serious. I tightened my grip on his little hand. It was a start.

TWELVE

This working from home business was fantastic.

Patrick was running around with a piece of toast in his mouth, trying to find a clean shirt. I sat on the sofa in my pyjamas, calmly eating my cereal and watching Jack run a plastic truck along the skirting board.

By the time Patrick left, Jack was ready for a sleep and I put him into bed.

The message bank on my mobile phone was beeping accusingly at me and I'd run out of space on the whiteboard which had become my to-do list. But I decided a coffee was the most pressing need.

I took my time frothing milk and then espressed my usual two shots of coffee into the largest mug I could find. After a moment's hesitation I added a third, just to be safe.

Jack slept for an hour, which gave me enough time to check my emails and make a couple of calls. I had made the wonderful discovery that his compulsion to deposit things into the rubbish bin could actually be used to my advantage. So when he woke, I sat him on the study floor where he transferred the contents of my briefcase (which I'd cunningly filled with scrap paper) through the swing-top lid. I was pretty confident that this particular child entertainment technique wouldn't be listed in the *Perfect Parent* handbook but it worked for me. The satisfaction I obtained from outwitting an eighteen month old was slightly worrying, but I chose not to dwell on it.

Trying to concentrate on an agreement for the sale of a business, I vaguely registered Jack disappearing out of sight. A few minutes later he returned. I noticed he was carrying the plastic packet containing the earplugs I had used to block out the early morning traffic before his arrival. Absently I reached out to take it from him. My stomach dropped when I realised it contained only one earplug.

'Where's the other one, Jack?' I asked, despite the fact that his vocabulary consisted mostly of the names of earth-moving equipment. 'Did you drop it on your way out here?'

I rushed into the bedroom and pulled open the bedside drawer where the packet must have come from. Nothing there. A check of bedroom and living room floors didn't reveal one either and I picked Jack up.

'Jack, you didn't eat that earplug, did you?' I asked. I snatched up the packet. *KEEP OUT OF REACH OF CHILDREN*, it proclaimed in large letters. *CONTENTS ARE NONTOXIC BUT ARE A CHOKING HAZARD.*

No kidding, I thought to myself. Trying to think rationally, I figured that since Jack hadn't choked already, it was probably all right.

As I was staring at him happily banging two CD cases together, my mobile rang.

I answered it absently.

'Hello Julia, Gordon here.'

This wasn't supposed to happen. Part of my grand 'working from home' plan was that clients and work colleagues only had my mobile number – which I wouldn't answer if Jack was around. The choking scare had made me careless.

'Gordon. How are you?' I tried to sound calm as I judged Jack's vital signs.

'Fine. I've just been looking at my statement again and think that one or two things need tweaking.'

I took a deep breath. *War and Peace* couldn't have been revised as many times as Gordon's statement.

'Of course, Gordon,' I answered. 'Let me just find it.'

Wedging the phone under my chin, I hurried into my study and shuffled through a pile of papers on the desk until I found his statement.

'Okay.' Racing back into the living room, I perched on the edge of a lounge chair from where I could see Jack.

He walked towards me and reached for the phone. Discovering it to be out of his reach, he grabbed at the pen in my hand. Desperately I shook the pen in an attempt to dislodge his fingers. When that didn't work, I tried to write with his fingers still attached to the pen but could only make an indecipherable scrawl.

'Are you with me?' Gordon asked. I realised that I had only heard about half of what he'd been saying.

'Most of it. Maybe you could just run it by me quickly again?'

He repeated what he'd said. Another tug at the pen finally pulled Jack's fingers away and I quickly began scribbling over the statement.

Jack looked at me with an affronted look on his face.

'Ah, sorry, Gordon, but could you wait for a moment?' I asked.

I was learning to expect chaos and had prepared for this kind of contingency. With Jack in tow I headed back to the study and, pulling open my filing cabinet, I took out the packet of Tiny Teddies I'd stashed there a few days ago. After ripping it open, I placed it in front of Jack.

Suppressing a stab of guilt, I sat down at the desk. At least the biscuits should dislodge the earplug if it was still wedged in his throat.

'Right, Gordon. Fire away.'

His 'tweaking' involved major redrafting of large parts of his statement and I wrote rapidly for the next five minutes.

Finally losing interest in the biscuits, Jack stood and picked up Harold. My blood chilled. Nothing that involved Harold ever seemed to work in my favour. As if in slow motion, I saw Jack walk towards me, squeezing Harold as he did. Knowing what was coming, I stood and backed up until my heels were pressed against the wall. It wasn't far enough, though, and when Jack released Harold's stomach, the guttural croak filled the room.

'Julia? What was that?' Gordon asked midway through his sentence.

'Ah, just a boat's horn,' I improvised. 'I'm outside the office – near the river.'

'Really? It sounded like a frog.'

'Frog?' I laughed nervously. 'No, of course not.'

As I watched, Jack depressed Harold's stomach again. Squeezing past him I bolted down the hall into the bedroom and slammed the door behind me.

As I did, I heard a series of croaks, which became gradually louder. The realisation that I was being stalked by a small child and a plastic frog didn't help my concentration levels.

'What are you doing near the river?' Gordon asked. 'Off for an early lunch at a fancy restaurant?'

'Ah, no, I'm just on my way to a meeting.'

'Not compromising your focus on my case, I hope?' Gordon asked.

Oh, for God's sake. 'No, Gordon. Trust me, no other client has more of my attention at the moment than you.' That was my first honest statement for several minutes.

As I watched the door, the handle turned.

Surely Jack couldn't open the door, even with the help of the dastardly Harold, I thought in terror. *Nightmare On Elm Street* had nothing on this scenario.

I retreated to the far side of the room.

'Was that the lot, Gordon?'

'Yes. I think so. Thank you, Julia. You'll have the revised statement to me tomorrow morning?'

Tomorrow morning. For a statement that had been finalised before his call and wasn't needed for a month? Jack should have another sleep in the afternoon, but I had three other jobs I'd been planning to do then.

'Of course, Gordon. It will be there.'

There had to be better ways to make a living.

I realised I hadn't heard either Harold or Jack for at least a minute. Silence was even more worrying than the croaking. I said a hurried goodbye to Gordon and dashed off in search of the latest disaster.

I found Jack a moment before he pulled my entire stack of dinner plates onto the floor.

'Buy child-proof locks,' I squeezed onto the side of the whiteboard.

As my adrenaline levels subsided, I thought about my plans for the rest of the day. Now that Jack was awake I'd return some emails and do a bit of other work that didn't require too much thought. After lunch we'd head out to playgroup and then I'd bring Jack home for a late-afternoon sleep which would let me knock over the work that needed a bit more concentration.

On the weekend I'd cleverly smuggled away a box of blocks that Jack had spent ages playing with. I figured that if he hadn't seen them for a while, I'd be able to leave him to it for at least an hour.

'Look, Jack!' I produced the box with a flourish from the top of the bookshelf.

He toddled over and plonked himself down in front of it.

'Excellent,' I muttered, settling myself in front of my laptop.

Two minutes later he stood and headed out into the living room.

'What? Jack, what's the matter? It's your blocks!'

I picked him up and put him back beside them. 'Look.' I picked a couple out and banged them vaguely together, not too sure exactly what one did with blocks.

Jack looked at me blankly.

'Here – have a look at this blue one!' I'd made an effort to at least look at some of the toddler books I'd bought and remembered something I'd read about subliminal colour education and mentally patted myself on the back.

Jack reached out for the block, took it from me and dropped it on the floor with total disdain.

'Right . . .' I realised I'd just been dismissed.

He walked back over to the desk and reached up for a stack of papers poking over the edge. It fell onto his foot with a thump.

His face creased and he let out a half-hearted cry.

Surveying the stack of jumbled pages, I took a deep breath. 'Here – let's do this together.'

I sat him beside me and handed him a few of the pages as I tried to restore some order to the remainder. He looked at them for a moment before crumpling them between his hands.

'Oh Jack.'

I took them from him and put the unsorted mess back on the desk – in the middle.

Jack's eyes lit up when he saw a file sitting on the other side of the desk. Beating him to it, I piled it and every document I could see into the middle of the desk.

Maybe, I thought, he'd just occupy himself if I ignored him. Turning my chair to the desk, I sat with my back to him. I pulled up some of the emails that needed replies, trying to concentrate.

Dead silence from behind me.

I paused with my fingers over the keyboard, head cocked, trying to pick up some sound. Surely if he was engaged in major destruction, I'd be able to hear something. I typed a few words, stopped and turned my head as far as I could to one side. Nothing. Slowly I turned my head back to the centre and around the other way. Still nothing.

Unable to bear it any longer, I turned around to see Jack positioned right behind me, playing gently with Harold's warty legs. I snapped my head back, but not before he'd spotted me. He started a low whine and walked around to my side, holding his arms up.

'You can sit on my lap as long as you don't touch anything. Okay?'

I picked him up and positioned him on my lap in front of the keyboard. Immediately he lunged for the keys, sending a row of gobbledygook spitting across the screen.

'Jack, this really isn't helping.'

I looked around the room desperately. He'd already done banging the saucepans this morning, and throwing the CDs on the floor seemed to have lost its appeal.

Just then my mobile rang. I stuffed it under some cushions. There was no way I could get through another conversation without a major incident from Jack. Whoever it was would just have to leave a message.

I racked my brain for something that would keep him occupied for longer than thirty seconds. I simply had to get these emails out. With sudden inspiration, I unplugged my laptop and, with Jack toddling along behind, headed for the bath. Turning both taps on full, I scoured the bathroom cabinets, tossing into the bath every object that could possibly interest him. As an afterthought I squeezed in a huge dollop of my amazingly expensive Lancôme bubble bath, which I'd previously been eking out in teaspoon-sized portions.

So excited was Jack that he managed to climb in before I had taken off his white T-shirt, which immediately went the same shade of blue as the water.

A small sacrifice, I thought, as I perched on the toilet seat and opened the computer again. Somehow I doubted the marketing people at IBM had meant customers to take the name laptop quite so literally.

Amazingly the blue bubbles kept Jack playing happily for long enough to allow me to deal with the most pressing correspondence and when I finally pulled him out it was time for lunch.

I knew I should go back to the playgroup. People had been really nice once the quiche incident had loosened things up. But I didn't feel up to it today. Next week, I assured myself. Instead I headed out to the park, driving the long way around to avoid passing the kindergarten.

It was only the third week that I'd been hanging out in children's playgrounds but already I hated them with a passion. The mind-numbing tedium of standing around watching Jack was only broken by the occasional panic when he did something life-threatening. Finally my watch edged closer to the time when he usually had his afternoon sleep and I dragged him reluctantly to the car. After pulling up outside the house, I turned around to see him fast asleep.

Okay, this wasn't a disaster, I assured myself. I'd pop him

into his cot and he'd sleep for a couple more hours, which, according to my day's schedule, was when I would have time to do some serious work.

Unfortunately Jack had clearly not read the memo about how the day was to run.

He woke as I took him inside. Twenty minutes of screaming later, I gave in and picked him out of his cot just as the first drops of rain started. After exhausting every single indoor activity I could think of, I threw him into the car in desperation and drove to a building site he loved going past. Delighted, he peered out the window, pointing at all the equipment. Optimistically, I pulled out Gordon's statement and started work on the amendments.

Glancing up a few minutes later, I saw the workmen who were sheltering under a large tree off to one side pointing at my car and conferring. Horrified, and with a screaming Jack, I drove off, unable to face explaining to a policeman why I was lurking beside a building site.

I'd fallen into a pattern of feeding Jack at five-thirty each day. But by four forty-five I was desperate to stop the grizzling and, with a worrying thrill of power, decided to declare it dinnertime.

Figuring there wasn't much point in hiding the problem, I'd confessed to Carla about the state of Jack's eating habits, which still hadn't advanced much. Feeling rather like the blind leading the blind, we had assured each other he would have to eat something healthy eventually. No child had ever starved to death because they didn't like eating vegetables. Had they?

We'd agreed the only way to handle it was to present a united front, and the hundreds and thousands packet had been hidden at the back of the cupboard. Carla had reported that he'd been fine with bread and strawberry jam for lunch yesterday and, bizarrely, had devoured a plate full of marinated olives. Unable to face a fight tonight, I cooked him fish fingers for dinner, promising myself I'd introduce vegetables tomorrow.

Finally, at six o'clock, I heard Patrick's key in the lock.

'I thought you'd never get home!' Patrick hadn't even closed the door before I descended on him. 'Today has been the longest day of my entire life.'

Patrick looked at my crazed eyes and skirted around me.

Undeterred, I followed him.

'What happened to the bliss of working from home?' he asked with a smirk as he pulled his tie and jacket off and threw them over the back of a chair.

The morning seemed so long ago I could hardly remember it.

'Working from home is not all it is cracked up to be,' I said with deep feeling. 'Don't suppose you'd bath him for me?' I asked hopefully.

Patrick grabbed Jack and swung him into the air. Jack giggled.

'I think I could just about manage that,' he said, sitting him on one shoulder and heading for the bathroom.

Delighted, I stood up, planning to start some of the work I hadn't done that day, but Patrick turned back to me. 'On the condition you bring me in a glass of wine.'

The two of them disappeared, Jack still giggling, and I opened the wine, poured two glasses and took a large sip. By the time I reached the bathroom, Patrick had just managed to get Jack out of his clothes. Despite the fact that he had already spent a good part of the day submerged, he was enthusiastic about getting in again. Until he saw the bathwater. He took one look at the water-coloured water and started wailing.

Patrick looked at me, confused. 'What's that all about? He loves the bath.'

I tried to look innocent but clearly failed.

'Julia – what did you do?'

In answer, I poured in about twenty dollars worth of bubble bath. As the water turned blue, Jack started to giggle.

'I think you may have created a monster,' Patrick frowned, looking at the bottle. 'And a very expensive monster,' he added.

'Yeah, but if it keeps him happy, who cares?' I answered, taking a glass and sitting on the floor with my back to the wall. I knew I had a mountain of work to do, but first I needed some grown-up conversation.

'Good point.' Patrick sat down beside me. 'So, tell me about your day, dear.'

I looked sideways at him, my lack of amusement at his comment very clear.

'All right, all right, it was a joke. Sorry. Sheesh.'

I tried to think of something vaguely interesting to tell Patrick about my day. There was nothing, unless I mentioned the incident at the building site, which I was doing my best to forget. I'd been desperate for adult conversation all day and now couldn't think of a thing to say. I was still struggling for a topic when the telephone rang.

Patrick bounded up and ran into the living room. 'Geoff!'

It seemed to me he greeted his old university friend with more enthusiasm than normal.

'Tonight? No . . . nothing. Yep, that sounds great, see you there in half an hour.'

He stuck his head around the door. 'I'm heading out. Drinks at The Victory. You'll be okay, won't you?'

'Fine,' I replied leadenly. 'See you in the morning.'

Jack was now tipping his twenty-dollar bathwater all over the floor. I tried without success to muster the energy to stop him. Instead I tipped the remainder of Patrick's wine into my glass, poured in another dollop of bubble bath and leaned back against the wall.

THIRTEEN

The words 'Conrad the Crane' jumped out at me. The only problem was that they were at the bottom of a three-page letter of advice I'd just typed, not the book I'd read Jack five times that morning.

Pushing back my chair, I rubbed my eyes, which were gritty from lack of sleep. It had been after 2 a.m. when I'd finished a quick review of a document I should have known inside out days ago, and Jack had woken fresh as a daisy at five-thirty.

I'd had three meetings that day and had managed to do enough work to scrape through all of them without looking totally incompetent. But as well as having to go back and do properly what I should have done before the meetings, I now owed one letter of advice and two amended agreements to the relevant clients.

Even assuming that the letter I'd just finished would make some sense once I'd taken out all references to storybook characters, I had days of work ahead of me. And tomorrow was a 'not working from home day' as I'd already begun to think of them.

Maybe another coffee would help, I thought doubtfully, eyeing the two empty foam cups on my desk. Grabbing my handbag, I headed for the office door. My briefcase sat on top of the cupboard and I picked that up too, hoping people would assume I was on my way to a meeting.

After leaving the building, I turned left, walked the length of the block and turned left again into a little side street that housed a dimly lit cafe—bar that would have looked more at home in Sicily than Brisbane. I threw my bags down and sank onto the padded bench. The waiter wandered over to me.

'Coffee?' he asked with raised eyebrows.

'Yes please, Brad,' I answered.

He walked back to the kitchen and I pushed my hair out of my eyes and tried to think clearly.

What was wrong with me? I'd worked when I was tired before. A number of the deals I'd been involved with had required late nights and, on a few occasions, all–night sessions, but I'd managed to hold it together. This felt different, though; it seemed forever since I'd had a decent night's sleep and the worst thing was that I couldn't ever imagine a time when I could catch up.

Brad returned with a perfect-looking cup of coffee.

'I added an extra shot,' he murmured as he put it down in front of me.

Great. Not only did I feel bad, I clearly looked like crap too.

Working from home was a terrible myth. I'd vaguely imagined that sometime in the distant future when I had children, it would be the perfect compromise. My vision had been of me sitting in my pyjamas, coffee at my elbow, tapping away peacefully on the keyboard while my beautiful children played happily at my feet. The only similarity between this vision and yesterday's chaos was that I was still in my pyjamas at lunchtime.

How on earth did women get anything done? The answer was obvious. They looked after the children, put them to bed and then started their own work. Sleep was definitely the optional extra in the equation.

Maybe I should think about leaving Jack with Carla every day, so I could keep working full-time? As appealing as that option sounded, I knew it wasn't the right one. Jack's life had just been turned upside down and my priority had to be to give him some sense of stability. He needed to know that I was going to be around a lot.

Surely if I could just get back on top of my work it would be manageable. At the moment the backlog was so overwhelming that all I seemed to be doing was putting out fires.

My state of mind hadn't been improved by a phone call from Robert to say he had some problems with his business, which meant he'd have to delay his trip to Brisbane for a while. He seemed to have slipped back into the role of the occasional uncle he'd no doubt played in Jack's life before Anita's death. I hadn't been expecting him to be around a lot, but having someone to share the responsibility with would have been great.

The only good news that had come out of the call was that Robert told me that his lawyer had called Thomas Driscoll to let him know of Anita's death. Apparently he'd been shocked, but quite clear about the fact that he held no responsibility for Jack. So it was just a matter of formalising things at this end. There would be a custodial hearing, but as no one would be contesting the issue, Jack should stay with me.

I wondered briefly what kind of man would leave his son in the care of strangers – and what Anita could have seen in him in the first place. Shaking my head, I decided there wasn't anything to be gained from that train of thought.

The first thing I had to do, I decided, was to get some sleep. I wasn't taking any work home with me tonight and was going to bed as soon as Jack did.

I drained my coffee and stood up. Dropping some money on the table, I waved to Brad on the way out. As I stepped onto the street my phone rang in the depths of my handbag and, still walking, I pulled it out.

'Hello?'

'Hi Julia, it's Tony. How are you?'

I stopped dead. I hadn't heard from Tony since the breakfast episode and had given up any hope that he would call. Maggie had thought the whole story was hysterical when I'd recounted it to her and had put the odds of him ever calling again at about a hundred to one. But that hadn't stopped me thinking about him.

'Great, thanks,' I lied.

He must be trying to get hold of Patrick. The production meeting with Tony's boss had been deferred until he returned from a business trip. But Tony and Patrick had been planning to get together to talk about the concept.

'I was wondering. Do you have anything planned for tonight?'

'Ah no,' I answered, deciding that a 7 p.m. appointment with my bed probably didn't count as a plan.

'Would you like to go and see a movie?'

I hesitated. Sleep was an absolute necessity and if I wasn't going to sleep I should be doing some work.

About to refuse, I shook myself. I had no social life, no boyfriend and very little prospect of obtaining either in the near future. Any work I could accomplish tonight would only be a drop in the ocean anyway. The fact that I was considering turning down a date with a decidedly attractive man, who knew I came as a package with a child who could demolish a coffee shop in ten minutes, showed how sleep deprived I was.

'That sounds great. I'll just have to check that Patrick's home tonight to look after Jack, but I think he will be.'

'Excellent. There's a new independent film showing at the Palace that I'm keen to see. It's won all kinds of awards.'

My heart sank. I was hoping he'd suggest a mindless Hollywood blockbuster. My life was wall-to-wall gritty reality at the moment, I didn't need to go and pay to see more on a big screen.

'Sounds good,' I managed with what I hoped passed for enthusiasm.

We arranged to meet for the seven-thirty show and I called Patrick at work.

'Yeah, okay,' he agreed when I explained the situation. 'I can manage as long as he's asleep before you go. I feel so crook after last night, I only want to go to bed anyway.'

Carla had fed and bathed Jack by the time I picked him up and I was standing outside the cinema ten minutes before the show was to start. I leaned against the wall, trying to look cool and relaxed. The minutes ticked past and the number of people heading into the cinema slowed to a trickle and then stopped. Twenty minutes later I started to wonder if I'd been stood up. Maybe this was payback for the wallet.

Just as I was about to leave, Tony walked around the corner. He was talking intensely on his mobile and smiled apologetically, mouthing, 'Sorry' at me.

I watched him as he spoke into the phone. His beige trousers and short-sleeved black shirt looked rumpled and the dark shadow on his chin suggested he'd had a long day. Not as long as mine, though, I was sure.

Despite his weary appearance he still looked good. Finally he finished the call and turned to me. 'I'm really sorry. I'm still trying to iron out some problems we've got with our news show.' He looked at his watch. 'Fifteen minutes late, let's just hope the show hasn't started.'

We went inside the building, bought tickets and pushed our way past a red velvet curtain into the cinema.

The movie had already started and the weird camera angles, flashes of sepia and close-ups of mind-boggling drug use confirmed my opinion of art-house movies. After ten minutes I still had no idea what was going on and I certainly didn't care. Independent cinema could be wonderful, but it could also be very bad, and as far as I was concerned, this definitely fell into the second category.

Sometime later I came to suddenly, wondering how long I'd been asleep. Sneaking a look at my watch I saw it was only about ten minutes. Wiping the dribble from the corner of my mouth, I looked sideways at Tony. He was staring straight ahead, apparently absorbed by the action on the screen. He appeared not to have noticed that I'd had a quick nap mid film.

I tried to concentrate, but had no grasp of whatever thin plot there was and spent the rest of the film trying not to fall asleep again. Finally the credits rolled and we filed out of the theatre.

'What did you think?' asked Tony.

I couldn't tell him the truth. If I confessed that my favourite type of movie was a romantic comedy starring Meg Ryan or

Gwyneth Paltrow or, if possible, both, he'd see me for the cultural philistine I was. My idea of developing sophisticated movie tastes was deciding that I fancied Nicholas Cage rather than Matthew Broderick.

'Ah, it was . . . great,' I lied. 'Very, umm, insightful.'

'Really?' he asked. 'That's interesting. I've read some good reviews but I thought it was awful. Those camera angles drove me mad.'

Why did I never learn? Thirty-one years old and I was still giving people the answers I thought they wanted to hear.

I had no choice now. If I admitted that I'd actually hated it, he'd never believe anything I said again. There was no choice for it but to go in boots and all. 'No . . . I thought the camera angles reflected the darkness of the plot.' One of the few things I had noticed about the movie was that most of the characters were dead by the end, so I figured it was probably safe to say the plot was dark.

Tony looked at me as if he couldn't work out whether or not I was serious. To my relief he changed the subject. 'So . . . Fancy a coffee?'

Despite my chronic need for sleep, I nodded. I had lost track of how much caffeine I'd had that day and figured a bit more couldn't hurt. At least there was no chance of it keeping me awake.

We sat down at a table in the cafe outside the theatre. As we waited for our coffees to arrive, I searched my foggy brain for something to say.

'Patrick seems to have come around to the *Kids in the Kitchen* idea. I think he fancies himself as a celebrity.'

Tony laughed. 'I can't quite promise him that, but I still think the show could work. All I can do is pitch it to John and see what happens. Listen, I'm sorry I had to rush off after breakfast the other day. How was the park?'

'Don't worry about it. Jack and I actually had a great time after you left.'

I was lying through my teeth. Jack had dropped his ice-cream on the ground and then screamed blue murder when I didn't let him pick it up. I was trying to introduce some standards of hygiene and figured I had to draw the line somewhere.

No taxi would take us without a child's seat and so I'd had to push a decidedly unhappy Jack the whole way home.

'That's good.' He seemed relieved and I was glad I hadn't told him the truth. 'How are things going with Jack?'

'Not too bad,' I answered carefully, resisting the impulse to lay my head on the table and sob out the story of the last two days. 'It's a big change,' I said instead. 'But everything's going fine.'

I paused, trying to think of a good way to change the subject again. It was starting to feel a bit like a game of table tennis, with neither of us wanting to say anything too personal.

'You must be some kind of wonder woman then,' Tony said. 'My sister Cassie is at home full-time with her three and my brother-in-law is pretty helpful, but some days when I go around there she's practically counting the minutes till she can have her first glass of wine.'

'Really?' I asked.

Yesterday I'd seen a lone beer at the back of the fridge when I'd been cooking Jack's dinner. My hand had hovered over it until I decided that drinking a beer alone at five-thirty in the afternoon was a slippery slope that had a pantry full of empty limoncello bottles at the bottom. It made me feel slightly better to hear that someone else felt the same way.

'Yeah, I have to admit that I'm not finding it easy trying to fit everything in at the moment,' I admitted.

'Is your boss cutting you a bit of slack?'

'It doesn't really work like that in a law firm,' I answered. 'If a client wants something done, then it gets done regardless of what else is going on in your life. The partner I'm working for missed his son's fifth birthday party a few weeks ago.'

Tony looked horrified. 'God, what could be more important than your child's party?'

'A hostile takeover of one of his major clients,' I replied. I'd never even thought about these things before Jack arrived.

Tony looked unconvinced. 'So you're doing a full-time job at the same time as looking after an eighteen month old?'

'Mmm.'

Tony looked at me closely. 'How much sleep are you getting?'

'Not much,' I shrugged.

'Cassie told me that she'd decided she'd just give up sleeping altogether after her third baby. She said she figured if she didn't expect to get any sleep, then anything she did actually manage would feel like a bonus.

'Right,' he continued, draining the last of his espresso. 'You need to get home to bed.'

Bed was what I'd been dreaming of since early that morning, but suddenly I was reluctant to go. There was something very comforting about sitting in a crowded coffee shop and having a good-looking man feeling sorry for me.

'Did you drive?' Tony asked as we walked out.

'Yeah, I'm parked over there.' I gestured towards a nearby side street.

'I'll walk you to your car.'

We walked the short distance in silence.

'Do you need me to follow you home?' Tony looked anxiously at my car.

I shook my head. 'As long as it starts I'll be fine,' I said boldly.

To my relief, the engine started on the first go, and I wound down the window. 'Can I give you a lift to your car?'

'No thanks, it's just around the corner.'

'Okay, then . . .' I suddenly felt silly. I hadn't even said goodbye and here I was sitting in the car practically revving the engine. He must think I was incredibly rude.

Tony rested his left hand on the roof of the car. He slowly lowered his face through the open window and kissed me softly on the lips.

My first thought was that I'd fallen asleep mid goodbye and was dreaming, but I'd never had a dream that felt that good.

He straightened.

'Off home with you. Let me know next time you want to see a dark and insightful movie.'

With a grin he was gone.

FOURTEEN

Reluctantly turning down offers to join some colleagues for Friday-night drinks at the bar across the road from the office, I put on my jacket and headed for the bus stop.

This weekend was the beginning of Operation Teach Jack To Eat Something Healthy and a trip to the supermarket was step one.

It had been three weeks since Jack's arrival and in that time he'd refused anything that wasn't full of sugar, full of preservatives or laden with oil. Even Patrick had conceded that Jack was probably on his way to developing scurvy.

While I was no child nutritionist, it seemed reasonable to think that putting some vegetables in the fridge would be a good start.

I had decided that food shopping on Saturday morning was the only activity less appealing than food shopping on Friday night, so after picking Jack up from Carla's we headed to the shops.

Trying not to dwell on how much fun everyone else I knew was having, I endured a torrid shopping experience and was on my way home when my mobile rang. My adrenaline levels surged at the thought that it might be Gordon checking yet again that everything was under control.

'Do you want the good news or the bad news?' I sighed with relief as I heard Patrick's voice.

'Um . . . the good news.' I quickly glanced back at Jack who was blissfully emptying my wallet onto the car floor. I knew there was a ninety per cent probability that I would lose at least one credit card, but I was willing to take the risk.

There was a pause. 'Well actually, there is no good news.'

'So, tell me the bad news.'

'I got fired.'

The silence seemed to stretch forever while I tried to think of something to say.

'What happened?'

'You know,' he continued as if I hadn't spoken, 'they actually gave me a cardboard box to take my stuff home in. I felt like Melanie Griffith in *Working Girl*. Do you reckon they buy them in especially?'

'Where are you now?' Judging from the background noise and his tone of voice, I guessed he had already found a pub in which to drown his sorrows.

A sudden flash in the rear-vision mirror caught my eye and I looked up to see a motorcycle cop gesturing rather impatiently for me to pull over. Cursing under my breath, I prayed that he hadn't been there for long.

I threw the phone onto the floor and pulled the car to the side of the road.

The policeman stopped behind me and slowly walked the length of my car, before leaning down and peering at me.

'Good afternoon, ma'am. My name is Sergeant Barlow.'

I smiled in what I hoped was an innocent manner.

'Are you aware that talking on a mobile phone while driving a vehicle is an offence?'

I thought about saying that I was Svenka from Sweden and no one had told me this rule but quickly decided I didn't have the cleavage to pull it off. Instead I nodded guiltily.

'Was there an emergency, or any reason for the offence?'

I turned for a quick look at Jack. He was entranced by the policeman's helmet and was waving his arms up and down and laughing at him. Reluctantly I abandoned the next lie that came to mind – that I'd been communicating with a doctor as I rushed a critically ill child to hospital. I shook my head.

'And are you aware that you were doing seventy-two kilometres per hour in a sixty zone?'

I shook my head again, relieved that I hadn't used my Svenka from Sweden defence. I was pretty sure speeding was a crime in Sweden as well.

'May I see your driver's licence, ma'am?'

I turned in my seat. Jack was still gripping my wallet, with notes, coins and various cards scattered over the back of the car. The policeman followed my gaze and when I turned back around, he was still staring at the chaos.

'Ah, is it okay if I get out? I'm going to have to open the back door to find my licence.'

'Do you think that's a good idea, letting your son play with your wallet like that?' he asked dubiously.

I had sudden visions of yelling hysterically, Basil Fawlty style, 'Good idea? Good idea? Of course I don't think it's a good idea!'

Thinking that might give him grounds for a 'driving while insane' offence, I made a noncommittal noise and opened the door. He stepped away and I opened the back door. I found my licence wedged between Jack and his car seat and brushed off a few squashed sultanas.

As I turned back I noticed that Sergeant Barlow, apparently searching for something more hygienic to look at, had moved closer to the registration sticker on the windscreen. As he did, I remembered that it had expired two months ago and although I'd paid my registration fee, I hadn't replaced the sticker.

Miraculously he made no comment and instead took my licence and looked at it.

'Could you tell me your current address, ma'am?'

Without thinking, I told him.

'And how long have you been living at that address?'

'Um. A bit over a year.'

'This licence says that you live in Red Hill.'

I wondered who would look after Jack while I was in jail.

'Ma'am, are you aware that it is an offence to not change your address on your licence within fourteen days of moving?'

I shook my head. The policeman had obviously decided that if he kept looking, he would find enough traffic violations to arrest me.

'All right. I have to book you for the speeding and the mobile phone offences, but if you tell me you'll change the address in the next couple of days, I'll let that one slide.'

I nodded enthusiastically.

He wrote out a ticket and handed it to me.

'Drive carefully, ma'am,' he said as he turned to leave, looking as though he thought the possibility highly unlikely.

I picked up the phone from where I had thrown it on the floor, hoping desperately that the call from Patrick had been disconnected.

'Patrick?'

All I could hear on the other end was Patrick's laughter. 'And you call yourself a responsible member of society.'

'It was your call that got me pulled over, thank you very much. And you have cost me –' I looked at the ticket, 'one hundred and eighty dollars.'

The mention of money brought Patrick's temporary good humour to an abrupt end. 'I'd offer to pay it for you, but now that I don't have a job, it would take me about a year to get it together,' he said gloomily.

'God – I'm so sorry about your job.'

'Yeah well, I guess it shouldn't really be a huge shock. It was pretty obvious that Jennifer was going to make life hard for me. I just didn't know she'd make it this hard.'

'You still haven't told me what happened,' I said.

A roar of revelry from the bar drowned out Patrick's reply.

'Look, why don't you come home for dinner? We can get some takeaway – my shout.'

'That sounds good. I was considering a bar crawl with my cardboard box, but I'm not really in the mood. I'll see you soon.'

As I pulled away from the kerb, I wondered how this sudden career dead end would affect Patrick. Although his lack of commitment to his job had always been something of a joke, his shock at suddenly being unemployed was real. I couldn't imagine it would be easy for him to get another job.

I'd just walked in the door when the telephone rang.

'Hi – it's Tanya.' I could tell from the background noise that she was calling on her mobile.

'Hi!' I replied, pleased to hear her voice.

'How's your day been?' she asked.

'Ah . . . Not too bad.' That was the best response I could manage. I didn't want to tell her about my panic-filled day at work, the traffic violations or the supermarket trip from hell.

Most of my shopping had been done while Jack screamed hysterically because I had refused to let him eat a packet of cockroach baits. Walking up and down the aisles, I'd avoided eye contact with anyone and done my best to pretend that the terrible sound wasn't coming from my trolley. An old woman had stopped in front of us, peered intently at Jack and then walked away muttering something that included the words 'not in my day'. It had taken all my self-control not to run after her and knock her walking stick out from under her.

'What about you?' I asked Tanya, desperate to hear about something fun.

'Well, since you ask, I'm pissed off and am about twenty minutes away from your place. I caught a flight out this afternoon and then hired a car. Don't suppose I could cook you and Jack dinner?'

'Of course – I'd love to see you!' I wondered briefly how Patrick would feel about Tanya's arrival and decided that he was so miserable, having someone else around could only be a good thing. And in any case, it seemed forever since I'd seen Tanya.

'Sure, come on over. Although I have to warn you, dinner might be more of a wake than a party.' I told her what had happened.

'I guess that beats my dramas,' she said. 'Greg and I had a fight and I told him I wasn't coming home until he apologised.'

This was a part of Tanya's new life I was starting to get used to. Occasionally being a country wife became too much for her, she and Greg would have a fight and she'd storm off to the city for a couple of days to blow off some steam.

'Bloody hell,' she'd said the first time it happened. 'Finding a bit of space isn't exactly a problem, but I've got to travel halfway across the state to find someone who isn't employed by Greg or hasn't known him since he was born.'

On these occasions she usually stayed with me and we'd spend Saturday mornings checking out the shops. Maggie would join us for coffee and cake at a cafe we'd been going to for years. And after lunch we'd all have a manicure and a facial, even though Tanya maintained that any benefit was gone within about thirty minutes of her being home. We'd head out for dinner and drinks, sleep late and then drive north and spend Sunday afternoon on the beach. By Sunday evening either Tanya or Greg would usually have apologised and she'd head home again.

As I hung up the phone, I wondered again about the wisdom of putting Patrick and Tanya together. At this rate we'd all be sobbing into our wineglasses by nine o'clock.

I looked at Jack and then at the bathroom. Sometimes the effort involved in wrestling him in and out of the bath and then dealing with the flooded bathroom seemed too much. Who would know if I didn't bath him tonight? I could just put him in his pyjamas before anyone arrived, maybe even sprinkle talcum powder on him if he smelled a bit. Knowing I'd feel guilty if I didn't, I sighed, picked him up and carried him towards the bathroom.

FIFTEEN

The doorbell rang just as I'd put Jack in the bath, which tonight was tinted a lurid red. I'd realised that if I carried on with my technique of using hideously expensive bath products, I'd be working just to support Jack's bath habits. The idea of food colouring had hit me in a burst of inspiration and Jack was delighted with his new array of colours.

Cursing under my breath, I picked him up and wrapped him in a towel. One of the many delights of Harold was that Jack insisted on taking him into the bath with him. As I walked towards the door, I tried to pretend that I wasn't being squirted in the face by a toad. What could Anita possibly have been thinking when she bought Harold?

Amidst the afternoon's dramas I'd forgotten that Maggie had mentioned she might drop around this evening. She didn't appear to notice the stream of red bathwater running down my face as I opened the door.

'Look what I bought,' she said, brandishing a big plastic truck in front of Jack. Placing it on the floor, she pressed a button. It tore across the room, emitting ear-shattering music.

Jack kicked to get down and, naked and dripping wet, headed towards it with a look of delight on his face.

Maggie looked up at me. 'It was on special at Mr Cheapy – I knew he'd love it.'

'That's just great,' I replied, my lack of enthusiasm lost on her. I decided immediately that the toy's speaker was going to have a terrible accident before Maggie was out the front gate.

It was clear that detaching Jack from the truck from hell to finish his bath would be way too hard. So, taking the line of least resistance, I quickly wiped him dry and struggled him into a nappy and his pyjamas. Meanwhile, I filled Maggie in on both Patrick's and Tanya's problems.

'Bloody hell,' she said doubtfully. 'This is going to be fun, isn't it? Why don't you just invite Nick Cave and be done with it?'

Patrick walked in ten minutes later, carrying his cardboard box, which he dropped on the floor.

'Hi.' I wasn't sure what to say. 'How are you holding up?'

He gave me a half-hearted smile. 'I'm fine.' After a moment he added, 'It's just a job.'

I nodded.

Giving Jack an unenthusiastic high five, he threw his suit jacket on the sofa, undid the top button of his shirt and loosened his tie. Jack toddled over to show him Maggie's truck and Patrick automatically picked him up.

'So, do you think Jennifer did it?' I asked tentatively.

'Had to,' he replied. 'There's been talk about redundancies for a while and ten other people got their marching orders today too, but Jennifer had assured me that my job was safe. Guess she changed her mind,' he added ruefully.

'Surely you can do something about it if she fired you because you broke up with her?' I said.

Patrick pulled a face and we all laughed as Jack tried to imitate him. In retaliation, Patrick pulled a cross-eyed look before continuing.

'Yeah, thought about that. But even if I could prove we were having an affair, showing that I lost my job because of that and not because I'm a crappy accountant who doesn't do anything anyway wouldn't be too easy. Besides, all the publicity and gossip that would go with it would suck and no one would want to hire me after that. No, I've just got to get on with it.'

He paused. 'Maybe it's a good thing. It will make me do something I should have done myself years ago. At least they gave me two months' pay. That'll give me a bit of time before you have to kick me out.'

Maggie looked inquisitively at Patrick. 'Hold on. I must be missing something. Who's Jennifer?'

'My boss. My married boss,' he corrected himself. 'Who I was kind of having a fling with and who wasn't too impressed when I told her I didn't want her to leave her husband for me.'

'I can't believe you didn't tell me!' Maggie exclaimed, looking at me. 'How could you keep gossip like that to yourself?'

'Patrick asked me not to tell anyone,' I replied. 'I wouldn't even have known myself except I overheard him on the phone.'

'Trust me,' Patrick said tiredly, 'the CIA could have learned something from the strategies that went into keeping this affair secret – until Jennifer went and told her husband, that is.'

'I thought that kind of thing only happened in the movies. That's very cool.' Maggie had recovered rapidly from her pique at not having been told. She looked admiringly at Patrick, obviously reassessing her opinion of him.

'Yeah, very cool until it lost me my job,' Patrick said flatly, putting Jack back on the floor.

'I guess that is a bit of a downer,' Maggie acknowledged. 'Not to worry,' she announced, 'tonight's cocktail will make you forget all your problems.'

The King's Head had recently opened a cocktail bar and Maggie's Cocktail of the Day had become the focus of interest amongst a lot of the young professionals working in the vicinity. She often stopped by our place to use us as guinea pigs for her upcoming concoctions, some of which had been less than wonderful.

She rummaged through a plastic carrier bag and pulled out some bottles. 'It's called a Pussyfoot – orange, lemon and lime juice, some grenadine and a couple of secret ingredients.'

'How secret?' Patrick asked dubiously.

'Trust me,' Maggie replied with a smile.

'Well, as long as it has a bucket-load of alcohol,' Patrick sighed.

'C'mon, it's not as bad as that,' Maggie said. 'I'll bet there are heaps of jobs around for accountants.'

Patrick just grunted.

The concoction Maggie made was bright red and looked anything but appealing. Reluctantly we each accepted a glass, waiting for Maggie to try it first. When it didn't seem to have any immediate side effects, Patrick raised his glass.

'Here's to new horizons,' he toasted unenthusiastically.

We clinked glasses and took tentative sips.

'Maggie, that is truly disgusting.' I didn't even try to break it to her gently. 'Why can't you stick with good old margaritas?'

Thoughtfully, she took another sip. 'Because everyone does margaritas. The whole point is that the cocktails we do are different – that's why people talk about them.'

Patrick stood up. 'Well they'll certainly talk about it if you serve that up,' he said. He collected his and my glasses and, despite Maggie's protest that the recipe just needed a little tweaking, poured their contents down the sink.

For once, after my shopping trip, our wine rack had something other than dust on it and Patrick pulled out a bottle of red wine.

I heard a car pull up out the front. Picking up both Jack and the truck from hell, I went out to greet Tanya. She jumped out of the hire car and hugged me, stepping back to look at Jack.

The word that first sprang to mind looking at Tanya was 'nice'. With her long straight hair invariably twisted and secured against her head, and her clothes that hid rather than revealed her body, she looked like she was born to be a high-school English teacher.

'Well hello there, handsome.'

Gently she took Jack's hand and shook it before turning to me.

'You didn't tell me how cute he was, Julia!'

'Didn't I?' I asked. It occurred to me that my conversations with Tanya had been full of complaints about how little sleep I was getting and what horrible things Jack had been doing. 'Yeah, you're right, he is cute. I guess I forget that sometimes.

Kind of like you forgetting how nice Greg actually is when you're annoyed with him,' I added mischievously. 'What did you fight about?'

'Oh,' she waved her hand dismissively. 'I was sick to death of cooking meat and three vegetables every night. So I decided I'd make a big effort and cooked a big chicken risotto for everyone – you know, to celebrate the end of the building work and all that. You would have thought I'd served them rat bait from the reaction I got. Greg told me that I should stick to the basics and – get this – that if I wanted to do something different, my desserts could use a little work. Anyway, we had a huge fight. He told me I was overreacting and should have known that "fancy" cooking wouldn't go down well with the boys. God, I realise that artichoke and olive terrine probably wouldn't be ideal, but I didn't think a bloody roast chicken risotto would start a riot.'

She took a deep breath. 'Sorry. I'll call him in the morning and everything will be fine. I would have come down next weekend to see you and Jack anyway. By the way, I've arranged to stay with my aunt tonight. Sorry, Jack darling, but I don't fancy sharing a house with you given what I've heard about your sleeping habits. But I am dying to cook for some people who don't think that antipasto is a phobia of Italian food.'

That was another thing about seeing Tanya these days. I'd heard a scientist once explain that the greatest difference between men and women was not their hormones, or even their anatomy, but the number of words they were allocated each day. According to this theory, the average man could comfortably manage 550 words each day, while women could easily manage 2550. If Tanya was to be believed, Greg's interest in talking was even less than the average, so by the time she made it to the city she was desperate for conversation.

She headed back to the car, still talking over her shoulder. 'So have you heard from the hunky Tony?'

'No, not sure I will after my ridiculous comments about that bloody movie.' Tanya had received a blow-by-blow telephone account of the movie and my postshow analysis, none of which improved in the telling.

Tanya hauled some shopping bags out of the back seat of the car. She always got so excited about the array of food in the local deli that she bought twice as much as she needed.

Jack seemed a bit unnerved by Tanya's non-stop conversation and clung to me a bit more tightly than usual. As Tanya slammed the door shut and pointed the keyring at the car to lock it, I saw an old MG round the corner. My stomach lurched and I told myself sternly that there were hundreds of old MGs in Brisbane. But not hundreds of old MGs pulling up in front of my house, I corrected myself.

Tanya turned to follow my gaze and we both watched Tony open the door and step out.

'Hi,' he said.

'Hi,' I stuttered in response, conscious of how bad I must look. I'd dressed for bathing Jack and had on an ancient pair of jeans, a threadbare U2 tour T-shirt with unidentified stains down the front, and a pair of sneakers.

He walked up to us, swinging his car keys in one hand, the other behind his back.

'Hello, champ,' he said, ruffling Jack's hair, then looking at me. 'I was at the gym and thought I'd drop by on the off-chance you were home.' Dressed in a grey T-shirt and black shorts, he looked pretty damn good for someone who had just been to the gym.

'And . . .' he continued, 'I was walking through the Mall today and saw a man making these.' From behind his back he produced a pink balloon twisted into the shape of a poodle.

Smiling delightedly, Jack grabbed at it.

'Boon!'

Clutching Maggie's truck in one hand and his 'boon' in the other, Jack looked like Christmas had come early.

I smiled at Tony. 'Thanks – it's great.'

'My pleasure.' He looked at me gently and I could feel myself start to blush. I stepped back slightly and realised that Tanya was standing off to one side, smiling awkwardly.

I introduced them. 'Tanya's in from the country for the weekend,' I explained to Tony.

'I had a fight with my husband and ended up here as I usually do. Julia very kindly hears all my emotional dramas.'

This early in a trip to town, Tanya was incapable of a two-word greeting.

'Let's go inside,' I suggested.

'Here, I'll take those.' Tony took the shopping bags from Tanya and followed us into the house.

Patrick was sitting on the deck, an almost empty glass of wine in his hand. Tanya threw her arms around him and patted him on the back. 'You poor love,' she said, then drew away and hugged Maggie warmly.

Patrick managed a half-hearted smile in response.

'Tony,' I said, 'this is Maggie.'

Maggie's eyes lit up and she looked from Tony to me. Desperate to head off the embarrassing question I had no doubt she was framing, I thrust Jack at her.

'Say goodnight to Maggie, Jack.'

'Goodnight, little man.' She kissed the top of his head.

Although I managed to convince him the balloon poodle would sleep better in the cupboard, no amount of reasoning was going to separate him from his truck.

Harold was already in the cot and I laid both Jack and the truck down. I closed the door, trying to pretend I couldn't hear the very unsleepy truck noises coming from the cot.

'I'm really sorry you lost your job, Patrick,' Tanya was saying as I walked back onto the deck.

'You've lost your job?' Tony asked.

'Yeah,' Patrick sighed. 'My cardboard box and I were made redundant today.'

'That's really bad. You didn't see it coming?'

'Nope. So unless you can reinvent me as the new Naked Chef, I'll have to get back out into the job market.' He paused. 'Actually, I've always felt Jamie Oliver wimped out by wearing clothes. If it helps, I don't have a problem with nudity,' he added hopefully.

'Got it.' Tony smiled. 'I'll bear it in mind.'

'Anyway, let's not talk about my career, I'm just getting

more depressed. What can I get you to drink?' He looked at Tony and Tanya. 'There's wine open and beer in the fridge.'

Everyone settled around the table with their drinks. The heat of the day had gone and it was a lovely evening.

'How's the book going?' Patrick turned to Tanya, clearly determined not to talk about his problems.

'Still no word – I'm thinking about putting the whole thing in the bin. Maybe I got it all wrong and it's crap.' Tanya had finished writing a novel three months ago and had so far only received a stack of rejection letters.

'C'mon,' I said. 'It's always difficult at the start. I heard that the guy who won this year's Booker Prize was rejected by heaps of publishers before he was finally signed up.'

'Yeah, and imagine how dumb those publishers feel now.' Maggie had finally given up pretending she liked her Pussyfoot and had poured herself a glass of wine. 'Not to mention poor,' she added.

'But all is not lost.' Tanya smiled. 'I actually got my first cheque as a novelist this week.'

I was confused. 'But I thought you'd only written one book?'

To my surprise, Tanya flushed a deep red. 'Promise you won't laugh?'

Intrigued, we all shook our heads.

'Well,' she said, and paused with a smile on her face. 'About six months ago I got sick of not earning any money, so I spent a week and a half writing a romance novel and sent it off to Black Label Press. I didn't hear from them for ages and figured they hated it. But a couple of weeks ago I got a letter saying they liked the concept, but the manuscript needed a bit more sizzle. So I added a scene where the hero and heroine had sex in some sand dunes, sent it back and they told me they loved it. It gets released in July.'

Patrick couldn't restrain himself any longer. 'You write porn? That's fantastic!'

'It's not porn, it's erotic romance!' Tanya pretended to be offended.

I glanced at Tony, who seemed highly amused by the whole situation.

'Who cares what kind of novel it is?' I interrupted. 'You're going to be published. What is it called?'

'I haven't decided yet. Maybe *In the Heat of the Night*?'

'Nice,' Patrick nodded approvingly.

I looked at him. 'Since when were you an expert on porn – erotic romance?' I corrected myself.

Patrick ignored me. 'Will you write another one?' he asked.

'Yeah, I'm actually halfway through number two,' she admitted. 'When I started I thought it would be hard to adapt my normal writing style. But the funny thing is it came really naturally. It's great fun. You know how I always said I felt I had a book in me?' The question was directed at Maggie and me and we nodded. 'Well, I'm thinking maybe this was the stuff I was meant to do – not that exercise in navel gazing that's sitting in my bottom drawer.'

'So, do you need some male role models?' Patrick asked, preening.

'Funny you should mention that,' she smiled. 'The one criticism the publishers had was that all of my male characters were two-dimensional. That actually didn't help the situation with Greg, not when I told him that it was probably a reflection on the men around me.'

We all winced.

'So when can I read it?' I asked.

'Never.' She certainly wasn't prevaricating about that. 'I'm using a pen name and no one I know is ever going to read my stuff. And by the way, I lied about the title.' She gave a mischievous grin.

Tony seemed to be enjoying himself and showed no signs of leaving. 'So are we talking lots of sex?' he asked, grinning.

'What you may not know is that there are various levels of eroticism in Black Label's books. I figured if I was going to do this I might as well jump in with both feet, so I'm writing for the Fantasy series. Not exactly X-rated, but we're not talking shy retiring virgins who faint after a decent kiss. It's actually quite liberating being able to throw your hero and heroine into wild lustful situations,' she added.

'I hope you didn't mention that to Greg.' I raised my eyebrows.

'Unfortunately yes.'

I could see why she was in Brisbane and he was in the middle of the outback.

'So what do you do, Tony?' Tanya managed to ask the question with a straight face, despite the fact that we'd spent about half an hour on the phone analysing exactly that subject.

'Well, for the moment I'm the assistant producer for a community TV station. But it's looking highly likely that may not last much longer.'

'Do you still have your picketers?' Patrick asked.

'No, thank God. I guess going round and round the parking lot at TV53 wore a bit thin.

'I've had angry mothers and children demonstrating outside the studio in protest at my axing of a kids' show,' he explained for Tanya and Maggie's benefit. 'And given that I haven't yet come up with a reasonable alternative, I'm not exactly kicking goals.'

'Maybe both your and Patrick's problems are going to be solved when his show becomes a huge success.' I'd decided I needed to head off the conversation before it became too tragic.

'You never know, I guess.' Tony smiled doubtfully. 'John is back on Monday and that production meeting is finally going to happen next week.'

Both Maggie and Tanya knew the details of every conversation I'd ever had with Tony, so the idea of Patrick's show wasn't new to them. But I didn't want Tony knowing that.

'Tony is talking about the idea of Patrick hosting a kids' cooking show,' I informed them.

I could see Maggie trying not to smile as she nodded, an interested look on her face.

'Really?' Tanya put what I thought was an unnecessary amount of surprise into her voice and I frowned at her.

'Yeah, but it will probably just be a dire failure like every other part of my professional life.' Patrick was getting more morose by the second.

'Ah, well, I can relate to that,' Maggie sighed. 'We've had the quietest week in living memory. You'd think I'd be used to pub fluctuations and know not to panic, wouldn't you?'

'Have you always worked in pubs?' Tony asked.

'Pretty much. My dad bought his first one when I was about five, so I've been around them as long as I can remember.'

'And you still decided to work in pubs even when you were old enough to do something different?' I had noticed this before about Tony – he seemed genuinely interested in other people's stories.

'I know. If I'd been a proper teenager and rebelled against my parents I would have become a teetotaller.' Maggie smiled. 'I don't know,' she shrugged, 'there's just something about pubs that I like. God knows what would ever happen if I decided to settle down and have a real life. Not that that's looking like being a problem any time soon,' she added, looking sheepish. 'Guess who I'm seeing tonight?'

'Maggie!' Tanya and I exclaimed in unison. I pasted my most disapproving expression on my face. But we all knew it was a half-hearted gesture.

Marcus was dark, stubbled and gorgeous. He was the lead singer of a high-profile band. He was also an ex-boyfriend who Maggie just couldn't quite manage to leave behind. They'd become inseparable within weeks of first meeting. Marcus's band was just starting out at the time and Maggie had joked about being their first groupie. She'd designed their first promo T-shirts and sold them at gigs, raving about the music to any-one who would listen.

But then, after they'd been together for a couple of years, Maggie's father had had a stroke. He'd recovered but retired from work at the pub. Almost overnight Maggie was trans-formed from a duty manager, able to change shifts to work around the band, to being the one making decisions and on call twenty-four hours a day. The band and Marcus had started to take a back seat, Maggie no longer able to disappear in Marcus's kombie for three days at a stretch. Around the same time, the band had decided to give up their day jobs and move to Sydney.

Marcus and Maggie had both tried hard to keep the relationship going, but the pressure of their different lives had finally become too much, and two years ago they had agreed to go their separate ways.

Except that neither of them seemed to be able to stick to that decision.

Maggie swore they didn't speak to each other regularly, but every time Marcus was in Brisbane, the routine was the same. He'd call her. She'd go to see him play. They'd end up in bed and they'd both be a terrible mess when the time came for him to leave. After the last such scene, about six months earlier, Maggie had made Tanya and me promise to talk her out of seeing him again. But we'd all known it was a lost cause.

If I hadn't been so intent on getting Jack ready for bed, I would have guessed where she was off to as soon as she'd arrived. She had on her high-heeled boots, fitted black jeans and a halter-neck top that was certainly not suitable for working in the pub.

'I know, I know – he called last night and asked me to come to their show.'

'What about the text-messaging man? Won't this break his heart?'

Maggie rolled her eyes. 'Hardly. The second time I saw him I gave up the whingy girlfriend routine and acted normal. And he never called me again! I swear I will never understand men!'

'Hey!' Patrick called out from the sink where he was opening another bottle of wine. 'Like you women come with a manual!'

Anxious to avoid an all-out Mars vs Venus conversation, which was never going to end well, I turned to Tanya. 'So, Ms Erotic Romance, what's for dinner?'

'Well . . .' Tanya paused for effect. 'How does a little seafood and fennel risotto followed by roasted honey peaches with mascarpone sound?'

We all made suitably appreciative noises and Tanya headed into the kitchen.

Tony looked at his watch. 'I actually have to get going. I'm supposed to be meeting someone in twenty minutes and I haven't even had a shower.' My spirits sank. I'd been thinking he might stay for dinner, but not surprisingly he already had plans.

He stood up. 'Thanks for the drinks.'

For a moment he looked at me and I thought he was going to say something, but he just waved. 'See you later – enjoy your dinner.'

And with that he was gone.

'Okay, so now what do I do?' I asked when I was sure he was out of earshot. 'Is he keen? Is he after my money? What?'

'Well if he's after your money, he has seriously bad information.' Patrick had accidentally opened my last bank statement and had been shocked by my lack of financial standing.

'I'm thinking he's a full suitcase man.' Maggie took a sip of wine and nodded sagely.

'Sorry?'

'There's a group of women who hold a book club in the pub once a month. Basically it's an excuse for a piss-up – to my knowledge they don't even talk about books. Last time they were in I sat down and had a drink with them and they were telling me all about this theory they have come up with about men. They reckon that any man who is older than thirty and single has baggage – it's just the size of the baggage that varies.'

Tanya was leaning against the rail, listening.

'According to them, guys who have been a bit scarred but could potentially get over it have carry-on luggage. But,' she held up a finger, 'the ones who are totally screwed up have a matching set of suitcases.'

'And you think Tony has lots of baggage?' I asked, no really wanting to hear the answer.

Maggie nodded. 'I kind of get that feeling,' she said. 'But hell, what do I know about relationships – I'm about to go out and get my heart broken again. And I even got dressed up to do it.'

'I reckon everyone has something they're trying to get over.

Maybe Tony just needs someone to help him deal with it.' A true romantic, Tanya always managed to put a positive spin on hopeless situations.

Yeah, I thought. And Jack and I are just what he needs.

With Tony's departure the mood of the group darkened. Even Tanya's typically sensational meal didn't do much to cheer things up. Maggie headed off to meet Marcus after dessert and Patrick disappeared downstairs to his bedroom. Tanya and I were left by ourselves.

She turned to me. 'I'd better get going too. Feel like hitting the shops tomorrow?'

I hesitated. 'I'd love to, but it just won't work with Jack. I took him into one of the clothes shops on Brunswick Street last week. He screamed until I let him out of the stroller and then lunged at one of the clothes racks. The top bar came off and all the clothes slid into a big heap. God knows how I'm ever going to buy clothes again. Maybe I'll just have to do everything by mail order.'

'Mmm.' Tanya didn't seem thrilled by the idea of us as shopping companions.

Searching for a compromise I said, 'Look, why don't you and I meet for a coffee at the normal place? I doubt that Maggie will make it, given Marcus is in town. I should be able to keep Jack under control if I feed him enough biscuits, and you can show me what you've bought.'

I was pretty sure this was a mistake, but refused to miss out on the shopping experience altogether.

'Okay, that sounds like a good plan.' Tanya picked up her keys and I tried not to feel sorry for myself. 'Well, I'll see you tomorrow then,' she said. 'Say eleven?'

I nodded glumly.

Tanya kissed me on the cheek and left.

I looked in on Jack, something I'd fallen into the habit of doing before I went to bed each night. He was fast asleep, head wedged against the cot and face pressed up against Harold's warty back. Asleep, he looked like an angel, incapable of the diabolical acts he was no doubt dreaming up right now.

I wondered if Anita had done this every night with Jack — given him a kiss and wished him goodnight like I did. He looked so warm and cuddly I was tempted for a moment to bring him into bed with me, but thought better of it. After covering him, I headed for bed, trying not to picture the glamorous and exciting woman Tony was probably squiring around the town at that very moment.

SIXTEEN

When I first opened my eyes two mornings later, I couldn't figure out what was so strange. And then it hit me. My bedroom was full of light. Not just grey pre-dawn light, but blinding yellow light.

I felt the confusion that usually came from waking in an unfamiliar bed. Looking around blankly, I tried to figure out what was going on. My eyes fell on the digits 9.45 on the clock radio beside the bed.

My God. What had happened? There was no way Jack could have slept until now.

Throwing the sheet back I dashed across the room and out of the door. I registered that Jack's door was open even as I threw myself inside. The cot was empty. I tried to think rationally as I stared at where he should be. The chances of someone breaking into the house and stealing Jack without waking either Patrick or me were remote, weren't they? At the thought of Patrick, hope flared.

'Patrick,' I yelled, belting down the stairs to his room. He wasn't there.

I climbed the stairs slowly.

All right, Patrick and Jack were both missing. The most logical and least paranoid scenario was that they were together. But this had to be balanced against the fact that Patrick had never ventured out of the house with Jack. I speculated wildly – maybe Jennifer had broken in to abduct Patrick and Jack had witnessed the event.

My eyes fell on a piece of paper taped to the glass doors leading to the deck, presumably in an attempt to differentiate it from the surrounding mess.

Stepping over several damp towels and Maggie's truck, which had mercifully run out of batteries, I pulled it down. *Jack and I have gone for a walk. Back about 11.*

I had no idea how I could have missed either Jack waking, or the pandemonium that must have been associated with Patrick and him leaving the house together. Although my chronic lack of sleep might have had something to do with it.

Almost eight hours uninterrupted sleep. And – I took a look at the kitchen clock – sixty-eight minutes more of Sunday morning freedom. Patrick had definitely earned himself some major brownie points with this effort.

What should I do? I eyed the room I was standing in. There was hardly a surface that wasn't covered. Pots and dishes were stacked precariously in the sink and there was a puddle of what I hoped was water in the corner.

I was frozen with indecision. The house could never have been described as neat while Patrick and I had lived together, but since Jack's arrival it had been bordering on disgusting.

But the fleeting thought of doing a whirlwind clean was banished almost immediately, as was the idea of finishing off the letter of advice I'd been preparing last night. The weekend paper was sitting on the bench, fat and enticing. Feeling vaguely guilty, I pulled the terrace doors open and settled myself in a reclining chair.

Ignoring the news section, I skipped straight to the colour magazine. Even those lightweight articles couldn't hold my attention, though, and I flicked through it vaguely, starting when I thought I heard a noise at the front door.

I strode to the door and opened it, to find no one there. Returning to the deck, I paced its width in agitation. What was wrong with me? Had I lost the ability to relax like a normal human being?

I checked the clock again. Sixty-five minutes.

An idea struck me. Even allowing for being home ten minutes early and for a five-minute drive each way, I could have forty minutes at the New Farm Deli.

Leaping into action, I ran into my bedroom, shedding pyjamas as I went. On went yesterday's clothes – a definite advantage to leaving them lying on the floor – and two minutes later I was out the front door.

I had deliberately never even walked past New Farm Deli with Jack. The previous day's coffee with Tanya, while not a complete disaster, had well and truly confirmed that coffee with Jack was not a relaxing experience for anyone within earshot, and I wasn't going to compromise the place that made the best lattes in Brisbane.

As I crossed the footpath a couple left my favourite table. Settling into a chair, I looked around in something approaching ecstasy. A cup of coffee in a cool cafe on Sunday morning, with no one systematically demolishing the place. It didn't get much better than this. I couldn't believe that this state of nirvana was something to which I'd once given little thought.

'Morning.' The waiter looked at me questioningly.

'A latte, please.' I decided food was an optional extra that could only complicate my tight time frame.

The newspaper I'd brought from home sat on the table in front of me. But these fleeting minutes of peace seemed too precious to spend on world events. I walked over to the pile of magazines in the corner, suppressing my impulse to skip.

The one on top was a recent copy of my favourite women's magazine. Absolutely perfect. I picked it up and returned to my table where a sensational-looking cup of coffee was sitting waiting for me.

Settling myself into the chair, I sneaked a look at my watch. It was only 10.20.

As I flipped through the first twenty pages of ads, my elation evaporated. How could I sit here getting excited about some time to myself when Anita was dead? She'd never have the chance to see her son again and here I was treating his presence like a millstone around my neck.

I was starting to get used to this emotional seesaw. When I was at work or running around after Jack, I managed not to think much about Anita. But at quiet moments like now, or when I was lying in bed, all I'd be able to think about was her death. I found myself wanting to tell her what was happening and then realising I couldn't.

I bit my lip. Feeling guilty every time I was happy wasn't going to achieve anything. Anita was dead, but my not enjoying living wasn't going to bring her back.

Deliberately I took a slow sip of coffee and turned to the first article. It was a regular piece called 'A Day in the Life of . . .'

This edition featured a woman called Angie Dawson. She was glammy, thirty-fiveish, in head-to-toe designer gear and surrounded by three children. The bold type under the heading read:

When she's not jetting off to the States for important pow-wows with clients, management consultant Angie bakes cakes, plays backyard cricket and throws fabulous dinner parties for her friends.

I hated her already.

I hated her even more after I read the next two pages, which followed her day from 6.30 a.m. (I should be so lucky) until 12 p.m., when she no doubt engaged in bed-spring-rattling sex with her movie-star handsome husband. Thankfully, that part was left to the imagination.

6.30 a.m. had her getting up with her youngest child (gorgeous husband and she took turns) and then waking her older two children an hour later. I stared sightlessly into the middle distance, picturing the sheer bliss of having to wake Jack. Although it seemed a somewhat unlikely scenario, having to kick him out of bed at eleven in the morning and tell him he was a lazy sod was something I longed for with every fibre of my body.

At 8.30 a.m. Angie left for work in a stunning suit on which, despite close examination, I couldn't spot one Vegemite smear.

The morning saw her flitting from desk to conference room, saving companies with her insight. 1 p.m. saw her eating a salad for lunch at a trendy new restaurant with a bunch of friends who all look similarly superwomanish. 2 p.m. – who ever did lunch in an hour? – saw her back at her desk, printer churning out inspirational reports all afternoon. 6 p.m. and she was leaving the office, walking in her front door at 6.30 p.m. to a house full of fed, clean and pyjamaed offspring. 7.30 p.m. and they all tootled off to bed in Von Trapp family high spirits, leaving Angie and divine-looking husband entertaining a table full of fabulous and witty guests until midnight.

There were two possible things happening here, I decided. Either this woman was lying or – and I prayed it wasn't true – this was how efficient, well-organised women actually dealt with the combination of a career and children.

Where were the midnight wakings, dirty nappies, whining children and food throwing? Where was Harold, for God's sake?

10.40. Reluctantly I drained the last of my coffee and stood up. Maybe I just needed to be more efficient. What I needed was to take control. Time management, that was the key. Lists, priorities, goals, objectives . . . If Angie could do it with three kids, I could do it with one.

The phone was ringing as I unlocked the door.

Instantly I imagined it was Patrick ringing to say something terrible had happened to Jack.

'Hello?'

'Hi.'

'Tanya . . .' I sighed with relief. 'So you made it home okay?'

Greg had called to apologise and Tanya had flown home the previous afternoon.

'Sure did. And I brought back a suitcase full of exotic ingredients. I'm going to teach Greg about good food even if it kills me. If I have to cook steak and chips once more, I'm simply going to have to chop off my own ear.'

I laughed. 'God, you really do love a challenge, don't you? Why didn't you marry that chef you used to go out with? You could have saved yourself all this bother.'

'Well, for starters he was addicted to cocaine, and secondly he was a total dick.'

'Ah yes,' I agreed. 'There is that.'

'Have you heard from Maggie?' she asked.

'No. You?'

'Uh-uh. I called the pub, but the guy I spoke to said no one had seen her since Friday. I assume she's still with Marcus.'

I sighed. 'Ah well. She's a grown-up. She knows what she's doing.'

'I guess so. I just know how bad she's going to feel when it's over again.'

'Yeah, I know.'

'Hey, guess what?' Tanya brightened. 'I had an email from Black Label Press while I was in Brisbane. I pitched them an idea of a series of books set in the outback and they seem keen.'

'Really?' I asked doubtfully. The times I'd visited Tanya I'd spent most of the time covered in dust. The most intimate male conversation I'd had out there was with a sixty-year-old station hand who'd insisted on telling me about his haemorrhoids.

'Yeah, there's some fantastic material,' Tanya enthused. 'Taut thighs gripping saddles, midnight trysts in the shearing shed . . .'

I burst out laughing. 'You're really enjoying this, aren't you?'

'It's fantastic – best job I've ever had. How's Jack going? Still in love with Maggie's truck?'

'Yep – he insisted on sleeping with it again last night. I reckon Hideous Harold's days are numbered.'

'You should be so lucky. Anyway, I must go. Let me know if you hear from Maggie.'

We said our goodbyes and I put the phone down. Taking a long look around the kitchen, I decided that if I left cleaning it any longer, the health department would be knocking at the door.

I had just about managed to clear the floor when I heard Patrick's key in the lock. He walked in, carrying two large plastic bags, followed by Jack who had been transformed into a rather baggy, but very cute, Spiderman. He was wearing a webbed costume that was at least two sizes too big – the web-launching wristbands looking like bangles on his little wrists.

Clutching what looked like a Batman mask in one hand and Harold in the other, he stood in the doorway beaming at me. He'd obviously had a great time and showed no signs of needing his normal morning sleep.

Assuming that a dramatic reaction was required, I screamed and ducked behind the sofa, much to Jack's delight.

Patrick interrupted as I pretended to cower in terror at the sight of an advancing Jack.

'Julia, where've you been? Spiderman is one of the good guys.'

'Oh.' I shrugged and stood up.

'You know this being poor thing isn't all bad. Check out what we found at a garage sale down the road.' He opened the bags to reveal a collection of clearly second-hand trucks, diggers and footballs. 'All this for fifty bucks.'

'But I've already bought him toys. I spent a fortune.'

'Nope,' Patrick declared with certainty. 'All wrong. This morning Jack spent nearly half an hour tucking that bloody toad into the pram, putting a hand towel over him like it was a sheet.' He looked at me accusingly, clearly expecting me to be as mortified as he was.

'So?'

'So? What do you mean so? He's a boy. He's supposed to be running trucks up and down the walls, not making up beds. I can't believe you bought him a pram – he'd never have been able to show his face on the street again if the neighbours' kids had seen him with it.'

I shook my head. '*Babies and Toddlers* magazine says it's wrong to gender stereotype kids and that they should be exposed to different kinds of toys. You're lucky that I didn't buy him a doll.' I wasn't sure I really believed this theory, but the pram had been on sale and it had seemed like a good idea at the time.

Patrick looked mortified at the thought.

I reminded myself that Patrick had kept Jack occupied all morning. He could buy him guns if he kept this up.

'Thanks for giving me a sleep-in. I really appreciate it. I feel better than I have in weeks.'

Patrick waved my thanks away. 'I actually wanted to test something one of the guys at work said — ex-work,' he corrected himself. 'He reckoned that having a baby was a great way to pick up women.'

I tried not to feel disappointed that my brother's motives hadn't been more honourable. 'And did it work?'

'Ah — no. I took him to the park — nothing. I even got him to run up to a woman who was sitting on a bench reading. But she just smiled at him and went back to her book.'

I tried not to laugh. 'I thought you were over women.'

'Oh, trust me, I am. It was just a sociological experiment.'

Jack was fully occupied making satisfied male noises with his new machinery.

Patrick, apparently pleased that he'd saved Jack from a fate worse than death, decided that his next task was to teach him to shake hands. 'Firm grip, that's the key,' he proclaimed.

I opened my mouth to comment, about to suggest that learning to feed himself might come slightly ahead of hand-shaking, but stopped as I saw Maggie walk in the door.

'Hi there. You're just in time to learn how to shake hands.'

When she barely managed a smile, I looked at her carefully. I knew from past experience that she was likely to be fragile. She was dressed in old jeans and a baggy T-shirt — a clear sign that she was suffering. Hair pulled back into a clip at the back of her neck, she smiled wanly.

'Have a good time?' I asked.

'Yeah,' she sighed. 'But it's Sunday again, isn't it. It's funny, every time we do this, I think the weekend will last forever. But Sunday always comes. You'd think I'd learn.'

'How's Marcus?'

'Just the same. Heaps of fun, getting chased by groupies. You know . . . He was seeing someone for a few months but they broke up. I shouldn't be glad but I am.'

She looked so sad I couldn't bring myself to say any of the meaningless platitudes that sprang to mind. 'You know, I don't think it's going to end for you guys until one of you falls in love with someone else.'

'Which I'm perfectly happy to do.' Maggie threw her hands up. 'It's just that every single man I meet is a complete dufus.'

Patrick put on an offended face and Maggie held a hand up apologetically.

'Sorry, Patrick, I should have qualified that. I meant every single man who started high school before I left. Although maybe cradle-snatching isn't an option I can afford to ignore any more . . .'

'Oh come on, Maggie,' Patrick tried half-heartedly, then gave up. 'Ah – I've got to make some calls. I'll be downstairs if you need me.' He escaped the discussion of female emotions with patently obvious relief.

Maggie sat down on the sofa and made an effort to distract herself.

'Hello Jack. Cool outfit!'

Jack beamed at her before heading purposefully towards his bedroom.

'So have you heard from the beautiful Tony?'

'Not a word. Mind you, he didn't call me for ten days before we went to the movies, so who knows? Maybe he's just the forgetful type.'

'Mmm. Told you he had issues. Listen, maybe one of us should give the text-messaging man another go?'

I raised my eyebrows.

'Yeah, all right. I'm just depressed.' She looked up at the ceiling and then back at me. 'Does finding someone you want to be with really have to be this hard?'

'I don't know,' I answered honestly.

'Whatever happened to the fairytales?' she asked. 'I'm over the love at first sight stuff, but I could definitely do with the living happily ever after bit.'

I hadn't seen Jack since he'd headed to his room and I was just about to check on him when he reappeared, Maggie's truck in hand. He came up beside her, making determined 'brmm brmm' noises.

Maggie's face softened. 'Ah, so you like the truck, Jack?'

'Like it?' I answered. 'I think you might have made a friend for life with that present. Unfortunately the batteries have run out though, so he can only push it around.' I tried my hardest to look sad.

'I remember that from when I was a kid,' Maggie said. 'You'd get a great present, it would work for a couple of hours and that was it. So . . .' She rummaged in her bag. 'I bought a few extra batteries.' She brandished a handful of packets that looked like they would keep the truck in business for a year or more.

Taking the truck from Jack, she ripped open a packet and replaced the batteries. She flicked the on switch and the familiar noise ripped through the air. Jack gave Maggie a look of adoration and followed the truck as it took off towards the kitchen.

I watched the miniature Spiderman following the truck and swallowed the words of protest that were on my lips. When did I suddenly become so grumpy? I could put up with a bit of noise if it made Jack happy.

Maggie turned back to me. 'I know it's stupid, but I saw a movie years ago when this couple met and fell in love. There was this montage of them doing fabulous things, like riding horses on the beach and kissing under waterfalls. That's what I want – a happy time and then pretty soon after that, another happy time. I know there have to be some bad times in there, but it's got to get better than this.'

Patrick chose that moment to stick his head out of the stairwell. Not seeing any overt displays of emotion, he bounded up the last few steps.

'I've got an idea,' he said.

'Does it involve finding a fabulous single man without hang-ups for each of us?' Maggie tried to smile.

'Ah, no. I was actually going to suggest that we all head to New Farm Park for lunch.'

'Really?' I asked. Patrick's usual Sunday afternoon venue was The Victory.

He looked embarrassed. 'I actually had a good time with

Jack this morning – I thought we could try out a couple of the footballs I bought.'

'Well, he should probably have a sleep. But heading out after that is a great idea.'

I had finally accepted that working while Jack was awake was impossible, which meant that I didn't feel constantly guilty about not doing anything. Although I still felt panicky whenever I thought about how much I had to do, I figured that removing one negative emotion had to be a step in the right direction.

'What about you, Maggie?'

She shook her head. 'Thanks, I can't. I didn't make it into work yesterday, so I need to go and check what's going on. Besides, trust me, you don't really want me around today.'

She stood up. I put my arms around her and gave her a hug.

'Bye, Jack,' she called across the room to where he was repeatedly driving the truck into the skirting board.

Intent on the task, he didn't turn around.

'I'm going to have my work cut out for me improving on that present,' Maggie smiled.

'Just promise you'll make the next one quiet?' I pleaded.

With a wicked smile, Maggie turned around and headed for the steps.

'Do not call Text-messaging Man!' I yelled after her.

SEVENTEEN

Patrick walked ahead, his rusty old VB esky in one hand and a rug in the other. Jack and I trailed along behind, stopping every few seconds for Jack to pick up every slimy and disgusting object he could see. Any vague resemblance we bore to a normal family disappeared when Patrick shook out the picnic rug under a shady tree.

The only rug I'd been able to find was one of Patrick's from his university days. It was lime green and had the words *College Property – do not remove* emblazoned across it.

Completely unconcerned at the public display of his theft, Patrick sat down and flicked back the lid of the ancient esky.

'Well,' he said, surveying the contents. 'Can't say the food looks too inspiring but the last-minute stop at the bottle shop was an act of genius.'

He extracted a cold bottle of white wine, two plastic glasses and a bottle opener.

Jack had been so difficult during my trip to the supermarket on Friday night that I'd managed to forget just about everything I had intended to buy. As a result our picnic consisted of an old block of cheese, a single boiled egg, a day-old baguette and jars of jam and mayonnaise. I had hoped the fact that it was to be consumed in the beautiful outdoors would transform it into a feast, but judging by Patrick's comment, that hadn't happened.

I leaned back and looked around. Despite the average food, this wasn't too bad at all.

Jack toddled off, chunk of jam-smothered baguette in hand. He found a bark-covered garden bed and, laying his baguette carefully on the ground, proceeded to bash two pieces of bark together.

Patrick poured two glasses of wine and handed one to me.

'Why haven't we ever done this before?' he asked.

'Probably because we used to have lives and money,' I responded.

'Ah, yes.' Patrick nodded.

'Have you heard from Mum and Dad this week?' I asked.

Patrick nodded. 'They sent me a text message a few days ago. To be honest I only understood about half of it – Dad uses some of the most bizarre abbreviations. But the general gist of it was that they were having a great time.'

Jack had finished with the bark and was striding purposefully towards the flower garden.

'Even in a park that child can find things to destroy,' I sighed, beginning to stand up.

'I'll go.'

Patrick sprang to his feet and grabbed the football he'd brought along. He picked Jack up and turned him around.

'Okay Jack, here goes your first football lesson. Remember me in your biography.'

I took a sip of wine and moved so that I could lean my back against the tree.

Rather quickly, Patrick abandoned the drop-kick tutorial and resorted to trying to convince Jack to run into the stationary ball.

'Yes!' he yelled in triumph, punching the air, when Jack made contact with the ball, which moved sideways about ten centimetres. Having completely lost interest, Jack wandered past the ball and off towards some children playing a short distance away.

'Right, well that was a huge success,' Patrick said in disappointment. He seemed to have been envisaging an afternoon of end-to-end kicking with Jack.

I laughed. 'Sit down and drink your wine, we can keep an eye on him from here.'

Jack had stopped and was watching the children play an improvised form of hopscotch. He tilted his head, entranced by what they were doing. Copying them, he bent his knees and lurched forwards, his feet not leaving the ground.

I felt my heart contract. He was so little and had so much to learn.

Picking himself up, he spotted a dog in the centre of the park and headed off towards it at a determined trot. One of the mothers at the playgroup had talked knowledgeably about the 'comfort zone' around a parent, which a child would apparently never leave. If Jack did have a comfort zone, it was about the size of New Farm.

The dog was on a leash and so not an immediate threat, but I dragged myself to my feet and followed him.

As Jack neared the dog, it barked at him. He stopped in shock and whirled around. Unable to see anyone familiar, he burst into tears.

I broke into a run and reached him quickly.

'Jack. It's all right, it's all right.'

I knelt on the ground and put my arms around him.

He kept repeating something as I pulled him into my arms. He tucked his head under my neck and as I spoke soothingly to him I realised what he was saying. It was 'Julia'.

My throat tightened and I held him closer. 'It's all right, Jack, I'm here.'

I picked him up and carried him back to our rug. Disaster over, he scrambled out of my arms and headed off in the other direction. But I was left with an emotion I couldn't identify.

When I turned back to Patrick, he was watching me. 'You're starting to love him, aren't you?'

'Of course I love him, he's Anita's son.'

'That's not what I meant. You're starting to think about him like he's here for good, not just someone you're looking after for a while.'

Patrick's question made me realise that somewhere during

the last few weeks, Jack had turned from being a terrible burden who had transformed my life, into a terrible burden to whom I'd become rather attached.

The small amount of affection Jack had to give me to make me happy was ridiculous. After him saying my name, I felt like I'd do anything he asked. Which luckily was a pretty safe commitment, given his limited vocabulary.

'I guess you're right.' I looked over at Patrick, who was waiting for me to elaborate. 'To be honest, I actually find it very hard to remember what I did before he arrived.'

'Sleep?' Patrick suggested.

'Well yes, there is that. The problem, though, is that nothing's ever just about Jack and me. I always feel as though Anita's part of the equation, too. I hope that won't keep happening forever.'

Patrick looked up at the sky. 'Maybe that's not such a bad thing,' he said, turning back to me. 'Maybe it just won't always be sad when you think of her.'

'See, that's the problem. I don't just feel sad when I think of her. I also feel . . . I don't know.' I struggled to put my feelings into words. 'Guilty and panicky.'

Patrick looked at me and I knew I wasn't explaining myself very well.

'You know, I think I actually feel worse now about Anita being dead than when it first happened. I can almost accept the fact that I'll never see her again. But as I get more attached to Jack, her missing his life and him not having her in his, seems more and more tragic. Add onto that the worry that I'm not doing anything as well as she would have and I'd be an insomniac if I wasn't always so tired.'

'But you never saw Anita with Jack. She might have been an awful mother.'

'Do you really believe that?'

'Well, no . . . But she certainly wasn't a saint and I think you're doing an amazing job.'

'Thanks.' His words meant a lot. Jack wasn't exactly giving me a lot of constructive feedback. Now I'd started, I wanted to tell someone what I'd been feeling for weeks. 'You knew Anita, she was always so bloody happy.'

'Yeah, you're right,' he agreed. 'She's the only person I've ever met who could manage to be cheerful with a hangover.'

'Exactly. Take yesterday morning for example. Jack pushed his bowl of cereal and milk onto the floor. I didn't yell at him, but not far off it. The first thing that struck me when he looked up at me with his big eyes was that Anita wouldn't have been cross. I'm worried that I'm going to spend my life comparing myself to her and trying to do what she would have done.'

'Well, that's got to stop,' Patrick said, filling up my glass. 'Anita left Jack with you because she knew you'd love him and look after him. There's no point in spending the whole time trying to guess how she would have done everything.'

'Okay. Supposing I do that. But you know the first thing Jack's going to say to me when he's old enough to figure out how to hurt me?'

'You're not my mother?'

I nodded.

'You're probably right.'

'Well,' I asked, 'what on earth do I do then?'

Patrick looked at me. 'I have no idea. But I think you've just got to deal with now and let the future look after itself.'

'I guess so.' I sighed. Jack was still watching the children and I wondered if I could pay them to come and hang out in our backyard.

'Well, what about you?' I asked. 'Where to from here?'

'I have no idea. The whole reason for the lay-offs, even apart from Jennifer, was that the market is in a slump. I doubt that any of the other big firms are hiring. I know I should be, but I'm not actually that bothered about it. Something might come of this television thing with Tony. But in any event I'll get more time to go out in the boat.'

Patrick had a little aluminium runabout he took out on Moreton Bay whenever he had a chance. I wasn't entirely sure what he did on it, though I could count on one hand the number of fish he'd caught in the last year.

'How are you feeling about living with Jack? It wasn't exactly the deal when you moved in.' I'd been putting off this conversation, but I figured I had to address it sometime. 'Do you want to look for somewhere else to live?'

'What? Do you want to me to move out?'

'No. Of course not – especially after what you did this morning. But do you really want to live with us indefinitely? Having a toddler running around the living room is going to cramp your style no end. What happens next time you want to bring someone home?'

'I swear, if I even look at a woman before I turn forty, please hit me over the head. Trust me, I've had enough of the weaker sex for a long time. Besides, I'm working on the theory that once Jack starts paying the rent on his room, we'll be able to split it three ways and I'll be in clover. Do you think two is too young for a paper run?'

'Nah – he should have the walking thing sorted out by then.'

I'd taken my eyes off Jack for about ten seconds and when I looked up I saw him headfirst in someone else's picnic basket. While Jack didn't seem to move that quickly when I was watching him, he seemed to have a turbo charge that kicked in when I wasn't.

Pushing myself to my feet I jogged over to him.

'Sorry,' I apologised to the owners of the basket. I pulled a plastic plate out of Jack's mouth, wiped it on my shirt and put it back in the basket.

'Jeez,' Patrick said when we rejoined him. 'It's just as well Jack's cute. If I'd done that I'd have a black eye by now. Maybe I can train him as a pickpocket and do the rounds of the parks each day,' he said in sudden inspiration. 'Forget the paper round.'

'Great idea, except I reckon you'd end up with a bunch of chewed serviettes rather than hard currency.'

'Mmm . . . I'll keep it in mind for when things get really bad.'

Jack was having a second go at his piece of baguette, which was covered in saliva and dirt. That was good, I told myself. One of the women at playgroup had mentioned a study that had found children had to be exposed to germs to develop their immune systems. I had immediately vowed to stop worrying so much, but had the feeling Jack was overdoing things. Even I'd felt sick when I'd seen him lick some dried chewing gum on the footpath yesterday.

As we were packing up to head home, I heard the telltale tinkle of music and my blood ran cold. I could have counted on one hand the number of times I'd seen an ice-cream van in the last five years. But now one seemed to be lurking around every suburban corner.

Patrick noticed that I'd frozen on the spot. 'What's wrong?' he asked. He registered the music. 'Oh.'

Patrick had found my run-in with Grant, my ex-boyfriend, hilarious and had told everyone he could think of.

'You know, maybe you should just face up to your fear. Go talk to the man – apologise or whatever. Kind of like getting back on the horse. Being terrified of a guy who sells soft serve is kind of sad.'

I hated to admit it, but he had a point. Earlier in the week I'd been walking to the corner shop and had done a four-block detour to avoid the ice-cream van. I couldn't keep living like this.

I hesitated.

'Go on. I dare you to ask him out for a drink,' he added with a grin.

My heart sank. As kids, Patrick and I had devised an elaborate system of dares and challenges. Whether it was a competition to see who could hold their breath underwater the longest, or a dare to try to convince the old lady across the street we only spoke French, you could never back down once a challenge had been issued.

'C'mon Patrick, I'm nearly thirty-two. I don't do dares any more.'

'Okay,' Patrick shook his head sadly. 'I guess that makes me the lifetime winner then.'

'I'm not even sure he'll talk to me. And besides,' I added, trying to sound mature, 'for all I know, he's married with twins by now.'

Grant and I had been classic high-school sweethearts. For nearly four years we were the couple who held hands at lunchtime and walked home together after school. We had known each other since primary school and started going out in grade eight. By the time we hit senior, everyone assumed we were going to get married and live happily ever after.

That was until an American exchange student called Bob arrived at school. Bob's southern accent had set every female heart in school racing, and despite my coupled status, I was not immune. To add to his already considerable attractions, Bob was almost a full year older than we were. When our group of friends was invited to his eighteenth birthday party, Anita and I planned our outfits for a week. Grant, though, came down with the flu the day before and had to stay home.

Not only was this the coolest party we had ever been to, it was also one of the first ones with alcohol. By the time I had downed four bourbon and Cokes, I was feeling so light-headed that when Bob asked me to go for a walk I didn't hesitate. We'd barely made it to the front gate before he kissed me and, without thinking, I kissed him back. By the time Anita came out to check on me, we were rolling around on the front lawn. She marched up and dragged me home, calling my parents to tell them I was staying the night at her house.

The next morning, having been sick several times and with a crushing headache, I went round to Grant's place and confessed. The look of hurt on his face was the thing that had stayed with me over the years. We broke up and hardly spoke to each other for the rest of the year. To top it off, Bob was incredibly offended when I wouldn't sleep with him and badmouthed me to anyone who would listen.

All in all it was not one of my finest moments.

Up until that point I had been completely convinced I was in love with Grant and that we were going to spend our lives together. He was the first guy I slept with and I was sure he was going to be the last. We even knew that once our kids had grown up, we were going to move to a house in the country where Grant was going to write a bestseller.

And then, just like that, it was over. All this time later, I still occasionally wondered how different my life would have been if I hadn't been so stupid.

So if I'd had to choose the top ten people I'd have most hated to see standing in that ice-cream van, Grant would have been way up there.

'Yeah, and maybe he's as single as you. You won't know unless you ask – besides, he's a nice guy.'

While we were going out, Grant had treated Patrick a bit like a younger brother, taking him to football games and the occasional concert.

'So what's in it for me if I do?' This was also part of our system. The reward for a successful dare had to match the level of difficulty.

'I'll do three nights' babysitting if you come back with an ice-cream for each of us – and a date.'

Even if my reputation wasn't at stake, this was an opportunity I couldn't pass up. Three nights of free babysitting – surely that was worth a bit of humiliation.

Slowly I pulled my purse out of my bag and dragged my feet towards the van. I looked back over my shoulder to see Patrick waving me on encouragingly. Rounding the van, I joined the back of the queue. I saw with a lurch of my stomach that it was indeed Grant's van.

The queue shuffled forwards disappointingly quickly and it was my turn.

'Yes ma'am . . .' His voice trailed off as he recognised me.

In the fifteen or so years since we'd left school, Grant had changed from a gangly seventeen year old to a handsome, broad-shouldered man. His blue eyes had deepened a bit and he wore his brown hair fairly long and pushed back from his face.

'Look, Julia, I'm sorry but I'm in the middle of the park. I haven't come within two kilometres of your place lately, surely the music can't bother your kid here.'

'No, no. I – uh – actually came to apologise. I'm sorry I yelled at you. I've only just started looking after Jack and he didn't do much sleeping the first week. He'd just gone to sleep when your music woke him and – well, you know the rest.'

I could hear disgruntled noises in the queue behind me.

'That's okay.' He smiled. 'You're forgiven. So what's the deal?' he asked conversationally. 'Do you babysit him?'

I didn't think the people behind me would put up with an explanation of the events of the last couple of weeks. 'It's a long story.'

I could imagine the look of polite discomfort on his face when I asked him out and he had to tell me about his twins. I knew I couldn't do it. I waved vaguely and stepped to one side.

'Hang on,' I lunged back towards the counter with sudden urgency. 'I need three ice-creams.'

'No problem.' He filled the cones with soft serve and handed them over to me.

I took a deep breath. 'Ah, I don't suppose you'd be free to catch up after work sometime?'

He looked surprised and I braced myself for the rejection I knew I deserved. I vowed Patrick was going to pay for this. The family behind me had fallen silent. Obviously they didn't often see their ice-cream man picked up by a customer.

'Uh – yeah sure.'

'Sorry?' I started, having been fully expecting a negative response.

He looked at me in confusion and I quickly tried to recover.

'I mean, great.' Now that I had actually asked him, I suddenly couldn't think of anything worse. 'Great,' I repeated. 'Well then, I'll call you, shall I?'

He smiled. 'You could do that. Or we could meet tonight.'

I started to mumble something about being busy until I realised that I was going to have to deal with this sometime.

'Ah, yeah okay.'

'Right, well . . . I knock off at five. How about I meet you at Luxe at six?' he suggested, naming a local bar.

'That sounds good. Well . . . I'll see you then.'

He shook his head when I handed him a ten-dollar note. 'You can buy the drinks tonight – the ice-creams are on me.'

By the time I reached Patrick, a feeling of triumph had replaced the humiliation. I offered Patrick's cone to him with a smug smile.

'Ha! I have four words for you. Tonight . . . Luxe . . . six o'clock. Hope you didn't have any plans.'

He stared at me. 'You're lying! There's no way you asked him out!'

I ignored him. 'I need to call in my first babysitting credit. I've got a date.'

EIGHTEEN

'How could you have dared me to do such a thing, Patrick?' I demanded.

I didn't give him a chance to respond. 'Because of you, I now have a date in half an hour with someone I haven't seen since I had a corkscrew perm.'

The flush of success I'd felt at meeting the dare had disappeared before we'd even left the park. Rather than wild and exciting, I now felt certifiable.

'I haven't seen this guy in more than a decade. How did he end up selling ice-cream anyway? He could be some kind of weirdo by now.' I was warming to my theme. 'I bet he preys on helpless mothers who buy ice-creams for their kids. If you think about it, it's the perfect cover.'

Patrick didn't seem at all remorseful. 'It's not as if you're meeting him in a graveyard at midnight. And besides, you were the one who asked him out – not the other way around. Pretty tricky for a serial murderer to arrange that.'

I had to concede that point.

'You'll be in a public place. You'll be fine.'

After seriously considering standing Grant up, I decided I had no option but to go. To 'face the music', as Patrick had said with a grin, lacking any sympathy for my predicament.

I felt slightly guilty about Tony, but decided that was one

thing I didn't need to fret about. Although I hadn't asked for it, Patrick had given me what he called 'the view from the other side of the fence' and his measured opinion was that Tony wasn't keen.

'Contrary to what women think, the length of time between calls isn't important – it's what days they happen on that counts. If a guy doesn't call for three days, it might just mean he's been busy at work, but if he hasn't called over a weekend, you're history.'

Although I pretended to ignore my brother's brutal honesty, I thought he was probably right. If there had ever been anything going on between Tony and me, there certainly wasn't any more.

Besides, it wasn't as though I was going on a date with Grant. We were just catching up for old times' sake.

Reluctantly I left at ten to six, having fed and bathed Jack in record time. His bottle was ready to go and I was pretty confident that as long as Patrick remembered Harold, everything should be all right.

'Bye.' Patrick waved cheerily as I headed down the path.

I pulled up across the road from the bar at two minutes to six. Unless he was sitting inside, he wasn't there yet. Sighing, I stepped out of the car and locked it. How did I manage to get myself into these situations?

I'd give him fifteen minutes and then leave, I decided, taking a seat at one of the outside tables. As I did, Grant walked around the corner. Exactly on time.

'Uh, hi,' he said, looking down at me.

'Hi,' I managed in response. 'Ah, do you want to sit down?'

He sat and put his hands on the table edge. Self-consciously he moved them to his lap, then back to the table edge.

'Look,' I blurted, 'I don't know what came over me this afternoon. Contrary to what you probably think, I don't usually pick up men in parks . . .' My voice trailed off. 'So, what I'm saying is that if you'd rather give this a miss, that's okay with me.'

'What, and have nothing to tell the other ice-cream van guys tomorrow morning? No way!'

I laughed for a couple of seconds too long, having no idea what I'd say when I finished.

'So,' he said when I finally stopped. 'It's been a long time.'

'Yeah, about fifteen years.'

Grant nodded. 'Whenever I hear a Phil Collins song I think of you, so I guess that dates us pretty badly.'

I was still struggling with the concept that I featured in Grant's thoughts at all, let alone in relation to Phil Collins, when he spoke again.

'Do you look after kids for a living?'

'Sorry?' It took me a moment to follow his thoughts.

'Today in the park you said you had only just started looking after the little boy – is that what you do?'

'Oh no. I'm a lawyer.'

He smiled. 'That was all you wanted to do when we were in school. That's great.'

I was relieved he didn't crack a lawyer joke or tell me all lawyers were scum. It still surprised me how many people felt free to tell me their low opinion of all members of my chosen profession.

'Do you like it?'

I paused. 'Yes, I think I do. Usually, that is. There are a few things going on at the moment that are making it all pretty tricky.'

Silence descended.

I had a sudden burst of inspiration. 'Do you want a drink?' I waved the laminated wine list at him.

He fumbled as he took it from me and for some reason I felt better. At least I wasn't the only one feeling nervous.

'I think I'll just have a beer,' I said. 'What about you?'

'A beer sounds good.'

There were no waiters in sight. 'Why don't I go inside and order,' Grant suggested.

His chair shrieked against the tiled floor as he pushed it back. As he disappeared into the bar, I wondered if he'd return.

I'd decided that one elbow on the table looked the most natural pose when he came back with two frothing glasses. I'd also decided that I couldn't ignore what had happened between us.

'Look, I'm really sorry about what I did when we were in school. I've never forgotten how stupid I was.'

Grant slowly traced a line in the condensation on his glass. Finally he looked up. 'It's okay. It was a long time ago – we were probably taking the whole thing too seriously anyway.'

'Yeah, I guess so,' I said without much conviction.

'So how's Bob these days?' he asked with a smirk.

I laughed. 'Who knows? Probably back home charming some southern belles. Actually, he's probably been married and divorced five times by now.'

'And you're not?' he asked.

'What, married or divorced?'

He smiled. 'Either.'

'Nope. You?'

He shook his head.

It sounded unlikely that there were twins.

'I thought you went to teachers' college?' I asked.

Grant shook his head. 'I was a teacher but I quit after a couple of years. I loved it at the start, but after a while I got a bit disillusioned.'

'I don't blame you. One child is more than enough for me – I couldn't face a whole room full of them.'

'Actually it wasn't the kids, it was the system. Rules, different theories, power struggles . . . Teaching the kids felt like a bit of a distraction – not the reason we were all there. So one day I saw an ad in the paper. And here I am.'

'So how does the ice-cream van thing work? Is it like taxis and you drive them for someone else?'

'Well, sort of – except I'm the owner. I have three vans now and I don't drive much any more. The guy who usually works this run broke his leg a couple of weeks ago, so I'm driving until he's better.'

'Have you been doing it for long?'

He nodded. 'I bought my first van about five years ago.'

'And you like it?'

'Yeah. Although the whole idea of doing it was that I'd be outside all day – you know, be my own boss and all that.'

I nodded and he went on.

'It was great. If business was slow I could read my book. And it's hard to find a happier human being than a kid who has just been handed an ice-cream.'

'But?'

'But then a guy who had a run over the south side of town wanted to retire. It seemed like a good idea to buy his business, so I borrowed some money to do it. And then another run came up. Now I spend all day in my office. Ah, the price of success.' He smiled self-consciously. 'So what else have you been up to?' he asked as if he felt he'd been talking too much.

I realised that I had to tell Grant about Anita. They'd been friends at school as well and he was going to find out about it sooner or later.

'Well, things have been a bit mad lately.' I paused, wondering how to say it. 'You remember Anita?'

Grant's smile was immediate. 'Of course – how is Anita these days?'

Tears started sliding down my face and his smile instantly disappeared.

I had a sudden vision of having this same conversation with Grant a month ago and being able to cheerfully answer something like, 'Oh, she's great – would you believe she's living in Italy?' We could have complained about how jealous we were and then moved on to another topic. Instead, the reality hurt so much that I could hardly breathe. When I could speak again, I haltingly told Grant what had happened.

'Oh God. I can't believe it. I'm so sorry.'

'Yeah.' I couldn't think of anything else to say.

'How old is Jack?'

'Just over eighteen months.'

'And you don't have any of your own children?'

'No, so it's been a pretty big learning curve.'

A look of horror crossed his face. 'And I woke him up – what, two weeks ago? That must have been the first week after it happened.'

'Yuh.'

'I can see why you screamed at me.'

I was slightly taken aback. 'Screamed' seemed somewhat of an exaggeration of my strained statement of my feelings.

'What are you going to do?'

It was a great question and one for which I didn't have an answer.

'Um, more of the same, I guess – except I am going to have to make some changes. I'm discovering pretty quickly that my old weekend activities don't mix well with a toddler.'

'What did you used to do?'

'Oh, I don't know. Eat, drink, shop – sleep.'

He grimaced. 'Yeah, I see what you mean.'

As if he could sense that I didn't want to talk about it, Grant changed the subject and the conversation became easier.

'Can I get you another?' A waiter stopped beside our table, looking at our almost empty glasses.

We both hesitated, looking uncomfortably at each other.

'I'll come back,' he decided diplomatically.

As the waiter walked away, I realised that I was actually enjoying myself.

'Ah, would you like another drink?' I ventured.

Grant looked at his watch. 'Thanks, but I can't. My flatmate moved out last week and I've got two people lined up to come and see the house – I really should get going.'

'Sure,' I nodded, hiding my disappointment.

I called the hovering waiter back over and paid him.

'Well, I guess I'll see you around,' I said as we stood up to leave.

'Yeah, sure.'

Do not suggest meeting again, I instructed myself firmly. Do not. Do not. I was determined to preserve some shred of dignity.

'Well – hope you find a flatmate,' I said instead.

We smiled awkwardly at each other and I turned to leave.

'Uh, Julia?'

I looked around.

'Would you like to have dinner sometime?'

'Sure. That would be good.' I smiled.

'Really? Great!' He looked surprised but pleased.

'How about you come around to my place one night during the week,' I suggested, conscious of my limited babysitting credits.

'Are you sure? You don't mind cooking?'

I shook my head. 'Don't worry, I'll do something easy.'

'Okay then, how does Wednesday sound?'

'Wednesday's fine,' I replied. 'Do you remember where I live from the ice-cream incident?'

'How could I forget? I'll see you about seven?'

'Make it seven-thirty, that way Jack will definitely be asleep.'

'Right, well, I'll see you then.'

I stopped at the edge of the road, waiting for a break in the traffic.

'Julia?' Grant was standing next to the table, a smile on his face. 'Do you think you could get a perm between now and then for old times' sake?'

Laughing, I ran across the road. This could actually be fun.

NINETEEN

I stared at the doctor.

Of course it wasn't possible.

I'd been looking and feeling very ordinary since I'd started back at work, but had just put it down to lack of sleep. Yesterday, however, a stream of work colleagues had looked at me in concern and asked if I was feeling all right. Finally I'd given in and booked an appointment with a doctor on the off-chance that he could prescribe some miraculous multivitamin that would substitute for eight hours' sleep a night.

In between trying to stop Jack from destroying the doctor's surgery, I'd managed to recite the whole story to him without breaking into tears. That had to be considered progress, I thought in an attempt to be positive.

Instead of prescribing a drug to fix all my problems, the doctor had asked if I could be pregnant.

Although it seemed a lifetime ago, it was only about six weeks since I'd slept with Michael. And I couldn't for the life of me remember whether I'd had a period since then.

My feeling of blind terror must have showed, as the doctor continued hastily, 'Look, it's highly likely that the way you're feeling is simply a result of the stress you've been under. I'd just like to do a test to rule out the possibility.'

He handed me a small plastic jar from his bottom drawer.

'When you're finished, take it to the front desk and we'll do a test.'

I pushed Jack's stroller down the corridor to the toilets, refusing to even consider the consequences of my being pregnant.

Jack and his stroller wouldn't fit into a cubicle, so I needed another plan. Deciding that as a first step the greater the distance I could put between my fellow toilet-goers and myself the better, I pushed him towards the toilet furthest from the door. If I was quick, I could leave him propped outside where I could at least see the bottom of the stroller.

Good plan, but as soon as I closed the door Jack let out a piercing wail. Peeing into a jar is not an easy activity under the best of circumstances and I knew there was no way I'd manage it with the racket he was making.

Opening the door, I lifted him out of the stroller, ignoring the interested glances of the two women standing at the sink.

'Right, Jack. Stay right there just for five seconds,' I commanded. I propped him on his feet in the corner of the cubicle.

Unscrewing the jar, I looked at the opening in consternation. Doctors certainly didn't try to make things easy.

Jack plopped down on the floor and dived for a small object lying in the corner. Hygiene was not my strong point, but scavenging on a public toilet floor didn't seem ideal. Pulling him up again I put him next to the roll of toilet paper. The amount these doctors charged for a consultation, I figured they could bear the cost of a toilet roll.

Jack's eyes lit up.

Taking advantage of the distraction, I sat down and focused on the job at hand. Intent on what I was doing, I didn't notice that Jack had turned back to me until a small hand grabbed for the full jar.

'Nooo, Jack!'

I jumped, only just keeping a hold on the jar.

I fended Jack off with one hand, holding the jar above my head with the other. I ran through the possibilities in my mind. If I stood up, Jack would be straight into the toilet bowl. If I put the jar on the floor while I picked Jack up, it would almost certainly get tipped over. Judging the distance, I let go of Jack and lunged for the hook on the back of the door where I'd hung my handbag. Dumping it on the floor, I landed back heavily on the toilet seat, beating Jack's hand by no more than a microsecond. The contents of the jar swirled dangerously close to the top, but miraculously didn't spill.

The bag was open and Jack dived for its contents, which were normally off limits.

I found the cap on the back of the toilet seat, screwed it on quickly, reassembled my clothing and stood up. Hefting Jack onto my hip, I ignored the fact that he was wrenching the arms of my sunglasses in different directions. I threw my bag over the other shoulder and burst out of the cubicle.

The room was miraculously empty, although the possibility that it had emptied because of the sounds the madwoman in the last cubicle was making crossed my mind. I stood Jack up and tried to figure out which parts of our respective bodies I needed to clean. Settling on a wash of my hands and a wipe of his, I leaned my hands on the sink and took a deep breath.

Would it ever get any easier? Surely women with children didn't spend their entire lives lurching from one humiliating experience to another?

I looked into the mirror and noticed that my eyes were bright red and had great black rings under them. As I watched, they filled with tears. This wasn't the way things were supposed to be.

I glimpsed a movement in the mirror behind my reflection. Spinning around I saw a cubicle door close. Jack was nowhere to be seen. As I lunged for the door I heard a click. No – it wasn't possible.

The door refused to budge, locked from the inside. Jack, with his love of all things bright and shiny, had obviously been fiddling with the lock and somehow managed to twist it.

'Jack? Are you all right?' I asked.

His answer was a wail as he decided that being alone in a small space was not a desirable situation.

Surely he couldn't drown in the toilet bowl. I tried to remain calm.

There was no room to climb over the door, even if I could somehow vault up there off an adjoining toilet. There was, however, a gap at the bottom of the door. I looked at the rather grubby floor, calculating how long it would take me to run down the corridor to the doctor's surgery to get some assistance. Too long, I decided, lowering myself onto the tiles. With an effort I was just able to squeeze through the gap and slither along the floor. Jack's cries stopped abruptly as my head appeared at his feet. By curling around the toilet bowl I managed to get my whole body into the cubicle and struggle to my feet. Tearing off a strip of toilet paper, I wiped the side of my face, which was worryingly wet.

Jack looked up at me with a delighted smile on his face.

'Fantastic. You think this is fun,' I grumbled. 'All I need is for you to turn into a serial toilet-door locker.'

His amusement was infectious, though, and I couldn't suppress a smile as I looked down at my T-shirt and skirt, which hadn't looked too good before but now looked as though I'd slept in them for a week.

I remembered the reason for my visit and my smile disappeared. 'All right you. Let's go.'

The doctor was mercifully swift and I was called into his office less than five minutes after I'd handed over my embarrassingly warm bottle.

'Well you're not pregnant,' he announced.

The roaring in my ears drowned out his next words. Only now that I knew it wasn't going to happen did I allow myself to visualise what it would be like trying to deal with Jack, a baby, no husband and, the way things were going, no job.

'So you really need to take better care of yourself,' the doctor was saying sternly as I tuned back in. 'You need to get some more sleep . . .' He paused as he saw my face. 'All right, that won't be easy, I know. But if you're going to be up early, try to get to bed early. Go to sleep as soon as Jack does. You need to remember that you're no use at all to him if you get sick.'

I nodded earnestly, while mentally prioritising the jobs I had to have done before nine the next morning.

His next words made their way through my thoughts. 'Do you have anyone who can help you? Your parents perhaps?'

I still wondered on a daily basis if I was being an idiot not telling Mum and Dad what was going on. If I'd known how hard it was going to be, I would have been text-messaging them before Jack's plane had even left Rome.

We'd got this far though. While I wasn't in great shape, Jack was no longer the sad and lonely little boy who had arrived.

But he was still unsettled by the way his life had been turned upside down and I worried that introducing Mum and Dad now might upset the very tentative balance Carla, Patrick, Jack and I had found. I didn't want to risk that, but it was very tempting to ask them for help. All I wanted was to go to sleep and let Mum sort everything out for me.

In deference to the doctor I stopped on the way home and bought some broccoli. Somehow I had always felt that regardless of the rest of the meal, my nutritional wellbeing was assured if there was broccoli on my plate.

Jack didn't seem to agree and was in the process of tearing his to pieces and stuffing it down his shirt when Patrick trudged down the hall and onto the deck.

'Not a good day?' I asked, glancing at him.

'No.' Patrick's hair was more dishevelled than usual and he looked truly miserable. 'I have managed to lose my second job in less than a week. That must be some kind of a record.'

'What do you mean? I thought you were just pitching an idea.'

Patrick sat down heavily at the table. 'I know, but I might as well be realistic. Tony and I met with the guy who owns the station this afternoon. He said to forget the whole kids' cooking show idea unless we could come up with some kind of angle to make it different. He's given us another chance to pitch an idea tomorrow, otherwise he's putting the old program back on.'

'I thought your idea sounded great,' I protested loyally, resisting the urge to ask if Tony had mentioned me.

'You have no idea what a jerk this guy is. I don't know how

Tony can work for him.' He was silent for a moment and then added, 'And he has the worst comb-over I have ever seen.'

I laughed. 'I thought that my day was bad, but I still have my job. At least I hope I have.' I suddenly remembered that I'd been ignoring my mobile all afternoon. I pushed the thought out of my mind.

'All right, let's think about this. What was comb-over man's objection to your concept?'

'He said it was unoriginal, boring and not even slightly entertaining.'

'Okay . . . Well at least he didn't beat about the bush. Let's think about this – there must be something we can come up with.'

'Julia, you are a lawyer, I am an accountant – ex-accountant. Can you think of a less creative combination? There's no way you and I will be able to think of something vaguely interesting.'

'That's a bit unfair,' I said, offended.

'Tell me the last slightly creative thing you did,' Patrick demanded.

'That's easy. I, uh, I pulled together a pretty gripping state-ment from an art expert in Florence the other day.'

Patrick looked at me and raised his eyebrows until I was forced to concede. 'Yeah, all right, but I'm not paid to be cre-ative. That doesn't mean that a vibrant, dynamic mind doesn't exist under this conservative lawyerly exterior.'

I wasn't sure that I believed what I was saying. I had a nasty sus-picion that any vaguely artistic tendencies I'd ever had had been smothered under years of trawling through dry legal documents.

'Anyway, you don't exactly have any wildly exciting artistic types with goatees and berets banging down your door to help you right now, do you?' I asked.

'I guess not,' Patrick shrugged.

I removed the remaining pieces of broccoli from Jack's plate in resignation.

'Well, the way I see it, you need a theme – something that ties all the shows together and makes them a bit different.'

'Hmm . . .' Patrick said. 'Except that themes are tacky. That's something comb-over man and I would probably agree on.'

I shook my head. 'Well, apparently they're not. I read an article last week about Sydney's top party planners and they all seemed to agree that themes are the way to go.'

'What?' Patrick said. 'Are you trying to tell me that cool people with stacks of money have "Dress as One of your Parents" parties?'

'Well, no. They were talking more about themes like "Medieval Madness" and – oh I can't remember, but they had a two-metre high slippery slide made of ice. Can you believe you can actually hire baby crocodiles in Sydney to use as table centrepieces?' We were definitely getting off track here. 'My point is that if you can come up with a general idea, it will hold everything together.'

'What about *Charlie's Angels*? I could have three gorgeous women cooking for me. I could direct them from a speaker phone – no one would even have to see me.'

Before I could say anything he continued. 'No, wait! I've got it. I could have a car that can talk – like in *Knight Rider*. Remember David Hasselhoff?'

'Patrick, those are fantasies, not themes. Anyway, I thought you were too young for *Knight Rider*?'

'No way. I used to arrange my lectures around the daytime repeats while I was at uni. Great show.'

'So did you talk about budgets in your meeting? Did you get the feeling they would spring for a computerised car?'

'Good point. I think the technical term for the budget they have in mind is "bugger all". Look, forget it. I don't know what I was thinking anyway. I just need to sort my resume out and find a real job.'

He brightened. 'You'll never guess what I found in a corner store near the studio.'

He ferreted around in his shoulder bag and pulled out a plastic bag. Withdrawing the contents, he brandished a small bottle at me in triumph.

'Magenta, I found magenta!'

'Are you serious?' I asked incredulously.

In the last week my collection of food colouring had grown

from two ancient bottles to an array of over ten, which were lined up proudly on the bathroom sink. In a serious comment on both Patrick's life and my own, we had become embroiled in a competition to find new and different colours. I had thought that a bottle green I'd picked up last week had been the pinnacle, but magenta left it for dead.

'You know, it's a shame the show isn't for kids Jack's age,' I said. 'All you'd have to do would be to add food colouring to just about anything and they'd think it was wonderful. That'd fit your budget too.'

Patrick pursed his lips. 'Maybe that's not so dumb. What about a colour theme? Each week we could pick a colour and make food that colour. Like pink – we could cook sausages and make strawberry daiquiris. Nonalcoholic of course,' he added when he saw my expression.

'That might not be such a bad idea,' I said thoughtfully. 'You could do a yellow day with scrambled eggs and . . . lemon tart,' I suggested.

'Julia, it's for kids. What kid wants eggs and lemon tart? No, I'm thinking Twistie sandwiches.'

'Twistie sandwiches? Are you serious?'

'No, I guess not – it wouldn't really amount to cooking, would it? They're good though,' he added. 'Banana split – that'd be perfect. And, I don't know, yellow fried rice or something.'

I could see he was getting excited. 'Our logo could be a picture of fairy bread with hundreds and thousands. Kind of a dedication to Jack.'

'Hang on,' I interrupted. 'What happens when you run out of colours?'

'At this stage I can't even think past the pilot show,' he replied with a wave of his hand. 'I'll worry about that problem when I come to it.'

He sprang up from the table and headed for his bedroom. 'I've got to try to get my ideas into some kind of script.'

His head reappeared around the living room door briefly. 'Thanks Julia. I take it back. You're a genius.'

TWENTY

It was five-thirty. Grant was arriving for dinner in two hours and I was still in the city, foodless and with no idea what I was going to cook.

As I hurried towards the bus stop, I remembered that I hadn't called Maggie. Marcus was still in town and had arranged to meet her for a coffee that afternoon. This was definitely not part of their normal routine.

'What's it all about?' Maggie had asked when she'd called me earlier in the day. 'I mean, we do drinks, we do bands, we do sex. But we certainly don't do coffee. It's just not part of the deal.'

My mobile battery was predictably flat. I looked at my watch. I didn't have time to stop. Spotting a phone box, I swerved towards it.

'Hi Maggie, it's me. So, what happened?'

'Marcus is moving back to Brisbane,' she said flatly.

'But that's great news, isn't it?' I asked, confused.

'He wants to try again. Figures we should find out once and for all if we should be together. So he's going to base himself here for a while.'

'So why aren't you jumping up and down in excitement?'

'I don't know. I pretended to be pleased when he told me, but I feel like running away. What if it doesn't work?'

'Well at least you'll be able to finally move on and find someone else.'

'Yeah, I guess so. But then I'd have nothing.'

I began to understand. At the moment, as deeply unsatisfactory as the relationship was, Maggie knew that Marcus wanted to be with her. In the scary singles market that was a comfortable fallback position.

'I still think you've got to give it a try. And think how amazing it would be if it did work out.'

'Yeah, I know.'

I could tell she hadn't really heard a word I'd said.

'Look, I'll be fine. I just need to get my head around it all. I'll talk to you tomorrow. Okay?'

I hung up the phone slowly. Unable to bring myself to rush, I walked down the street, miraculously arriving at the bus stop at the same time as the Paddington bus.

A burst of laughter hit me as I opened the shop door. Carla poked her head around the door to the house.

'Hi Julia. Come on in.'

Three of Carla's regulars, whose names I couldn't extract from the constant stream of chatter, were seated in the lounge room. Jack was in the middle of the room, clearly loving the fact that every person's attention was focused on him as he trundled a toy truck along the floor. Smiling, he pushed the truck towards me and noisily ran it over my foot. I let out a squeal and pretended to limp. As he giggled, I couldn't suppress a buoyant feeling – he seemed as pleased to see me as I was to see him.

Carla looked at her watch. 'I'll get Jack's things together. I know you need to get going if you're going to have time for a shower and to put some make-up on.'

I looked at her blankly.

'Tonight's the date with your ex-boyfriend, isn't it?'

I nodded in surprise.

'Patrick told me,' she explained. 'He's such a nice boy.'

Patrick had collected Jack on Monday evening. He must have told Carla about my date then. A thought struck me –

surely he hadn't told her about my yelling at Grant or, God for-
bid, what I'd done to him at high school?

I looked at Carla, but if she did know, she didn't seem
perturbed.

'Come into the kitchen for a minute,' she said. 'Jack will be
fine here.'

On the stove was a large pot, which seemed to be responsible for the amazing smell that filled the place.

'I hope you don't think I'm interfering, but I didn't think
you'd have time to cook anything. So I made a pot of my meatballs this afternoon. You don't have to use it tonight if you don't
want to,' she went on hurriedly. 'Just stick it in the freezer for
some other time.'

I stared at her, trying to take it in. 'You cooked me dinner?'

Carla nodded and then hurried on, 'But it's only meatballs
– I picked the recipe up when I was in Italy. It's supposed to
take five hours to cook, but I cheat a bit. Just give it to Jack if
you don't want it.'

I shook my head. 'From the wonderful smell, it's about ten
times better than anything I could have made even if I had the
time. I thought I'd have to go to the shops on the way home –
I didn't even know what I was going to cook.'

I took the lid off and looked at the tiny meatballs in the rich
tomato sauce, breathing in the aroma.

'Just pick up some bread on your way home and make a
green salad.'

I hugged her gratefully.

'Thank you for everything. I truly don't know what I
would do if I didn't have you to look after Jack – and me,' I
added. I was starting to think that if Mary Poppins did turn up,
I'd tell her the position was filled.

Carla waved her hand. 'It's nothing. I love having him
around. Now off you go.'

After putting the pot into a styrofoam box and extracting
Jack from the admiring circle, she ushered us out the door.

Every time I collected Jack from Carla's I expected him to
object to coming home with me. Her shop was so warm and

full of life and I always felt vaguely like a fraud coming in to pick him up – as though I was an actor playing the part of someone's mum. But he seemed happy to see me and, with him blowing her kisses, we left the shop and headed out to the car.

Without any shopping or cooking to do, I suddenly didn't have anything to stress about. Jack would be in bed within an hour and then I'd have plenty of time to get dressed before Grant arrived. Hell, I thought extravagantly, I might even have time to shave my legs.

When we got home I poured myself a glass of wine and opened the concertina doors leading to the deck. A loosely wrapped package was sitting on the table. Surprised, I picked it up.

Just then, Jack managed to pull the fridge door open, knocking himself over in the process.

Carla had told me that except for marinated olives, for which he had a passion, Jack had refused all offers of food that day. Putting the package down, I ladled some of Carla's meatballs into a small bowl and heated it in the microwave.

I hauled Jack into his highchair and placed the bowl in front of him, not holding out much hope he'd eat anything so wholesome. Past experience had taught me not to even attempt to feed him, so, prattling about my day, I turned back to the counter and opened the package.

Inside was a videotape without a label and a folded piece of paper, obviously ripped out of a notebook.

I opened it.

Dear Julia,
According to the closest thing I have to an expert on such matters (my sister), time to yourself is your greatest need right now. On her advice, I set my video (a technical feat designed to impress you) to tape every episode of Playschool *this week. By my calculations that is three hours' worth of coffee-drinking time.*
Hope it helps!
Tony

I didn't know whether to be touched or annoyed. What was this supposed to mean? If Tony was trying to keep me guessing, he was doing a good job. He hadn't called since Friday night, but here he was doing something lovely and making comments about wanting to impress me.

I put the package down on the table and then picked it up again. Having to explain to Grant where it had come from wasn't the way I needed this evening to start. I felt a stab of irritation that Tony had managed to make me feel guilty.

Immediately I felt bad. Tony probably hadn't even given any thought to what was going on, because nothing was. We'd had a horrific breakfast, been to an appalling movie and he'd dropped around for a drink. Not exactly enough to constitute a committed relationship. If I had some form of life, I wouldn't be analysing every development like this.

Taping *Playschool* was a pretty thoughtful thing to do and I was being ridiculous expecting anything more. No one in their right mind would contemplate a relationship with me right now.

Programming my video machine was something I'd been swearing I'd do ever since I moved in. Until I did, I could only tape a program if I was watching it – somewhat defeating the purpose. I couldn't help but be impressed that Tony had used the timer on his video, and I found myself daydreaming about how nice it would be to have a guy around the house.

I was on about page two of my mental handyman list when I turned back to see Jack had emptied the bowl and was licking it clean.

Trying not to give a loud whoop of excitement, I heated some more meatballs and handed him another bowlful, which he devoured just as quickly.

After that, the evening should have been a piece of cake. Jack should have been in bed by seven and I should have had a leisurely half-hour getting ready. Except that Jack screamed blue murder when I put him down, and didn't stop. At seven twenty-five I was still pacing the hall, having had a tense shower and thrown on a bright paisley skirt and a loose black off-the-shoulder top. He was usually happy to go to bed. Why did he have to pick tonight to protest?

What was worse? A screaming child who was out of sight, or a wide-awake child toddling around the lounge room? And more importantly, would I ruin his sleep patterns forever if I let him get up?

Patrick's key turned in the lock and he came face to face with me in the hallway. He'd been due to meet with Tony and John at five to see if they liked his new theme idea.

'So?' I asked, holding my breath.

The smile on his face gave me the answer before he spoke.

'He went for it! I've got the go-ahead for three shows. If viewer response is good, we'll do some more.'

'That's fabulous! Congratulations.'

He walked down the hallway still talking. 'He liked the yellow foods best – so it's yellow fried rice and banana split for the first show.' He stopped. 'You do have some cookbooks, don't you?'

'Yes . . .' I wasn't sure that fried rice and banana splits actually had recipes, but decided to keep that to myself.

Patrick stopped, Jack's screaming finally making its way through his euphoric haze.

'My God, where does the child get the energy to scream like that? I couldn't do it for more than five seconds.'

'I have absolutely no idea, but he has been doing it since seven o'clock and Grant is going to be here any moment.'

'Oh. He'll stop soon,' he said without much conviction. 'I think he's winding down. Look, I just dropped in to tell you my news. I'm meeting a few guys at Maggie's pub to celebrate my new career.'

'Wouldn't fancy taking Jack, would you?'

Patrick looked at me, not sure whether I was joking or not. I wasn't sure either.

'Ah, I remember seeing a sign saying no children are allowed in the bar,' he improvised. 'Otherwise I'd love to – really.'

'Liar.' I managed a momentary smile. 'So what do you think I should do?'

'Well, you can't let the little guy cry. Maybe he's not tired.'

I had to concede he certainly hadn't looked tired when I'd put him into bed, but I had been in desperate need of a shower.

Instantly I felt guilty. Wanting to impress an old boyfriend wasn't exactly a great reason for just throwing Jack into bed. Full of remorse, I flung his door open.

He stopped mid wail, mouth open, and stared at me. I gently picked him out of his cot.

'I'll do you a deal. You can stay up until you are tired but the first time you yawn, you are back into bed. Sound okay?'

He looked at me solemnly as if he was weighing it up and I took that as an affirmative answer.

Patrick smiled at Jack as we emerged from his room. 'Hey, little buddy.'

All trace of misery gone, Jack wriggled to be set down. I hadn't managed to clear away any toys in days and he grabbed his Bob the Builder ball and rolled it in Patrick's direction.

Patrick rolled it back and I took advantage of the momentary diversion to slip into the bathroom and put on some make-up.

Staring into the mirror, I wondered how I looked to Grant. How different was I from the girl he'd gone out with in school?

I was surprised at how excited I was by the prospect of seeing him. Maybe running into him was a sign that we should try it again. Perhaps it wasn't too late to make it work.

I heard Patrick calling me and I quickly turned off the light and headed back to the living room.

Patrick was trying to extricate himself from underneath a very un-tired looking Jack, who was doing monster impersonations.

'Help . . .' Patrick called weakly. 'I can't . . .' Much to Jack's delight Patrick died a very dramatic death complete with a death rattle and seizures. Jack looked up at me, pleased by his handiwork.

I pulled Jack off and Patrick opened one eye.

'You know,' I said, 'I really think that routine would be a hit at the pub.'

'Uh-uh. I'm out of here.' He stood up, dropped a kiss on Jack's forehead and headed out the door.

Five minutes later, the doorbell rang.

'Hello there.' Having opened the door with Jack on my hip,

I decided to pretend this was how I usually conducted romantic dinners. 'Come on in.'

'And you must be Jack,' Grant said. Suddenly shy, Jack burrowed his head into my shoulder. I turned and headed into the living room.

'Whatever's for dinner smells fantastic,' Grant enthused as he entered the living room.

'Italian meatballs,' I announced proudly.

He looked at me. 'Wow, your cooking skills have improved since high school. I remember a string of disasters coming out of your cooking classes and have a clear memory of having to chew through the heaviest scones I've ever tasted.'

'You said you liked them!' I said in mock affront.

He grinned. 'I lied.'

'Don't be fooled. Some things might have changed, but my cooking hasn't improved at all. Dinner was going to be something very basic until I discovered the lady who looks after Jack had made this for us.'

'Well I'm glad I brought red wine.' Grant handed a bottle to me. 'This place is great.' He looked around.

'Thanks. I bought it about a year ago. Patrick lives downstairs.'

'Really? You get on all right?'

'Yeah, it actually works pretty well. Once I came to terms with the fact that I was living with someone who had no idea who Maxwell Smart was, everything was fine.'

Grant looked as shocked as I had been. *Get Smart* had been our staple Sunday-afternoon entertainment the whole time we'd been together.

Jack wriggled to be let down and I put him on the floor.

'I'm sorry about his being awake,' I apologised. 'He should have gone to sleep half an hour ago, but for some inexplicable reason didn't. Maybe he got wind that the ice-cream guy was coming.'

He smiled, but I couldn't help feeling that for Grant, having a child around at dinner would be like me having one of my clients hovering. The thought didn't make me feel any better.

'Would you like some wine?' I asked.

'Thanks.'

Grant leaned against the kitchen bench as I opened the bottle.

I could see Jack heading towards me, but tried to ignore him. The bottle was open and I was filling two glasses when I saw him trip over a toy and fall. Instinctively he threw out an arm and grabbed onto the nearest object, which happened to be my elastic-topped skirt. It slid over my hips and landed in a pile around my ankles.

Frozen, I looked down at a prone Jack, and then at the puddle of material on my shoes, my bare legs and the off-white cotton underpants I'd been vowing to throw out for at least a year.

Placing the bottle slowly on the bench, I bent down and pulled up my skirt with the small amount of dignity I could muster. Jack seemed to realise he had done something very bad as he was uncharacteristically silent.

Taking a deep breath, I looked over at Grant. He had discovered a damp patch on the wall and was looking at it as though he'd never seen anything so fascinating.

Suddenly I had a picture of how I must have looked and snorted with laughter. After a moment Grant joined in and we both relaxed a little.

I picked Jack up and kissed him on the cheek. 'How do you keep coming up with these stunts?' I whispered.

Jack yawned and rubbed his eyes. I was terrified of a repeat of his earlier screaming, but more terrified of having Jack wreaking his special brand of havoc all evening.

'Right. You're off to bed,' I decreed. 'Won't be a moment,' I flung over my shoulder at Grant.

Entering Jack's room, I went to put him into the cot. Until I realised that it was Haroldless.

Stunned at my idiocy, I picked the disgusting creature up from the other side of the room and put both him and Jack into bed. Jack turned on his stomach, drew his knees up under his chest and closed his eyes. Still shaking my head, I returned to the living room.

'Okay,' I exhaled as I lowered myself onto the sofa.

'You look as though you've been doing this kid thing forever,' Grant commented.

'Trust me, if that skirt thing had happened before, I'd never wear anything without a very tight waistband.'

He laughed. 'Yeah well, apart from that.'

'I don't know. Sometimes I think I'm getting the hang of it and then something comes along and I realise all over again how incompetent I am.'

I took a sip of my wine. 'Take yesterday for example, when I was working from home . . .' I made a face. 'Well, actually, I was doing no work from home . . . I had a letter I really had to get done and Jack wasn't cooperating. He was walking around with a plastic cup half full of water. He started drinking some of it and I encouraged him because it was keeping him happy. I didn't really think too much about it. Until I followed him into the bathroom and saw him dipping the cup in the toilet.'

'Oh,' Grant screwed up his face.

'Yeah, exactly. He hasn't shown any ill effects, though, so I'm hoping I'll be able to avoid confessing to the doctor how a Brisbane child contracted cholera.

'Anyway.' I changed the subject. 'Did you find a flatmate?'

'Nope, not yet. One guy didn't show up and the other one asked me how I felt about nudity.'

'Really? What, just around the flat or everywhere?'

'Don't know, couldn't quite bring myself to ask.'

'What did you tell him?'

'I said I hadn't given it a lot of thought. But I'm thinking if he asked about that before he even asked how much the rent was . . .'

'Mmm – sounds a bit of a worry.' I stood up. 'Well, I'm hungry, let's eat out on the deck.'

Dinner was sensational and the conversation flowed easily. The warm Italian food and the candlelight created an easy intimacy and by the time we'd finished eating I felt it couldn't possibly have been fifteen years since we knew each other, or that our relationship had ended so badly.

Pouring both of us another glass of wine, Grant pointed to the guitar which sat in the corner inside the doors. 'Is that yours?' he asked.

'No – Patrick's. He's determined to teach himself how to

play. I'm not sure what's worse, Jack's crying or Patrick's rendition of "Jingle Bells".'

'Do you think he'd mind if I played it?'

'Not at all. I didn't know you could.'

'I learned when I was at college,' Grant answered, tuning the guitar. 'Do you like Bruce Springsteen?'

'He's great.'

Grant strummed a few bars and then launched into 'Fire', an old Springsteen love song. He had a lovely low voice and, combined with the lyrics, the result was mesmerising. He simply shouldn't be allowed to do that around defenceless women, I decided.

As I watched him sing, I was struck by a strange realisation. I had once known just about everything there was to know about this guy. We'd told each other everything – all our dreams and plans. I knew his parents had fought bitterly when he was young and that he'd been secretly relieved when they got divorced. I knew his first dog had been called Skywalker – a tribute to his favourite movie. But now, fifteen years had passed and, while he looked the same, if a bit taller and broader, I hardly knew him at all.

He finished and we were both quiet for a few seconds.

'That was lovely,' I finally managed when I trusted myself to speak.

'Thanks. Playing the guitar is one of my favourite things. I used to keep mine in the back of my first van for when business was quiet. Now it sits in my office and gets played maybe twice a year.'

'Maybe you can ditch the canned music you play in the van and play Springsteen instead,' I suggested hopefully.

'Sorry,' he shook his head. 'It has to be "Greensleeves" – just wouldn't be the same otherwise.'

We moved into the living room for coffee and he asked if there was anything I wanted him to play.

'Um,' I tried frantically to think of something cool to suggest, but my mind was absolutely blank. I decided to dodge the question. 'Do you really know enough songs to take requests?'

Grant laughed. 'Don't underestimate me – I've learned a thing or two since we last met.'

I had the distinct feeling he wasn't just talking about music.

'What about Phil Collins?' I asked, remembering his comment.

Suddenly I realised that every single Phil Collins song I could think of was a love song. I was going to have to sit here, whilst Grant played 'One More Night' to me. Ritual humiliation seemed to have become a part of my life, even with Jack sound asleep.

Grant smiled slowly. 'Sure, how about "Billy Don't You Lose My Number"?'

I nodded with relief – I couldn't remember many of the lyrics but at least it was upbeat.

Just as Grant started to play, I heard Patrick let himself in downstairs and then his footsteps on the internal stairs. My heart sank. There were some definite downsides to not living alone.

Grant stopped playing and looked up as Patrick reached the top of the stairs. My brother stood there, swaying slightly, obviously having done a fair amount of celebrating.

'Hi,' he said, clearly concentrating on not slurring his words. 'Long time no see.'

I figured Patrick would realise he was interrupting a private moment and disappear, but the alcohol had clearly blunted his social radar and it quickly became obvious that wasn't going to happen.

'Good to see you again.' Grant stood up and shook Patrick's hand and to my dismay Patrick dropped into an armchair.

There was a brief silence and then Grant turned to Patrick. 'Hope you don't mind my borrowing your guitar?'

'Not at all. It's good to see it being used.'

'Have you been playing for long?' Grant asked.

Patrick shook his head. 'A mate of mine taught himself to play "Let It Be" and "Sounds Of Silence". He trots them out on every first date – reckons you only need to know two songs and it impresses women every time.'

Patrick hadn't mentioned this before and I shot Grant a look, wondering if I'd just fallen for the same technique. As if he guessed my thoughts, he looked back at me and shook his head.

'I know three songs,' he mouthed at me silently.

I laughed.

'Don't laugh. He swears it works,' said Patrick, having missed the exchange.

Oblivious to my glares and attempts at telepathy, Patrick stayed where he was.

After half an hour, Grant stretched and stood up.

'Well, I should get going. Thanks for a lovely evening, Julia. It was good to see you again, Patrick.'

I walked him to the door.

'I really enjoyed tonight. Thanks,' Grant said.

'Me too.'

'Well, I'll see you later.'

Where, I wondered?

'Ah, maybe you could give me your number?' he said.

How was it that this whole dating thing didn't get any easier just because we were older?

'Okay – just give me a second.' I darted into my bedroom and grabbed a card out of my wallet. 'The mobile is generally the best way to find me,' I said as I handed it over.

'Great, well . . . goodbye.'

'Bye.'

There was a moment's silence and I wondered if he was going to kiss me.

'Grant?' Patrick's voice came from behind me. 'You know, it would be great to get together and play a few tunes. I'll buy the pizza and the beers if you teach me your repertoire. Actually, just the ones the chicks like would be fine.'

He winked slyly at Grant. I had the distinct impression Patrick had regressed to the ten year old he'd been when he'd known Grant.

'Thanks. Let's do that,' Grant replied, casting an amused glance in my direction. He paused awkwardly. 'Well. I'll see you both later.'

I watched him disappear into the darkness before I headed back inside to chop my younger brother into small pieces.

TWENTY-ONE

The doorbell rang and I looked at my watch. Seven-thirty at night was a strange time for someone to drop in.

Patrick was sitting at the table on the deck, attempting to write a script for the first cooking show he was supposed to be taping the next day. Oblivious to the fact that he was trying to concentrate, Maggie was talking him through her latest cocktail as she created it. She maintained that she was fine about Marcus's move, but she didn't want to talk about it. I just hoped she'd get used to the idea.

I'd been sitting in the study, trying to determine how much work I absolutely had to have finished by the morning.

I opened the door to see Tony standing there.

He smiled apologetically. 'I always seem to be dropping in on you unannounced.'

'Oh no, not at all,' I lied, wondering if he had some kind of phone phobia.

'Have I caught you at a bad time?'

'Um . . . no . . . I . . . Do you want to come in?'

'I'm not interrupting anything?'

I shook my head and stood back to let him in. 'Maggie's creating new cocktails and Patrick's reluctantly road-testing them. I'm sure they'd be delighted to have another guinea pig.'

If I was to ignore the pile of files by my laptop, he'd actually arrived at a comparatively good moment. Jack was fast asleep and I'd done a half-hearted clean of the house that afternoon, which meant that for once it didn't looked like something the health department would be getting complaints about.

As I followed Tony, I wished I'd called to thank him for the tape. I'd kept putting it off, not sure how, or if, I should respond.

'Thanks for the tape.' I spoke to his back.

He turned and flashed me a grin. 'So you got it then? Was it a hit?'

'Absolutely – your sister definitely knows what she is talking about.'

I didn't think it was necessary to mention that Jack had watched the whole thing already – twice.

Before we reached the kitchen, Tony stopped so suddenly I almost bumped into him.

He turned towards me and spoke softly. I could feel his breath on my cheek. 'I was kind of hoping you'd be home when I dropped it in.'

'Really?' I tried to keep my voice light. 'And why was that?'

I was surprised to see some colour creep into his face and wished I hadn't been quite so flippant.

Just as he started to answer, Maggie poked her head around the kitchen door. 'I thought I heard voices. Hi Tony.'

I quickly stepped back from Tony and, like a true friend, Maggie pretended she hadn't noticed anything.

'This is perfect timing,' she continued smoothly. 'I'm sure Tony will respect this drink, unlike Patrick,' she added pointedly.

I followed Tony into the kitchen, wondering what he'd been going to say. I couldn't get a handle on him. Just when I was about to put him firmly in the too-hard basket, he'd turn up again, acting as though we'd exchanged ten phone calls since the last time we'd seen each other.

'Couldn't we have a gin and tonic tonight?' I asked Maggie hopefully.

'Nope,' she replied shortly, consulting her notes.

'Hi,' Patrick greeted Tony from the deck, obviously as surprised as I was to see him.

Maggie put the lid on the blender, turned the dial and the red mixture swirled around for several seconds. The shattering noise made conversation impossible and Tony and I headed out to the deck. Pulling four glasses out of the overhead cupboard, Maggie poured a generous amount of the drink into each and handed them round. Tony took a glass, wisely realising that resisting Maggie was fruitless.

'It's called a Scarlett O'Hara,' Maggie announced as we each took a tentative sip.

The horrific taste I'd expected didn't materialise and I realised with shock that it was actually very nice.

Patrick and Tony both had surprised looks on their faces and each took another larger sip.

'That's actually good,' Tony said.

'See!' Maggie glared at Patrick.

Tony and I sat down with our drinks.

'Have you come to check up on me?' Patrick joked. He gestured at the pages. 'It's coming along, although God only knows if it's any good.'

Tony looked uncomfortably into his drink. 'Ah, no – I've actually got some bad news. I've been offered another job.'

'Isn't that good news?' I was confused.

'Yeah, it's good news for me . . .'

'But not so good for me,' Patrick finished.

'No. There's no way John will carry on with the cooking show when I'm gone. I haven't told him yet, but my guess is that he'll want me to leave straightaway.'

I looked over at Patrick. He looked really disappointed and I felt a big sisterly urge to protect him from the nasty world.

Patrick shook his head. 'Ah well, there goes my shot at fame. Don't worry about it, mate. You've probably done me a favour – I've been using it as an excuse not to look for a real job.'

'I'm sorry to pull the rug out like this, but it's an opportunity I can't pass up.'

'Yeah, of course. It's not a problem. Tell us about the job.' Patrick pushed the writing pad to one side and took another mouthful of his cocktail.

Tony's face brightened. 'I had two interviews with these guys a couple of months ago,' he said, naming one of the commercial stations, 'but then heard nothing. I'd assumed they didn't want me until I got the call this afternoon. I can't believe it's actually happened.'

He stood up, drink in hand, and walked around the deck, his excitement visible.

'So what shows will you be producing?' Patrick asked.

'Believe it or not, the main one we are trying to get off the ground is a new cooking show.' He looked at Patrick. 'I know, I must have poisoned a king or something in my last life and am paying my dues now. Apparently the concept is to have a chef who goes to a different person's house each week. I don't know anything about the other shows – all I know is they're low budget.'

'Well they can't be any lower than the zero TV53 allocated to this one,' Patrick said, gesturing at the writing pad.

'Yeah, I guess. And you know what? I don't even care. This is the break I've been after for years. Finally it looks like I might actually be able to do what I've always wanted.'

Maggie refilled everyone's glass and dropped the blender into the sink. 'Well, I must love you and leave you. I need to enlighten my staff as to the secret Scarlett O'Hara recipe so they can prepare for the stampede of drinkers wanting to try it tomorrow night. Congratulations on the job, Tony.'

After shooting me a look of encouragement I prayed no one else had seen, Maggie made her usual noisy exit, clattering down the hall and slamming the door behind her. I thanked God that Jack was a heavy sleeper.

I gestured at Tony's glass. 'Now that Maggie's gone, I can offer you a proper drink if you'd like.'

'Actually I don't mind it – although I'm meeting my parents for dinner, so too many probably isn't a great plan.'

'A celebration dinner?' Patrick asked.

'Yeah.' Tony leaned against the railing. 'Definitely a celebration for them – I've never really done what they hoped for. I'm their only son and they always expected that I'd do something respectable, be a doctor like Dad, or something else they could tell their friends about.' He half smiled. 'Sorry, that sounded mean. They've always stood behind me, but I know they secretly wish I'd done things a little bit more by the book.'

This was a different Tony to the confident, outgoing person I'd seen so far. The breakthrough in his career, or possibly Maggie's cocktail, seemed to be making him much more open than normal.

'What did you do before you went to film school?' I asked.

He paused and I expected him to answer vaguely and change the subject. I had the feeling he didn't like talking about himself and he often seemed to dodge personal questions.

Instead he answered slowly. 'I was a professional golfer for about five years. My uncle taught me to play when I was very young and I turned out to be pretty good. Mum and Dad thought it was great until I told them I'd decided to join the professional circuit. I always knew making it to the top was a long shot, but I decided that the regret of not having given it a go would be worse than doing it and failing.'

'I knew your name was familiar.' Patrick was clearly impressed. 'Didn't you play in the Australian Open a couple of times?'

I was relieved that Patrick was here to make intelligent comments. While he religiously devoured the sports pages of the newspaper each day, I couldn't even sit through the sports segment on the news. I'd never held a golf club in my life and always had a mental block when it came to remembering how many holes were on a golf course.

He nodded. 'I turned professional when I was nineteen and played the circuit until I was nearly twenty-four.'

'The circuit sounds like a lot of fun,' Patrick commented.

'It was.' Tony smiled. 'I played a mixture of big events and smaller ones where I'd stand a good chance of making some money. In between, a few friends and I would find a beach and surf for a couple of weeks.'

'Why did you give it up?'

'I'd had problems with my shoulder for years but kept telling myself it would be okay. Finally, after my third injury in six months, I realised it just wasn't going to last the distance.'

He wasn't smiling any more.

'So I pulled out. It's not like I was that old when I finished. But all my friends were already well into their careers. Playing golf was really all I'd ever wanted to do and I didn't know what else to do with my life.'

'Kind of like me and accounting,' Patrick joked.

Tony laughed and the mood lightened. One of the strange things about spending time with Patrick was realising that my little brother was actually an intelligent adult. Well-judged comments like that from someone who had spent years with a plastic dog turd in his pocket still surprised me.

'A friend of mine owned a restaurant and I started helping him out. I enjoyed the business and ended up managing a couple of restaurants. The hours were bad, though, and it never really felt like something I would do forever.' He paused. 'This is kind of embarrassing to admit, but one day I was in an electronics shop and Oprah was playing on all the TVs. Some guy was talking about success and said you had to follow your passion. I decided my passion was films, so I found a good film course and well – here I am.'

With the realisation that he was a true film buff, the humiliation of my inane comments about the movie we'd seen hit me afresh.

There was a brief silence.

'Sorry,' Tony said. 'I don't often tell people the story. It's not a state secret, it's just not something I feel like talking about all the time.'

'Don't apologise.' I had decided it was safe to talk now we were off sports. 'I'm really glad things seem to be working out.'

'Just think,' Patrick added, 'no more picketing mothers.'

Tony laughed. 'Unless they find out where I've gone and follow me there.'

'TV53 doesn't know what it's missing.' Patrick shook his

head mournfully. 'The less likely it is to happen, the more convinced I am that I would have been great.'

'Look at the bright side,' I said. 'At least you'll be able to go shopping without being mobbed by lustful women trailing toddlers.'

Patrick didn't look as though this was any great consolation.

Tony looked at his watch. 'I really should get going. I've cancelled the last few times I've planned to see my parents and our booking's for eight.'

I tried to pretend I wasn't disappointed.

'Well I hope things go really well for you.' Patrick stood up and extended his hand.

Tony shook it and turned towards me.

'I'll walk you out,' I said, hoping he would finish what he'd started to say earlier. It had definitely sounded like something I wanted to hear. With Patrick's television career finished, there would be no reason for Tony to drop around again, and after the sit-up ball incident, I had no intention of ever again showing my face in the gym.

Tony opened the door and turned to face me.

'Thanks for the drink. I guess I'll see you around.'

He waved and ran down the stairs.

Right. Well obviously what Tony had left unsaid hadn't exactly been torturing him.

I slowly closed the door. It occurred to me that this was the second time in two days that a good-looking man had headed down these stairs without kissing me. And this time I couldn't even blame Patrick – or Jack. Morosely I trudged back inside to my pile of unfinished work.

TWENTY-TWO

I sank onto the vinyl bus seat with relief.

Jack had woken determined to make life difficult and everything from feeding him breakfast to putting on his shoes had been a battle. So it was with a guilty delight that I'd closed the front door of Carla's shop and walked towards my toddler-free day. No doubt I'd be wishing I was anywhere but at work within two hours, but for the moment I allowed myself the optimistic thought it was going to be a good day.

Reaching into my handbag I pulled out my phone and turned it on.

'You have four new messages,' the recorded voice intoned. My stomach dropped. This was not good.

'First message recorded at 3 p.m. on Thursday, March Four.'

Yesterday. How could that be? I always had my mobile on. Unless – my stomach lodged somewhere near my left ankle – I hadn't turned it back on after Jack had gone to sleep yesterday.

To my great dismay, Jack was starting to refuse to go to sleep in the afternoons. I had relentlessly analysed the circumstances each time it happened and had decided that the problem seemed to occur if he was disturbed in the critical ten minutes after I'd put him to bed.

Extreme situations called for extreme measures and I'd taken to shutting every door and window in the house and putting rolled-up towels across the bottom of his door. Usually I turned my mobile back on and reconnected the phone line once he was asleep but I couldn't remember doing either yesterday. Which explained why the afternoon had been so blissfully free of calls.

'Julia, it's Brian Randall. We've got a situation with Procan. I need your input. Please call me as soon as you pick this message up.'

Brian Randall was a partner in Jennings Walker's litigation group. Procan, a large pharmaceutical company, was engaged in some serious litigation with another company which Procan alleged had infringed the patent of one of its bestselling drugs. Although Brian and his lawyers were handling the dispute, I was looking after anything that affected the ongoing operations of the company.

No need to panic, I told myself. Most of the stuff I was doing was pretty routine, definitely something I could handle today.

Message two – 3.20.

'Julia, it's Kerry.' Kerry was my secretary.

'Something big is happening with Procan and everyone is looking for you. I've called your home number a stack of times but can't get through. Call me soon – please.'

Two messages to go. This made medieval water torture look like a walk in the park.

Message three – 3.45.

'Julia. Gavin here.'

No, no, no. Gavin was the head partner of the corporate section. Despite telling myself it was ridiculously childish, he terrified me. Had on the day I started and still did. He was frighteningly intelligent, was on the board of a handful of companies and had only recently started acknowledging my existence.

'Julia. Neither your home number nor your mobile number seems to be helping us locate you. Do call when it suits.'

The sarcasm dripped down the line and the palms of my hands were suddenly clammy.

Message four – 5.30.

'Julia. It's Mark. It's probably best if you come to see me first thing in the morning. Bye.'

The Brisbane River appeared on my right. Maybe a suicide attempt would evoke a bit of sympathy. I dismissed the thought immediately. These people were lawyers. Appealing to their emotions was hopeless.

The bus, which usually spent ten minutes mired in traffic, barrelled down the snarl-free streets and deposited me in front of my building in what seemed like moments.

I stopped on the edge of the road, my fellow commuters parting around me. I watched the bus as it shrank into the distance and tried to suppress the feeling that my career was still on board.

Kerry smiled sympathetically at me as I approached her desk. 'Mark's in his office,' she said softly.

I tapped on the glass panel beside Mark's door and he looked up. In contrast to the quagmire that was my desk, his was always clear except for the one document he was working on at the time.

'Hello Julia.'

'Should I come in or just head down to HR to pick up my final cheque?'

I'd decided an attempt at humour might defuse the situation, but he looked as though he was actually considering the option.

'Sit down,' he said finally. 'Procan settled the patent litigation yesterday.'

'You're kidding! The other side walked out of negotiations last week.'

Mark shrugged. 'All I know is that they reached a settlement yesterday and had to announce it to the stock exchange.'

As Procan was a public company, information that could affect its share price had to be formally announced before it leaked. That was exactly the type of work I was there to do.

'When they couldn't find you, Brian contacted Gavin. I was out at a meeting, so Gavin handled it all himself.'

I rested my head in my hands for a second. Opening my eyes, I looked across at Mark.

'God, Mark. I've been having trouble getting Jack to sleep lately. So I turned off all the phones – and forgot to turn them on again. It's such goddamn bad luck that something like this happened.'

He nodded. 'I figured it was something like that. Look, it's not a total disaster. I talked to Gavin last night and told him what you've got going on. Stay away from his side of the floor for a while and it will sort itself out.'

I felt a breath of relief. Maybe this would just blow over and we could all forget about it.

'There's one thing, though,' Mark added. 'We don't think now is the right time to put you up for partnership.'

I felt as though Mark had thrown a brick at me. I swallowed hard. 'One afternoon I'm out of contact and that ruins every-thing I've done here?'

Mark took his glasses off and pinched the bridge of his nose. Pushing them back into place, he shook his head slightly. 'Look Julia, the first thing to say is that this isn't a life sentence. Next year things will probably look totally different. But now . . .' He trailed off.

I wasn't consoled. Next year was an eternity away in a law firm. Anything could happen. The economy could slow, which would mean less work and definitely fewer new partners. A new and brighter star might take my place. I'd worked myself inside out for this opportunity now, not sometime in the future.

'It's not just this business yesterday. It's the whole situation with Jack. What you're trying to do is huge and I admire the effort you're making to stay on top of everything. But . . . but it's not enough. You used to be the last person in the office, clients knew that if you said you'd do something, you would. Now you have to be the first out of the office and I know some things have been slipping.'

'Just give me a chance, Mark. Things will get easier, once it all settles down.'

'You think you want this, Julia, but trust me, you don't. The first couple of years I was a partner were the hardest I've ever had. On top of my normal workload, I had to start managing

staff, doing admin stuff and all the crappy jobs the bigwig partners don't want to be doing. If you think you're just keeping
your head above water now, believe me, you'd be swamped. I
only just managed, with Andrea not working and looking after
everything not connected with this office. Doing it by yourself
would be impossible.'

I knew what he was saying made sense, but I couldn't see
past the fact that the carrot which had been dangled in front of
me for years had been yanked away.

'So suddenly I'm not up to scratch and I'm on the scrap
heap?' I didn't even try to keep the anger out of my voice.

Mark shook his head. 'Nope. You're good at what you do –
very good. And we've put a lot of time and effort into training
you. But what's happening at the moment isn't working for
anyone here. So what we think you should do is step back a bit.
Maybe let someone else handle one or two of your clients.'

Well at least Procan was off the list. That was a start.

'Okay.' I nodded slowly.

I pushed myself out of the chair and walked to the door.

'Ah, Julia?'

I turned back towards him.

'One thing, though, when you're thinking about whether
you can give away a couple of matters and lighten your load . . .'

'Yes?'

'Don't even consider trying to get rid of Gordon's statue
case.'

'Oh well. When I lose that trial, not making partner will be
the least of my worries. Jonathon will have me washing dishes
in Chinatown for the rest of my life.'

On that cheery note I left.

TWENTY-THREE

'Patrick, I really don't think that anyone is going to notice whether the extractor fan filter is clean.'

He gave me a withering look, scrubbing harder with what looked suspiciously like an old pair of his underpants. 'I'm not doing it for the show – I've been meaning to do it for ages.'

This statement didn't have a lot of credibility coming from a man who vacuumed his bedroom about twice a year.

It was a week since my partnership prospects had disappeared. Thankfully Maggie had talked me out of my first impulse, which had been to march around to Gavin's office and confront him with the huge injustice that had been done to me. The anger that had fuelled this idea disappeared before lunch and I finally figured out that what I felt most was hurt.

Jennings Walker was a business. It was there to serve its clients and make money. But I'd worked myself inside out for years and knew I was well thought of. Somehow I'd thought that gave me some kind of credit to work with. For the first time, however, I realised that I was just one of a legion of young lawyers who'd passed through the place. No one would remember my name in a year's time if I left tomorrow.

I'd gone through the motions the last week or so, flicked a few files to other lawyers, and my workload was slowly coming back under control. Without the incentive of moving to the next level, everything looked pretty dreary and I felt as though I was just putting one foot in front of the other. I knew I had to fire myself up again if promotion next year was really going to be a possibility, but I couldn't muster the energy.

In stark contrast, Patrick was as excited as I'd seen him since he'd confessed Jennifer had seduced him in the work kitchenette.

Tony had called him yesterday to say that the woman who'd agreed to have the first cooking show in her kitchen had cancelled. He'd asked if Patrick would be interested in taking her place – with the show to be shot in our kitchen today. Far from being insulted that he was a last-minute ring-in, Patrick had accepted enthusiastically. I suspected he was still harbouring dreams of fame.

I'd arrived home last night to find whimsical sketches of coffee cups propped at the back of the counter and a new Alessi juicer that looked like an alien space ship off to one side. There was also a full set of gleaming saucepans, a marble chopping board and a chef's knife. More worryingly, there were two new vases, each filled with what Patrick claimed were native flowers.

'I thought the whole idea was to shoot the segment in a real kitchen. I wouldn't even recognise this place as ours.'

Despite Tony having told Patrick that the 'normal people' on the show were simply a way of making the chef look good, Patrick was on tenterhooks.

'Well, if you're going to be on TV, you have to make a bit of an effort.' He'd finished with the extractor fan and had moved on to the fridge, which he'd only cleaned yesterday.

'This must have cost you a fortune. How did you afford it all?'

Patrick looked uncomfortable. 'Same as everything else – credit.'

Patrick was so nervous, he hadn't even eaten and had barely said two words, even to Jack, all day. Despite Jack's best efforts, the entire house was still spotless at lunchtime and I was under strict instructions to make sure it stayed that way.

This whole thing was so out of character that I was starting to worry about how much being unemployed was weighing on

Patrick. In the two weeks since he'd been fired, he'd been knocked back by the other three major accounting firms in town. He didn't seem to want to talk about it except to voice his conviction that Jennifer was using her influence to prevent him finding another job in the industry.

Patrick wasn't the only one flustered – Tony's call had unsettled me as well. Another week had gone by with no word from him and here he was turning up again. Sure, it was Patrick he'd called, not me. But if he really didn't want to see me again, would he have arranged to shoot the show in my house?

The truth was he probably hadn't even given it any thought.

'So do you know who the chef is?' I asked as I blew on a party sausage before handing it to Jack. Unfortunately, his love of Carla's meatballs hadn't ushered in a new approach to food and a worrying amount of his diet still came from the frozen food section at the supermarket.

'Some guy called David Green. He's head chef at a restaurant in town.'

'Do you know if he's been on television before?'

Patrick shook his head. 'I hope so though. I've just remembered how uncomfortable I am whenever anyone produces a video camera. Can you tell me what on earth made me think I'd be any good at this?'

'This is totally different to amateur stuff. You'll be great,' I assured him with as much conviction as I could muster.

'You think so?' he asked desperately.

'Absolutely.' I nodded sagely.

'What time are they coming?'

He looked nervously at his watch. 'In half an hour.'

We both looked at Jack, who was jumping around the room astride the broom, making horse noises and crashing into every available surface.

'Don't suppose you have a playgroup to go to this afternoon?'

''Fraid not.'

He looked at me pleadingly.

I'd been keen to see what happened, but it was clear that a television shoot and Jack couldn't coexist in this small house.

'Okay,' I relented, 'I'll take him swimming.'

'Thank you,' Patrick sighed with relief.

I'd taken Jack to the local pool earlier in the week. My expectations of our outings were becoming more realistic – I figured that if I expected total catastrophe, anything else was a bonus. As neither of us had drowned, I'd deemed the expedition a success.

Now, after two hours of unsuccessfully trying to convince Jack that splashing harmlessly in the baby pool was way more exciting than throwing himself into three metres of water, I was exhausted.

We returned home to find a van and a couple of cars parked outside and the house crowded. For a low-budget half-hour show, there certainly seemed to be a lot of people in the kitchen and spread around the deck.

I took Jack straight to his room and put him down for a sleep, blessing the fact that he was so tired he couldn't muster the energy to put up a fight.

My swimming costume had soaked through my T-shirt and shorts, making very undignified-looking patterns, and I decided to change before venturing into the kitchen.

'Hi Julia.'

I heard the familiar voice behind me as I was quietly pulling Jack's door shut. I turned and saw Tony standing in the doorway. I couldn't help the lurch in my stomach at the sight of him.

I glanced down at my front, trying to gauge how bad the watermarks looked. Bad.

'Over here, Tony,' someone called from the kitchen, and with an apologetic wave he was gone.

I escaped to my bedroom with relief and threw on a dry singlet top and trousers. With so many people already involved, the last thing I wanted to do was get in the way. Trying to convince myself I wasn't avoiding Tony, I went into the study and closed the door.

Other than a couple of shattering crashes, which I hoped weren't Patrick's new vases, and a few teeth-jarring scrapes along the floor, there wasn't too much noise coming from the kitchen, but I still couldn't concentrate. After about half an hour I stopped pretending to work and looked in on the filming.

Despite the fact that the crew had been there for over three hours, it didn't seem as though much cooking had been done. I perched on the back of the sofa, trying to be as inconspicuous as possible.

Patrick and another man, who I assumed to be David Green, were standing in front of the bench, each with identical knives and chopping boards. David was instructing Patrick on the proper way to dice an onion.

'No, no, no. That's not finely diced, that's massacred. Here, try again,' he was saying in a deep voice.

He scraped the irregular chunks of onion into the sink and handed Patrick another.

'You need to work with the grain of the onion – don't fight it,' he coached.

I could see why they thought this guy would work on TV and wondered whether they hadn't chosen him more for his looks than his cooking skills. For some reason I'd been expecting someone French and small, with a neat little moustache. David looked more like a footballer than a chef.

Although Patrick was well over six feet, he looked short in comparison. On the back of one of David's hands was a tattoo that I couldn't quite make out, but it looked like some sort of spider. His face was handsome in a beaten-up sort of way, as though he'd survived his fair share of bar brawls.

As I watched, the camera focused on Patrick, who started to painfully cut up his onion into rough, irregular cubes. Beside him, David's knife flew and within five seconds he had a perfectly diced onion. With Patrick still labouring away, he turned to the stove.

Boredom had clearly overcome Patrick's nerves and casting a glance over his shoulder, he waved a tea towel in front of the camera while swapping chopping boards. 'Ta da,' he announced, looking proud. 'Just a little trick I picked up in chef school.'

He quickly turned and dropped the perfectly cut onion into his pan on the stove.

David turned back to find himself left with the huge chunks of onion. 'Right. So it's going to be like that, is it?'

Tony, who had been standing off to one side, spotted me and came over. 'How's it going?' I asked as he leaned on the wall next to me.

He shook his head. 'We're running way behind schedule. The lights blew one of the fuses, so we had no power for an hour. I'm afraid your kitchen will be out of action for a while yet.'

I waved my hand. 'Gives me the perfect excuse not to cook. You can stay all week if you want.' As soon as I spoke, I realised how much like an invitation that sounded. 'I mean . . . the crew can . . .' I decided to cut my losses and change the subject. 'How's Patrick going?'

'Well, I think. He was nervous when we started, but because he has been in front of the camera for so long, he's pretty much forgotten about it. He and David seem to have hit it off, which is good.'

'Are you taping this?'

'Yeah. We rehearsed it a few times without the food and then got some pretty good stuff doing it properly. We've got a heap of food though, so I told them to play around with the script a bit. We might be able to edit some of the impromptu bits in if they work.'

Having salvaged the onion and set it cooking on the stove, David was talking to the camera again. Patrick spotted me and smiled slightly.

'Fresh ripe tomatoes are the key to this dish. The first step is to remove the skins.'

One of the crew appeared with two steaming bowls filled with tomatoes and hot water.

'All you need to do is gently pull the skins off each one.' David plunged his hands in.

Patrick copied him, slipping his hands into the water, and instantly let out a howl. 'Shit!' He rushed over to the tap and turned on the cold water, running his injured hands underneath. 'Mate, that's not natural. That water must be close to boiling.'

David laughed as he placed each skinned tomato on the board.

Hands still under the tap, Patrick turned to face the camera. Putting on a David Attenborough voice, he whispered as though trying not to disturb some elusive jungle creature.

'Now, one of the wonderfully unique things about chefs is that they are stark raving mad. Although able to withstand high temperatures, they are remarkably out of touch with the rest of the world, as evidenced by the fact that they have not yet discovered the modern invention of tinned tomatoes.'

David stepped in front of the camera. Using the same voice, he mimicked Patrick. 'Another truly bizarre species that lives in this habitat is the unemployed accountant.'

I looked nervously at Patrick, but he was smiling and seemed to be enjoying himself.

'This species believe they are able to do away with the traditional skills of hunting, gathering and cooking, relying instead on takeaway pizza and the local Indian restaurant. However, they are suddenly left floundering in a frightening world of fresh vegetables and uncooked meat when their income is removed.'

Patrick threw his head back and laughed.

'Now, if we could get back to the cooking?' David arched his eyebrows at Patrick. 'It is important to make sure that the onion is only sweating, not frying.'

'Okay, yes. Sweating good. Frying bad.' Patrick pointed at his pan. 'Perfect.'

'No Patrick, that is definitely frying. This is sweating.' David pointed at his own pan.

'Oh, right. Sorry.' Patrick adjusted the flame under his pan and made a face at the camera.

'Now pour some balsamic vinegar over it.'

Two identical bottles appeared on the counter. This was my kind of cooking, I thought.

David gripped the neck of the bottle in his fingers, turning it on the side. He slurped an amount into the pan, stoppered it with his thumb and then added another bit.

Patrick watched him. 'How much was that?'

'Oh, I don't know,' David replied airily. 'A good couple of slurps, until it colours nicely.'

'Okay,' Patrick said uncertainly.

Copying David, he turned the bottle on its side and awkwardly tipped it. The vinegar poured out in a rush. In a panic Patrick tried to use his thumb to stop it and somehow dropped the whole bottle in the pan with a resounding crash.

David picked the bottle out of the pan calmly. 'See,' he said to the camera. 'Beautiful colour.

'You can just pour it normally,' he said to Patrick, rather kindly I thought.

'No way – it looks too cool. I wouldn't even have to cook to impress the girls if I could do that. Just offer to put the dressing on the salad and they'd think I was a cooking legend.'

'Dressing that you'd made earlier of course?' David clarified.

'Make dressing? No way! Haven't you tried the ready-made ones they've got in the supermarket?' He looked serious but I could see a trace of a smile around his mouth.

David didn't seem to notice he was being wound up. 'Patrick, Patrick, Patrick. If there is one thing you will learn before I leave today, it is how to make a proper dressing. You simply must not buy one of those terrible concoctions.

'Now.' David drew a deep breath. 'Where were we?'

'Onion a-sweating.' Patrick opened the oven door and a waft of cooking meat came out. 'Meat a-cooking. We just need some mashed spuds and tomato sauce, right?'

'Where have you been for the last five years? You never, ever call it mashed potato – it is mash, as in potato mash, or sweet potato mash. Don't they let you accountants out at night?'

Patrick shook his head in mock sadness. 'Well, they let us out. It's just that no one invites us anywhere. Social death to be seen talking in public to an accountant, you know . . . It's why accountants intermarry. Lawyers are about the only other lot that'll have us, and even they feel they're doing us a favour.'

The banter continued throughout the making of a tomato relish, which Patrick insisted, to David's obvious irritation, on calling a sauce. David showed Patrick how to 'plate' the food and finally Tony interrupted.

'All right, you two, I think that's enough. Thank you.'

'Tony, mate, you're going to have to do something about the quality of the students you send me.' David smiled. 'Got to admit, though, that was more fun than I thought it would be. You're not going to use that last one, are you?'

'I don't know. I'll wait and see how it looks, but I thought it was pretty entertaining. You pair work together well.'

The crew was already packing up and wheeling large items down the hallway.

'What happens now?' Patrick asked.

'We'll edit this over the next couple of days. If it looks good, we'll take it to a management meeting and see if they like it enough to produce a series.'

'Do you want to stay for a drink?' Patrick asked. 'Celebrate the end of filming?'

I promised myself I'd be extra nice to Patrick for ever more.

David answered first. 'Afraid not – I need to get back to the restaurant and prep for tonight's session.'

Patrick turned to Tony expectantly.

'Sorry, mate, got to get back to the studio and look at this stuff.' And with a brief goodbye, he was gone.

All right. There was now absolutely no doubt that I had imagined Tony kissing me after the movie – and quite possibly the whole date. He'd hardly spoken to me since and certainly shown very little interest. It had obviously been a desperate fantasy that was the product of a sleep- and sex-deprived mind. I was clearly a very sad person.

At least now the show was finished, I wouldn't have to see him any more. That was good news.

TWENTY-FOUR ·

Although I wasn't quite lurching from one disaster to the next in the way I had been a month ago, my ability to pack things Jack would need while we were out was still somewhat patchy.

Typically what happened was that I'd decide I couldn't be bothered with carting a pile of stuff and head out with nothing but a handbag. However, a dire situation involving some form of bodily fluids would inevitably arise and I'd be forced to deal with it with nothing more useful than a soggy tissue. As a result, on the next outing I'd take more paraphernalia than eight children required, cart a ten-kilogram bag around for hours and use absolutely nothing.

I knew there was middle ground somewhere but was still trying to find it. Faced with my first beach expedition with Jack, I accepted that my groovy little sunflower beach bag wasn't an option and reached for Patrick's old backpack.

He'd been going to come with us. But when I saw the packet of cigarettes on the table this morning I knew we were on our own. Patrick didn't smoke – unless he'd had way too many beers. The smell of alcohol hit me when I peered in his door and I didn't even attempt to wake him. Instead, I scribbled him a note and threw Jack and all our paraphernalia in the car. Just as I was about to pull onto the road, my mobile rang.

'Hi Julia. It's Grant.'

I felt a jolt of pleasure. I hadn't heard from him since our dinner last week and had wondered if I would.

'Fancy catching up for breakfast?'

My heart sank at his suggestion. There was nothing for it. If I was going to attempt some form of romance I was going to have to find a man with children. At least he would understand the terror that such a suggestion inspired in me. But even as I thought it, I recoiled from the Brady Bunch type future which swam before my eyes.

One thing was certain, though – after the breakfast debacle with Tony, I was not taking Jack out to eat until he could drive me there.

'Actually we're in the car, heading for Southbank for a swim. I don't suppose you feel like coming along?'

'That sounds like a great idea. I'll meet you there.'

We arranged a place to meet and I let out a silent whistle as I hit the phone's disconnect button. A morning with Jack for date number two – there was no doubt this was a high-risk activity, but I didn't see that I had much choice.

I had discovered Southbank after a particularly bad case of cabin fever had forced me to call the Brisbane Tourism Office and ask if they had any suggestions of good places to go with toddlers. Although I had been vaguely aware of the cafes and restaurants in the Southbank complex, the very understanding woman on the phone had informed me there was an artificial beach in the middle, which would be perfect for Jack.

It was indeed. The huge lake, which sat beside the river, ringed by a perfect golden beach, was wonderful and had kept Jack busy for hours.

Today, as we walked past one of the upmarket cafes, I saw a woman seated at a table on the footpath. She was wearing a white T-shirt and blue jeans cut off at the knee. Her long dark hair was pulled back from her face and, as I watched, she pulled my favourite section out of the weekend paper, leaned back and took a sip of coffee.

I averted my eyes. What a waste she was making of a

wonderful morning, I told myself determinedly. It was so much better to actually be going to the beach, not just sitting near it.

As we reached the sand, Jack struggled to be put down. When his feet hit the ground he looked up at me with a delighted smile and took off for the water as fast as his little legs would take him.

Backpack bumping painfully, I caught him and threw my towel on a likely spot of sand. I quickly dressed him in bathers, slathered him with sunscreen and pulled his hat down on his head.

Once again he took off for the water at the stumble that constituted his run. I strolled behind him, sure that he'd stop when he reached the shallows. Except he didn't. He was up to his thighs when I reached him and was definitely heading deeper. The child had zero sense of self-preservation.

I picked him up and deposited him on the edge of the water where a string of children were playing. As I did, I realised he was seriously outclassed by the other kids who were clad head-to-toe in fluorescent lycra. Jack's bare shoulders glowed in the bright sun and I looked around guiltily to see if anyone else had spotted my negligent parenting.

His eyes lit up and he headed towards a group of girls who were delicately covering a sandcastle in shells. Turning him around, I realised I was going to have to provide some enter-tainment. Any lingering hopes I'd had of reclining on my towel and chatting enchantingly to Grant disappeared.

It had been a long time since I'd done anything more active than read a book on a beach. Luckily my initial shopping trip before Jack's arrival had included a bucket and spade. I dug half-heartedly until I had a tiny pile of sand. Jack leaped on it in delight and our roles became clear. I was the sandcastle maker and he the sandcastle destroyer.

At first I kept half an eye out for Grant and tried to project a lithe and athletic appearance which he could admire as he walked towards us. However, I quickly tired of keeping my back straight and sticking my chest out and started actually enjoying myself. Jack laughed delightedly at my squeals of mock horror at his destruction of my castles and discovered a whole new source of fun when he accidentally flicked some wet sand onto me. By the time a shadow fell over us, wet sand was sticking to most of my upper body, and my sunglasses, which I'd originally perched in my hair, were hanging off the side of my head.

'Looks like you pair are having fun.'

I looked up and wiped a strand of hair back from the side of my mouth. Grant was wearing a pair of surf shorts and a T-shirt and was looking decidedly appealing.

'Hello. I'm glad you made it.'

'So am I.' He smiled, eyes hidden behind dark sunglasses.

I looked down at myself. Men found female mud wrestlers sexy, didn't they? Maybe this was a similar thing.

In any event, he didn't seem to be even looking in my direction.

'She calls this a sandcastle?' he asked Jack as he surveyed the wreck of my last creation.

'Come on now, I've been working under pretty difficult conditions. I have approximately two seconds before my demolition team moves in.'

Grant didn't seem impressed with my excuse. 'What we need is a plan. And some wetter sand.' He picked up the spade and walked along the sand a couple of metres. Jack toddled obediently after him.

I debated whether I was expected to follow, but decided it was a male-only activity and wasn't going to last long anyway. Stretching my toes out in the shallow water, I tipped my head back and enjoyed the feeling of sun on my face.

A couple of minutes later I turned around. Grant's sandcastle was ten times the size of any of mine and growing rapidly as he shovelled sand on top. Jack was engaged in throwing tiny handfuls in its general direction.

'Very impressive.' I stood over them, hands on hips. 'How on earth did you convince Jack not to destroy it? Promise him a lifetime's supply of ice-cream?'

Grant looked up in surprise. 'He hasn't tried to knock it down. He clearly knows quality when he sees it.'

I sat down beside them and hugged my knees. 'You're not working today?'

'Yeah, I brought the van with me, but I figured I could start a bit later than normal. Thanks for dinner the other night, by the way. I really enjoyed it.'

'You're welcome. I had a good time too.'

We smiled at each other.

Jack stood up and began pointing frantically at several seagulls which had landed on the grassy area bordering the sand.

'They're seagulls, Jack. Do you want to go closer?'

His answer was a definite nod. He held out his hand and I took it in mine, feeling a pang of tenderness for him as I did.

'Excuse us,' I said to Grant.

As we headed for the seagulls, I wished I'd thought to put my T-shirt on. Since the day I'd bought it, my swimsuit had insisted on riding up if I did anything more strenuous than breathe deeply. Unable to bear the thought of how bad it no doubt looked, I reached behind me every few steps to pull it down. My only hope was that Grant wasn't watching.

As we neared the birds, Jack took off, arms and legs flailing as he tried to catch them.

This was clearly not the first time these birds had been attacked by a child. They took one unworried look at him, flapped their wings casually and flew only a few metres away. Undeterred, Jack continued towards them and the whole process repeated itself. I followed behind him, wondering how long he'd persist. Finally the birds flew over his head and we began the whole cycle again – this time heading back the other way.

Eventually we made it back to Grant. Instead of abandoning the sandcastle project as soon as we had left, Grant had turned it into what looked like a five-bedroom Tuscan villa complete with palm trees and swimming pool.

'Ta da. I give you the House of Jack.'

Apparently unimpressed, Jack jumped, clearly set on landing on the sandcastle and demolishing it. Greatly overestimating his abilities, he landed in exactly the same spot he'd started from.

He advanced on the sandcastle again, this time wielding a spade, and clumsily reduced it to ruins. Grant looked only amused at the destruction of his labour and I sat down beside him. Jack pottered around depositing stones in his bucket.

'Do you go to the beach much – the real one, I mean?'

'My folks live on the Sunshine Coast, but they're overseas so I haven't had a chance to take Jack yet. What about you? Do you still surf?'

Grant nodded. 'Yeah. Every time I go out I vow I'll make the effort and do it every weekend, but somehow it doesn't seem to happen.'

That topic came to an abrupt end and I wondered where the easy conversation from the other night had gone.

'So. How's work going?' Grant ventured.

'Oh, not too bad. I spent yesterday going around pool shops trying to find someone who would testify that cleaning a pool once a fortnight is perfectly normal.'

Despite my disillusionment at work, I hadn't lost sight of the fact that things would suddenly get a whole lot worse if I didn't somehow snatch victory from the jaws of defeat that were threatening Gordon's trial.

'You're kidding, right?' Grant looked incredulous. 'I thought you'd spend your days marching in and out of courtrooms, striking deals and rushing out to cocktail parties at night.'

'I'm going into a courtroom for the first time in five years next Friday.' Even uttering the words sent a shudder of dread down my spine. 'And trust me, it will not be glamorous.'

'No cocktail parties?'

'Nothing you'd give up dinner with your grandmother for.'

'Ah, see, I was right. Mobile ice-cream sales, that's the new glamour industry.'

'I've heard that,' I nodded seriously.

'Yep, what people forget is that kids of famous people want ice-creams too. You'd be amazed the people I've served ice-creams to.'

'Really?' I asked.

'Ah, no,' Grant laughed. 'I was just making it up. Although,' he continued, 'I did once sell an ice-cream to the guy who does the weather on television.'

'Well that is impressive,' I said with mock awe.

'You've shattered my illusions anyway,' Grant continued. 'I've never met a woman lawyer. I thought you probably drove a snappy red convertible and kept turning down people asking you to become a judge.'

'Well actually my car is silver and it spends more time in the mechanic's than out of it. This week has seen me bumped from any chance of a promotion, and at the rate I'm going, I'll be lucky if I still have my job this time next month.'

There was a pause. To spare Grant the stress of finding an adequate response, I jumped in. 'What about you?' I asked. 'Do you miss teaching?'

'Sometimes.' He hesitated. 'Remember Mr White at school?'

I nodded.

'He was just so cool – somehow he made learning fun and taught me how great reading can be. I've just always wanted to be that kind of teacher.'

I decided this would be a bad time to admit that for years I'd harboured a secret crush on Mr White.

'But once I became a teacher, it wasn't that simple. There was all the staffroom politics, and the constant bombardment with wonderful new theories and techniques. And then there were the parents . . . Some of them were great, but some of them – God! They usually had the most painful kids and would come in to see me, complaining about the most ridiculous things. I taught for five years, and by the end I was just going through the motions. I decided I needed to change some things – so here I am . . .'

He looked over at me. 'Sorry, this is much too heavy for a beautiful morning at the beach.'

'That's okay,' I smiled. 'It's usually me telling people my life story these days.'

We both looked at Jack who had wrapped a towel around his shoulders and was advancing on us, growling in a way that would have been menacing if he weren't three feet tall and smiling. Nevertheless Grant and I both put on suitably terrified faces.

He flung himself at me. I squealed and fell over backwards, a wet and sandy Jack and a large towel on top of me. To my surprise, he didn't get up immediately, or even try to throw sand in my face. Instead, he put his arms around me, his head on my chest, and gave me a hug.

He was up and off again in a moment, but there was no mistaking his affection and I felt unreasonably happy.

I tried to sit up without using my hands and failed. Even if I couldn't get to the gym, there was absolutely no reason I couldn't do some sit-ups at home, I told myself sternly as I used my arm to lever myself up. Peering out from under the towel, I tried to see if Grant had noticed how pathetic my stomach muscles were. Thankfully, he seemed to be looking the other way.

'Seeing all these hot, sweaty kids doesn't make you itch to sell them ice-creams?' I asked.

At the words 'hot and sweaty', I found myself looking at his rather lovely chest. I jerked my eyes upwards, pretending to look at something else.

'To be honest, no. I'm a bit over it all at the moment. I've had a couple of complaints in the last few weeks – it's a much bigger deal when it's not just you.'

'See!' I shook my head. 'It's that music – it's got to go.'

He laughed. 'The complaints were actually about the quality of the ice-cream from one of the vans. Mind you,' he added, 'if all complaints worked out as well as yours, I wouldn't mind.'

He looked at me and we both smiled.

Suddenly I realised that I couldn't see Jack and I spun around in panic. He was only a few metres behind us, watching a woman with a chihuahua.

I looked back at Grant but the moment was gone. How on earth was I supposed to make meaningful eye contact with an attractive man while looking after a cyclonic toddler?

Grant chuckled, looking in Jack's direction.

Jack was miaowing at the top of his voice at the chihuahua,

much to the amusement of everyone in earshot. Everyone except the dog's owner, who looked stonily ahead.

'Oh dear,' I muttered under my breath.

'Kind of hard to blame him,' Grant replied quietly.

'Let's just hope the owner doesn't realise he's with us – she looks scary.'

Grant looked at his watch. 'I have to get going,' he said in what I hoped was a regretful tone. 'Can't keep my public waiting – the kids get pretty mean if I'm not there on time.'

He stood up and picked up his towel and keys. 'Well, thanks for a great morning. Bye Jack,' he yelled in his direction.

'See you then. We might even buy an ice-cream from you next week when you drive by.'

Grant looked suddenly uncomfortable. 'Ah, I won't actually be around after tomorrow. I've got someone else to handle the inner-city van next week.'

'Okay then,' I replied, slightly confused at his reaction.

'Yeah, I'm taking a week's holiday.'

'Half your luck. Where are you going?'

'Ah, I haven't decided yet.'

'Oh – right.'

The conversation had switched back to being awkward again.

'Well. I'd better go. I'll give you a call when I get back.' He smiled and headed for the road.

Jack tugged at my legs, saying his word for 'hungry'.

As I rummaged in my bag for some food, I cast a look at Grant's retreating back. 'What on earth was that about, Jack? Come on, you're a man. Explain it to me.'

He looked at me silently.

Shaking my head, I handed Jack a biscuit and slumped down on the sand beside him.

TWENTY-FIVE

I've heard it said that most recovering addicts have had a defining moment which makes them realise they need to make some changes.

Mine was a sudden, horrifying glimpse of my future in which I had become the kind of person no one wanted to sit next to at a dinner party.

It started on Sunday. By amazing coincidence Jack and I headed to New Farm Park at almost exactly the same time we'd seen Grant there last time. Jack insisted on walking the last half of the way and as we cut across the lawn, Grant's van tinkled past on its way out of the park. He didn't see us, but I was close enough to know it was him and to see the blonde girl sitting beside him.

Normally that wouldn't have been such a big deal, but not only was she very attractive, she was also sitting in the middle seat of the van and Grant's arm was around her.

I stopped dead, looking after them. For some reason I'd assumed Grant wasn't seeing anyone. But maybe he was. After all, there was nothing between us, but why on earth had he spent time with Jack and me yesterday if he was with someone else? The thought that he was trying to pay me back for my actions of years ago crossed my mind, but I dismissed it. He was too nice for that.

The more likely answer was that he was keeping his options

open. There was no rule against seeing two women at the same time. That theory also explained why he didn't want to tell me where he was going on holiday – or with whom.

Our history, the fact that our current relationship had spanned a whole two weeks, and my interest in the elusive Tony, made it hard for me to feel angry. But it didn't stop me picturing Grant and his floozy arriving at a lovely unit on the Gold Coast and cracking open a bottle of complimentary champagne on the balcony.

And as the week wore on without a word from Tony to distract me, I began envisaging Grant and the mystery blonde in ever more romantic settings. My current picture was of them sipping tequila sunrises beside a swim-up bar in the Maldives.

But it was the 'Pop Goes the Weasel' conversation that convinced me I had to change my life.

Patrick had arrived home from a day on the boat, just after I'd put Jack to bed.

'Have a look at this, would you?' I said, proffering an open book of nursery rhymes.

'What am I looking at exactly?' Patrick asked.

'The lyrics to "Pop Goes the Weasel". Have a read of them.'

He scanned the page and looked up again. 'Okay . . . read them – I'm obviously missing something here.'

'But have you read them properly?' I demanded.

'Julia, have you been drinking?'

'Of course not,' I answered haughtily. Patrick didn't need to know that was only because the cupboard was bare. I silently congratulated myself for thinking in nursery-rhyme parlance.

I took the book back. 'Listen to this. It talks about the monkey chasing the weasel around the mulberry bush, but when the monkey stops to pull up his socks, the weasel goes pop!'

'Yes . . .' Patrick was starting to look worried.

'Does that make any sense to you?'

'Um – no. It's a nursery rhyme.'

'But what do you think it means? I'm thinking there must be a hidden drug reference or something, but I just can't work it out.'

'Julia, to be honest I don't care. It's a nursery rhyme, for God's sake – they're not supposed to make sense. And you shouldn't care either.'

I looked at him. 'I'm losing it, aren't I?'

'Not losing it,' Patrick said a bit more kindly. 'But I think your perspective is getting a bit . . . a bit confused,' he finished.

'Am I boring?'

'No, not at all.' He said it a bit too quickly. 'What you're doing is amazing. Working really hard and managing to figure out how to look after Jack at the same time. But – all that – well, it doesn't leave time for much else, does it?'

'No.'

'Look. I've been pretty crap, I know. I've been feeling sorry for myself about not having a job and now there's this television thing.'

'Jack's not your responsibility.'

'No, but you are my sister.'

He gave me a strange look. We weren't big on talking about emotions in our family. I felt a bit odd about Patrick becoming all caring and considerate.

He obviously felt the same, as he continued in a lighter tone. 'And it reflects very badly on me to have a sister who . . . has lost perspective. I still owe you two babysitting nights for asking Grant out, so why don't you take a night off and go and do something fun?'

'Okay, I will,' I said decisively. Patrick was right – I needed to get out more. The prospect of an occasional night with grown-ups was as appealing as a fifty per cent pay rise would have been a month ago.

'All right, see if I can get this straight. Weekend in Fiji with handsome man – exciting. Afternoon at local park – boring. Ahhh . . . Morning spent stacking blocks on top of one another . . .' I paused, 'boring. Evening eating and drinking with group of good friends – exciting.'

'Yes, that's a big improvement,' Patrick smiled, obviously relieved to have escaped the dangerous territory of his sister's mental instability. 'And on weekend with said handsome man or evening with friends, do not discuss nursery-rhyme lyrics.'

'Right,' I nodded seriously. 'Got it.'

We decided Patrick would look after Jack on Monday night and then moved on to something else, but I thought about our conversation a number of times afterwards.

My existence consisted entirely of work, looking after Jack and evenings at home, generally by myself. Given the not-so-good direction my job had taken, I couldn't even justify my lack of a life on the basis that I was dedicating myself to my career. I tried to think about what I used to talk to friends about before Jack arrived. Nothing very intelligent or exciting leaped to mind. But I was pretty sure that nursery rhymes hadn't featured.

Something had to change if I was going to keep my sanity and any of my friends. The difficult thing was to decide what to do to make myself more interesting.

Maggie wasn't any help when we met for a quick lunch together on Monday.

'Are you sure this is the right way to go about it?' she asked dubiously. 'Isn't trying to make yourself interesting a bit deliberate? It's something that just happens, isn't it?'

I shook my head firmly. 'I've thought about this. It's fine if you have lots of time to do a whole bunch of stuff. You can afford to relax and let things happen because in the course of, say, a week, you do a whole lot of things which provide you with interesting snippets. But I have a four-hour window. I can't afford to muck around – I've got to spend my time wisely.'

'At least wait until next week and I'll go with you.'

Again, I shook my head. Maggie sighed. 'All right then, what are you thinking of?'

'Well.' I pulled the entertainment guide out of the paper 'There's no shortage of options. But I was thinking maybe kick-boxing?'

Maggie spluttered her mouthful of mineral water over the table, obviously picturing me attempting a head-high kick.

'Okay,' I acknowledged with a small smile. 'Maybe that's not quite me. What do you think about some kind of course?'

'Maybe you should go for one-off things to begin with. Work up to a commitment.'

'You're right. Oh, I don't know.' I folded the paper and threw it on top of my handbag. 'Re-engineering your life is exhausting. I'll think about it later.'

'I need to get back to the pub.' Maggie looked at her watch. 'Marcus gets here on Thursday, and I'm taking Friday off, so I need to get a day ahead of myself.'

'He doesn't waste any time, does he?' I asked, watching her face carefully. This was the first time she'd brought up the subject of Marcus.

'No. He says now he's decided, he just wants to be here – he's moving in with a friend until he finds a place to live.'

'And you're okay about it?'

'Yeah, I think I am,' she smiled slightly. 'Still a bit nervous though.'

'It'll be great,' I declared. 'Right, let's get back to it – I can hardly see over my in-tray.' Thankfully Mark was still managing the First Gen matter by himself, but Gordon's trial was due to start on Friday and I had a million things to do before I left for the day.

By five-thirty I still hadn't decided what I was going to do that evening. The pressure of it all was getting too much and I found myself wishing that I could just forget about it and have an early night.

Patrick was waiting in the kitchen when we arrived home. Lifting Jack into a bear hug, he looked at me jubilantly.

'Do you want the good news or the bad news?' After the last time, I wasn't taking any chances.

'Um – the bad news.'

Patrick smiled broadly. 'There is no bad news – Tony called about the show.'

'And?'

'And . . .' Patrick could hardly stand still he was so excited. 'The management committee loved it.' He put on an American accent. 'It's been green-lit, baby!'

'That's fabulous. When will it be aired?'

'That's the best bit. Tony decided to use the last take we did – the one where we were mucking around. The people he showed it to thought the chemistry between David and me was great and that the whole thing was really funny. They've canned the idea of doing it at a different person's house each week and want me to do the whole series with him!'

'Bloody hell!'

'Yeah, exactly. The details need to be sorted out, but I've been invited to some big studio party on Thursday night so I can meet some people. How good is that?'

'This calls for champagne,' I decided. 'You start Jack in the bath and I'll be back in ten minutes.'

'Uh-uh.' Patrick shook his head. 'This is your "I am going to get a life" night. You're not going to get out of it that easily. We'll celebrate tomorrow night. Go and get ready.'

At seven o'clock I was standing out the front of the house, wondering what the hell I was going to do with myself for the next four hours.

Well one thing was for sure, I wasn't catching public transport at this time of night. I pulled out my car keys and sat inside the car. Turning on the interior light, I flicked through the pages of the newspaper Patrick had thrust at me as I'd left.

Seeing a band was an option. But it was only seven o'clock. None of the musicians would even be awake yet and I couldn't face a day with Jack tomorrow on only a couple of hours' sleep. Besides, a whole night in a bar by myself didn't sound like much fun.

I flicked through the theatre reviews. Why did anything with any form of theatrical credibility have to be wrist-slashingly depressing?

At the bottom of the page was a section on art galleries. I noticed that tonight was the opening of a new exhibition at a gallery on Brunswick Street. I'd never heard of the artist and knew nothing about painting. But it sounded like an excellent tidbit of information to drop into a conversation – actually *every* conversation I had in the next week – and as an added bonus I figured there was a good chance I'd score a free glass of wine. Decisively I flicked off the light and turned the key in the ignition.

As I approached the gallery, I could see that it was full of people and my steps faltered. Who exactly was I going to talk to? I couldn't spend an hour looking at the paintings. Close to the gallery was a bus shelter and I sat down, trying to get up enough courage to go in.

I was tempted to turn around and go home. But summoning the look of concern on Patrick's face when I told him my nursery-rhyme theory, I stood up and walked to the door.

There was a waiter holding a tray of drinks standing inside and I picked up a glass of wine. My plan had been to head straight for the paintings, but the closer I got the less I wanted to see. Given that I didn't know a soul, though, I had no other option and I was still wandering from one to another when a woman spoke to me.

'Ah, excuse me?'

I turned to her with a smile. Obviously this was what sophisticated people did at gallery openings. I needn't have worried about meeting people.

'Ah. I just thought I should tell you that you have something on the back of your skirt.'

From the distasteful look on her face, I knew we weren't talking a small something.

'Right.' I couldn't think of anything appropriate to say. 'What is it, do you know?'

She shook her head uncertainly. 'Well, I'd say chewing gum. But it's a very odd colour.'

Duty done, she gave me a pitying look before threading her way through the crowd.

My first thought was of the length of time I'd been standing with my back to a room full of people. I felt the colour rise in my cheeks and cursed the impulse which had made me sit on the bus stop seat, which I could only assume was the source of the unidentified goop.

I looked for somewhere to put my wineglass, focusing on the quickest possible exit route.

'Julia!'

My blood chilled as I recognised the voice which haunted my dreams.

'Gordon, hello,' I stammered. He didn't appear to notice my lack of enthusiasm.

'Hello Julia. I didn't know you were an art buff!' He took my arm and pulled me towards a group of people.

'Oh well, you know, a well-rounded lawyer is a good lawyer.' I thanked God that none of my friends had heard those words come out of my mouth, but Gordon nodded in agreement.

'This is my lawyer,' Gordon announced to the circle in front of him. 'She's going to blow the other side out of the water at our trial on Friday.'

Gordon's confidence in me had the result of making me even more terrified that we were going to lose badly. I smiled wanly at the faces turned unenthusiastically my way.

My back was now to the door and any exit would involve presenting my soiled rear view to Gordon for at least ten seconds. Not the way to inspire confidence in a client.

For once Gordon's mercurial nature, which was the bane of my professional existence, worked in my favour. Within minutes of greeting me, he spotted someone he knew across the room and disappeared. Pointedly ignored by his previous companions, I took the opportunity to bolt for the door, thrusting my glass at the same waiter who had served me.

I tried not to run as I headed for the side street where I'd left the car. As I turned off Brunswick Street I stopped and swivelled my skirt around. The woman at the exhibition hadn't been joking. It was truly disgusting. I reached out to touch the raised mess, but pulled back at the last minute.

Suddenly I felt tired. At least I couldn't humiliate myself publicly if I was at home with Jack.

I couldn't even summon the energy to turn the car radio on and stared glumly at the road as I drove. Patrick wouldn't be thrilled to see me back so early, but sitting in the car at the front of the house until ten o'clock seemed a bit sad, even for me.

A crowd of merry cinema-goers was streaming out of the local theatre as I drove past. On impulse, I pulled over. I had to make the most of my night off. A movie – that was the answer. Something mindless, something totally lacking in credibility, something fabulous.

I looked at the screening times and saw that the latest James

Bond movie was starting shortly. Perfect. And as if I needed another excuse, it looked as though I'd have time for a glass of wine in the street-front bar before the movie started.

I twisted my skirt around so that it wouldn't dirty the seat and sat down. Intent on the wine list, I didn't notice the figure standing beside me until he spoke.

'You look like you're enjoying yourself.'

'Tony! Hi.' I felt a strange sensation in my stomach, as though I'd just driven over a speedbump too quickly.

'What are you up to?'

'Patrick kicked me out of the house and told me to come home after I'd had some fun. I'm waiting to see the James Bond movie – I figure two hours of gratuitous sex and violence should do the trick.'

As I spoke I looked behind him, half expecting to see a gorgeous redhead tapping her kitten heels. But he seemed to be alone.

'Do you want to sit down?'

'I'd better get going.'

We spoke at the same time and then smiled awkwardly at each other.

I broke the silence first, regretting my invitation. 'I was just going to ask if you'd like a drink, but if you have to get going, that's fine.'

'Yes . . . I mean . . . no, I'm not in rush. What time does your movie start?'

I looked at my watch. 'In fifteen minutes.'

'Okay, I'll grab a drink from the bar. Do you want anything?'

I put in an order for a glass of wine. While he was gone, I glanced down at my lap. Of course the gum was still there in all its sticky glory. I looked quickly at my reflection in the window.

'I didn't think James Bond would be your scene,' Tony said with a smile as he returned from the bar and sat down opposite me. 'I thought you were into movies with meaning.'

He was clearly winding me up and I decided to come clean.

'Oh all right.' I took a sip of wine. 'I am actually the Queen of Hollywood Trash. I have absolutely no idea what that movie you and I saw was about. Not the foggiest idea. Are you happy now?'

He nodded, smiling. 'Very.'

'What about you?' I demanded. 'Did you understand it?'

'Nope.' He didn't seem the least bothered about admitting it and I vowed to be honest about my opinions in the future.

'Why didn't you tell me?'

'I wasn't sure whether you were pretending, or if you really liked it.'

'Well, at least James Bond shouldn't be too taxing. You can usually spot the bad guys because they die.'

Tony laughed. 'Ah, except for the women. You can survive a lot longer in a Bond movie if you're beautiful.'

'Good point,' I acknowledged with a grin. 'So what are you up to? Are you on your way out?'

'No, I'm heading home,' he answered. 'I met a friend for a drink in a bar over the road and was on my way home when I saw you in here. So I thought I'd stop and say hello.'

'I'm glad you did. People would talk if I started drinking alone.' I decided to ignore the fact that I'd already been doing a fair bit of that in private, which was probably even worse.

He smiled. 'So is Patrick looking after Jack?'

I nodded. 'I won a bet,' I boasted, forgetting for a moment that I was no longer ten years old.

'Really?' he asked, interested. 'What was the bet about?'

Telling him I'd picked up my ex-boyfriend was clearly not an option. 'Um . . . I walked down to the local shop wearing my great-grandmother's wedding dress.'

The dare was one I had won, but it had happened twenty years ago. I had a nasty feeling I'd only fit one leg in the dress these days.

Fantastic! Now Tony would think I was some kind of marriage-obsessed woman with no respect for her forebears. But he laughed and I dared to look up from the tabletop.

'So did you win only one night out for your efforts?'

'No, three . . .' I broke off before telling him this was the second night and rushed on. 'I actually started off at an art gallery up on Brunswick Street. Tonight's the opening of a local artist's exhibition and I stopped in to have a look.'

'Sounds good.'

About to lie and gush about how fabulous it was, I stopped. 'Actually, it was deadly dull. The paintings looked like Jack's highlighter pen efforts on the sofa. And just as I was about to leave, I ran into a client whose case I think I'm about to lose.'

'Hence the James Bond movie?'

'Exactly – I should have just come here in the first place. Great news about the cooking show,' I said, changing the subject. 'Patrick can't believe his luck.'

Tony nodded. 'Yeah, Patrick and David both come across really well on film and the management committee seem keen. At least we've got the go-ahead to do the first series. After that, who knows?'

'So is the new job working out?'

'Yeah – it's great. The only problem now is that I'm competing with everyone else. TV53 was crappy but I was practically in charge. Now I'm just one of the troops again and I need to work out a way to make my mark.'

'Is there a rush, though? Now that you're in, can't you just take it slowly?'

'I'm about five years behind everyone else because it took me so long to get started. I have to make things happen now.'

There it was again. That burning ambition. Reluctantly, I glanced at my watch, wishing I hadn't mentioned the movie. What I really wanted was to stay here, talking with Tony and hopefully having several too many drinks.

'Well, I'd better go. Can't keep James waiting.' I was conscious of the gum on my skirt and was hoping I could work out a way to leave after Tony did.

'Actually . . .' It was Tony's turn to seem awkward. 'Would you mind if I came with you? I've been wanting to see this one for ages.'

'Then why on earth did we see that terrible thing the other week?' I laughed.

'Well I wanted to see that one too – and thought it would impress you more than taking you to see something like this.'

I tried to hide my surprise at this admission. Instead I delivered what I hoped was an enigmatic smile, unable to quite believe how much my night had improved in the last half hour.

I decided that Tony was the type of guy who might let me go through a door first – a chivalrous act that would be a disaster in my current chewing-gum-soiled state. Feeling rather strange, I left my skirt back to front and managed to hold my bag over the mess as we walked the short distance to the cinema.

We settled into our seats just as the lights went down.

As the opening credits rolled, I felt Tony touch my hand. 'I'm glad I ran into you tonight,' he said quietly.

I was grateful for the darkness, which hid my face. 'Me too,' I whispered back.

The movie was mind-blowingly predictable and sexist – the perfect choice considering I was only giving it about five per cent of my concentration. Although we hadn't spoken again, I was very conscious of the weight of Tony's arm against mine. I had a fleeting moment of guilt when I thought about Grant, but squashed it quickly by conjuring a mental image of him and the blonde – who by now made Christy Turlington look ordinary – lying naked on a bearskin rug in a snow-covered European chalet.

In any case I had nothing to feel guilty about – yet. I felt the small quiver of excitement in my stomach grow as I tried again to follow the not-exactly-complicated plot.

When the final credits started to roll, I looked sideways at Tony.

'So was that an improvement on the last one?' he asked.

Even though I was going with honesty these days, I simply couldn't tell him that I was a bit confused about what the bad guys had been trying to achieve.

'Much better,' I hedged. 'Did you like it?'

'I did actually. I counted eight explosions and four totally implausible stunts. A perfect night at the movies.' He tactfully didn't mention the three stunning women who had appeared in various stages of undress.

We filed out of the cinema and paused outside. I knew this was nothing more than a casual encounter but I was still reluctant for it to end.

'Do you have your car?' I asked.

'No, I'll just walk home.'

'Well, if my car will start I'm happy to drop you off.'

'I'm the gambling type.' He grinned. 'Let's go.'

TWENTY-SIX

Miraculously the car started first go, and Tony directed me the short distance to his flat.

He turned to me. 'Thanks for the movie – and the lift.'

I smiled. 'My pleasure.'

Tony cleared his throat. 'I know it's late, but would you like to come in for a drink?'

I hadn't wanted the night to end but neither had I been quite prepared for this. I thought of Jack and hesitated.

'Umm . . . Thanks, but I really need to get h–'

To my great surprise, he leaned over and touched my lips with his own, cutting off my words.

'Will it really matter that much if you are home a little late?' he asked.

Maybe it was the remaining adrenaline from the James Bond movie, or maybe it was the memory of the gorgeous nuclear physicist who managed to sleep with every man she met and still maintain her professional integrity. In any event, something made me shake my head.

'I guess not.'

'Stay there,' he commanded. He climbed out of the car and walked around to open my door. Feeling faintly foolish, I stepped out, surreptitiously swivelling my gum-laden skirt back to its normal position.

'Thanks.'

'My pleasure,' he said, smiling.

Tony unlocked the security door, letting us both into the dimly lit foyer. The lift doors opened as soon as he pressed the button and we stepped inside. Although we didn't speak, he took my hand and his palm felt warm against mine.

When we reached his apartment, Tony turned the key in the lock and pushed the door open, releasing my hand as he did so. He flicked on the lights. I followed him into the living room, which had white walls and stark black furniture upholstered in suede. My first thought was of the devastation Jack could cause here in less time than it took for Tony to throw his keys on the table.

I caught myself. This was my time off. Right now I had enough to worry about; I didn't need to add what Jack would do here to the list.

'So – this is home.' Brilliant comment, I thought.

'Come and I'll show you around. As you can see, the kitchen is here.' He gestured towards the chrome bench, which was all that separated the kitchen from the living room. 'The spare bedroom is in there.' He threw open a door leading off to the left and I saw a flash of colour. 'And mine is over here.' He strode across the living room and slid back a door, which opened onto a bedroom that was even more stylish than the lounge.

The dark timber of the built-in cupboards matched the bedside tables, and the soft-looking throw on the perfectly made bed completed the picture.

Tony's apartment was about as different from my house as it was possible to be.

I had a vision of how my bedroom had looked before I'd left and for a moment I forgot my nerves. 'Please tell me you don't always live like this?' I'd tried to keep my voice casual, but even I could hear the note of desperation.

Tony laughed. 'Well actually, the cleaner did come today – trust me, I hardly ever make the bed.'

Given the decor, I found that very hard to believe, but decided the less said the better.

'Can I get you a drink?'

Tony closed the bedroom door behind us and we moved back into the lounge. He dimmed the lights, then stepped behind the kitchen bench and opened the fridge door.

'A glass of wine would be great, thanks.'

Pulling out an open bottle of wine, he poured two generous glasses.

'Take a seat.' Tony opened some cabinet doors to reveal the stereo.

As strains of Massive Attack floated through the room, I pondered whether I should choose the single armchair or the couch and downed half the wine trying to decide.

Although it seemed pretty clear that Tony was interested, I certainly wasn't comfortable enough with him to sprawl across the couch. But then if I sat in the armchair, surely I was sending out a message that I wasn't keen?

Taking the coward's way out, I chose the armchair, but just as my rear connected with the suede, I remembered the gum. Instantly I sprang up. But it now seemed to have reached its maximum elasticity and stretched from my skirt to the chair.

At the same instant Tony turned back towards me.

Not seeming to notice my dilemma, he came over to stand beside me. His glass made a hollow knocking sound on the coffee table as he put it down. He leaned over and kissed me on the lips, one hand behind my head.

I was still traumatised by the gum situation and the kiss caught me off guard, but after a moment I relaxed and began to enjoy it. It felt like a lifetime since I'd been kissed properly and I'd forgotten how good it felt.

Pulling back, he looked at me. 'I've been wanting to do that all night. Do you mind if I do it again?' His voice was low as he whispered in my ear.

'Um . . .' My hesitation broke the spell and I knew I had to come clean.

Tony looked hurt. 'Is there something wrong?'

'No . . . Well actually . . .' Not looking at him, I pointed at the gum behind me.

I was willing to bet Nicole Kidman had never found herself in this situation.

He burst out laughing. 'Is that all? I can fix that.'

I gasped as I felt the zip on the back of my skirt slide downwards.

His hands ran over my hips, taking the skirt with them. I tried frantically to remember what my underwear looked like and relaxed when I remembered I was wearing one of my few matching sets. Sure, they weren't exactly black lacy wisps of nothing, but it could have been a lot worse.

He tugged at my waist and I stepped towards him. As I did, my shoe tangled in the top of my skirt, which the gum had suspended off the ground. Tripping, I landed with my full weight on Tony's chest. He staggered backwards, only just stopping himself from falling. I looked up at him and had a sudden vision of the way we'd met. At least he could never claim that I'd pretended to be in any way coordinated.

'Sorry,' I managed weakly.

'Maybe it would be safer if we sat down,' Tony suggested, pulling me with him onto the couch.

Kissing me again, he gently pushed me backwards until I felt the soft suede under my head.

His hands and body felt wonderful. As Maggie would say, it had been a long time between drinks.

Tony pulled at the top of my shirt, expecting the button to give. Which it would have had it been a button rather than a row of twenty couplets. After tugging fruitlessly for a few seconds he pulled back and looked down.

'You've got to be kidding,' he exclaimed as he saw the task at hand. 'I only mastered bra clasps a few years ago. What on earth is this?'

I laughed and Tony smiled, eyes focused on my shirt. I certainly hadn't considered its ease of removal when I'd dressed.

I moved to help him but he brushed my hand away. 'It's all right – I think I have it worked out.'

Quickly he made his way down my shirt front, rapidly flicking the couplets open with his thumb and forefinger.

'Actually, I like it. Particularly what's underneath,' he added as he slid his hand under my open shirt.

He slowly touched my breasts, finally reaching around my back and unclipping my bra.

'Ah – very masterful,' I managed, pleased to hear what sounded like a reasonably normal-sounding voice coming out of my very not-normal-feeling body.

He pulled my shirt off and dropped it on the floor. My bra followed seconds later.

'Ah, no,' I said as he went to push me down again. 'For every piece of clothing I lose, you lose one too.'

His eyes flicked to the pile on the floor.

'Yes,' I clarified. 'That means three.'

'Uh-uh. The skirt was an emergency – it doesn't count.'

Considering it a small price to pay for ruining his chair, I let the issue pass. I shuffled forwards, undid the buttons on his shirt and pushed it back off his shoulders.

Men's upper bodies had always been one of my weaknesses. And despite a long scar running over his left shoulder, Tony's was definitely one to be weak about. His collarbone led straight to nicely squared shoulders, which joined a pair of biceps bulging out at very pleasing angles.

'That's one,' I announced, depositing his shirt on the floor and fumbling with his belt buckle. I tugged the belt out of his trousers and Tony took it from me.

'That would be two,' he announced as he flicked it behind me. 'My turn.'

'Okay,' I laughed, and my knickers joined my bra in seconds.

Up until then, it had seemed like a game, but I realised it was way too late to back out now. Tony's hands ran over my stomach and my hips and I was suddenly certain that I didn't want to back out anyway.

'Roll over,' he whispered, and he lazily massaged my neck and shoulders as if he had all the time in the world.

I couldn't remember when I'd last enjoyed being touched this much and dimly wondered where he'd learned his technique.

And then, as his mouth joined his hands, I stopped thinking completely and gave myself up to enjoying being with him.

I woke with a jolt in Tony's bed with no idea of the time. Tony's body was curled up behind mine and for a moment I closed my eyes and just enjoyed being next to him. We'd ended up in his bed at some point and I must have drifted off.

I was relieved to see that the sky outside the windows was still dark. I hated the thought of Jack waking up and coming into my room to discover I wasn't there and I knew I needed to get home. But I lay still for a moment. It felt so good to be here like this.

Finally I rolled over as gently as I could. The dim light was still on in the lounge and I watched Tony's face as I touched him.

'I have to go,' I whispered.

He stirred and opened his eyes. 'I know. I wish you didn't.'

'Me too.' Reluctantly I pulled myself away and sat up.

'Julia?' Tony's hand was on my back. 'Lie down again for a minute.'

I knew what that meant. I was sorely tempted but shook my head. 'I'd love to, but Jack . . .'

He interrupted. 'No, I . . . I just want to tell you something – please.'

I lay back down, not sure what was coming.

'I don't know if this is the right time – I just wanted you to know I'm divorced.'

Right. Baggage. Big time.

I was still trying to think of an appropriate response when Tony spoke again. 'We didn't have any kids and we've been divorced for nearly a year, but . . .' He sounded as though he regretted bringing it up. 'It makes a difference to some people.'

I thought about it for a minute. Did it make a difference to me?

Actually I thought maybe it did. He'd loved someone so much he'd asked her to marry him. He'd got dressed up and looked into her eyes and promised to be with her forever. I knew I was a hopeless romantic, but did that mean he could never be completely in love again?

'Were you together long?' I asked.

'I guess – Joanne and I met soon after I stopped playing golf and got married after a couple of years. It was all great while the money was coming in from the restaurant stuff and there was lots going on. But when I started the film course things started going downhill and got gradually worse. I'm still not quite sure what happened. It just seemed like we ran out of things to say to each other.'

'Oh.'

There was a moment of silence.

'Look, I don't want to bore you with it. I just wanted you to know.'

'Okay, thanks.'

Unsure of the protocol in this type of situation, I sat up again and tried to remember where my clothes had ended up. Naked, I headed out to the lounge room and dressed as quickly as twenty clasps would allow. Still unsure what to say, I returned to the bedroom and sat on the edge of the bed.

'I'll talk to you soon,' he promised.

I couldn't prevent the small fizz of happiness I felt at his words.

'I'd like that,' I replied, not sure whether I meant it. I stood and paused awkwardly. 'Well, cheerio.' The words were out of my mouth before I realised what I'd said, and sure that any attempt to improve on them would only make things worse, I gave a small wave and left.

'Cheerio?' I mouthed to myself as I headed for the front door. Where in God's name had that come from?

TWENTY-SEVEN

'Oh my God, look over there,' I said as I spotted a swimming legend who'd won five gold medals at the last Olympics.

'And isn't that Brad Hastings?' I asked as a well-known newsreader walked past.

'Julia, please be cool,' Patrick pleaded. 'I have to work with these people.'

He was joking, but only just. While I was here strictly as a tourist, Patrick needed to impress these people. Some of them at least.

He had arrived home yesterday, after a meeting at the television station, with an envelope addressed to me. Inside was a ticket to a party celebrating the station's forty-fifth anniversary and a note that said, *Love to see you there! Tony.*

I didn't know whether to be pleased or offended, considering his lack of contact since Monday night.

I'd spent Tuesday unable to decide if I regretted my wanton behaviour and trying to figure out exactly how I felt about being involved with a divorced man.

My mobile rang repeatedly during the morning, but none of the calls were from Tony. Maggie's advice had been not to wait, but to call him myself – advice that I knew was sensible but that I couldn't quite follow. Finally, at almost four, his number had flashed up on the screen. But in a sudden attack of cowardice, and with Jack looking at me like I was mad, I'd watched the phone ring without answering it.

No matter how many times I played the message Tony left, it never got more romantic. 'Hi Julia. It's Tony . . . I . . . um, I guess I missed you. Talk to you soon . . . Bye.'

Since then there'd been nothing. At least now I knew I wasn't inventing something that didn't exist. We'd had what I, at least, had thought was fabulous sex and he'd left one message. This wasn't exactly the stuff of one of Tanya's novels. I'd even called my own mobile to make sure it was working properly. It was.

'Well, that's just wonderful,' Maggie said when I played the message for her on Wednesday night. 'Not exactly a man of many words, is he? But the party sounds good – you need to go, look stunningly gorgeous and totally ignore him.'

We decided on a dark blue Lisa Ho dress I'd bought on sale several years earlier, although I had my doubts that it would be good enough to make the transformation Maggie had in mind.

Next we called Tanya and put her on speaker phone.

'Well, as an erotic fiction writer, I feel obliged to ask the next question. Was the sex good?'

I blushed. 'Um – yeah, I guess.'

'Okay, on a scale of one to ten, what would it be?'

'C'mon Tanya . . .' There was a silence on the other end of the line. Maggie was regarding me seriously.

'All right then . . . if you must know, it was about a seven.'

'Oooh!' Maggie's eyebrows were suddenly raised. 'Seven's good for the first time – very good.'

'Yeah, but what about the ex-wife?'

'Well, it is a bit of an issue,' Maggie agreed. 'I wish I hadn't been quite so accurate about his having baggage.'

'Yeah, but hang on,' Tanya's staticky voice came down the line. 'Who doesn't have a past by the time they're our age? Julia, you've got Michael. Maggie, you have Marcus, although admittedly he may no longer be a past. But anyway, my point is that at this age just about everyone has someone they really cared about in their history. Whether or not you signed a piece of paper is a bit of a technicality, isn't it?'

Tanya's words lifted my spirits. 'I guess you're right. I loved Michael, but that wouldn't stop me loving someone else. Tony really does seem different, you know – he's just . . . I don't know . . . caring.'

'Yeah, well, I'm not sure that caring is one phone message in three days,' Maggie supplied.

'No, you're right,' I agreed. 'But maybe the ex-wife is part of that. I can kind of understand him not wanting to jump back into a relationship after having been through a divorce.' This wasn't a new thought. I'd spent a lot of time dwelling on it over the last few days.

'Yeah, it could be. But if he doesn't want to get involved, why did he invite you home the other night?'

Maggie had a point. I wasn't exactly a candidate for a no-strings fling.

'So do you think I shouldn't go?'

'No!' Tanya yelped from the phone. 'She doesn't mean that. Just don't get hurt – that's all we're saying.'

I arrived home at six-thirty the next evening, having arranged for Carla to put Jack to bed at her place. Carla had offered to have him on his first sleepover, but I'd decided he was still better off waking up in his own bed in the morning. Instead, I planned to pick him up on my way home in a taxi.

Feeling unaccountably liberated at the absence of his normal bedtime rituals, I poured myself a glass of wine and showered quickly.

The party was in one of the tall office buildings in the middle of town. A large part of one floor had been taken over for the event and all the fittings stripped out. Everything was white, from the floor and walls, to the waiters' uniforms and their trays. I was used to functions where you almost had to put a waiter in a headlock in order to grab a warm glass of bad wine. Here I had people offering me lychee martinis and white cocktails whenever I glanced around.

When I finished my first drink, a new one was in my hand within seconds. I told myself to slow down. Gordon's court case was tomorrow and I was nervous enough about it as it was – I didn't need to add a hangover to my problems.

'C'mon Patrick.' His discomfort at my being so uncool as to star-spot was rather touching really. 'You have to loosen up. This is a party. You're supposed to have fun. These are media types – they'll think you're a nerd if you're uptight.'

'You're right – I need to relax.'

He looked so uncomfortable trying to appear at ease that I laughed. 'Just finish your drink and have a look around. I didn't realise that people lived like this.'

'It's not like it happens every week. This is an important –'

Patrick's words stopped abruptly and I looked over at him. He was staring at the other side of the room with a look of horror on his face.

'No! No! Goddamn it, not here!'

I followed his gaze but could only see a crowd of people. 'What's wrong?'

'It's Jennifer. She's over there.' He gestured wildly.

'Jennifer . . .'

'Jennifer – bloody Jennifer. Jennifer-who-ruined-my-life Jennifer!' He looked around desperately for a means of escape but it was too late.

This was not good.

'She's on her way over. She must have spotted me as soon as we got here – maybe even before! Surely she's not going to destroy this for me too.'

I felt a chill of apprehension as I watched the ring of people around us. From what I'd heard, this was one scary lady.

A woman slipped between two groups and stood in front of us. Despite the fact that Patrick had described her as being of normal height with brownish hair, I had always pictured Jennifer as looking something like Zena the Warrior Princess.

The woman standing in front of us did in fact look fairly

normal, if a little on the glamorous side. She was about five foot four with sleek, dead-straight black hair that stretched halfway down her back. She was one of the few women in the room wearing trousers, but they were so obviously well cut and expensive, she didn't look out of place. 'Patrick. How are you?'

'Hello Jennifer. I'm fine thanks.' Patrick had pulled himself together and looked surprisingly calm, although I could see his hands clenched behind his back.

Jennifer turned and shot me a look of pure contempt.

'Um – this is my sister Julia.'

At that she managed a chilly smile before turning her attention back to Patrick. Obviously the fact that I wasn't Patrick's girlfriend raised my popularity slightly.

'I've heard about your show.' The words seemed to hang in the air. Although I knew no one else was taking the slightest notice, I imagined the people around us holding their breath. 'My partner is in the industry.'

I willed Patrick to be silent, but he couldn't help himself. 'You mean your husband has changed j–'

She gave him a pitying look and shook her head. Clearly this was a new partner – the husband was history.

'Congratulations,' she continued. 'You look like you've landed on your feet.'

I wondered what was going to come next. Even if she did think he'd treated her badly, having him sacked had to be quite enough payback. Surely she wouldn't try to ruin this for him too.

'Thanks.' Patrick was obviously hoping the same thing.

'You were a lousy accountant. But it looks like you might have found what you are good at – so maybe it was all for the best.' She let out a tinkling laugh. 'So, if you ever need any accounting help, just give me a call.'

I felt as though I'd wandered into a scene from *Days of Our Lives*. This woman had done just about everything in her power to ruin Patrick's career and here she was acting as though she'd done him a favour.

She leaned in and kissed him on the cheek and then swivelled back the way she had come, but not before she had slipped a business card into his hand.

I resisted, but only just, the temptation to ankle tap her.

Patrick blinked, looking down at the card. 'Is that it?'

'I think so,' I breathed. 'Did she just hit on you again?'

'Um. Well I don't think she really wants me to call her for accounting advice,' Patrick answered. 'She's not bad looking, is she?'

'Patrick! The woman ruined your career. She's a monster.'

'You're right.' He didn't sound convinced.

'I think one drastic career change a year might be enough. If you go near her again you could find yourself emptying bins at dawn.'

'All right, all right. But she did sound kind of keen, didn't she?'

'Who cares? She's a bunny boiler – leave her alone.'

He breathed out heavily. 'This calls for another drink.' As if he had read Patrick's mind, a nearby waiter headed towards us and handed him another martini.

I looked around in what I hoped was a casual manner. I knew absolutely no one. I took another big sip of my drink as I felt my earlier courage start to fade.

'Come on, Patrick. You must know someone we can chat to. If we stand here by ourselves much longer we're going to look like total outcasts.'

It was his turn to look around. 'Nope, not a soul. I'm not exactly a regular at station boardroom lunches, you know. My only chance is to recognise a cameraman or . . .' He paused as Tony walked in the door.

'Patrick,' I hissed, grabbing his arm. 'Turn around! It looks pathetic if we're standing here with smiles on our faces, just waiting for him.'

'What?' Patrick looked at me strangely. 'But we are. We don't know anyone else.'

It was at times like this that I realised women were wasting years of their lives trying to read intricate subtexts in the conversations of their menfolk.

'That is not the point, Patrick. Turn around.'

I grabbed his elbow with fingers of steel and pulled him towards me.

'This is great, Julia. Now he'll find someone else he knows and leave us stuck here by ourselves.'

'Julia, Patrick. Hi.'

I felt a touch on my arm and turned around just as Tony leaned in to kiss my cheek.

'Tony! Hi . . . Been here long?'

Over Tony's shoulder, I saw Patrick roll his eyes.

'No, I just got here. What a great party! They didn't exactly put this kind of show on at TV53.'

'Mmm, I know what you mean. My firm's idea of going wild and crazy is having a slide show at the annual dinner.'

Tony was treating me exactly the same way as he always had. So were we supposed to pretend that Monday night hadn't happened?

'Hi Patrick.' Tony turned towards him.

'How are you going?' They shook hands.

'Have you spoken to any of the guys from the program?'

'No . . . Can't actually spot anyone I've ever seen before.'

'Right. I'll get on the case.' And with a wave he was gone.

'Well he was a great help, wasn't he?' Patrick said glumly. 'This room is full of beautiful women and the only ones I manage to talk to are my sister and the woman who destroyed my career.'

As he spoke, a blonde girl in a backless white dress appeared at his side.

'Hi. I'm sorry if I'm interrupting anything.' She looked uncertainly at me before directing her gaze back at Patrick. 'I just wanted to say that I've seen your show and think you're great.'

'Really?' Patrick asked uncertainly. 'Are you sure you have the right person?'

'You're Patrick Butler, aren't you?'

'Yes! I mean yes . . .' He tried to adopt a nonchalant expression, but looked exactly as he used to before he opened his presents on Christmas morning.

If she noticed, the blonde didn't give any sign. 'I'm Audrey. I work in production.'

'It's lovely to meet you, Audrey. This is my sister Julia.' He said the word 'sister' so loudly that a couple of people in neighbouring groups turned their heads.

She smiled briefly. Casting me an apologetic look, Patrick turned his body towards her, leaving me standing by myself.

Right. What now?

Suddenly the night was looking a lot less fun.

This was ridiculous. Patrick aside, Tony was the only person I knew in this room and I'd had sex with him three nights ago. Surely I wasn't overstepping the mark by expecting a bit of small talk?

Before I could change my mind, I strode over to where I could see him talking to a circle of men. He smiled as I approached and I relaxed slightly.

'This is Julia Butler. Julia, this is . . .' He reeled off four names, none of which I even registered.

I smiled vaguely at them.

'Are you in television, Julia?' asked the man beside me, an overweight fellow with a receding hairline.

'Ah no. I'm a lawyer,' I replied. That reply was always a conversation stopper. 'I do a bit of entertainment law though,' I ventured, vaguely remembering writing the terms and conditions for a radio station car park years ago.

'Really?' Receding hairline looked slightly more interested.

Beside me, I saw Tony turn his head.

'There's Arnold,' he said. 'Would you all excuse me, I must have a word to him.'

And he was gone, leaving me alone with the four suits. Splendid. How on earth was I going to get myself out of this one? There wasn't even a bar I could pretend to go to.

After a few minutes of increasingly strained conversation I decided the only option was a trip to the toilet. Just as I was about to make my excuses and leave, the lights dimmed and the wall at the other end of the room was rolled back to reveal another huge room beyond.

It was the same size as the one we were standing in, but there the resemblance ended. The walls were bright yellow and the floor a brilliant blue.

If the last room's theme had been sophistication, this room was like a funfair. There were banks of clowns' heads moving left and right, waiting for punters to throw table-tennis balls at them. Several whippet-like girls were turning somersaults and doing other contortions that made me ache just looking at them. The waiters here were dressed in bright colours and circulating with trays of bizarrely coloured cocktails and tubs of popcorn.

Had this been where the evening started, everyone would have huddled in the corners. But the first few drinks had loosened the crowd up and the noise rose audibly as the party-goers moved into the second room.

It was then that the music struck me. 'Greensleeves' – played very tinnily and coming from somewhere at the back of the room.

I peered through the people in front of me, trying to spot the source. Obviously I was obsessed, I told myself sternly. I'd be dreaming the music soon.

The music stopped and the crowd parted to reveal a miniature ice-cream van. Standing in front of the van was Grant, handing soft serves to the queue that had already formed in front of him. A queue of women, I noticed immediately. Very skinny women who looked as though they hadn't had an ice-cream in the last twenty years.

I froze. What on earth was he doing here? There was no way this could be a coincidence. I tried to think logically. The only possible link between Grant and this event was Patrick. But surely Patrick would have told me if he'd known Grant would be here.

Grant was intent on handing a toppling ice-cream to a dark-haired glamour in three-inch heels. As he finished, he looked up and saw me. There was no mistaking the surprise on his face. He certainly hadn't expected to see me here.

He smiled and automatically I smiled back. Somehow I

managed to register that he didn't look tanned. Obviously he and the blonde had spent the whole time ignoring the beach or the ski slopes. A torrid sex life probably did that to you, I thought sourly.

I considered pointedly looking away and resuming an intense conversation with my companions. Except that I didn't have any companions. They'd obviously taken advantage of my lapse of concentration to slip away. Given that I was standing by myself, the only option seemed to be to head in Grant's direction.

I hovered uncertainly behind the queue, but Grant beckoned me forward. Reluctantly I walked up to him, feeling the daggers sink into my back.

'See, I knew you were lying when you said your job wasn't glamorous,' he smiled. 'A do like this is just hard work, I suppose?'

'Actually, my being here has nothing to do with work. Patrick is embarking on a television career. What about you? This is a long way from serving melting ice-creams to whinging kids.'

'You could say.' He couldn't help a look at his customers, whom he was still managing to serve while talking to me. 'Someone from the studio approached me in the park a couple of weeks ago. Offered me a ridiculous amount of money to do this. God, I would have done it for free!'

'Well at least you were back from your holiday in time,' I said coldly.

'Yeah, I arranged it like that,' he answered calmly.

'So how was it?'

'Oh. Fine thanks.'

Conversation suddenly dried up.

The queue was not happy. Its members were being served their ice-creams without any interaction from the ice-cream man himself and there was a growing murmur of disapproval.

'Well. I'll let you get back to your fans. I'll see you later.'

I turned around. To my great relief I spotted Patrick and Audrey deep in conversation off to one side of the room. Having Grant watch me look for someone to talk to would have taken my humiliation to new depths.

'Patrick!'

He jumped. 'God, Julia, loosen up, would you? This is a party.' I didn't find his parroting of my words from earlier even slightly amusing.

'Do you know who is over there?'

Patrick followed my eyes and spotted Grant.

'Oh.'

'So this is your doing?'

'No! Well kind of,' he conceded. 'Some of the guys from the show were on the committee that had to brief the party planners. They were talking about the fact that they couldn't find anyone to replace the dagwood dog vendor they had lined up for tonight – apparently he'd given food poisoning to everyone at a school rugby tournament the week before and lost his licence. I mentioned that you had picked up a good-looking ice-cream van guy a couple of weeks ago and they were interested. So I told them that he was at New Farm Park on Sunday afternoons. That was it. They must have followed up with him.'

'You picked up the guy who sells soft serves?' Audrey asked, clearly impressed.

'Thank you very much, Patrick,' I growled. 'Perhaps you could tell a few more people.'

'Julia.' I felt a hand on my shoulder.

'Having fun?' Tony asked.

'Yeah, it's fabulous.' I pasted a smile on my face.

'Well come over here with me. There's someone I'd like you to meet.'

This was more like it.

We joined another circle and Tony introduced me to a group of thirtysomething studio employees. They were interesting and friendly and didn't seem to hold my job against me. I chatted away happily, delighted to be talking to someone who was neither my brother, nor someone I'd recently had sex with.

One of the women asked how I knew Tony and I had the whole group in stitches recounting the gym incident. But when someone asked how long we'd been together, I stuttered and fudged an answer. Tony only smiled enigmatically.

The lights dimmed suddenly and the wall at the end of the room was removed. Even though people were half expecting it this time, a roar of approval rose from the crowd as it moved forwards.

Fire-engine red walls contrasted with a black floor and the room was lit only by spotlights. Two platforms were suspended high on the longest wall and on each, a man and a woman danced wildly to the music, which had abruptly switched to a techno beat. Here the staff were dressed in black leather and carried trays laden with shot glasses. The noise level rose dramatically as people responded to the atmosphere, loosening ties and throwing back drinks.

All except Tony, that was. I watched as he calmly looked around the room, spotted a man several metres away and moved towards him. They shook hands and struck up a conversation. Watching him only made me feel tired. I had probably been that ambitious once, but it seemed a long time ago. His determination to make it as a producer reminded me of some of the people I had worked with. It was almost as though nothing was more important than career success – not even love or family.

Maybe I could just use him for sex, I thought hopefully. Regretfully I abandoned that option. If I had any doubt as to whether I was cut out for that kind of behaviour, the 'cheerio' line should have cleared that up.

Why did it always go like this? Ten days ago I was juggling two fabulous men. Now one of them was with an up-and-coming supermodel and the other was making it pretty clear that he was much more interested in pursuing his career than pursuing me.

Tony looked over at me and smiled. I smiled in reply and grabbed a shot from a passing waiter. The sambucca burned my throat as it went down and my eyes pricked.

I sneaked a look at my watch. Eleven o'clock. Despite the fabulous surroundings and beautiful people, I wasn't actually having any fun.

I walked over to Tony and touched his arm. 'I'm heading off.'

'Really? Aren't you having a good time?'

I looked around. 'Not really. The party is pretty amazing, but I don't know anyone and I'm not really one of life's networkers.'

Tony's face changed slightly at the obvious edge to my voice.

'I get so little time to myself these days. To be honest I don't feel like wasting it doing something I'm not really enjoying.'

It seemed like a very long time since the night I'd tried to convince Tony I was an art-house movie buff. Honesty was incredibly liberating.

Tony turned as someone beckoned to him from another group. He'd only been in the job two weeks but seemed to know more people at this party than I'd met in the last ten years. He was obviously doing something right.

He waved at them and turned back to me. 'Okay. I'll give you a call.'

Suddenly I'd had enough. I was over waiting for calls that didn't come. I was tired of flip-flopping between elation when he gave me some kind of signal that he was interested and disappointment when he didn't call.

'Actually, don't worry. I know we're not twenty any more and we've all got baggage of one sort or another by now.' I figured Tanya wouldn't mind if I borrowed a line from her speech. 'Hell, my baggage has a vegetable phobia and sleeps with a toad.'

I'd gone too far to stop now. 'But you're looking to prove something to the world and I don't think having me and Jack around is going to help. So why don't we just give it a miss?'

I'd thought I'd be making things easy for him, that he'd be delighted that he didn't have to make the break. Instead, I was surprised by the look of hurt that spread across his face.

'Sure.' He looked down at his hands briefly. 'If that's what you want, that's fine. I guess I'll see you around then.'

'Yeah, well you'll probably see me at my place when the next episode is filmed.' As I said the words I vowed not to be there, even if it meant a whole afternoon chasing earth-moving equipment in New Farm.

'Of course.' The person in the other group called Tony again. 'Have a good night.' Tony was moving away even as he spoke.

I gave him a half-wave and turned around, trying to look as though I broke up with guys at fabulous parties all the time.

Concentrating on not tripping over in my heels, I tried to ignore the disappointment that squeezed my chest. Now that I knew it was over, I finally admitted to myself that I'd hoped what Tony and I had could have become something special.

Clearly not.

I headed towards what I thought was a door, only to discover it was a prop. I couldn't face retracing my steps past Tony, so I squeezed past the cardboard wall, deciding to wander back through the earlier party rooms.

Stepping out of the red nightclub, I hit the funfair, which was now in the process of being dismantled. The fluorescent lights were on, and with half the decorations already down, it had lost its magic.

Grant was in a corner, packing things into boxes. I thought about putting my back to the wall and creeping quietly towards the doorway. Instead I walked over to him.

He looked up as I approached. 'Hi there. How's the party?'

'It's pretty cool – they've done a great job.'

'Sounds like the equivalent of "she has a nice personality".'

I smiled. 'I didn't know anyone except for Patrick and one other guy. I'm not really in the mood.' Without giving myself the chance to change my mind, I spoke again. 'Listen, I know the truth about your holiday. Why didn't you tell me?'

His face flushed red. 'I wanted to tell you but couldn't bring myself to. I don't know, it's not the kind of thing you want to talk about to someone you've been seeing.'

'No, I can imagine that,' I answered dryly. 'So was it good?'

'Good? Well yeah, I guess so.'

'That's marvellous,' I answered, my voice dripping with sarcasm.

If he noticed, he didn't give any sign. 'Do you want to have a look?' he asked.

I stared at him incredulously. What was wrong with this guy? He took off for a romantic holiday with another woman and then wanted to show me how fabulous it had been. What did he think I wanted to see – holiday snaps?

Leaning down, he gingerly pulled up the leg of one of his trousers.

'See, beautiful job. I should be back in bikinis in a fortnight.'

'What?'

'My varicose veins – all gone. Can't say the process was a bundle of fun though.'

It was slowly dawning on me. 'So that's what you were doing? Having an operation?'

He looked at me strangely. 'Yeah. I thought you said you knew.'

I couldn't believe it. He wasn't hiding some rendezvous with a supermodel. He'd just been too embarrassed to tell me about his operation.

'What did you think I was doing?' he asked quizzically.

I couldn't see a way to avoid telling him the truth. 'Well, I saw you with your arm around a blonde girl at the park. And you didn't seem to want to tell me about your holiday and – well . . .' I broke off. For some reason I couldn't quite remember the perfectly logical train of thought that had led me to the conclusion he was off cruising the Greek Islands with her. 'Well, I decided that you were off having a romantic holiday,' I finished lamely, feeling like a total idiot.

'With my sister?' he asked with a smile.

'Your sister is nine years old!'

He raised his eyebrows.

'Was nine years old, fifteen years ago . . .' I trailed off.

'Mmm. She's actually a very grown-up twenty-four now and her husband of not even six months has decided being married is not his cup of tea.'

'Right.'

None of Grant's boxes looked big enough to hide in, so I had no choice but to stand there looking at him.

He laughed. 'Julia. I'm not seeing anyone else.'

'Okay.' Although Grant was being very understanding, I still felt pathetic. It was definitely time to end this night. Tomorrow had to be a better day.

'Right – well now we've cleared that up, I'm going to get going.'

'How about I do you a deal?' he asked. 'If you help me carry these boxes outside, I'll give you a lift home.'

I looked down at my shoes doubtfully. He sighed and, bending down, picked up a container about the size of a large book.

'Think you can manage this?'

I nodded. 'Um, if I carried two of them, do you think we could stop off to pick Jack up on the way?'

He laughed and muttered under his breath, 'Give them an inch . . .'

The underground parking lot was deserted. We loaded the equipment into the ice-cream van and ten minutes later I opened Carla's back door with the key she'd left outside.

Carla was asleep on the sofa bed in the back room, an equally sound asleep Jack lying beside her.

Quietly I lifted Jack, inhaling his warm smell as he clung to me without waking. He felt like a huge trusting puppy and I kissed his head. Even though he would be awake in less than six hours, I was glad he was coming home with me.

Opening her eyes, Carla smiled and waved us out.

With some difficulty, I strapped Jack into the seat belt between Grant and I, his head resting in my lap. He was still fast asleep when we got home and I carried him upstairs and deposited him in his cot. He rolled over and a shaft of light fell across the side of his face. I smoothed his hair back gently from his face. Had it really only been five weeks since he'd arrived? In that time I'd been sleep deprived, publicly humiliated and lost my chance at partnership. But if someone tried to take him away from me now, I'd fight them to my last breath.

I thought of Anita. The familiar sadness stole over me, but for once I didn't feel guilty or panicked at the thought of the responsibility she'd left me.

We'd manage.

'Goodnight Jack,' I whispered.

At the sight of Grant standing in the lounge room, I felt unaccountably nervous. 'Fancy a glass of wine?' I asked.

He nodded, just as the latch on the front gate clicked.

Surely Patrick couldn't have convinced Audrey to come home with him this early? That would be too quick, even for an up-and-coming superstar.

There were footsteps on the wooden steps at the front and then a knock on the door. It wasn't Patrick then – he'd use his key.

Grant looked at me. 'Expecting anyone?'

I shook my head.

'Julia? It's Tony.'

His voice floated through the window beside the door and I was momentarily paralysed.

This couldn't be happening.

Pulling myself together, I walked to the door and opened it.

'I know it's late,' Tony said by way of greeting. 'But I'm not going to let you end it like that.'

He stepped onto the landing and, catching sight of Grant, stopped dead.

I had a sudden vision of how this must look. It was almost midnight, less than an hour after I'd left Tony, and I had a strange man in my house.

'I – um. This is Grant. He's . . .'

'Forget it,' Tony said. He turned on his heel and ran down the stairs without a backward glance.

Should I have told Tony and Grant about each other? I'd been trying to figure out if there was anything going on between myself and either of them, so saying anything would have looked like ridiculous overkill. Now, though, I wished I had.

Grant raised his eyebrows in question when I looked around at him.

'Sorry – this must look bad. I've seen Tony a few times, but I told him tonight that I didn't think it would work. It was such a low-key thing, I didn't think it was worth mentioning. But maybe I should have, I'm –'

Grant interrupted. 'It's all right. Relax. You don't owe me any explanations.'

'Really? Okay – great. Well, I'll get that wine.'

Grant followed me into the kitchen. I reached into the overhead cabinet for wine glasses and as I put them on the bench, I felt his eyes on me. Stepping closer, he lowered his face to mine and kissed me softly and then again, more insistently.

As he did, I felt a wave of warmth for him – but nothing more. It was a lovely kiss and it brought back some old memories. But there was no rush of feeling like I felt with Tony.

Goddammit. What was wrong with me? Grant was great looking and fun to be around. So why wasn't my heart beating any faster? For some reason the spark we used to have between us was gone – and as much as I wanted to tell myself it didn't matter, it did.

As gently as I could, I pushed against his chest. Grant straightened and looked at me.

'You want to know something?' He spoke in a gentle voice. I nodded, although I wasn't sure I did.

'I have the feeling you're going to break my heart again.'

In that moment I would have loved to be able to tell him he was wrong and to ask him to stay with me forever. Maybe I had some deep-seated problem with commitment which drove me to screw things up whenever I was close to someone. Was I going to spend the rest of my life turning away good men and pining over others it could never possibly work with? In any event Grant didn't deserve to be part of my problems. The very least I owed him was to be honest.

'I'm sorry – it's not you. I just . . .' I didn't know how to explain how I felt and trailed off.

'It's not quite right, is it?'

After a second's hesitation I shook my head.

He smiled sadly. 'You know, maybe the problem is that we have too much terrible eighties history together. I mean, I can remember you wearing blue legwarmers and earrings shaped like a fried egg in a pan. Damage like that can take a lifetime to heal.'

I laughed. 'Listen, Mister Skinny White Leather Tie, I don't think you're exactly innocent in the fashion crimes department.'

'What about that denim outfit with about two hundred white lace frills?'

I threw up my hands in mock surrender. 'Okay – you win. I don't want to hear any more.'

We smiled at each other and there didn't seem to be a lot more to say.

He broke the silence. 'You know, I think I might pass on that wine. It's getting late.'

'Grant . . . I'm really sorry.'

He gently touched my hair. 'So am I.'

As I shut the door behind him, I made a mental note to check my horoscope in the morning. Two men gone in one night. It was hard not to come to the conclusion that the universe was trying to tell me something.

TWENTY-EIGHT

The magistrate asked Adrian, our barrister, to begin. As he did, I stared at the witness statement in front of me. A third of each page was totally obscured by a huge black ink stain.

Barely breathing, I picked up the document to find a lidless black felt pen underneath. I looked at the statement again, praying I'd been wrong and that it was a photocopy. It wasn't – our original statement from the Italian art dealer was largely illegible.

This was crucial to our argument and the signature wasn't even visible.

Earlier that day I'd put the documents I'd need on the study desk – but obviously close enough to the edge for Jack to poke a pen in the middle without my noticing. The fact that I had a crashing headache from last night's cocktails hadn't helped, but still, I couldn't believe I had been so stupid.

Beside me, Adrian paused and I jumped, throwing my arm across the offending page. Oblivious to my panic, he continued with his explanation of the nature of our case.

Heart racing, I tried to think rationally. Maybe we could just submit a photocopy? If the other side were cooperative that might work – but I knew Leonie's lawyers would insist on their right to refuse to accept anything but an original document as evidence.

All right, maybe we could live without this particular document. But I knew that if we did, we had no hope of establishing that it was not at all unusual for someone to have an expensive statue in their backyard. Given that the witness lived in Milan, having him sign another one wasn't exactly an option either.

Adrian sat down and Richard, Leonie's barrister, stood up.

Gathering my courage, I touched Adrian's arm and pushed the damaged statement in front of him.

His head snapped up.

Original? he scrawled on the pad in front of him.

I nodded.

Adrian looked at me and blinked his eyes once.

I'd heard about, but never seen, 'the blink' which was something of a legend amongst the younger lawyers in Brisbane. Adrian was frighteningly intelligent. In addition, he was generally acknowledged as being amazingly tolerant of the lesser legal souls around him, particularly lawyers who didn't have his experience. When something disastrous happened, he'd simply close his eyes briefly, then reopen them and deal with the situation.

Bad? I scribbled, hoping he had a brilliant strategy to deal with the problem.

V. Bad, he scribbled back.

How on earth was I going to explain this to Gordon and Jonathon? I cursed my incredible stupidity. What was I thinking leaving precious documents within Jack's reach?

Adrian scanned his notes, obviously trying to figure out how soon we'd have to own up about our butchered statement.

I realised I'd heard nothing of what Richard had been saying. Tuning back in, I heard him describing how Leonie, an ardent gardener, constantly tended her thriving tree. He stated that the trees on Gordon's side prevented Leonie from knowing the statue was there. Palms upturned, he asked the magistrate what person in downtown Brisbane would ever suspect that there could be an Italian sculpture in their neighbour's backyard.

Half turning, I saw Gordon with arms folded and a smirk on his face. He obviously believed that our Italian art dealer would sink that argument.

Perhaps I should hightail it to Carla's, grab Jack and start driving, I thought desperately. Reality hit quickly, though – there was no way I could escape Gordon and Jonathon's combined wrath.

Richard finished his opening words and sat down. It was now up to us to present our case.

Adrian was still seated, making notes on the page in front of him. No doubt trying to construct something out of our decimated case. Every eye in the courtroom was on him.

He stood. This was it – we were about to go down in flames.

I held my breath. If I was Adrian, I'd point at me, tell the room that the whole thing was my fault and demand to be given a solicitor who had some clue about what she was doing.

'Your worship,' Adrian addressed the magistrate.

'Actually Mr Badley,' the magistrate interrupted, 'I have something to say first.'

We all looked at him in surprise.

The magistrate spoke slowly. 'It seems to me that this matter is one you have already spent a great deal of time and money on and are intending on dealing with in great detail. Let me give you some guidance. If I have the feeling that you are wasting the court's time with a dispute that should have been sorted out between two educated and successful individuals . . .' he paused and stared at Gordon and Leonie in turn, 'then I will make a decision that reflects my feelings. Now, if I could make a suggestion it would be that you go away and see if you can't come up with a solution.'

This was all legal speak for, 'If you don't get your acts together and stop behaving like two year olds, I'll make you sorry you appeared in my courtroom.'

It was all I could do not to genuflect in front of him. I'd been facing certain disaster – now there was the faintest glimmer of hope on the horizon.

'Yes, your worship,' said Adrian, as quick to grasp this twig as I was. 'Perhaps you could adjourn the case for an hour and we'll see what we can resolve.'

Richard was on his feet and nodding. It was never a good career move to disagree with an irritated magistrate.

'That will be fine. I will ask my clerk to arrange two conference rooms and will see you back here at . . .' He looked at his watch. 'Four o'clock.'

We all filed out. Gordon turned to us in the corridor. 'What on earth is going on?'

'This happens occasionally if a magistrate decides that his time is being wasted,' Adrian explained. 'If we insist on fighting this out in court, then he will decide the case; but no matter who wins, the award will only be a nominal amount. On top of that you will probably each have to pay your own costs.'

'Too bad,' Gordon blustered. 'It's the principle that is at stake here.'

But he didn't sound convinced. I hoped he was remembering that I'd warned him long ago that the magistrate might do this.

Adrian walked over to where Leonie was standing with Richard and her solicitor, a mousy-looking fellow called Trevor, whose appearance disguised an aggressive streak that hadn't helped the process so far.

This was it. Now was the time to confess to Gordon. As the lack of the document affected his case, I had to come clean.

Now.

'Uh, Gordon . . .'

'Mmm,' he muttered, busy glaring at Leonie.

I couldn't do it. I simply couldn't admit that my eighteen-month-old ward had destroyed one of our most important pieces of evidence and that Gordon would probably lose as a result.

Instead, I tried another tack. 'Perhaps it is worth considering talking this over. If it doesn't work we can still take it all back before the magistrate.'

Adrian rejoined us, presumably having decided that Richard was looking as unsuccessful as he in persuading his client to look for a compromise.

'She's right, Gordon. Even if the magistrate decides in your favour, he'll find a reason to make the award tiny. As well as paying your costs so far, you'll also have to pay for the costs of a few days in court. If we can sort this out here, then at least you'll be spared that.'

Adrian looked at me, eyebrows slightly raised. I shook my head imperceptibly, shamed by my cowardice. To my surprise, I saw a glimmer of a smile on his face before he turned back to Gordon.

Gordon looked over at Leonie, who refused to meet his eyes. Which was no great surprise, given the amount of paper vitriol exchanged over the last few months.

I'd never really understood this case. Something about Gordon's attitude always struck me as strange. He was a well-respected businessman, involved in significant negotiations on a daily basis, and his refusal to compromise on this seemed strangely out of character.

Although I'd seen normal, rational people lose perspective where money, religion or sex was involved, none of those categories applied here. It wasn't really about money – the amounts involved were insignificant for both of them. The statue didn't have any religious significance, and given that Gordon was gay, it couldn't be sex. Whenever I'd been through this thought process before, I'd come to the conclusion that neighbours' brawls deserved a category all to themselves.

And yet something still didn't seem right.

Although the magistrate had offered a tiny ray of hope, this just wasn't going to work. We were all going to end up back in front of him and the mutilated witness statement was going to end my career. I had a sudden vision of telling my parents that in the short time they'd been away, I'd managed to acquire a child and lose my job. I took a deep breath. Desperate times called for desperate measures.

'Adrian?' I interrupted his conversation with Gordon. He looked at me. 'I think a private conversation might be helpful.'

'Really?' He looked dubious.

I nodded sagely, attempting to convey a confidence I didn't feel, and they followed me into one of the conference rooms. We sat and they both looked at me expectantly.

'Gordon, are you gay?'

Well, if nothing else, I thought miserably, I'd shocked the notoriously poker-faced Adrian. He stared at me as if I'd lost my mind.

Gordon looked at me impassively for several seconds, during which time all of the things I'd dreamed of for my career flashed through my mind.

Finally he spoke. 'See. This is why I like you, Julia. You're prepared to do things other lawyers wouldn't even contemplate.'

I decided anything I said at this stage could only make things worse, so I kept my mouth firmly closed.

'The answer is no. Somehow a rumour got started a few years ago and I've never bothered doing anything about it. I like to keep my personal life private and in a way the rumour made it easier.'

Maybe a rumour like that was what my love-life needed. It certainly couldn't make things any worse. I felt sick every time I pictured Tony's face last night.

I took a deep breath. I was only halfway there.

Gordon held up his hand. 'To pre-empt you, the answer to your next question is, yes, I have slept with Leonie.'

My relief was so great I felt light-headed and had absolutely no idea what to say next.

Thankfully Adrian had recovered and was back with me. He rested his forefinger along the base of his nose thoughtfully and then spoke. 'Now, does that relationship have anything to do with this case?' he asked diplomatically.

For the first time ever I saw Gordon look slightly shame-faced. 'No, not at all. We have known each other vaguely for years. One day she was walking her dog when I was hosing the garden. We started chatting, she came in for a drink. And well, one thing led to another.'

'And . . .' Adrian broke off. 'Sorry, I feel like a shonky divorce lawyer asking these questions, but I do think this is relevant if we're going to sort all this out.' He tactfully omitted the fact that it would have been helpful had we known this information six months ago.

'Ah . . . Was this an isolated incident or something which was repeated?' It was painfully clear this was not a topic Adrian often discussed with clients.

Gordon snorted. 'Definitely a one-off. The next day I left some flowers at her place with a note and then called her twice. She never replied. A month later her branch broke David and . . . well, here we are.'

Yes, here we are, I thought.

'Okay. Look, it's possible that the emotions which have made this case so,' I paused, 'painful for everyone, might be able to be dealt with. How would you feel if I had a chat to Leonie?' I asked tentatively.

Gordon glared at me and I was sure that finally I'd gone too far.

He pushed the stack of papers in front of him roughly. 'Fine. If you think it will help resolve this disaster, go ahead.'

I stood up before he changed his mind. 'All right, I'll be back in a minute.'

I paused at the door to the other conference room and then knocked lightly. They looked surprised to see me by myself.

'Ms Baker,' I began, taking a seat at the end of the table. 'My client has just told me something that I feel may be relevant to resolving this situation.'

They all looked at me expectantly.

'He, ah . . . he said that shortly before the incident with the statue, he had sexual relations with you, Ms Baker.'

Rumpole always used the term 'sexual relations'. I figured that, as no part of my training had prepared me for this, I had to work with whatever I had.

Richard and Trevor's faces mirrored Adrian's and it was clear they'd had no idea either.

Leonie gave a short laugh. 'Yes, that's right. Did he also mention the fact that he is gay?'

'Actually he told me definitively that he's not – he said it was a rumour he's always just ignored.'

She sat back in her chair. 'Well of course he'd say that,' she managed without much conviction.

'He said that he left a note and some phone messages afterwards, but that you didn't call him back. He was very hurt.'

I was warming to my topic and felt I could be excused one small white lie.

'Really?' she asked.

'Absolutely.' I was about to say that he'd felt they had something special, but stopped myself just in time.

Richard and Trevor had clearly decided to stay well out of this conversation and weren't saying a word.

Leonie spoke again. 'The day after we slept together, I told a friend what had happened. She said that everyone knew he was gay. I thought he was just using me – trying something different for a change.'

'So you didn't return his calls, and when he brought an action about the statue, you were determined not to let him win,' I finished for her.

'Uh-huh.' She smiled ruefully. 'Sounds kind of pathetic, I know.'

'Look, I've got a suggestion. Why don't you and Gordon go for a coffee and have a talk about things. If you still want to go ahead with the action, that's fine. But maybe you'll be able to sort something out.'

Leonie looked awkwardly at Richard and Trevor and stood up. 'All right. I'll do it if he will.'

I left her outside Gordon's conference room and went in.

I quickly filled him in on what Leonie had told me. 'She wants to have a coffee to talk about things. What do you think?'

Gordon put his head back and looked up at the ceiling. 'Fine. Let's just get this over with.'

He stood up and left the room, closing the door behind him.

Adrian looked at me expectantly and I held my finger to my lips.

After what I judged a sufficient length of time, I opened the door a crack and peered out. Seeing nothing, I opened it right up. The corridor was empty.

'Well they've either gone for a coffee or are beating each other up somewhere,' I said.

'I don't know what to say,' Adrian managed. 'That was the

most gutsy thing I've seen in twenty years at the bar. Also the most risky,' he added.

I could only manage a small smile. 'It's not over yet. It could still go terribly wrong.'

Five tense minutes later my mobile rang.

'Julia, Gordon here. Look, Leonie and I are heading off. Can you sort that court stuff out for me?'

The tension drained out of me and I leaned back in the chair. 'Absolutely, Gordon. It will be my pleasure.'

It took less than thirty seconds in front of the magistrate to finish the whole business and I burst out of the court half expecting to see dozens of photographers and journalists waiting to witness my victory. I refused to let the small fact that there were only a couple of police officers and a woman on a cigarette break dent my high spirits.

If losing Gordon's case would have been a disaster for my career, maybe I could use this unexpected success to my advantage. My bookseller had come through with a horrendously priced, but pristine, copy of Jonathon's book, so my career prospects were looking a whole lot better than this time last week. Having Jonathon on my side might just be enough to push me back on the partnership track. If I still wanted it, that was. Suddenly I wasn't so sure.

Anyway, that was a question for later. This was celebration time.

I'd expected the case to last for a couple of days and had made sure there was nothing urgent to be dealt with at the office while I was away. Carla didn't expect me to pick up Jack until tonight. So for a couple of hours at least, I was a free agent.

I turned to Adrian. 'Fancy a drink?'

With barely a glance at his watch, he shook his head. 'Sorry, I'd love to but I can't. But,' he added, 'if you promise never to do anything like that again, I won't talk to Jonathon until this evening. Let him think it went all afternoon.'

'Mmm,' I pretended to hesitate and then smiled as he started to walk off. 'It's a deal,' I shouted at his retreating back.

The forecourt of the building was completely deserted and

suddenly I was at a loose end. I took my mobile out of my bag and turned it on.

'You have two messages.'

The first message was from Maggie. 'Hi, just wanted to let you know Marcus and I have just had a very normal, enjoyable lunch. And get this, we didn't have sex! Just a nice civilised lunch. I think it's going to be okay.'

I smiled and pressed the delete button.

The second message was from Patrick, who sounded like he was still on a high from his night with Audrey. I had filled him in on last night's events over breakfast.

'Okay, here's the deal,' his recorded voice began without preamble. 'I'm not sure if this is going to make me popular or very unpopular, but I called Tony today.' He paused as if waiting for a response from me. 'I don't understand why you women have to make things so complicated when it's really very simple. It's like the Jennifer thing all over again . . .' He paused again. 'So anyway, I called him and left a message on his voice mail telling him it was all a misunderstand—'

Having exhausted his recording time, his voice cut out.

Before I had time to think about the message, I heard a voice behind me.

'I don't want to miss my child's birthday party.'

I turned around to see Tony.

'Sorry?'

He took a deep breath. 'When we first met, you told me about a partner at your firm who missed his son's birthday party because he had to work. I don't want that to be me.'

I shook my head. 'I don't suppose anyone does — I think it just happens.'

'Julia.' Tony put a hand on my shoulder. 'I've been trying to figure out how to say this since Patrick called. He told me you were here. After you left the party last night, I was talking to some boring old fart. Suddenly I pictured myself like him in another twenty years, rich and successful and miserable as all hell. So I left the party and came around to your place, but when I saw you with that other guy . . .' His words trailed off.

'Grant's just –' I started to explain, but he cut me off.

'I know – Patrick told me. Don't worry about it.'

The sun was in my eyes and I put up my hand to block the glare. But I still couldn't read Tony's expression.

'Ever since I quit golf, I've felt like I had to do something brilliant in my career to compensate. And then when my marriage broke up I felt it even more. Kind of like I'd messed everything else up, so I'd better at least get it right in my job. And then I met you.'

He paused.

'You manage to roll with the punches and keep laughing, and I love that. Suddenly I'm not sure I'm prepared to sacrifice everything to get to the top. I can't even remember who I'm trying to prove myself to any more. What I want most now is to see if you and I can make it work.'

This all sounded nice, but not very realistic. People didn't change overnight – it didn't work like that.

'But it's all starting to happen for you. This is not the time for you to begin a relationship with anyone, let alone someone who has a child.'

'I know,' he acknowledged. 'That's why I've been a bit hot and cold.'

That was a serious understatement. We were talking Sahara Desert and Siberia here. I decided to let it slide.

'Right from the start I've enjoyed being with you and Jack. But each time I left you, I started thinking about all the reasons it made absolutely no sense to see you again. When I landed this job, I decided I definitely wouldn't take it any further. That it wouldn't be fair to either of us. But then I saw you walking into the cafe outside the movies when I was picking up my takeaway . . .'

I raised my eyebrows.

'Uh. I wasn't going to tell you that. I actually lied when I said I'd met a friend there. I'd caught a taxi from work to pick up some takeaway Indian I'd ordered. When I saw you I dumped it in a rubbish bin – you have no idea how hungry I was during that movie.'

Despite myself, I laughed. 'Come on though – why me?' I was serious again. 'There are plenty of girls you could find who come without as many issues as me. Aren't you making things hard for yourself?'

'It's because you are you that I've realised how much I'm missing out on. Until now there's never been a contest whenever there was a conflict between my work and my personal life. I love being at your house. There's always something happening with Jack or someone else and it makes me realise how quiet my place is. All of a sudden I'm sick of working fourteen-hour days and coming home to an empty flat. And doing it again the next day. I want to make this job work, but I'm not prepared to give up everything for it.'

He seemed to have a surprisingly rosy view of the times we'd spent together. It occurred to me that maybe he'd subconsciously blocked out the memory of the breakfast debacle. I'd certainly tried.

'Trust me, it's not all cocktails and riotous fun at home. Do you really have any idea what it would be like having a relationship with Jack and me?'

The words sounded strange, but they were true. We came as a 'two for one' deal and anyone who wanted to be around me would have to want to be around Jack too. One thing the last few weeks had made me realise was that pretending otherwise was a sure way to give myself an ulcer before my next birthday.

'Think about it – no sleep-ins, definitely no breakfasts, no movies, no –' I was on a roll and could have continued for hours, but Tony held up his hand.

'I get the picture. But Julia – it's okay. I actually love the idea of having Jack around – he's a great little kid.'

'Tony, you don't know what you're letting yourself in for.' I realised I'd missed out the endless hours at the park, a critical omission, I felt, but I didn't think this was the time to mention it.

'Did you know what you were signing on for when Jack arrived?'

'Well, no. But that was different.'

'Maybe not as different as you think. I want to make it work with you and I'm prepared to do whatever it takes.'

Finally I allowed myself to believe he was serious. I remembered my advice to Maggie – not trying something because it might not work out wasn't the answer.

'You know, maybe we could give it a try.'

I put my briefcase on the ground beside me.

'Perhaps we both just need to pack a bit lighter,' I added with a smile.

'Sorry?'

'Don't worry,' I answered as he pulled me towards him. 'It's fine.'

ALSO AVAILABLE FROM PAN MACMILLAN

Kris Webb and Kathy Wilson
Sacking the Stork

Sophie presumed 'making sacrifices for your children' meant giving up Bloody Marys and champagne for nine months. When she thought about it that is . . .

But then two blue lines appear on her pregnancy test.

How does a baby fit in with a hectic job, a chaotic social life and the absence of Max, the Y chromosome in the equation, who has moved to San Francisco?

Support and dubious advice are provided by an unlikely group who gather for a weekly coffee session at the King Street Cafe. It is with Debbie the glamorous man-eater, Andrew the fitness junkie, Anna the disaster prone doctor and Karen the statistically improbable happily married mother of three, that Sophie discovers the ups and downs of motherhood.

And when an unexpected business venture and a new man appear on the scene, it appears that just maybe there is life after a baby.

SACKING THE STORK tackles the balancing act of motherhood, romance and a career, while managing to be seriously funny.

'Bridget Jones has a baby'
SUNDAY AGE

'Filled with wry insight, *Sacking the Stork* is about the search for balance'
GOLD COAST BULLETIN

'Written by sisters who live on opposite sides of the world, this book combines humour with a keen look at lifestyle choices'
DAILY TELEGRAPH

Liane Moriarty
Three Wishes

It happens sometimes that you accidentally star in a little public performance of your very own comedy, tragedy or melodrama.

The three Kettle sisters have been accidentally starring in public performances all their lives, affecting their audiences in more ways than they'll ever know. This time, however, they give a particularly spectacular show when a raucous, champagne-soaked birthday dinner ends in a violent argument and an emergency dash to the hospital.

So who started it this time? Was it Cat: full of angry, hurt passion dating back to the 'Night of the Spaghetti'? Was it Lyn: serenely successful, at least on the outside? Or was it Gemma: quirky, dreamy and unable to keep a secret, except for the most important one of all?

Whoever the culprit, their lives will have all changed dramatically before the next inevitable clash of shared genes and shared childhoods.

Ilsa Evans
Odd Socks

Unlike her best friend Camilla Riley, compulsive list-maker Terry
Diamond prides herself on her organisational abilities. Also unlike
Camilla, Terry is tall, blonde, self-confident, and has a chest that
could stop traffic – or at least would do wonders for airbag design.

But none of the above stops chaos bursting into her life when her
daughter not only gives birth on the living-room rug but decides to
move home with infant in tow. Meanwhile, Terry is starting to suspect
her pink-overall-wearing boyfriend may not even be Mr Right for Now
– especially as she has just fallen in love with a mysterious, elongated
stranger who dresses like the father in a 1950s sitcom. Will all this
mayhem make the play-it-safe Terry do what she needs to do to turn
her life around?

The author of *Spin Cycle* and *Drip Dry* is back with another hilarious
celebration of chaotic normality.

Louise Limerick
Dying for Cake

Life has taken an unexpected turn for the women in a mothers' coffee group. Baby Amy has disappeared, and her mother, Evelyn, broken and distant in a psychiatric hospital, won't utter a word.

Desperate to find Amy, desperate to understand, the women cope with the loss in their own ways. But Evelyn's withdrawal has altered them irreversibly, and each begins to look for something to satiate the cravings they had not allowed to surface before . . .

Joanna is dying for cake. Clare is longing to paint again. Susan wants to claw back all the time she's lost. Wendy is trying to forget the past. Then there's Evelyn. Nobody knows what Evelyn wants. But how can she not want her baby back?

Dianne Blacklock
Almost Perfect

Mac and Anna appear to have the perfect marriage, but their relationship is cracking under the strain of infertility. Anna cannot let go of the increasingly elusive dream of having a child, but Mac doesn't know how much longer he can cope with her pain and disappointment.

Georgie and her sister-in-law have made The Reading Rooms bookshop a successful business, but Georgie has not been so successful in her love life. Her brother Nick wonders if she's waiting for the impossible – the perfect man.

And then Liam walks into The Reading Rooms and Georgie finds herself at a turning point. As do Mac and Anna, when finally the hurt and frustration sets Mac on a path that will have unforeseen consequences for them all.

Dianne Blacklock, author of *Call Waiting* and *Wife for Hire*, expertly crafts a novel of interweaving characters which asks that crucial relationship question: if there is no such thing as 'perfect', how do you know when to settle for *Almost Perfect*?